Kevin William Bowden, born on July 27, 1949, in Liverpool, England, is the eldest of four brothers. The house he was born in is long gone, demolished as part of Liverpool's "slum" clearance program. It lacked hot water and electricity, and the toilet was an outhouse at the end of the yard, with yesterday's "Liverpool Echo" newspaper hung on an old rusty nail.

He lived there until he was seven. His father worked in radar at Liverpool docks, having served in the Royal Navy much to his mother's disapproval, who declared she would never marry a sailor. His mother worked at "Ogden's – Tobacco" as a stripper, a family joke referring to her job of stripping tobacco leaves.

Kevin lived with his Nan and Nin (his mother's mother and grandmother) in a two-up, two-down end-of-terrace house. Nan nursed Nin until she died at the grand age of 96. They shared the same bed at the back, while Kevin, his mother, and father slept in the front bedroom.

Kevin spent most of his adult life as a site carpenter, having tried his hand at various other occupations, including car salesman, pub manager, folk singer, clairvoyant, palmist, tarot card reader, asbestos surveyor, and counselor/therapist.

He has been married to Lisa for 25 years. Together, they have seven children: Kevin's two sons and a daughter, and Lisa's four daughters. They are also proud grandparents to 14 grandchildren. They currently live on a boat on the south coast.

During the 2008/9 recession, they lost their home and 90% of their business. Kevin retired in December 2015 after a mental breakdown, but he has since recovered.

Kevin started writing just over a year ago, inspired by a vivid dream. "It was as if I was watching a full-length movie, so clear, so detailed," he describes. The dream was about a young girl who lost the lower part of her legs in a freak accident.

Within a few days, he began writing *The Quest: Lucie No Legs*, compelled by the vivid images and persistent dream. He had never written before and has struggled with dyslexia throughout his life. "I am dyslexic," he admits. "I thank goodness for spell-check."

He is now three-quarters of the way through the sequel, "The Quest: Secrets of Cove Manor," a more mature story that continues the lives of Kevin O'Keefe and Elisabeth Churchill, filled with intrigue, secrets, and murder. They eagerly await its completion and publication.

Kevin W. Bowden

THE QUEST: LUCIE NO LEGS

Kevin W. Bowden
1st March 2024

AUSTIN MACAULEY PUBLISHERS™

LONDON • CAMBRIDGE • NEW YORK • SHARJAH

A CIP catalogue record for this title is available from the British Library.

ISBN 9781035815227 (Paperback)
ISBN 9781035815234 (ePub e-book)

www.austinmacauley.com

First Published 2024
Austin Macauley Publishers Ltd®
1 Canada Square
Canary Wharf
London
E14 5AA

I would like to express my deepest gratitude to my Uncle Bob, whose unwavering support, infectious enthusiasm, and endless encouragement were instrumental in bringing *The Quest - Lucie no Legs* to life.

Chapter 1

My name is Kevin O'Keefe, born 27 July 1900 in a large, bustling fishing village some eleven miles North-East of Belfast named Carrickfergus.

My father's a boat builder and fisherman, my mother in service's at the Castle. Both were born and raised here in Carrickfergus. Born a day apart on the 28th and 29th December 1853. They were childhood sweethearts and had known each other all their lives. They were made for each other. Folks would say, "William and Whinny, well, they had eyes only for each other when they were still in the womb."

It was as if they had an invisible cord between them, almost magical, spiritual, and tangible. And it was envied by all who knew them. It was said they always seemed to know where the other was at any given time, and would do each other's bidding without words. Often, they would squeeze the other's hand as a way of kissing. At any rate, I had a very loving and happy upbringing, Da and Ma would make each other laugh. Ma would burst out laughing whenever Da attempted to sing to her a romantic song. Try as he might he could not keep a straight face, and both would end up in tears of laughter.

I understood what a truly loving partnership was, and wanted the same for me one day. I sensed it in my heart and soul. I was just happy being with them. My mates would call, but I seldom went out.

I suppose with them being older parents, things where calmer and if they did argue, they would end up laughing and agree they were both right and that was the end of it. They taught me what was important and what was not.

"As long as you have each other, health, wood for the fire, enough pennies to clothe yourself, and a roof above your head the rest can go fly," Da would say quite often.

We always had wood for the fire and when Da would go fishing with Jack Cattin, we always had food. We were not well-off by any means, but we never went without.

Another of Da's sayings was, "If you can use these," he'd look at his hands, "you will never be out of work."

They had only me. I found out later from my auntie Kathryn that there were complications bringing me into the world and was told I was lucky my mother didn't die. Ma was 47 years old and I was a total surprise. That must have been a terrifying and traumatic time for them both. Auntie Kathryn says Da never left Ma's bedside for over two weeks and wouldn't let anyone tend to his beloved Winny. Not even Ma's sister Kathryn.

I will mention at this point that there is a Welsh connection in the family. My great-great grandma came from a little village in North Wales called Mold. The family name was Owen, and I believe my great-great grandad's name was John Owen-Kelly, a bit of Irish and Welsh. My auntie Kathryn's name is spelt the Welsh way. I was told Kelly is a popular name on the Isle-o-Man. I just might travel there one day and have a look for myself.

I would help Da out in the boat shed. This was most of the time as schooling was not for me. No matter how I tried, nothing went in. And being left-handed, well, Mrs O'Connor, our teacher, described my handwriting as, *"a drunken spider that climbed out of the inkwell and staggered across the paper."*

All I wanted to do was work with wood. I loved the smells: fresh sawn wood, the making of the glue, and the tar/pitch I loved it all. I would make all sorts of stuff from off cuts of wood lying around. When working with Oak, my hands would become black with an ink coloured stain that came from the wood. Nothing would clean it out of my hands, and it took day for the stain to wear away. But most what I enjoyed working on most of all was boats! Da had given me tools as young as five years old. The women folk in the village thought he was mad.

"He'll have the leg of the table if not his own," was the cry.

I could read and write, I found the pencil much better. Than a bit of dowel with a nib on the end was not for me. Pushing the pen and not pulling only tore the paper. I did try writing right-handed, but as both my parents were left-handed and so was I.

I did have friends, but I was always a bit of a loner and did prefer my own thoughts and company. I loved going down to the quay and just watching the goings-on, boats coming in and going out. I knew all the fisherman, especially Jack. Then again, he was known for miles around. His party trick was to bite the head of a live rat for a pint O' Porta. He was big and strong and always had a smile on his face. I remember once Ma asked him, "What are ya smilin about, Jack Cattin?"

"Ah, ya don't know what I'm thinkin about, Winny. And if ya did, your William wouldn't like it," he'd respond with a big laugh.

He never married and when asked why, his standard reply was, "I'm married to a mermaid who lives on the Giants Causeway and God love us can she eat fish." Every village has its fare share of characters, and this one was no different.

I loved the smell at low tide, that sweet, damp smell of the seaweed and the salt sea air. I would fill my lungs to bursting point with it. I'd just sit there silent in my own thoughts as I looked across the water, almost mesmerised with its rhythm. Day dreaming, but my mind was never empty.

Flashes of faces, people talking, places I didn't know, never been, and moving images of streets and buildings. I would try to clear my mind, yet with little success.

Perhaps these are people and places I have yet to see, I would often tell myself. Nan, Ma's mum, could read the tea-leaves, the Tarot Cards, and your fortune from the lines in your hand. So perhaps it was in my blood, too. I loved going around to her house as people would just walk in as the front doors were never closed except at night.

"Em, (her name was Emily) read me leaves, will ya?" they would say.

Nan would read whatever she saw in the shapes and pattens left in the teacup. Sometimes the Tarot Cards would come out. I was spellbound, just sitting there trying to take it all in. If I had a penny for every time I heard, *"She must have seen this coming,"* I would be rich!

One of the most memorable times was in 1912 when the whole village congregated at the water front, hoping to catch sighting of the largest ship afloat as it passed by—The Titanic. What a day that was to be sure. Music, food, the Black Porta, side shows, dancers, and the most horrendous cheer as this magnificent vision glided effortlessly past as if some heavenly force pulled her through the water.

The local fishing boats resembled toy boats bobbing up and down in her wake. Then, there was a strange silence, as if all the people standing there slowly became aware of this wonderful achievement before them and what they were actually looking at. This ship was built only a few miles away in Belfast and helped by some of the village folk. I was twelve and sitting on Da's shoulders.

In the silence I heard Da say to Ma, "I know sweetheart, I know."

She was looking up at him stone faced and just holding his hand.

"What do you know Da?" I said.

"Oh, nothing, my boy, nothing."

They both knew. It is well documented, so I won't bother to go into the details.

But after the tragedy, the village was not the same for quite a while. As I am sure it was the same elsewhere on both shores.

It was winter 1913/4 and Nan was not well at all. She gave up her rented house and came to live with us. She kept to her bed and was tended to by me Da and Ma. I would go in to see her and talk about life and daily goings-on around the village.

Nan was never short of visitors. All and sundry would call and ask if Em was still doing the readings. However, Nan soon stopped the readings. You could see she was getting old, you know showing signs of her great age. Skin grey and heavily lined, The folds of loose skin on her arms I remember one night Ma came out of Nan's room and told me she wanted to see me. It was the last day of December 1913. I was sitting, watching the flames in the grate, and making shapes from the red, yellow, and orange. Tonight it was horses galloping, I was in a world of my own as usual. I went in and sat beside the bed. The fire needed more wood.

"Shall I put more wood on the fire, Nan?" I asked.

"No, it's fine as it is. Would you let me look at your hands?"

I remember how big my hands seemed when held by hers. She seemed to vanish beneath the bedsheets, she was so tiny.

"You have the gift, but don't be frightened by it. Embrace and control it," she said. "When I go, and it will be soon, I want you to have the Tarot Cards. You will need no teaching, you'll know the meaning. But this I will say, your true love won't be what you expect and not from these parts. Yet, once you win her heart, my boy, you will have it all. Now go, I must sleep."

Our Em went that night in her sleep at the age of 96.

It has to be the best way to go, I thought. *So peaceful and without pain.*

As I'm sure you could imagine it was a big affair. She was well loved and the village did her and themselves proud. The Wake went on for days. It was a celebration of her life-lived, what she saw, how things must have changed in those nine and a half decades. I only wished I had had the foresight to ask what her memories where and why there was no mention of her husband, my grandad. I was never told and I never questioned.

It was a bright and warm October day 1916. The Great War didn't seem to bother us much. Most of the men had been called up. Da was too old and in a trade that made him and I exempt. Ma was still up at the castle, not surprisingly now used as a Garrison and Ordinance Store.

October the 13th, 1916 is a day I will never forget. It was about ten in the morning and Jimmy, one of the carpenters was making a brew. Da put down his smoothing-plane. I was sitting on some planks at the time and just happened look Da's way when he suddenly shook violently, as if hit by a steam train He staggered a few feet, then crumpled into a heap on the floor. For a few seconds I could not move, just stared. Jimmy and Pat ran to him, both knelt with their backs to me. Time stood still for what seemed a lifetime. Finally, Pat turned to me solemn faced. I had never seen him so pale.

"He's gone, Kev lad."

I could not move as the words sunk-in. They placed him on the work-bench and closed his eyes. I just stood there and watched, I don't think I blinked. Jimmy and Pat. moved slowly to the side. I eased towards him. He looked asleep. I held his hand in mine and looked at his palm probably for the first time. It was large hard and scarred.

It feels so heavy, I thought.

A red mist came over me like nothing I'd ever experienced before. I screamed in anger and started to throw things around the workshop. Wood, tools, paint anything I could get my hands on. Then as quickly as it came, it went, but I'd dissolved into a flood of tears by then. As my mind cleared, I could not believe the carnage. When I turned, the workshop was empty.

I collected myself and called out, "Jimmy? Pat?"

They appeared around the workshop doors and inched towards me, but stopped a few feet away, both ashen and stony faced. Mary, the owner's wife, they lived above the workshop flew in, ran straight up to me and threw her arms around me. Jimmy started to say something.

"Not now, Jim," Mary looked me in the eye. "Not now." She smiled and held my hands.

By now there were about a dozen people standing inside the workshop, and I was getting a strange feeling. My blood ran cold and I started to shiver.

Why is everyone so quiet, and just staring at me? I got myself together and looked at Mary, who still had hold of both my hands. "What was Jimmy going to say, Mrs O'Hara?" I asked in a very controlled and strangely cold way.

She burst into tears, just as Mr O'Hara, the boatyard owner, appeared at the doors and came in. He strode up to Mary and me, put his arm around my shoulders, and walked me off.

"Tis best you come up to my office and we can talk there. I will make arrangements for your father so don't concern ya-self just now."

I went first up the wooden stairs to his office above the workshop, closely followed by Mr O'Hara and Mary. She closed the office door behind us.

"Sit ya-self down, Kevin lad and Mrs O'Hara will make us a nice strong cup of tea, wont ya, Mary?"

I turned to see Mary looking at him with a face like thunder, but softened to a small smile, "That I will. I want to be here when you—"

She was cut short by, "WONT YOU, MARY?"

She muttered something under her breath and left.

"Now, Kevin, I liked your father a lot, a fine craftsman, a team leader, and well thought of by folk. He was foreman as you know. He will be missed." He spoke quietly. "I see you have your father's temper." He must have heard of my rampage in the workshop.

I've never witnessed this, I thought. *I just can't imagine Da losing his temper.* I was about to apologise, "Now, I want to offer you a full-time position here, the money we can talk later about that. I will promote Jimmy to Foreman and you can follow him. All the tools that ya father used were, as you know, all his own and now will become yours. I have seen ya work, and I think you will become a strong member of the team here at O'Hara's Boatyard. Now." He was just about to say something else when he was cut short by Mrs O'Hara coming back, flustered and carrying with the tea and a bottle of whiskey.

"Have ya—" she began.

"NO, I haven't, Mary," replied Mr O'Hara. "Ah, that's a grand idea. A wee nip in the tea is what's called for, just to calm the nerves."

What the hell is going on? I thought. My mind started to come back from where ever it had been the last hour or so. "Has anyone gone to fetch me-Ma?" I almost shouted.

They both looked at each other with the same solemn face I had witnessed in Jimmy and Pat a few moments before. Mary could not control herself any longer.

She burst into tears and blubbered, "We are all so so sorry, Kevin." She could not speak for sobbing.

I stared at Mr O'Hara my mind had just exploded. He started talking before I had time to speak.

"So sorry, Kevin lad, but ya Ma has gone as well. At least they are together now as always they were."

I sat there frozen in time, numb, and in shock. I turned, picked up the bottle of whiskey, and drank. Mary went to stop me but. his hand went up to stop her, "Let him be, Mary. Let him be."

I came to in the early hours of the morning feeling ill as I never had before. I had the lingering taste of vomit in my mouth and my head throbbed. I opened my eyes slowly, closed them, and tried again. I was in a small room with no light lying on what felt and smelt like old hessian sacks—rough and fibrous with a smell of their own. A voice spoke from the darkness.

"So, Kev lad, you're awake and more so to the point, alive."

I jumped up, banged my head on a roof timber, and sank to the floor in a heap. I could not speak or focus, and now knew the meaning of Blind Drunk. A candle was lit, and I could make out a shape, but had no idea who it was.

"Who are you?" I demanded, weakly.

"It's Jack, Kev lad, Jack Cattin. Now that I know you are still with us, thank the Lord, I'll leave ya be."

I sank into a deep sleep only to be awoken by Mrs O'Hara.

"Are you up to coming down, Kevin? I have a nice strong cup of tea waiting for you, and NO whiskey this time, God love ya."

I descended the Sail-Loft ladder and strode deliberately into the day-light that seemed to penetrate my eyes-balls like needles. Sitting around the table was Jack Cattin and Mr O'Hara with Mary pouring the tea.

"Would you like something to eat?" She asked.

The very thought of food made my insides turn. "No thank you, Mrs O'Hara. Just the tea, please."

"Oh, call me Mary, Kevin."

I just smiled at her and she smiled back. She was pleased with this I could see as they had no children. The tea quenched my thirst, but it took three cups.

There was a uneasy silence. I spoke first.

"Please tell me what happened to me-Ma."

They looked at each other, seeking who was to speak first. Mary was just about to when Jack spoke.

"Ya Ma was on her way down from the castle, one of the horses bolted." He hesitated. "It hit ya Ma with such force, she felt nothing. I'm sure it was instant." He stopped and I got the feeling there was more. I just looked at him until he lowered his head.

"Now, I don't want you to worry about the arrangements, Kev lad," said Mr O'Hara.

"Not now," piped up Mary, "No, best spoken now, Mary. No use pussy-footing around. The lad's up to it, aren't you?"

I nodded.

"I have taken care of the arrangements. It's been decided the Village will chip-in and I'll cover any shortfall. So you have no worries on that score. It would appear you will now be living with your auntie Kathryn. I'm sorry, but I will need the house. The O'Malley family will be moving in as soon as—"

Mary cut him short. "Sean, for God's sake, give the lad some time to recover and sort himself out."

"Yes, Yes, of course, Mary, but these things need to be said. I will give you Jimmy and Pat for the day, Kev lad."

The cottage came furnished, I thought. *Except for a few personal things, mostly Ma's. Her spinning wheel, sewing box, a few cups and plates, etc. Da's pipes, a few tools, that's about it.* "Thank you, Mr O'Hara, but I will do the move to Auntie Kathryn's myself."

"As you please, as you please," was his reply.

"I want to see me-Ma," I said to all three.

"She's with your father," said Mary. "Both are at the cottage. I'll go with you."

"Thank you, but no. I'll go myself," I said. "Thank you all for all you have done. I will repay you all, I promise."

"As you will, as you will," said Mr O'Hara. "I tell you now there is no need. Up to you, lad, up to you."

I walked out into the sunlight. I was aware I badly needed to change my clothes. The smell of stale drink and vomit made me want to heave. It was about a five minute walk home from the boatyard.

Home! I thought. *Not for much longer.*

14

I began walking slowly at first. Then I straightened myself up, took a deep breath, and marched up the hill. This was the first day of the rest of my life. What was I going to do? I felt strangely confident within. That the strength, wisdom, and guidance of me-Ma, me-Da, and Nan within me, I was going to be just fine.

People I had known all my life, some just on nodding terms passed me by as I continued up the hill. Some had a kind word, others gave a knowing smile and a nod of the head that said so much without words ever being spoken. The village seemed strangely quiet.

I rounded the corner. The same corner I had turned so many times before. I looked at our front door, stopped dead in my tracks at sight of so many people standing on the door steps. They were looking at me and I stared back. Men had their arms around their women folk, some with tears in their eyes. Even the children were quiet. Boys and girls held onto their mothers skirts.

The moment was broken when the front door opened with a familiar creak. It was a joke Ma and I would have with Da. He wanted everything to work as it should, but would not oil the door's hinges. He always said, *"A creaking door lasts the longest."* It made no sense but so what.

Auntie Kathryn appeared in the doorway. I walked up to her and noticed her eyes were red from crying. I gave her a hug. She clung to me before letting go and moving aside. I went into the house. The place was full of light. There must have been over a hundred candles around the room all placed there by the people of the village. I had no idea how much they had respected, or how much love there was for me Ma and Da.

There were two wooden pine coffins laid out on the large kitchen table. Standing next to them were two figures. One I knew was Jack Cattin, he must have passed me without me knowing, no mistaking the size and the other was Father Kelly. I felt calm and confident, as if I knew this was a new beginning. I also didn't feel grief or no loss.

Was this going to grab me at some future point in time? I wondered. *Am I suddenly going to collapse in a jabbering heap on the floor? No.*

I stepped over to where they both lay and looked at them. They appeared to be sleeping. They looked old; I had never thought of them that way. But they were both over sixty. Perhaps this made the loss a bit better, I don't know. They had been dressed in their Sunday best. Ma had a bunch of flowers in her hands.

They both look so peaceful. I smiled and said, "You were always together and you always will be forever more." I bent down and kissed them before turning to Father Kelly. "I won't have them buried in separate coffins. I will make a coffin so they can hold hands and be together."

He was taken aback for a brief moment. "If that is what you wish, I don't foresee any problems."

"What a lovely idea, Kevin," said Auntie Kathryn.

"I will start now," said I. "Can I leave the arrangements to you good folks?"

"Aye to be sure you can, Kev lad," spoke Jack.

I needed to get started right away and went back to the workshop.

Jack ran after me. "You might want to change ya clothes, lad."

"Oh, yes," I went back inside, changed, and started to leave. I stopped by Ma and Da and looked at all who gathered there.

"I'm going to be fine, I just know it. I feel it in here." I placed my hand on my heart before pointing to my head. Some folks relaxed, while others nodded in acceptance.

I got back to the boatshed full of energy. It was as if I had absorbed Ma and Da's being, it was now in me. I went straight to the workshop and looked for the timber needed for the coffin.

Mr O'Hara must have heard me and came in to the workshop. "What's ya doing, lad? I closed up for the day and gave Jimmy and Pat the day off. You should be at home with ya loved ones around you at a time like this."

"I am making me-Ma and Da's coffin. It is going to be a wide enough for both of them to lay together. Father Kelly said it will be fine." I faced the work-bench. "It'll be done in one day. I want it in Oak and will pay you back." I turned, but he had gone. I carried on and a few minutes later Jimmy came in.

"I hear what you are trying to do, Kev. I know where there is some Oak planking just right for the job. The old man was saving for himself, so he was." The old man being Mr O'Hara.

The Oak had already been prepared, six planks measuring seven feet long by fifteen inches wide... Jimmy and I glanced at each other. A moments thought is an hour in words. We both worked together, Jimmy was very thoughtful, he just helped with—"shall I do this while you do that?" sort of thing never taking the task away from me.

We completed the task in six hours, Auntie Kathryn came with some bread and cheese for us both, Jack Cattin with a bottle of ale. The casket was ready for its first coat of first quality boat varnish which thinned 50/50 with white spirit.

This was to allow the varnish to really soak into the Oak. Second layer 75% varnish and 25% white spirit. Finally 100 % varnish.

It was now, way past midnight, but the job was done. Jimmy left soon after it was completed. I sat back and studied this wide coffin lit by the candle light. I was about to finish off the bread and cheese when a very familiar voice said, "That's a funny looking boat. Wouldn't fancy me chances in a swell, Kev lad." It was Jack Cattin. "Mind if I join you, lad?"

I smiled, he joined me.

"You okay, lad? Folks are a bit concerned."

"I have never felt better, Jack. I know this all sounds strange, but I do. I feel re-charged somehow. I wanted to ask you about what you said about Da and his temper, I never saw Da loose his, ever."

Jack stared at me for a few moments. "You never knew ya da when he was young. Oh, don't get me wrong, he was not a tear-a-way by any means. In fact just the opposite. He could not stand for any injustice or bullying, and helped a lot of people in this village stand up for their rights. Things like wages, rents, and the like. Your Ma and Da were well respected and I think you have witnessed a bit of that today eh, Kev lad. I only saw your da lose it once and believe me that was enough."

"Well?" I shouted, "And?"

Jack looked at me, straight faced. "It was way back when me and him were in our twenties. A soldier from the Castle knew ya da, but he had no idea that your ma was with ya da. He was in the pub with two of his mates and he well, he made a remark about ya ma.

"Ya da very calmly as ya da would, asked this bastard to apologise. The stupid bugger just laughed at him and the three of them squared up. I put down me pint and stood up. I had a feeling a fight was in the running. Ya da asked this bloke to apologise again.

"Instead, the soldier took a swing at him. Now, I had never seen ya da fight ever. and me, well, I was always fighting. One left-handed straight hook took this soldier's face right off, he was out for the count with teeth and blood everywhere. The other two stepped forward.

"Like a flash, ya da had both by the throat and I mean the throat. They were gasping for their lives. It took me and two others to get him to let go. The poor sods were touch and go, they could hardly catch their breath. One was spitting blood, God love em. Well, to finish the tale as ya ma was employed at the Castle and well respected, the C.O. transferred the three of them and nothing more was said or spoken.

"*'Thank God I never challenged him,'* were my first thoughts when ya da was in the thick of it. I want him on my side in a fight, that's for sure. Ya da said afterwards it was like a red mist came over him, and for the life of him couldn't remember any details. So, Kev lad, be careful and look out for any signs. I think you know what I mean."

"I know what you mean, Jack, and thanks."

I locked-up and walked back home while Jack headed to the harbour, probably to sleep on-board. It must have been about 5 a.m. as dawn was starting to break I went in, said God-bless to Ma and Da. Auntie Kathryn was asleep in their room. I got into bed fully clothed, and suddenly felt exhausted.

I awoke to the sound of people talking in the front room, I got myself together and splashed my face with cold water.

Still nothing there to shave, I thought. *Da would call it "Bum Fluff."*

I saw Ma and Da were gone. Auntie Kathryn seemed a bit better and told me to sit down. Mrs Dunn from next door was at the table.

"You have got to eat, Kevin. Keep up your strength, my lovely boy, sit. I have some fresh skate Jack Cattin dropped it in." Mrs Dunn winked at me.

From the kitchen Auntie Kathryn was having a go at Jack.

"I don't know why he has took it on himself to do all this stuff. After all he never did so much when my poor sister was alive. I have seen more of him these past few days than in a month of Sundays."

Mrs Dunn had been a top secretary to a firm of solicitors in Belfast before retiring. She turned to me and winked again. I was confused.

"I think the lady protesteth too much," she said.

God knows what she is talking about and He won't tell, I thought.

"I happen to know that Jack Cattin has a thing for your auntie Kathryn," Mrs Dunn remarked. "And I think she for him. It's been going on now for years. Folks wonder why. I have a feeling what's happened will bring them closer, you mark my words, Kevin. You know, Kevin, I think you're going to be alright."

Auntie Kathryn joined us carrying some fish and crusty fresh baked bread. I love the smell of newly baked bread as well as the crust. Ma would say, *"Your hair won't curl if you don't eat your crusts."*

I smiled at Mrs Dunn.

"And what have I missed?" My auntie asked. "What are you two smiling about?" She inquired.

"I think Old Jack Cattin is a good man," I added, "and I thanked him for his help."

"He's not that old," Auntie Kathryn coloured up and ran back into the kitchen.

"*Well, well, well,*" thought I.

Mrs Dunn and I suppressed a laugh and started to eat. It was about eight in the evening when Father Kelly came round.

"I have arranged the service for tomorrow. How does that suit you, Kevin?"

"I think it's fine, Father, and thank you."

"That's all very good. The service is at 10 o'clock. Oh, Kevin, the coffin has been taken to the Chapel of Rest and you can see your folks any time."

"Can I follow you back now, Father?"

"Yes you can, let's be going now."

I followed Father Kelly up to the church.

"You know where to go now, Kevin, so take as long as you need. God bless you."

I headed to the Chapel-of-Rest and went in. There they were, lying together holding hands as I had asked them to be. The coffin looked good.

I wonder if this has ever been done before. Of course, it must have been done surely, though nobody had heard of it.

I looked at them both. "Da, look I have your fishing knife. You know I always wanted it. You know I'll take good care of it. And, Ma, I thank you for all you have done for me, you taught me right from wrong. You both showed me what is really important in life, and that laughter is a great healer you said once, *'Everybody laughs in the same language.'* I will make you both proud."

The morning came bright and sunny, the church was packed to the rafters. Everyone in there, Sunday best and all, I had never seen so many flowers. Father Kelly said some wonderful things. I felt proud to have been so lucky to have been blessed with such well loved and respected parents. As they lowered the coffin into the ground, it took eight men, two on each corner rope. I smiled. This was the final farewell, they were now at peace, together for eternity and next to where Nan lay. Jimmy made an Oak Cross and Pat hand-wrote in Gold;

William and Whinny O'Keefe—Together for Ever.

A stone had been ordered from Belfast. I was told this could take several weeks, and I must tell Auntie Kathryn the wording I wanted. I stood up and thanked everyone for their support and help. Folks drifted away with knowing nods and smiles. Only Auntie, Jack Cattin, and I remained by the graveside.

There were a quiet few moments before Auntie spoke, "Tomorrow we will move your things over to mine. Do you want to sleep at mine tonight?"

I jumped in with, "At home tonight, if that's fine with you, Auntie."

"Yes of course that's fine, Kevin."

"Kev lad," said Jack, "Mr O'Hara has agreed to have the wake in the workshop. He thought ya da would appreciated the gesture."

"Thanks Jack. Hey, could I ask a favour of you? Would you kindly escort Auntie Kathryn to the wake? I need to know she will be with someone who will look out for her now that Da's not around." Jack and Auntie's faces were a picture. this was just what Auntie wanted and Jack had hoped for.

"It would be an honour and a pleasure, if that's fine with you, Kathryn?" said Jack.

"I-I-I, well, yes, that will be fine." Auntie Kathryn tried to conceal her joy and excitement. They looked at each other.

Mrs Dunn was right. I smiled to myself.

Aunt Kathryn once said, *"Fishermen never die, they only smell that way."* She was not thinking that now, I bet. Neither had married and neither were by any means young. she must be 63-ish, a few years older than Ma. And Jack about the same, maybe slightly older.

A strange couple. She had worked for the banks in Belfast, held a very good job, owned her house, and appeared proper. Him, a fisherman and had been around a bit, but he did own his own boat and never seemed short of cash. I can't see my auntie helping Jack with the boat, but, you never know. Ma would say, *"Love has no hard and fast rules. It grabs folks in different ways, and to find your one true love, must be the greatest gift the good Lord can give. Ya da and I know this for sure, for we have been blessed."*

I left the church to head to the only home I have ever known. I stopped and looked at the front door before going in, I felt no remorse no sadness, there was nothing there for me anymore. I went in, it was quiet. I stood still for a moment, trying to make a connection. They were not there, they had gone.

I must go away, travel, start my life's journey. I thought. *They are with me in this. This is how it will be; I'll stay in the village until next spring and get some money together before starting my travels. I am stronger than I have ever been both in mind and body. I can use my hands and have enough knowledge to be able to make a living anywhere. I am confident and comfortable in my own self.*

I looked around. *Right, I'll get all the bits and pieces I want and the rest can stay put. I'll start with clothing.*

This took about five minutes. Not much, just summer and winter stuff of my own. I tried on Da's stuff, all too big except a good pair of boots, a nice leather belt with a big brass buckle. I'd have to make a few more holes in the leather to fit me, three handkerchiefs, his pipes and stand, and that was it. I put all Ma's clothes in a heap with Da's. Father Kelly can pass them out as he sees fit. There was no jewellery, what she had went with her.

Now, Da's tools, all the good ones, were at the workshop and they were now mine. I was eager to use them, and hoped some of his skill was still in them, I'll need it. I grabbed the knife and Nan's Tarot Cards, still not sure what I am to read in them. I'll have a look at them in time. There was nothing else of any value really, and decided to leave it all here.

Hopefully they may be of use to the new tenants. Same goes for the bedding.

I had asked Auntie Kathryn if there was anything of Ma's she would like. She said, "I would like the spinning wheel and rocking chair, as they belonged to our mother."

It must have been around 3 p.m. when Father Kelly came knocking at the door.

"Just popped around to see if I could be of assistance." He looked at the pile of clothes on the table, "Yes, Father, you can have them."

His eyes widened and he smiled. "I don't suppose any of the bedding, and bits will be left. I can't see your auntie Kathryn wanting any of it, and the new folks would really appreciate anything you could leave behind. I know they haven't got two brass farthings to rub together."

"They can have it all, Father, except the rocker and the wheel."

I caught sight of the rag-rug by the hearth made by Ma from old hessian sacks with bits of rag cut into small strips and threaded through. It was about six feet by four feet and very colourful. I drifted back to the time I watched her make it. I must have only been about four or five.

"I will also take the rug, Father."

"It's a good thing you are doing, Kevin. Now, are you sure you are alright?"

As I met his gaze man to man, I realised I'd grown-up in the past 24 hours.

21

"I assure you, Father, I am fine. Thank you for your concern and all you have done."

"Yes, my boy, I think you are. May God bless and guide you."

" I will bring the clothes to you tomorrow on my way to Auntie Kathryn."

"Don't bother, Kevin. I think they would be of use left here. So, you will be staying at Kathryn's from tomorrow? Good. I'll tell the O'Malley's they can move in the day after tomorrow. Well, I will see you later, it promises to be a good crack." He left.

I sat in the rocking chair, lost in thought while gazing about the room and out at the open door. Except for Da and Ma, I would miss nothing. It was as if I had been just waiting for this day to arrive. The moment was broken by a soft voice I knew well.

"Hello, Kevin, can I come in?" It was Mrs Dunn's granddaughter Nelly. Nelly Kelly, it was one of those names you never forget, and no relation to Father Kelly.

She lived on her parents farm some six or seven miles out of the village and would walk to visit her gran once every few weeks on Wednesday, market day. This was when the village came alive. Nelly was my age, with me being seven months older. I knew our parents had plans for us. We did get on well, and I knew Nelly was keen. But it wasn't for me. Something kept me from letting her get too close.

She was a good looker, the lads fancied her and sometimes it was hard to resist her charms. We kissed once a few months ago. It would have gone a lot further right there, but I backed off. If we had laid together, I would have had to marry her. That's only right and proper.

Is this visit planned? I wondered. *Had Mrs Dunn suggested Nelly try to catch me at a vulnerable time?*

"I just thought you would want me with you at this time." Nelly sat on the rag-rug.

She held my hand with both of hers, and gazed up at me with her head slightly to one side. I peered back at her, nothing was said. She was lovely, a classic Coleen with big clear emerald eyes, lots of burnished copper coloured hair hanging down to her waist, and flawless pale skin while wearing a dress that showed her ample breasts.

I'd never seen her looking so good. I felt my resolve weakening. To break the spell I jumped up and stood by the mantle a few feet away. However, she joined me. We gazed into each other's eyes. She threw her arms around me, her head on my chest. I could not help myself and held her close. We again made eye contact and dissolved into a kiss that said far too much.

"Oh, Kevin, I will always be here for you. You know that, don't you? It's you I want next to me."

I remembered a saying I had heard one of the fishermen say down at the harbour. One of them was getting married, another good man gone wrong, His mates greeted his announcement with roars of laughter. He simply said, *'High hopes fade by a warm hearth stone, he travels faster who travels alone.'* There wasn't so much laughter this time. Perhaps it went home for a few of them.

Why should this be? I thought.

Perhaps it was a bit naive of me. The moment was broken by Mrs Dunn's arrival.

"Oh, sorry, I didn't mean to interrupt, I can see you are alright." She winked at me.

"Mrs Dunn!" I cried. "Was there anything you wanted to talk to me about?"

"No, no, it will keep." She smiled and winked at Nelly.

I untangled myself from her arms. "Er, I need to have a wash and get changed for the Wake."

"Oh, er, yes. Can we walk there together? Me ma and da will call for my gran. What time do you think ?"

I'll have to go through with this, I thought. "About seven-ish."

Nelly's smile seemed to say, *I've got him!* She turned and floated out the door. My God she was something special. I had to get through the next five months. It was a very bitter sweet feeling.

It only seemed a few minutes passed before Nelly reappeared in the doorway. The sunlight shone through the dress silhouetting the wonderful contours of her young firm body. Did she know this or not? My gaze swept over her from head to toe, taking in this beautiful sight.

I swallowed. "You look—nice." I was going to say fantastic, yet stopped myself just in time.

My mind and body were doing things I had no control over. As I said before: A moment's thought is an hour in words. It was over in seconds. She smiled and came towards me.

Of course she knew, you dimwit! Why do you think she stopped in the door-way? My God, why me? I didn't think my thoughts were in anyway sinful so The Confessional was out.

Nelly came up, threw her arms around my neck, and me kissed me. She looked so happy, and God knows she felt good to hold.

I have got to say something to her soonish.

Nelly's parents were at the door with Mrs Dunn. I caught sight of their smiling faces. They must've been waiting just outside, I'm sure of it.

This is a bloody conspiracy. I won't be pressured by anyone. I will make up my own mind as and when.

They must have seen the stern look on my face, as they all turned serious. Mr Kelly cleared his throat.

"Right, then shall we make a move?"

All I could think of as we walked is what Nan said on her deathbed, *"The true love of your life is not what you would expect and not from these parts and when you have found her, you will have all you desire."* Why would she say that? She was seldom wrong about these things and she said I had "the gift."

"Well, come on," beckoned Mrs Dunn.

Nan, give me a sign for God's sake!

Nelly had her arm in mine and was uncomfortably close. I felt her right breast moving against my arm. Everything between us had moved so fast over the last 24 hours. Our first kiss after years of knowing her and keeping my distance was months ago. Now it was as if we were a couple. I knew I was beginning to weaken. Perhaps Nan was wrong, I was beginning to fall. A line from an old folk song came to mind,

'If you find love and she really loves you,

Hold onto her tightly and never let her go.'

It won't be long before Nelly says she loves me, I just know it. And I truly believe she does and probably always has. The more I thought back over the years, the gifts she made for me, she was always just there, happy, smiling, and attentive.

Oh, for Christ's sake get a grip.

We reached the boathouse and I was brought back to reality by the noise of the good folks, the music, lights, food, and drink. What a spread. The tables groaned under the weight, bottles of beer, homemade wines of all sorts, pies—

pork, chicken, beef and lamb. Cakes of all denominations, some large some small, and the centre of the main table an oak barrel of the Black Porter.

'Father Kelly met us at the door. I could see he was pleased at what he thought he saw. I removed Nelly's arm from around mine and placed it by her side. She stood still. I could not look at her face, but sensed she was not happy about this.

"Well, Kevin, I have to say, your parents would be so proud by the way you have handled yourself since their departure from this earth. May God bless them and keep them. Now, let's celebrate their lives for the fine upstanding people they were." He moved aside and bid us enter with a wave of his hand. Almost stumbling he lent against the wall to steady himself.

I thought he had been at the juice-o-the-barley already. I felt proud at the amount of people who came up to me and spoke fine words about my folks. What Da had done for them. I'd no idea how involved they had been. The Commanding Officer, he in full dress uniform, and his wife from the Castle came up and shook my hand.

"Your mother was a special woman. She had wisdom beyond her years and was a great comfort to my wife when she needed the understanding of a wise woman." His wife pulled at his sleeve.

"Yes, well, say no more. But this I will say to you, Mr O'Keefe, I need men like you with me, think about it." He turned and the both of them left. This was the first time I had been addressed as Mr O'Keefe, and it felt wonderful.

Nelly followed close behind me. She put her arm in mine and gave me a look of uncertainty, a small smile, and large eyes. I could not stop myself, sod it all. I wanted to be happy and the same for everyone there. I draped my arm around her waist.

"Can I have this dance please, Miss Kelly?"

She beamed, it made me feel so warm inside, and I had not touched a drop…

"It would be a honour and a pleasure, Mr O'Keefe," she curtsied.

It was a fantastic send off, it was a pity my parents couldn't be there to enjoy it themselves.

My best pal, Terry Duffy son of one of the villages fishing fleet, was only three years older than me and was shall we say really enjoying himself. He came up to Nelly and me, staggered, threw his arms around us both with tears in his eyes.

"You, you two, I mean you two, look just butiful, just look at ya, what a handsome couple you make."

"Terry." I held him up. "Terry, you have been at the Cryin Whiskey?"

"Better than the Fighting Whiskey," added Nelly.

He looked me in the eye. "If you don't make a onist woman of Nelly, you will regret it to your dying day. If ya live that long that is, so it is."

His big brother Mike came over, grabbed him, and hauled him away.

"I love you, my big brother," Terry slobbered.

"Yes, yes, yes and I love you, too, ya drunken bum." Mike smiled.

Terry kept repeating himself as the pair wandered off. I knew how Terry felt about Nelly. He would have her if he could, if she showed the slightest notion.

The wake was going well, everybody enjoying themselves. Drink and food everywhere.

"I need some fresh air." I smiled, "Oh, so do I." smiled Nelly.

We strolled outside. The night was clear, a thousand stars twinkled. In a few days it would be a full moon. We walked around the back, out of sight. I grabbed Nelly, and she gasped. I held her close, kissed her, and felt her sink into me. It was bliss. My hand went to her breast. I kissed her neck, my heart beating like a drum.

She pressed herself into me, then out, then in. My hand slid down her body. I was just about to go between her legs when we suddenly became aware of a low moaning. We looked to our left, our eyes widened as they became accustomed to the lack of light. There no more than ten feet away was Mike and Maggy. She lying on a stack of wood, skirt up around her neck, and him with his trousers around his ankles.

The two of them going at it like rabbits. They were totally unaware of Nelly and me.

After we had a good eyeful we backed away and walked around the front. Nelly stopped and stared at me. I felt myself becoming lost in her clear green pools of emerald. After a few moments I spoke,

"I know what you're thinking, Nel."

"When, Kevin?"

"Soon, sweetheart, soon," I replied, but with reservation in my mind.

"I am ready for you."

I held her hand and we returned to the wake. Father Kelly came into view. I tried to get away by joining the dancing. Too slow.

"Ah, what a lovely couple you two make. Are we to—"

I cut him short. "I think, Father, you will have more meat on the bone if you turned your attention to the couple sitting over there by the band." I pointed to the table where Auntie Kathryn and Jack Cattin were sitting.

With him momentarily distracted, I dragged Nelly into the dance. I knew what he was going to say.

Not now, I thought. *And not here.*

Father Kelly had a look of contempt as he grabbed my arm and whispered in my ear, "You and I need to talk, young man."

I stopped and looked him in the eye. "That would suit me fine, Father."

Nelly and I resumed dancing. As dawn broke, it promised to be a nice day. It must have been around five o'clock and there was only a few die-hards those who are the last to leave left. Most had gone to their homes as they had work that day. The band departed around two-ish. I stood alone as Nelly had gone with her parents about an hour ago. I felt for Nelly as she left looking a bit confused and unsure, as was I.

It's for the best, I thought.

Mr O'Hara was asleep in the corner with a glass in his hand, I took the glass from him and placed it on the table. He woke with a start, and mumbled something.

"Thank you, Mr O'Hara, for all you have done. I'll go get a few hours and I'll come back and tidy things up."

"No need, Kev lad, no need. All taken care of. See you at work first thing 7.:30 tomorrow. We can talk money then." He fell asleep.

What had just happened? I asked myself.

The last few days flew past, so much has happened, but I felt on top of the world. I had gone from a boy to a man. My whole attitude towards life and people changed, hopefully for the better. I was proud of my parents, their passing had been the beginning for me. I went home and slept like the dead.

I was woken with hammering on the door, I was still dressed.

"Oh, it's you, Mrs Dunn. What time is it ?"

"It's just gone six," she answered.

I had slept for twelve hours and more if it wasn't for Mrs Dunn.

"I just thought you could do with a nice bowl of soup. I bet you have not eaten since yesterday." She was right, "Thank you, Mrs Dunn." I went to take the bowl and plate of bread, yet she held tight.

"Our Nelly will be down later. She will want to be seeing you, I'll send her around for the dishes." She studied me, trying to gage to see my reaction.

I kept a straight face. "Good, I need to talk to her." I could tell this was not the reaction she wanted. I managed to get the food from her grasp and bid her goodbye.

I sat and ate. The bread was warm with a crispy-crust, and the soup more like a stew was very welcome, I had no idea I was so hungry, I could have eaten it twice over. All my stuff was now at Auntie Kathryn's, and she was expecting me today. I think.

God, I can't remember. Yes, I'm sure it's today.

There was a knock on the door, and in the doorway was a man, woman, and several children. The children burst in shouting. "This is wonderful!"

"Which is my room?" the eldest girl squealed.

I stood up. "You must be the O'Malley's."

Mrs O'Malley rushed in. "Oh, Mr O'Keefe, so sorry. But the children are excited as am I."

Mr O'Malley looked at me unsure of my reaction. "Father Kelly did say we could move in today I hope this is the case as we have vacated our old house, Mr O'Keefe."

I still can't get used to being called Mr O'Keefe. "Of course, Mr O'Malley, please bring your belongings in. I'll give you a hand."

"No, no need. Thank you all the same, it's not much." He seemed embarrassed.

"I'll get out your way, Mr O'Malley, I hope you will be as happy here as I have been. Only good memories here." I picked up the dishes and walked out into Mrs Dunn's open hands, "I'll tell Nelly to call at your auntie's then, shall I?" She did not look pleased.

"Er, yes please," I said, not really thinking it through. I set off to Auntie Kathryn's house.

I was shown my room.

She placed the rag-rug on the floor in front of the bed. "Have you eaten ?"

I lied, "No Auntie."

"Then I'll see you down stairs." She left to prepare a meal.

I settled myself in and not thirty minutes later Auntie shouted up the stairs, "Hot food on the table, Kevin. Don't let it get cold."

No chance of that, I thought.

It was another stew and bread with a glass of ale.

A glass of ale. Mmmm, this is going to be fine just fine.

Auntie joined me. "I've already eaten. Kevin, how are you?"

"I have never felt better, Auntie. The wake showed me just how well me-Ma and Da were thought of. I feel a new person, my own self, and thank you, Auntie, for taking me in."

"Oh, don't talk nonsense. It's nice to have you here, there's only you and me left. I hope you will be happy here."

"I am sure of it."

She smiled and held my hand.

"I trust Jack looked after you and saw you home."

She jumped up. "Yes, thank you. He was a gentleman." Her tone said she didn't want to discuss it any further. She disappeared into the kitchen.

I smiled to myself. *It won't be long before it becomes public knowledge.* I was pleased for them both.

There was a knock at the door, I knew who it might be. Auntie opened the door to Jack, not Nelly as I had thought.

"Both of you come in." Auntie beckoned.

Both?

Nelly and Jack crossed the threshold. There was an awkward silence. Jack spoke first, "Hello, Kathryn, and the same to you, Kev lad. I have a lovely bit of skate for you Kathryn and a nice bit of—"

"Nelly, do you fancy a walkdown the front?" I grabbed her hand and off we went before Jack could finish his sentence. He had that wicked look in his eye. I just knew he was about to add something like, *"and a nice bit of stuff for you or such."*

Nelly giggled in delight and soon her arm was around mine.

"Well, Nel." *Oh my God I called her Nel.*

"You have never called me Nel. That's what my family calls me."

"Oh, sorry, I—"

She cut me short. "No, no, it sounds lovely when you say it."

I knew it! What were you thinking? I changed the subject. "What do you think about Jack and Auntie Kathryn er, Nel?"

"Oh, it's fantastic. People have speculated over those two for years, and it appears they have finally got together. Just like us, Kev."

For God's sake, what am I saying? Have the gods taken over? Is this fate or a test? I thought before answering and she WAS waiting for an answer. It just came out, I was weakening.

"Just like us, Nel," I said, half-hearted.

What happened next, I knew would happen. She jumped into my arms and kissed me as she had never kissed me before, "I love you so much, Kev! I always have and always will. I will follow you to the ends of the earth."

You may have to, I thought.

"I will live in a midden as long as I am with you. Oh, I'm so happy" She shed tears of sheer joy.

I felt myself filling up, getting emotional and it was fantastic. *What a relief.* I held her tight. All was going to be fine, just fine.

My whole way of thinking changed and I embraced it. I had the most beautiful girl in the county, the girl they all wanted. She wanted and loved me. The words to that old folk song came flooding back:

If you find love and she really loves you, hold on to her tightly and never let her go.

I knew Terry would be pleased for me after what he said at the wake. But I also knew he'd be sad, as I believe he possessed strong feelings for her. One bridge at a time.

We just stood there, not a word was spoken for quite a while. There was no need, we understood.

"You staying at Mrs Dunn's tonight, Nel?" I asked.

"Yes, darling."

O my God, she called me darling. "I start back at the boat yard tomorrow start at 7.30 a.m. When are you back down here next…" I went for it, "sweetheart?" This is what Da would call Ma.

Nelly would have given herself to me there and then. This was unbelievable, I felt complete.

I think I'm falling in love, if this is what it feels like, I want the world to feel like it. I now know how Ma and Da must of experienced all those years. Why did the hell did I fight it so?

We walked back to her gran's, stopped on the path, and kissed. The door flew open and Mrs Dunn stood there, looking at me with a face like thunder, I smiled at her, bent, and kissed her cheek, Nel was smiling, too.

"Oh, come here you two. I'm so pleased. Oh, Nelly, you must be… Oh, Kevin, I thought, well, I don't know what I thought."

I interrupted her. "I will say goodnight to you both. I'm sure you have lots to talk about."

"I don't know what you mean, young man. Now, be off with ya," she scolded, but smiled.

As I walked away, I glanced back. Nel was standing in the doorway, her silhouette outlined by the room's light.

My God, I must be the luckiest man alive. I grinned all the way back to Auntie Kathryn's.

I reached home right as Jack was just leaving. "Evening Mr Cattin."

"Good night to you, Mr O'Keefe."

We were both smiling like idiots.

Has his night gone as good as mine? I wondered.

I bid Auntie goodnight and went straight up to my room. I undressed and got into bed, Oh yes, this was a fantastic bed. Goose and duck down filled. My mind was galloping faster than a race horse. I suddenly remembered the horses I'd seen in the fires flames the night Nan died. Oh my God, had I seen the future? It was a galloping horse that had ran over Ma. My blood ran cold as ice. I sat up and just looked into the dark of the room. Nothing.

After a few minutes, I settled down with the face of my lovely Nel in my mind's eye. I started to fantasise, imagining her undoing dress and letting it slowly fall off her shoulders, past her firm young breasts, down to her waist, finally to the ground. She stood naked in front of me. I was getting hard I could see that smile of hers that would warms the cockles of the coldest heart. I gripped myself, my breathing coming deep and fast, and my heart about to burst right through my chest. A knock on the door interrupted my fantasy.

"Kevin, I'm out early in the morning. So breakfast will be served then. I'll give you a knock when it's ready, ok?"

"Er—yes, Auntie," was all I could say. The moment was gone. *Will I ever get to sleep? Was Nel thinking the same? Was she still awake? Are her and her gran still talking? Probably all of it.* I gave a short laugh and settled to sleep.

During a breakfast of eggs, bacon, and, a large mug of tea, I got the feeling Auntie wanted to ask about Nelly, but was afraid I might ask about Jack. So little was said. Afterwards, I bid her good day and she left while I headed off to work.

31

It was too early to go to the boatyard, so I walked down to the front. It was going to be a fine day, the sun was starting to show itself bright and orange.

This can't be bad, I thought. *It's true what they say, 'the best things in life are free.'* Jack's warning came to mind, *'Nothing comes free except death.'*

I strode into workshop and greeted both Jimmy and Pat.

"Tell me what you want me to do," I said to Jimmy. "And I'll make a start."

This was met with, "Whoa, whoa, slow down. Carry on like that, and you'll be knackered by the end of the day. And so will me and Pat. First thing for you is make a brew, then we will discuss the day's schedule."

We sat down with our mugs of tea.

"First things first," says Jimmy, "how are you, Kev? Must say, you look on top of the world."

I didn't want to say anything about Nelly right now. "I am fine, just fine."

"Good," said Pat. "Right, lads, let's get started. We should have this one boat done by the weekend. It's already two weeks late, and the old man says he has an order for a 36 foot. Fishing boat. The timber is scheduled for delivery next week, so we need the space."

We stopped for dinner at one o'clock. It was then I remembered I had left mine on the table this morning, not being used to the idea as Da would have had both ours. I went to the toilet and heard Jimmy shout, "Kev lad, there's someone to see you. Now don't forget to wash your hands."

I detected a smile in his voice and came out. There was this vision of loveliness. and this angel was all mine. I tried not to smile, but could not stop myself. I glared at the other two sitting nearby, pretending not to notice. Jimmy gave me a knowing nod.

"What have you got that I haven't, Kev lad? I don't get my grub personally delivered."

"That's because you're old and you are ugly." Laughed Pat.

"Well, thank you for that Patrick not so O'Flattery."

I grabbed Nelly's hand. "Shall we go outside?" We sat down on a bench next to the lumber pile. this gave us a view down to the sea. "I thought you went back home in the morning."

"I normally do, but today I just thought for some reason I would stay. Can't think why. I met your auntie Kathryn with your dinner and offered to bring it myself. Hope you don't mind."

"Well, I don't know." I sounded unsure.

She playfully slapped my arm, it was bliss. "I won't be down again till next Wednesday, market day. I'll see you then."

We kissed.

"I thought of you in bed last night" The words tumbled out.

"I did it, too," she admitted.

We gazed at each other.

Strange thing to say, 'I did it, too,' I thought.

The moment was broken by Jimmy. "I hate to disturb you both, but we have a boat to finish. Come ed, lad." Nelly blew a kiss and walked away.

For a few seconds I watched as she walked, I wanted her so much it hurt…

"You coming back to work or what?" Laughed Jimmy, "Ok, ok, I'm here." I could tell they were both happy for me.

We all worked together well, and it felt good. I was part of a team. The day was spent planning the boat. Suddenly, Nelly's words came back to me, *'I did it, too.'* The penny dropped. My God, women can relieve themselves as well. I wanted to ask Jimmy or Pat about it, but felt too embarrassed.

Sunday came and I was invited out fishing with Jack Cattin. The cod had started to run. It was a great day, we were out by six o'clock in the morning. We got a varied catch, cod, dog, skate, and a tope. We got back around dusk, that must have been five-ish. Several of the boats docked within minutes of each other. Jack chatted with the others about the day's catch. There was a lot "Micky" taking, leg pulling and laughter.

"Kev!" shouted Peter from "The Alice," the largest of the fleet.

"What?" I replied.

"You still on with Nelly?"

I chose not to answer.

"She got little hands, then?" He continued.

I glared at him, knowing something was coming.

"Always find a girl with small hands." Laughter from the group. "It'll make you look bigger."

I laughed with them, not understanding what the hell he was talking about. I offered to take some skate to my auntie as it was her favourite.

"No, Kev, don't trouble yourself I'll bring it later once I've tidied up," Jack said.

"It's no trouble, Jack, I live there now."

We gave each other that knowing smile, "I'll see you a bit later, Jack." I headed off.

I walked around the back as I smelt a bit fishy, took my oil-skins off, and left them outside as I intended to wash them down later. The walk home wasn't very long at all.

"Well, you're home, Kevin, had a good day?" Auntie asked.

"Yes, thanks. Jack said he would bring you some skate a bit later once he got himself sorted."

She stiffened. "I hope it's not too late, that will never do. I'll put your tea on the kitchen table."

"Thanks, Auntie."

Off she went to sit in the parlour while I sat at the table. *Cottage pie, this can't be bad,* I thought. I heard voices and got up to investigate. It was Father Kelly. I went back, finished my tea, and put the plate in the sink.

"Kevin!" shouted Auntie. "Father Kelly would like to speak to you." She must have heard me put the plate in the sink.

I joined them in the parlour. "Hello, Father, how are you?"

"I'm good, thank you. But more to the point how are you, Kevin?"

"I am very well. Auntie has made me feel welcome, and I'm enjoying it at the boat yard. Following in Da's footsteps."

"Yes, yes. I thought I might see you in church today," Father Kelly gazed steadily my face.

"Weather, time, and tide waits for no man, Father, and people need to eat. Me-Da did the same, it was me-Ma who was the church goer with Auntie here. You said you wanted to talk to me, Father."

He was taken aback. "Well, I was concerned with the way things were going between you and Miss Kelly. However, I now am to believe the situation has somewhat improved over the last few days. She always had eyes for you and you—"

I interrupted him. "We are only sixteen, Father, and what will be will be." It was in my mind to tell about my plans, but I wanted to speak with Nelly first.

"I see. Will we be seeing you and Miss Kelly in church?"

"I can't speak for Miss Kelly, but I will not." His ferocious frown told me he was not pleased.

"Your mother would turn in her grave, and the grave not yet cold." He took a breath.

"Me-Da is holding her hand, he would stop her," I quipped.

His face reddened.

"I have been reading in the newspapers about this terrible war, the killing, the maiming, and the suffering people are doing to other human beings. Yet, when they all go to war with God on their side, it would appear over the thousands of years and hundreds of wars, that more suffering and death has been caused by religion than anything else put together.

"And if man could only live his life as close to the ten commandments as humanly possible, this madness would stop. If the church does not soften its views and listen to the needs of the people, I foresee the church losing its power and standing. You are a good man, Father Kelly, yet you could do so much more if you spoke less and listened more. This I will say, looking at the broken veins in your face, if you don't cut down on you food and drink, you will be dead within two years. What you eat and drink in one day would feed some families for a week. Look at the O'Malley's. I know Mr and Mrs Kelly are firm church goers and very involved with religion. If I find the relationship between Nelly and me weakens in any way, I will know who to blame and this would only prove my point that more suffering and pain has been caused because of religion."

I thought he was going to explode, a vein throbbed in his neck and his face had a slight purplish hue. Auntie Kathryn was pale. The situation was broken by a knock on the door.

"I'll get it," I said. "Hello Jack please come on in. Father Kelly was just leaving."

The man walked out, looking at no one and saying nothing.

"I am really sorry, Auntie," I apologised. "I just don't know where the hell all that came from." Some colour came back into her face, Jack stood there, his eyes darting between Auntie and me, unsure of what to say.

"There was a lot of truth in what you said, Kevin, and to be sure you are your father's son. Perhaps you have forgotten what your nan was known for. I think you may have her gift." Offered Auntie.

"Are you the same with politics, Kev lad?" snapped in Jack. "That was a bit sharp. I was listening at the door."

"I will put it all down to you being in mourning," said Auntie, "Ah, yes, Kev, that must be it," chipped in Jack.

"What do you mean Auntie, 'my father's son'?" I asked.

"Another time, Kevin, I can't think at present."

"Aye, another time." Jack put his arm around Auntie, smiled, and winked.

"I'm off to bed. Sorry if I upset you, Auntie, that's the last thing I wanted to do."

She was leaning into Jack. She glanced up at him then looked down. His arm tightened around her. She appeared quite happy with this development, and not at all her normal, stand-offish self.

Well, I thought, *every cloud has a silver lining.*

I lay in bed not at all sleepy. The room was dark, yet my mind was all over the shop. My father's son? Are you the same with politics? I don't remember Da saying anything about the church or politics. Well not at home, never. Now that I think about It he would go out some nights, where he went and who he saw, I never asked and was never told.

At breakfast Auntie seemed a bit quiet, perhaps it was just me. I caught her looking at me in concern. Maybe the events of last evening brought up a memories, or my outburst was so out of character she didn't know what to think.

"Auntie, can you tell me about my Da tonight after work?"

She nodded and spoke softly, "Yes, Kevin, you need to know certain things. Now off with you."

The day dragged on, and at last it was six o'clock. I set off for home. Tea was on the table. This time Auntie sat with me. Normally she would have had hers before I arrived. We sat in silence, eating.

"This is lovely, Auntie," I offered.

"And why shouldn't it be? The veg are from the garden, you'll not get fresher than that." She fidgeted. "Kevin, your father was a special man, I suppose you would say. He was a peoples champion. He had some rather unconventional ideas, and cared for the people in this village and surrounding areas. If they were being bullied or thought they had been treated unfairly over things such wages, rent, price of fish, price of food clothing… Pretty much all sorts of day-to-day things that affect simple folks, they would ask your father to help.

"And if he thought they had a real problem, he, as I think you are or will be, did not suffer fools. He'd help if he thought he could. This did not at times, impress the powers that be. The church being one, some of the land owners around here, business people, merchants and the like being another.

"Your father could have been a Magistrate or some such thing, but he would not compromise his beliefs just to fit in with their standards. As Jack – Mr Cattin said, his other pet hate was politics and politicians. He believed in Ireland for the Irish. This is, as you will learn, a sore-point. Well, any questions, Kevin ?"

"No, Auntie, I don't think so. Thank you. Will you save the papers for me to read?"

"I hope all this ends well, but what will be will be," she muttered under her breath. Aloud she said, "Yes of course I will. Kevin, you gave Father Kelly a real flea in his ear that's for sure. Make your peace with him, he does try his best."

I only nodded.

The Wake now seemed years ago. My new life had begun, and I believe for the better. I had a full-time job I enjoyed and the lovely Nelly Kelly in my heart, mind and everywhere else, a lovely new home, and fishing with Jack Cattin. What more could a lad want or need?

Chapter 2

A few weeks passed. The boat was completed and we started on the new one. A very high build, Rock-Elm on oak planked in larch, framing at six inches, centres of two inched by two inches. We were looking forward to the build. Mr.O'Hara said this could be the start of some good and profitable contracts, so we must get it right and delivered on time. The incentive, not that we needed one, was a big bonus.

I offered to pay for the arrangements he had made for Ma and Da, by working a day for nothing. But he would have none of it. He said it was an honour to be able to do something for Da for a change. So, Da must have helped him with some such in the past.

Auntie Kathryn and Jack were now officially walking out together. The village was pleased for them. Jack, when not fishing, even started going to church. This was more for Auntie's benefit than his. I believe his thoughts on religion were close to mine. It appeared Father Kelly had not said anything to Nelly's parents with reference to my outburst, as all seemed going well.

Over the last few weeks Nelly and I enjoyed each other's company with a picnic and a boat trip. Mr O'Hara let me take out the launch, a 15-footer we used to move boats around with. It was great fun. I happened to know Nelly does not like the water or boats. However, she had no idea that I knew.

I got the boat ready, started the old, temperamental paraffin/petrol engine, and got it warmed up. It was a clear and crisp late October day, no wind with a blue cloudless sky. Nel. appeared looking as lovely as ever with a basket of food and drink on her arm. I watched her face as she drew near. The smile was forced, the eyes wide and stern. I smiled to myself as she stood on the quay.

"Well, are you going to take this basket and help me on, or just stand there?"

I took the basket, and offered my hand. She took hold as if her life depended on it, she was shaking.

"Come on then, Nel, jump on."

Her eyes shot daggers at me, as if to warn that if she died, it was my fault… It was only a few feet below the quay-side. She jumped, I caught her, and she grabbed a hold of me as if her life depended on it. I held her close and started to laugh. She was still shaking.

"Nel, looked up at me."

"What is so funny?" Her face softened, and I just melted inside. "You knew, you knew."

She smiled, "Your, your gran told me." I admitted, "Do you think I would let anything happen to you?"

"You can be so—"

"Handsome?"

"No, well yes."

"Thoughtful?"

"Annoying is the word." She playfully slapped my arm.

"Careful, I bruise easy."

She smiled, kissed me, and whispered in my ear, "I will get my revenge. How far are we going?".

"Oh, just around the headland. The sea can get a bit choppy, but the views are fantastic."

Her face went paler than normal. I laughed.

"You can stop that right now, Mr Kevin O'Keefe. Or I will get out and walk back and take the basket with me."

We both laughed at the thought.

"So, Nel, you can walk on water?"

Tears ran down our faces as we laughed till we ached. Once recovered, I gave her the tiller.

"Now, remember pull to the left to go right and push to the right to go left. Nel looked at me."

"That makes no sense at all, Kevin."

"Just try it. Now, would I lie to you?"

"You're smiling at me."

"I will always smile whenever I look at that beautiful face of yours."

She relaxed. "You're right, it does work."

"I know. Now, have a play go left then right, or as I should say Port and Starboard."

We had a series of slow curves leaving a wake like a drunken snake behind us. I stood up and went to open the basket. Just then Nelly gave a sharp turn to port. I stumbled and managed to grab the seat, or I would have been over the side. I whirled about, ready to tell her to be careful, when I saw her guilty grin.

"You did that on purpose!" I retorted.

"Revenge is sweet sayeth the Lord," Nelly laughed.

"That was wicked, Nel. I could have been overboard, and I can't swim."

"Kevin O'Keefe, you are such a liar, I happen to know you are an excellent swimmer, and you said you would never lie to me."

"Any man who said he has never lied to a woman shows a complete disregard for her feelings." I smiled.

I sat down and we stared at each other. I've never felt so close to her as I did now. I knew also my Nel. felt the same. It was a magic moment in time we both would never forget. I wanted everything to stand still. Words I heard Ma say once to Da, can't remember the situation, were:

"If you want time to stand still, first, you must stand still and make time."

This was one of those moments. We sat next to each other, me to Port and Nelly to Starboard with both hands on the tiller, hers on mine. We sat in silence, the sea was, as Jack Cattin often said, '*as flat as a witch's tit.*' Only the noise of the engine and the odd call of a seabird. Neither of us wanted this moment to ever end. No words were spoken, there was no need, we understood.

We cut the engine and drifted with the tide. Nelly sorted out the food of cold meat, pork, cheese, homemade apple pickle, crusty fresh bread, and a bottle of Mrs Dunn's famous homemade Elderflower wine.

"Nelly Kelly, you never stole the drink!" I exclaimed.

"No, she gave it to me," she pouted.

"Your gran gave you the wine?"

"Yes."

This drink I know, is only offered and consumed on very special occasions. *Us men really don't stand a cat's chance in hell once the woman folk start to plan and scheme. We stand no chance at all.* I smiled.

We sat and talked, ate and drank, "This Elderflower wine is strong stuff, Nel. Best I finish it off."

"No chance."

"Nel, what do you know about this Easter Rising thing that happened back in April in Dublin."

She looked taken aback, "Er, I heard Father speak about it. It's the old thing, Ireland for the Irish. Why do you ask?" She looked concerned.

"It's ok, sweetheart, just something my auntie said about me-Da."

She kissed me. "I love it when you call me sweetheart. Say it again, please."

"No, Nel, you're limited to one a day."

She pushed out her bottom lip in a sulk, "Ok, ok. Sweetheart, sweetheart, sweetheart. sweetheart, sweetheart, sweetheart, sweetheart. That's a week's worth now gone. No more for a whole week."

"That's mean of you."

"Treat them mean, keep them keen. That's my motto" I kept my face serious.

"I hope not." She frowned angrily, "Where did you hear that? It's horrible."

"I overheard some soldiers from the castle."

"That might apply to some of the girls in the village, but not me, Kevin O'Keefe."

I held her close, and winked. "The tide is turning, sweetheart. Damn it, you got an extra sweetheart. Damn there's another one."

She laughed, hugged herself, and sighed happily as she looked out to sea her back to me. I looked at her. She must've sensed it because turned and winked at me. I bent down and kissed her. My hand cupped her breast. I felt her nipple harden against my palm. My hand trailed down to her waist around her back and I pulled her close to me. Her hands held my face, then she pulled away slowly her face only mere inches away from mine. For a few moments we searched each other's eyes. Then we kissed fast and hard.

My hand moved down between her legs. I touched her. She raised her body to meet me, shaking. I broke away. She was confused, unsure. I swallowed, grabbed the thick woollen blanket, and placed it on the deck boards. I stretched out and she laid down next to me. We held each other and kissed. She was no longer shaking, but wore a look of sweet surrender.

My hand slid down to her knee and lifted her dress. I inched up between her soft smooth thighs, until I felt her knickers. We stared at each other all the time. She closed her eyes as I pulled her knickers down. She brought her knees up, I slid the fabric over her knees and feet. My hand moved up until I touched her. She was wet. She arched her back and uttered a low noise like a small animal. I undid my belt and lowered my trousers. I was hard. Her hand moved down and held my penis.

We shared a smile as I rolled on top. She opened her legs and brought her knees up. I fumbled, then suddenly was inside her. She uttered a little moan and looked hurt. She must have seen the concern on my face.

"It's ok, Kevin. I'm ok," she whispered, her face softened.

I could not hold back any longer and exploded. She had felt this, arched her back, and grabbed me tight. I lay on my elbows with my hands around the back of her head while planting kisses all over her face and neck.

"Please don't move. Let me hold you like this forever," she whispered.

I had no intention of going anywhere. I was a man, and this vision of loveliness was my woman. I started to soften. I felt a bit... well, hard to say.

"We've done it. You have made me a woman, Kevin. I do love you so much. I always have, you must have known."

I waited for the right words to come into my head, but all that came out was "I love you, too."

Her reaction told me those were the right words. She beamed and flung her arms around me. I was on top of the world.

"We must be getting back, sweetheart." I got myself together, as did she.

I started the engine and headed back with Nelly at the bow and me at the tiller. I looked at her. God, she looked more lovely and possessed a kind of glow. She looked like a beautiful figurehead sitting there. She gave me a smile that could melt the coldest of hearts. She stared right at me. I then understood the look, she had got exactly what she wanted.

It started to feel cold it was about four o'clock. I intended to tell her about my plan to leave next spring. But could not bring myself to spoil the day as I felt it would. Soon, I must tell her soon.

Who am I trying to kid? A little voice in the back of my head demanded. *"You're not going anywhere."*

We got to the quay, and saw Jack on his boat. We waved and he waved back.

"I'll drop you of here. Nel, you wait here while I go tie-up at the yard. I'll only be a few minutes."

She stood on the quayside holding the now empty basket, I pushed off the yard, was just around the quay out of sight. I tied up, straightened myself up a bit, and started back to where I left Nelly. The walk took me past Jack, "Did you have a grand time of it out there, Kev, lad?" He asked. "Don't answer that. I can see by the look on your face. She is a handsome colleen to be sure, you take good care of her now."

"By the way, Jack, how is Auntie Kathryn?" I teased.

"Be gone with ya now." He smiled and waved me on.

I was almost there, just around this boatshed when I heard Nelly shout, "Get off me!" I rounded the corner. There was Nel. and around her were three soldiers from the castle. They stopped and watched me walk up to them.

"This the boyfriend, my lovely." This was spoken by the one in the middle. He was bigger than the other two, and stood between me and Nelly. She quickly ran around him and behind me. He was bigger than me and about five years older. He advanced towards, stopping about an arm's length away.

"Going to fight for the ladies honour? Or has someone had her cherry already?"

The others stood there laughing. My blood turned cold as ice, and I felt like a cat looking at its next meal, tense and still. I never took my eyes away from him. We both stood still it for what seemed like ages, but was probably only a few seconds. As I felt he was about to move, I spoke, "Is Thomas still the Commanding Officer?"

This took him by surprise.

"So, what if he is. What's it to you?"

"I know him very well. If you don't apologise to the lady, I will let him know and you and your comrades will be cleaning out the latrines for the rest of the war. And you will lose your stripes, Sargent."

"Bugger-off you," was his reply.

That was as far as he got. My left hand shot out. I had him by the throat, and was squeezing harder and harder. He fell to the ground. I let go, he was gasping for breath and coughing blood.

"Lord almighty, Kev lad! Not again, bloody hell. You almost killed him!" Jack had heard the commotion and was standing by my side.

I said nothing and glared at this mess on the ground. The other two helped him to his feet. They glared at me and one said, "You are bloody mad, mate."

"It's being mad that keeps him sane," Jack shouted as they led their comrade away, coughing a bit but breathing. He sighed and shook his head.in concern. "I told you to watch out for this, Kev. *'Read the signs'* I said."

I looked around Nelly. She stood some feet from me. I went to her, yet she moved back a step with a look of horror on her face.

"I-I'm sorry, sweetheart."

She started to run away.

"Nel! Nel!" I pleaded.

She stopped and turned towards me. "I'm going back to Gran's." She ran away.

"Let it lay for a bit, Kev. She'll be ok," Jack advised. "Just had a bit of a shock that's all. Come back to the boat and have a beer." We walked in silence. We sat in the main cabin "Catch this," He threw me a beer.

"Sorry, Jack, can't stay." I started to leave.

"Sit down, lad, have the beer then go. Clear your head first."

I hesitated, then complied.

"Good," said Jack. "I thought for a moment history was going to repeat itself. I went right back to that night with your father. You really will have to control yourself. If you're not careful, you are going to kill someone, and that you do not want. Imagine when in a few years you get your full strength. It doesn't bear thinking about, Kev lad, not at all."

I listened in silence.

He continued. "Think about that lovely girl and what it would do to her."

I finally made eye contact with him. I had trouble holding back tears of anger and lots of mixed emotions and thoughts. "What would they have done to Nelly if I hadn't been there, Jack? I couldn't stand there and do nothing."

"Well, yes, Lad, but I think you are going to have to find another way. What's wrong with the old one-two?" Jack got into a boxer's stance and started punching the air. "The old right, then a swift left. Well, er, the other way in your case."

I stood up.

"I really don't think they would have harmed Nelly. They have far too much to lose. And anyway, did ya see one of them? I've seen more meat on a butchers' pencil. See his legs? Muscles like knots in cotton he had."

We both laughed.

"Thanks, Jack. I'll go find her. Are you seeing Auntie later? If so, please tell her I may be late and not to wait up."

"Aye, Kev lad, I will" he replied.

I got onto the quay and looked back at him. *"'Being mad keeps him sane,'"* I repeated with a question in my voice.

"Well, it seemed to make sense at the time. Perhaps if we all admitted we had a little madness, it just might keep us more sane." He shrugged his shoulders.

I walked as fast as I could till I got to Mrs Dunn's house. I knocked, the door opened and was greeted with Mrs Dunn, hand on hips. I started to say something, yet she spoke first.

"She's not here, she has gone home."

"Did she—" I was interrupted.

"Yes, I heard it all."

"I was only protecting her, I didn't want her to get hurt."

Mrs Dunn softened. "I know, lad I know. She will come around to be sure. She loves you too much, give her time."

"What did I do that was so wrong?"

"She saw a side of you that to her was so out of character, it frightened her a bit."

I thanked her and left.

"Now don't try to find her now, it's getting late," she shouted after me.

I knew there was no way I could sleep, Nelly's home was about seven miles outside of town. It was getting dark.

Nelly must be a good way there by now, I thought. I started to run, yet after a few miles dropped to walk.

I saw the lights of the farm house about a mile away. No sign of Nelly, she must be inside. I got to within a few hundred yards and about to open the gate.

"YOU took your time!" Nelly exclaimed from out of the darkness.

"MY GOD! Nelly, sweetheart, are you trying to kill me? My heart is about to jump out of my chest."

"Another sweetheart. I *am* being spoilt, I am."

We grabbed each other, "I'm so sorry. It must have frightened you. I will never do that again, honest."

"No, Kevin, it should be me who says sorry for being so nesh. You did frighten me, though."

I held her tight. "I could have never slept until I had spoken to you."

"Me, too." She smiled. "I was thinking all the way home. I prayed you would follow me. I couldn't take it if we fought. I thought I would have to wait till dawn then walk back to town to see you."

We walked into the light and perched on a swing seat right outside the door. There was a wool blanket. We huddled it around us and sat in silence.

"You said you will never do it again, So," said Nelly, "if my honour is challenged again, you will not defend it?"

"I am not falling for that, young lady. Does your mind ever switch off?"

"Not where you are concerned, young man."

Time stood still, and after what seemed like hours, she broke the silence.

"There will be times like this, darling, when we sit silent in each other's arms. Nothing to say, yet it's all being said."

"I think I know what you mean, Nelly Kelly. I have to go, sweetheart. I have work in a few hours, and that's the last sweetheart for now. I'm all sweethearted out."

She smiled and we kissed.

"Till Wednesday, my love," said Nelly.

I started the long trek to town. I turned and waved. She stood in the doorway with the porch light behind her. She looked like an angel, my angel.

It took me two hours to get to Auntie's. I reckoned it must have been about three o'clock. I removed my shoes, crept in the back door, and got to the kitchen.

"AND what time do you call this?"

Twice in one night, can my heart take it? "So sorry, Auntie. I—"

"No need to explain, Kevin. Jack told me all. You're home safe, and that's all that matters right now. Best you get to bed, I'll wake you in time for work. Now off with ya."

"Sorry, Auntie, I repeated."

"Aye, it's all very well. Now off to bed with ya."

"Yes, Auntie."

The next several weeks passed without incident, Oh, I did see that sergeant once from across the street. I stopped and clenched my fists by my side. He hurried on, not making eye contact.

Perhaps Jack was right, I thought. *Perhaps I was a bit hasty.* I am not one for all the shouting abuse at each other and shoulder pushing. Should I catch up and apologise? No! It was he who was in the wrong, a bully.

It was market day, only three weeks to Christmas. Where has the time gone? Nelly and I were so happy, everybody was pleased for us. Lots of smiles and nods of the head as people passed us. We always held hands if we were not linking arms.

"So, Mr O'Keefe, what have you got me for Christmas?"

"Well, Nel, that would be telling."

"So you have got me something then?"

"I never said that, Miss Kelly." There was a few seconds of silence.

46

"Aren't you going to ask me what I got you?"

"Not fussed," I said. Which earned me a slap on the arm. "You will get what you are given and be thankful, young woman." Another slap. More silence.

Nelly stopped and stood in front of me with a serious expression. "You HAVE got me something, Kevin? I have made something for you."

I smiled at her. She was so annoyed with herself for letting it slip. "Oh, made something for me then have you?" I teased.

"Forget you heard that, forget now."

"I have, I have, don't hit me again. Nel, you know I bruise easy. I had no idea you were so aggressive."

"ME aggressive!" She laughed.

We walked on with her arm in mine. Out of the corner of my eye I caught her looking up at me. I imagined what was running through her head, *'he has, he must of, I'll kill him if he hasn't.'*

"Why do you keep studying my hands?" Nelly asked.

"Oh, erm, well, merely looking at the lines in your hands. You know Nan could read a person's future from them, and she said on her deathbed, I had the gift."

She gazed intently at me. "She said that to you? go on then, tell me my future."

"Well," I played for time by pretending to study her palm. "I see, I see."

"For pity's sake, what do you see, Kev?"

"I see, lots of, er, lines." Another slap on the arm.

"Be serious for once. People pay good money for this, you know," she offered.

"Then cross me palm with silver, my dear. Have you big earrings and a head scarf I could borrow? What shall I call myself?" I put my finger to my mouth as if in deep thought.

"I could think of quite a few," she snapped. "Now stop it."

I held her hand open palm up. I suddenly got a mental picture of Nelly's mother and a pain in my side. I tried to appear normal as I looked at her.

"You are going to have six children."

She smiled. "I like that."

"And you are going to be married—four times."

"You will get a slap in a second."

"No, Nel, I can't see anything. She must have got it wrong, shame really."

"Why?"

"I just thought of a name for myself, Keystal Kev."

We both laughed till tears ran down our cheeks.

"So, what do you two think is so funny?" It was Father Kelly.

"Hello, Father," we said at the same time. This started us off again.

"Well?" said Father Kelly. "I'm waiting. You can share the joke with me, surely."

"I was trying to read Nelly's future from the lines in her palm, Father. My Nan said I had the gift."

With this his face hardened. "Tis the devil's work, so it is. The church takes a dim view on such things."

I frowned. "The church must relax its views to survive."

He walked away.

"I think we have upset him," said Nel.

Mmmmm, I thought. *I know why.*

That night I sat in my room and thought about the feeling I had when I held Nelly's hand, and the clear vision in my head. I would tell no-one, best I thought kept to myself and passed it off. I was really looking at her hand to try and guess the size of her fingers. I had almost finished a ring made from an off-cut of seasoned oak. I had made it as fine as I dared. It had a block on the top about half an inch square by quarter inch deep. I inlayed in the top a heart made of rosewood. I needed to polish it and it was done.

What had she made me? I wondered.

Soon it was the last market day before Christmas, and as usual, I met Nelly on my dinner break. We perused the various stalls, had some hot chestnuts, and a glass of hot punch.

"Do you think it will be a white Christmas, Kev?"

"Let me put my Krystal Kev hat on, sweetheart."

She raised her hand.

"If you are going to hit me, use my other arm, this one's had enough."

We linked arms and bumped into Mrs Dunn.

"If you leave go of him, child, will he fall over?" She giggled.

"I'll catch you up, Gran."

We walked back to the workshop.

"See you at church on Sunday then," I said. It was one of those—a moment's thought is an hour in words—kind of moment.

"See you there." She gave me a quick peck on the cheek, as Mrs O'Hara came around the corner, "You two will have no lips left at this rate. And you, Miss Nelly Kelly, leave him alone he's been looking tired. I need him to work." Mrs O'Hara had a big grin on her face.

Nelly was blushing. She went to kiss me again, but thought better of it. Instead, she left. I watched her for a moment.

"Inside, young man, try to concentrate and get some work done."

"Yes, Mrs O'Hara."

"I told you to call me Mary, Kevin, I'd like it if you would."

"Yes, Mary."

"Go do some work, and don't let them two," she pointed at Jimmy and Pat, "overwork you. Or take advantage of your giving nature now."

Pat cast his eyes skyward and shook his head, all done in good humour.

'Twas the day before Christmas. We had three whole days off, today, tomorrow and Boxing Day off. Back to work, off again for New-Year's Day, and back to work the following day. Nelly and I were excited to spend some time together, family allowing.

I'd spend Christmas day with Auntie and I believe Jack, as the man had no family of his own. Nelly will spend it with her parents. Her older brother was away fighting, believed to be in France. Stupid war. No Soldiers, no war. Or is that too simple and naive?

I planned to meet Nelly at her gran's. I got there first. Mrs Dunn invited me in and sat me down.

"Well, Kevin, would you like a wee glass of my Elderberry wine while you are waiting?" She had a gleam in her eye.

"Yes please." I glanced around the room while she fetched the drink. It was spotless, polished to within an inch of its life, and the smell of Bees wax polish filled the air.

She returned. "Good health to you, Kevin."

We touched glasses and drank.

"Now, what have you got our Nelly? You *have* got her something, correct? I know she has something for you."

"I know she made something for me as she let it slip."

"Did she say what?" Mrs Dunn looked a bit worried.

"No, ma'am."

"Ah, that's all well and good. Now show me what you have for her."

I hesitated. "I made this ring." I showed her.

"My Lord, Kevin! It's—it's beautiful! You made this? Well, you wait there." She scuttled off, and returned a few minutes later. "Here take this." It was a lovely small wooden box lined with cushioned material. "That's velvet, Kevin, real velvet. Put the ring in that."

I did and it looked fantastic. "Mrs Dunn, were did you get it from?"

"Never you mind now. I was not always an old woman. I don't mind telling you I was quite a beauty in the day, if I do say so myself. I had admirers you know."

"Was there a special one?"

"There might have been." She had a faraway look in her eye. "That's enough of that now. You do know what it means to give a girl a ring now, don't you? Oh here they are now."

I quickly pocketed the box.

In came Nelly looking fantastic. I went to hug her when the look on her face screamed 'Nooo'! I stopped in my tracks. Her parents were right behind her.

Mr Kelly shook my hand. "Pleased to meet you at last, Kevin, Nelly has told us all about you."

Nelly brought her mother to stand in front of me. "This is Kevin, Mammy."

"Hello, Mrs Kelly, did you have a good journey?" I asked.

"Yes, Kevin, thank you for asking."

"It looks like it's going to snow," Nelly piped up.

"That would be grand now if it did," added Mrs Dunn. "A white Christmas, wonderful. Now, make yourselves at home, and I will go make some tea. There's also some fresh biscuits, my own recipe."

Mrs Dunn went into the kitchen. I glanced at Nelly, there was a silence.

"Are you staying for long?" I inquired.

Mrs Kelly spoke up. "If it looks like snow, we can't stay too long. The track back to the farm gets slippery in snow and the like."

In came Mrs Dunn with the tea and biscuits. "I'll be Mother," she said. "As I am right enough. Help yourselves to the biscuits."

"Don't say that with Kevin, Gran. He'll eat the lot, he's got hollow legs I'm sure of it. He could eat for Ireland."

"That's grand in a growing lad," said Mr Kelly with a smile of approval.

She likes me, I thought.

"Well, I now think it's time we gave each other their Christmas gift. I'll start. This is for you both." Mrs Dunn handed her daughter and son-in-law a package wrapped in brown paper and string, "Now, Shamus, I know you're going to like it as it's your favourite."

"Don't tell him, Gran," Nelly admonished. "it won't be a surprise."

"I will never be able to tell, Asumpta." He studied the shape of two bottles under the brown paper.

We all laughed.

"This is for you, Mammy." As Mrs Kelly gave Mrs Dunn a parcel wrapped in blue paper with a pink ribbon, Nelly leaned close to whisper in my ear.

"It's a bed cover that Gran liked on our trip to Belfast in the summer."

I nodded.

"My turn," said Nelly, excitedly. "This is for you, Kevin."

I was handed a parcel wrapped in the same paper as Mrs Dunn's. "Thank you, swe-Nelly. God, I almost called her sweetheart. The look of panic disappeared from her face. She stood in front of me with her head angled to one side with a look of, Well? Where is mine?"

I was quiet for a few seconds, "Oh, yes I almost forgot. It's here somewhere in my pocket… Oh, here it is." How I kept my face straight, I will never know.

Her mouth was clenched taut, and I could see the muscles in her cheeks flexing. I reached for her hand and placed the tiny box in her palm, and unwrapped it. The look of confusion was a picture a bit scary and unsure. Again, a moment's thought is an hour in words is what must have been going on in her mind.

"It's what's inside the box, Nelly, not the box. You cannot open the box until Christmas day, or I will cast a spell on your best cow."

She smiled at me, and those eyes went straight into my very soul. I could tell she wanted to kiss me. I wanted to do a lot more than kiss.

"What are you two whispering about?" Mrs Kelly demanded. "Let me have a look."

Nelly showed her ma the little wooden box. I could see that her ma recognised it and gave Mrs Dunn a sideways look.

Mrs Dunn, fidgeted with her hands, obviously a bit flustered. "Well, isn't this grand? We all have gifts to open first thing tomorrow morning. I'll start clearing up. Are you going to finish the biscuits, Kevin?"

"Yes, Mrs Dunn, if no one wants any more."

"No, you go to it," said Mr Kelly.

Mrs Kelly followed Mrs Dunn into the kitchen and I heard raised voices.

"I think it's about time we started back ladies," Mr Kelly called out in a loud voice.

"It's started to snow."

Mrs Kelly came out followed by Mrs Dunn, both had faces like thunder. Meanwhile, Nelly had been sneaking peeks at the little wooden box in her hands and searched my face for clues, but got nothing.

They said their goodbyes, we all wished each other a Merry Christmas, and they left. This just left Mrs Dunn and me.

"I hope nothing is wrong, Mrs Dunn."

"No, lad. Don't worry yourself."

"It was the box wasn't it?"

"Well—Yes, it was. Her father gave it to me on our wedding day with my wedding ring in it. It was given to me, so it was mine to give away. and that's an end to it. Now be off with ya. Your auntie Kathryn will be waiting, and maybe Mr Jack Cattin I shouldn't wonder." She winked at me.

I thanked her and left for home.

It was Christmas Morning, and I promised Auntie we would open presents at dinner time, I looked out my bedroom window, what a sight. Everywhere was white and it was still snowing. Perfect. There were no footprints for as far as I could see and everything was quiet.

I had a quick wash, or as Ma would say, *'More like a cat's lick and a promise.'* I sat on the bed. This was the first Christmas without them. I burst out crying for the first time. I looked up just as a white feather floated down and rested on my arm. Where it came from I had no idea.

"Hello, Ma," I whispered, the tears stopped.

Her words came flooding back, *'When feathers appear an Angel is near.'* She was with me. The tears flowed like rain, time passed. I got myself together and went down stairs.

"Good morning, Kevin, and a Merry Christmas to you."

"And to you, Auntie." I kissed her on the cheek.

"Be off with ya now, save all that nonsense for someone else."

"And who would that be Auntie?" I smiled.

"And who do you think I mean, young man? Sit and I'll make us some eggs and best back bacon. There's tea in the pot, so pour yourself one. By the way, Jack—Mr Cattin will be joining us for dinner."

"He has you, Auntie." I continued before she had chance to answer. "And he has us. He was a good friend of Da's, and—"

This time she cut me short.

"And that's why I tolerate his company. His table manners need improving, a diamond in the rough that's what he is. And he smells of fish."

I opened my mouth to speak. "I know you don't have to say it. Yes, he is a fisherman."

She softened. "Aye, he does look out for me I suppose."

I couldn't help myself. "I think the lady protesteth to much."

She turned from the sink where she was washing and preparing dinner. "Where on earth did you hear that?"

"Mrs Dunn, Auntie."

"And what does she know? Just wait till I see her Christmas or not."

"Everybody is so pleased, Auntie. You seem to be much happier over the last few months. Jack is a good man, but there is something fishy about him."

She couldn't stop herself from smiling. "Get away with ya. You could charm the birds from the trees, so you could."

That's not what Jimmy and Pat said I could charm off, I thought. *But, that's just man talk.*

There was a knock at the door, "That will be Jack, Kevin." She quickly tidied herself and checked her hair.

"I'll go, Auntie." She gave me one of those knowing looks. "Hello, Mr Cattin. Merry Christmas to you."

"And the same to you, Mr O'Keefe."

"Please do come in."

"Why thank you, sir." We both bowed and chuckled.

Jack whispered. "I'll leave the door a-jar. I have something outside on the step." He went into the kitchen. "Good morning to the lady of the house, and may I wish her a Merry Christmas."

"And the same to you Mr Cattin—Jack."

"And thank you for inviting me to join you both for Christmas dinner and as such. I have something that will, I hope, brighten up the occasion. It's on the door step. May I have permission to bring it in, ma'am?"

We had never heard Jack speak this way before, all very proper.

"I'm sure. If you must," said Auntie.

"Thank you, ma'am." He went outside and returned with, well, hard to explain. He placed it on the side table in the corner. "I saw this in a book. It's what they call a Christmas Tree in colder parts."

"Yes, I know about Christmas trees," said Auntie. "But—" I glanced at her and she understood the look. "Well, Jack, it's lovely and thank you."

Jack beamed. "No problem, glad you like it."

Now, let me try to describe it. Start from the base, a bit of wood a foot square, now I know what he wanted the wood for, with a hole in it and in this hole was a broom handle about four feet long. This handle had a dozen or so holes drilled in it at random places up and down, and in the holes were placed twisted-wire bottle brushes. These were the branches.

Jack was so pleased with himself. Auntie left the room. We looked at each other, puzzled. A few moments later in she came with a box of old ribbons, and proceeded to place the various coloured ribbons around the tree.

"There now, that's better." She placed two little parcels around the base. "Kevin put your present from Nelly here as well."

I did and also Auntie's present, Jack went to place his present to Auntie.

"I'll take that, Jack. I think I can guess from the smell what it might be."

We all chuckled. Auntie seemed happy, living alone in this house all those years must have very lonely at times and now she had us to fuss around.

Ever since I woke up, I wondered if Nelly opened her present from me yet, and if she liked it. God, I hope it fits.

We sat down for dinner. We had a plate of cold meats, pork and beef, with veg, and a bottle of Mrs Dunn's elderberry wine. I started to say something.

"Don't you say a word, Kevin."

"Auntie, I was—"

"No, wait till I see that woman."

"What woman?" Jack asked.

"Never you mind, Jack Cattin. Now, for afters I have made one of my rice puddings."

"That's grand, Auntie. I love your rice pudding," I looked at Jack.

"It's the burnt crispy bits around the skin I like, Jack," Auntie remarked.

"Less of the burnt, thank you," she said.

I offered to help wash up.

"That's alright, Kevin. Jack can help."

She received raised eyebrows from Jack and me.

"You go and open your presents, I'll start the washing-up."

"I'll have none of it, Kathryn," insisted Jack. "We will open them together."

Auntie was pleased you could see it. She was enjoying the company and the closeness.

"Right," said Jack, "ladies first."

"Well, I know what you have given me, Jack Cattin from the smell, and I thank you."

"My pleasure, Kathryn."

"Now, you two come on. We have church at eight o'clock, and it's two o'clock now."

Jack and I opened the gifts from Auntie. I got a knitted wool hat and scarf. Jack got a pair of knitted wool socks, all made by her own fair-hand.

"Wow, Auntie, fantastic. Thank you, I kissed her cheek and she excepted."

"Kathryn, just what I wanted," said Jack.

"Just what you needed you mean." she corrected him. He also kissed her. "And what do you think you're doing Mr Cattin?"

"I was, er, thanking you."

"Well, you have done that, so sit down."

He did and winked at me. I stood, looking at Nelly's present.

"Come on now, Kevin, it won't open itself," said Auntie.

I opened it slowly, a note fell out. I put the note in my pocket. *I'll read what it said later when I'm alone.* It was an oatmeal fisherman's jumper. I held it up.

"My word, Kev," said Jack "that's a work of art."

"Her mother spins so that would be from their own stock," Auntie commented.

It had ropes and anchors in the pattern, very heavy and thick. The work in the arms and all over the body was as if the ropes and stuff had been glued on, they were so proud of the background.

"Put it on, Kev lad, put it on."

I did It fit perfectly. Now with this and my hat and scarf, I could face the coldest of winters.

"Sorry, Auntie, I have to see Nelly. I'm going now."

"It's going to be dark in two hours," Jack objected. "You be careful as you go."

Neither tried to stop me.

"Give our best wishes to the Kelly's, Kevin. I don't expect you back till the morning." I looked at her then glanced at Jack, he only winked.

"I expect they will insist you stay. What with the time and weather."

"I will be careful, Auntie." I donned Da's boots and out I went.

It stopped snowing, it had settled about a foot deep and deeper where the wind made drifts. Yet it was soft and loose which made walking was easy. The was no cloud or wind, and except for the sound of children's voices a few streets away, close to where I used to live, there wasn't a sound.

Just outside of the village I looked back. The village looked like something from a children's fairy tale. All the roofs were white with snow, the smoke from the fires going straight up to the heavens. The sea was still, no boats out today. The tree branches were heavy with snow, and looked as if it would fall off if hit with the slightest movement.

I continued on. My God this jumper is warm. To think my Nelly made this for me. I unbuttoned my coat to look at the wonderful pattern. I touched the ropes, it felt as if could grab, pull them off, and use them. The fishermen here and in Scotland have a similar jumper. Nowhere as fancy as mine. Their wives would knit a particular pattern that would tell which village they were from if they were to be washed up on shore. Their bodies could then be taken back to their village.

I was about halfway there and it was getting dark and cold. I could feel the snow beneath my feet getting crisp. The sky was dark blue and the stars were appearing one by one.

What a beautiful night, maybe there is a God. Then I thought of the war raging hundreds of miles away, the suffering and death. How many thousands of good men would not be coming home? I thought of the women folk waiting for their men, children for the fathers who they will never see again.

I had a mental image of soldiers from both sides walking to meet each other, shaking hands, and wishing each other Merry Christmas. No, it could never happen, knowing that soon they would be trying to kill each other. What a stupid thought. But imagine if they did, then decided not to carry on the war. just stop and go home. Let the governments and leaders get on a field and fight it out. No, they're back home warm and fed.

I started to feel angry. I thought of my Nel and smiled. I buttoned up my coat, rolled my new woollen hat over my ears, and marched on.

The sky was covered in stars, I couldn't remember ever seeing so many. The snow crunched with every step. It was now dark and the cold biting my legs. My scarf was wrapped around my face, only my eyes faced the cold.

I rounded the last bend and there in the distance was the porch light. I could see the flicking of the fire in the window. The thought of standing in front of that spurred me to walk faster. I stopped a few yards from the house and thought, *My Nelly is in there. What is she going to say when she sees me?*

The curtain moved and there she was, the lovely Nelly peering through the window, then she was gone. I started to move, the door opened and there she was.

"I knew it! I knew it!" She shouted, running to me. "Oh dear, I've got my slippers on."

I ran to her. We hugged and kissed.

"What's going on?" I heard her father shout.

Mrs Kelly appeared. at the door. "Well. don't let all the hotness out. Come in you two, you'll catch your death." She coughed. I looked at her. "It's nothing to worry about, I've had it for weeks now can't seem to throw it off."

I kept staring at her, remembering my vision of her that day. when I held Nelly's hand and felt her pain.

"You must be frozen, Kevin, here have this." Mr Kelly handed me a glass of whiskey.

"Give me your coat and go stand by the fire." Mrs Kelly had gone to the kitchen.

I stood there by the fire with a glass of whiskey and my new jumper.

"Well don't you look grand standing there looking like the proper Squire," said Mrs Kelly. "Here now sit and have this chicken and a few bits to warm you up."

"I have my new jumper for that, Mrs Kelly."

"And very grand it looks, too, I do declare."

"Thank you, Mrs Kelly." I looked at Nelly.

She was standing there with her hands behind her back, wearing the biggest smile I'd ever seen.

"Thank you for the jumper, Nelly, It fits as if it was made for me," I joked.

"It was—Oh, very funny."

We continued to stare, then slowly she brought her left hand around, and there on her wedding finger was the ring. "It fits as if it was made for me."

"It was," I whispered.

We all laughed.

Mr Kelly gave the ladies a glass of sherry and us men had the Whiskey. "We'll all have a drink to wish each other good health and happiness"

We touched glasses and drank.

What a wonderful welcome, I thought, sat and ate. I had no idea I was so hungry.

"More, Kevin?" Mrs Kelly asked. Before I had chance to say anything she added, "Nelly tells me you have hollow legs."

"Thank you I'm fine Mrs Kelly." I was ignored.

"There's plenty left. I'll go and fetch a bit more chicken." In she came with a plate full. I ate that as well. "It appears Nelly was right."

Nelly sat next to me at the table as close as can be. We held hands under the table. Mr and Mrs Kelly sat by the fire, facing away from us. This left Nelly and I. out of ear shot.

"Wont the ring fit any other finger ?" I asked with a smile. The usual smack on the arm. "Sweetheart, I call it – A ring of intent."

"I've never heard that before, Kevin, what does it mean."

"It means my intent is to keep you, for the time being anyway. No, not that arm."

We talked and joked. It suddenly dawned on me why had her ma and da left us alone it was for Nelly to find out my true feelings. Just then, Mrs Kelly came over, "Kevin, we expect you to stay over tonight. We can't have you traipsing home at this hour, and with the weather and all, what would your Auntie Kathryn think of us if we sent you out in this? I have made up a bed in the spare room, Now, Nelly Clare, your father and I are going up, don't stay awake for too long. I'll say good night to you both, sleep well." With this off they went.

"Nelly Clare, you kept that quiet, sweetheart."

"Don't you ever call me Nelly Clare, promise?" Nelly frowned at me half-jokingly.

"I quite like it, it has a ring to it."

"Oh, you think you are so clever, Mr O'Keefe?"

I pulled back holding my arm, just in case.

"Do you like the jumper?"

"What do you think? I will never take it off, even when it gets wet and I smell like an old sheep. I'm so glad the ring fits. It was a guess."

"It's perfect. when I opened the box this morning it was still dark outside. I just could not wait. I saw it and cried, ran into Mammy and Da's bedroom, and woke them up. Well woke Mammy, Da can sleep for Ireland. Mammy said, *'This makes it real. He must love you to make something so fine and personal.'* You do love me, Kevin, you have said it."

This is the moment, I thought.

'Say it, please,' her eyes silently begged.

I held her face in my hands. "I have loved you since the first time I saw you all those years ago. You had a blue dress and black boots, your hair was in bunches, tied with… I can't remember the colour."

"I can, it was blue to match the dress. I remember that dress, Kevin."

I kissed her like I have never kissed her before. this time it was different and we both knew it. She broke away. We both stood there in silence.

"I er, it's late, Kevin. I think it's time we went to bed." She ran upstairs.

I followed a few seconds later in time to see her door close. To the left was an open door, this must be for me. I looked about my quarters, it was empty save for a single candle burnt on the bedside table giving just enough light. This must be Tom's room. I stripped, splashed my face as the whiskey made it feel a little numb, donned the night gown left on the bed, and got in.

I am never going to sleep. I was well awake and lay there looking at the ceiling. My heart was beating like a hammer in my chest. Something wonderful had happened. I felt it and couldn't stop thinking of Nelly.

I pictured her lying there in her bed, her copper hair spilling over the pillow. My mind's eye moved down to her breast, I bolted out of bed. I heard the latch on the door, open softly then close. I could just make out Nelly's outline in the dark room. My heart threatened to burst out of my chest. I reached out; she took my hand.

"I could not sleep," I whispered.

"Me, too, darling, I just want to be with you. I know it's wrong. Please don't think I came here to—" She hesitated.

"I hope you did. I feel the same."

She flung her arms around me. "You want to marry me?, Say it, ask me."

I held her hands in mine. "Nelly Clare Kelly, will you marry me?"

"Yes! Oh please yes! Oh my Lord, you do realise I may never sleep again, ever. What a time to ask me. I can't tell Mammy till morning. No, I can't tell her then, she will want to know when you asked me and I can't say I went into your room in the middle of the night."

I kissed her. "That was to shut you up, Nelly Kelly, before you wake everybody." I held her close.

For the first time I became aware she was naked under her night dress, as was I. I felt the firmness of her breasts against my chest. I pushed her away and put my hands down to hide my hardness. She looked down, covered her mouth with put her hands, and giggled. She walked past me and got into bed. I joined her.

We lay facing each other. My hand caressed her breast before trailing down to her belly. She moved against my hand as it found the bottom of her night dress. I lifted it. With this she sat up and removed it, letting it drop to the floor. I did the same. We were naked and in the same bed. It felt fantastic, much better than the boat.

My hand went between her legs, she rocked against my fingers, her mouth open, her breathing heavy and deep. She rolled over and was on top of me, her hand now grabbing me and I was inside her. I cupped both breasts then her belly, and slid around to her hips I held her as she moved. Her hand went down and she touched herself. After a few moments she held my hand and placed it between her legs.

I placed my open hand on her belly with my thumb between her legs I touched what felt like a vein. With that she took a deep breath, her head bent down, mouth open, she moaned then shivered. I exploded inside her, she felt this and gave a sigh.

Nel straightened her legs. We rolled over, me on top. As before, I held her head and kissed her neck. We were hot and sweaty. It was total heaven.

There must be a God after all, to create a feeling like that, I thought. *He must have wanted us to do it.*

Nel kissed me, got up, put on her night dress, touched my cheek, and was gone.

I just lay there. *What just happened? I have nothing to be ashamed of. What does she expect, coming in here dressed like that? It's only natural, she lives on a farm for God's sake, she knows what happens.*

I repeated that last bit again slowly in my head, *'She knows what happens.'* She was waiting for that to happen. *That's why the little giggle. you dimwit. Well,*

I'm glad I did not disappoint in that case. This is all going far too fast. When things got back to normal.

I must have fell asleep. I was awoken by various noises around the house. It was still dark outside. I swilled my face, rinsed my mouth out wiped under the arms, got dressed, and went down stairs. I was greeted by Mrs Kelly.

"Good morning, Kevin, sit ya self-down. Mr Kelly and Nelly will be down shortly. Eggs and Bacon for you?"

"Yes, Mrs Kelly, that will be fine."

"Fresh tea in the pot, help yourself to bread."

I sat down, waiting for Nelly. I wasn't sure what to expect. In she came. Our eyes met. She was trying her best to stop grinning, which started me off. We were acting like eight-year-olds.

Mrs Kelly looked at us both and smiled. "It's a sight for sore eyes, so it is, seeing you two so, so happy." I think she wanted to say, *'So in love',* but stopped herself.

"Now, Nelly, before you start go fetch your father's ointment. You know, Kevin, he has this terrible stiffness in his—"

I could not look at Nelly nor her me.

"What is the matter with you two this morning? Your father's stiffness is no laughing matter, Nelly Clare. Now off you go." She glanced at me. "I don't know what's got in to that girl this morning. It's probably got something to do with you, I shouldn't wonder. You do make her very happy and for that I thank you."

Suddenly I felt more grown-up, more of a man, it felt good.

Mr Kelly came in followed by Nelly. Mr Kelly was swinging his right arm, holding his shoulder with the other.

I looked at him. "Mrs Kelly told you about my stiffness in this—"

Nelly ran out of the room.

"This shoulder, I wrenched it years ago. I must sleep on it. Every morning I have to have that stuff rubbed into it. Nelly, NELLY!" he shouted. She came back in. "Do my shoulder, my lovely, I'm sure Kevin won't mind. It gets so stiff."

I focused my attention on my food and ate.

"She's very good at this, has the touch. You might need her to do the same to you one day."

Oh My God, please no more I can't stand it! I glanced up for a second. Nel was staring at the ceiling.

"Oh yes, that hit the spot, I can feel the stiffness going. That will do, lass."

Nelly washed her hands and sat down next to me.

"Kevin, would you like me to do you a sausage? Won't take a second, nice big ones from O'Hoggans."

"No thank you, Mrs Kelly." *Will this never end?* I thought.

We finished breakfast.

"I will help with the cattle and the milking if you would like me to, Mr Kelly," I offered.

"Oh, that would be grand. Nelly will show you what to do." He started to rub his shoulder again.

Please God no more mention of stiffness please, I promise to be nice to Father Kelly, honest.

Nelly and I worked well together, with lots of smiles and giggles. There was no time for talking. After dinner I thanked them for their hospitality.

Mr Kelly said, "You were excellent today and if you ever get fed-up with wood butchering, there's a job here on the farm for you."

Nelly walked me to the far gate. There had been no more snow, but it stayed cold. The snow crunch underfoot. overhead was a clear, blue sky, not a cloud to be seen, nor a breath of wind to be felt. The walk was silent, we held hands, and at the gate we held each other tight. Nelly looked up. I smiled at her lovely face, but she didn't smile back.

"Something wrong, sweetheart?" I asked.

Tear filled her eyes. "I don't want you to go. I know it's selfish of me, Kevin, this is silly."

I kissed her. "We have the rest of our lives together. Years and years of just us, and the five kids of course."

"Just the five." She smiled.

"For starters."

Her face became serious again. "Last night you asked me to marry you, do you still feel the same today?"

"Nelly Kelly, you are my life, you are every breath I take, you are in my thoughts night and day. I love you more than you will ever know." I stood straight and stared deep into her eyes. "Nelly Kelly, will you marry me for the second time ?"

"Yes! Yes! Yes! Oh, Kevin when can I tell Mammy?"

"I want to be there when you do, sweetheart. Do you think your father will want me to ask him first?"

Her eyes twinkled mischievously. "He's already married to Mammy."

We looked at each other. Everything in the world is good. I grabbed her hand and marched back to the house.

"What are you doing?" She demanded.

"What do you think I am doing? I'm going to ask your father to marry me."

She gave a scream of sheer delight. God knows I felt good, strong, manly. The scream had brought them out onto the porch.

"What on earth is going on?" Mrs Kelly looked alarmed. Not knowing what the commotion was all about.

I stood ramrod straight, still holding Nel's hand. "Mr and Mrs Kelly, I have asked your daughter to marry me and she has said yes." I was going to say more, but both women ran to each other hugged, tears flowing.

"Well," said Mr Kelly, "about time, lad. We thought you would never ask."

"Now, I am going back home. I will see you all next week, er, New Year's eve in town." I grabbed Nelly and kissed her, her eyes were wide.

"Till next week." I marched off.

I felt ten feet tall, like I could fight anyone and win. I don't remember much of the walk back to town. I stopped with the first sight of town, stood tall, and looked up to the sky.

I spoke out loud, "I hope I have your blessing, Ma and Da. My Nelly is a lovely girl and she does love me so much. I want to make you proud of your only son. I do miss you both. I know you are with me."

I started to step forward, but stopped. There on the unbroken snow lay a white feather. I could not help myself, the tears flowed like warm rain. I scooped it up and held it tight. I smiled and chuckled to myself. All was good in my world. A thought hit me, what was Auntie going to say?

"Well, Kevin, she is a lovely, hardworking and honest girl. She will make you a good wife. But, Kevin, this I will say, please give it time. You are both so young, there's so much to do with your lives, getting married, and all that's involved is not cheap. You will have to start saving and planning for the future, I know Nelly has been filling her bottom draw since she could walk, according to her mother. Are you going to tell anyone?"

"I will tell Terry and Jack, that's all for now."

"Yes, it will have to be done properly, her mother will see to that. I suppose they are in town for New Year's Eve?"

"Yes, Auntie."

"And the ring?"

I frowned in confusion.

"The one you made for Nelly."

"Perfect fit, Auntie."

"Is that all I am going to get, Kevin?"

"She loved it. Had it on all the time, except when milking."

"Well, what is the meaning of it, may I ask?"

"It is a ring of intent. Yes, Auntie, I'm 'intent' on keeping her for the time being."

"Oh, you think you are so sharp, lad. If you are not careful, you'll cut your-self."

By New Year's Eve the snow had all but gone, and people were gathering at the church. I went with Auntie and Jack. I looked around, no sign of Nelly. We all went in, still no sign.

After the service, I told Auntie, "I am going to Nelly's, something is wrong."

"Do you want me to walk with you," Jack offered.

" Thanks Jack, I'll be fine." *I'll be quicker alone,* I thought.

The night was star-lit, the moon was full and bright. I thought of Mrs Kelly's cough.

Hope Nelly is okay. I quickened my pace.

The trip took around two hours in good weather, a bit longer in snow. At last, the light of the farm appeared, I knew I had only fifteen to twenty minutes left to go. I arrived and knocked. Nelly opened the door, her face red from crying. She fell into my arms sobbing. I helped her in doors.

Mr Kelly was sitting still, staring at the fire, although no sign of Mrs Kelly. Nelly handed me a piece of paper. My heart sank.

We are very sorry to have to inform you that your son – Private Thomas Patrick Kelly has been killed in action. I threw it on the table. "This Bloody war!" I was angry and took a deep breath. I went to go to Mr Kelly, but Nelly grabbed my arm and shook her head.

"Not now Kevin."

"Were is your ma?"

"Up-stairs, she won't come down. She has been there since yesterday, refuses to eat or drink. I am really worried." Her lower lip trembled.

"What's happening to the livestock?" I asked with concern.

"The Duffy's from Top Farm have been taking care, but they have their own farm to take care of."

It broke my heart to see her so upset. "You stay here and look after your da. You must be strong, sweetheart. I am going to speak to your ma. I know what she is going through."

I hesitated outside her room, swallowed, then spoke, "Mrs Kelly? It's Kevin. I am so sorry for your loss. I do know what you are feeling and going through and it still hurts sometimes. But, they are still with me as Tom will always be with you, in your mind and heart. The pain will go, and there will be times when you cry over a memory or object that reminds you of better times. He loved you both and the farm. It will be very hard to come to terms with the void he left, yet you will in time. Life must go on. I will help wherever I can, as one day I will be your son-in-law. I want to be part of this family. Please come down, your family needs your strength and understanding. you are not alone."

I heard nothing, so I headed down stairs to the front room. Nelly was holding her father's hand and had her arm wrapped around his shoulders. I walked close, he reached out and grabbed my hand tight, tears swimming in his eyes.

With a trembling voice he spoke, "Thank you, son for being here. I'll be fine, just fine." He returned to staring at the fire.

"Mammy!" Nelly ran to her ma.

Mrs Kelly stood at the foot of the stairs. She glanced at me, trying hard to compose herself. Taking a deep breath, she went up to her husband and draped her arm around his shoulder. He held her hand tight. No words were spoken nor needed.

I stayed overnight. It was early hours before we all went to bed. Nelly and I were the last to go.

On the landing she whispered, "I don't want to be alone tonight."

I held her hand and led her back down stairs to the large sofa. "I'll go get some blankets." I found some in a nearby chest and we settled down on the sofa.

She was gone in seconds. I lay with my arms wrapped around her, staring at the ceiling.

And they say there is a God who looks after us all. If I ever meet the bastard, I will put him on the deck.

The morning came soon enough. It was early when a a knock sounded on the door. I opened it to Mr Duffy.

"How are they?" He inquired.

"Better, thank you."

"Oh, good. We'll just carry on." He started to leave.

"Can I be of help, Mr Duffy?"

"I think your place is here."

I nodded, he was right. He left. Mr and Mrs Kelly descended the stairs.

"I'll start breakfast," said Mrs Kelly.

I went to the sofa and woke Nelly. We all sat at the table. There was the odd smile and nod, otherwise we ate in silence.

Mr Kelly rose. "I'll go and tend." He joined the Duffy's.

"Nelly, sweetheart, you look after your mother. I'm going back. On the way I will tell Father Kelly." I kissed her. *What a start to the year. Every New Year's Day from now on will bring this memory back. It's going to be so hard for them with no body to bury. This is Father Kelly's job, and he is good at it.*

No matter how strong your faith is, this sort of thing makes you think twice. There will be a lot more mothers, wives, sisters, daughters, and sons that will feel this way before this Bloody war is over. Just hope we win. If we lose, then what has all the loss of life been for? Will man ever learn?

I was about halfway home when suddenly, I felt I was falling with this horrific pain in my lower legs. I screamed out, I was on the floor rolling in agony. I opened my eyes and looked at my legs—nothing. I tried to get to my feet, again the pain, I thought I was going to pass out, the pain was tearing through my body. Sweat poured from me. Then no pain, no marks.

What the hell was that? It must have been a really bad attack of cramps. Lord that was painful.

I hobbled a few steps and it was as if nothing happened. If it was cramps, I would still feel it in the calf muscle. Had I been attacked by a wild animal? That's what it felt like. I looked around, but had no idea what I was looking for. There was nothing.

I walked on a bit shaken. *Am I coming down with something? Was that a 'fit' of some kind? What a bloody day.*

I heard something on the track. It was a pony and trap driven by Father Kelly.

I stood to the side. He stopped the cart.

"Good morning, Kevin."

"Good morning, Father. I would wish you a Happy New Year, Father, but it does not seem right."

"I understand. I met Mrs Duffy she told me of the sad news, How are they, Kevin?"

"As well as can be expected, their alright. The Duffy's are helping."

"Ah yes, they are a good God-fearing family. Indeed, they are." He looked at me as he spoke.

"We must all help each other at times like this," I replied. "It brings out the best in people."

He cracked the reigns and moved on. I arrived home, a bit tired and disillusioned with the world in general.

"How are they, Kevin?" Auntie asked.

"They are fine, Auntie. I passed Father Kelly on his way up there." I sat down at the kitchen table.

"There's tea in the pot. do you want something to eat?"

"No thanks I had breakfast at Nelly's."

"And how is she?"

"She's strong, Auntie, she will be ok."

"And that's it then? No other news?"

It dawned on me. *She knows something. It's a bloody conspiracy. Us men don't have a chance, not a hope in hell.* I looked at her and smiled.

She raised her eyebrows. "In God's name, lad, have you named a day?"

"No, Auntie, it hasn't been mentioned."

"Good, you took my advice then. Two or three years or so, I would imagine, When all this terrible business is over I will talk to Mrs Kelly."

I shook my head. *Not a hope in hell!*

Chapter 3

The War of was just four months old.

"Yes, I agree, Captain, it is a problem. However, we have to do something, remember who her Father was."

"Well, yes sir. Did you know she speaks German Italian and French? Her mother was French."

"I had no idea, Captain, no idea at all."

Liz was sixteen years of age when her French mother and English father, a serving Army captain, were both killed in a bid to get back home from an undercover operation in Poland. They were captured, tortured, and the bodies had been left where they could be found by the French.

Liz was never told the truth. As far as she was concerned, they died at sea and their bodies where never found. Her father received the George Cross. Liz never knew her mother's true position or involvement in British-French Counter-intelligence.

"Jean, ask Captain Miller to come in, would you please?"

"Yes, sir." Jean disappeared into the next office. "The Major wants you in his office, Captain."

"Now?"

"Yes, now, sir."

Captain Miller followed Jean back to the Major's office. The captain admired Jean's form as she walked in front. She knew he would be so teased him a bit by exaggerating her wriggle.

"Last time I saw a movement like that I had the back off my Swiss Watch." He smiled.

Jean stopped at the door, blocked the way slightly, and gave Miller a very old-fashioned look. that indicated she knew exactly what he was thinking. He brushed past her and grazed the back of his hand across her lower belly. She drew her belly in with a sharp intake of breath. Miller glanced over his shoulder and smiled as he walked into the Major's office. He and Jean became an item some weeks ago and only last night did they bed each other.

"Come in. I have had a call from Brigadier Kingsley based over on the Isle-O-Man. It's classified, but will soon be common knowledge. The Powers that Be are going to use the Island for the Internment of the German, Austrian, and Italian folks here in the U.K Poor sods, there has been a lot of unrest in the major cities, shops burnt and ransacked, being called spies, and worse. So it is for their own safety."

"Right, Major, thank you for that," offered Miller.

"It was just for your ears at the moment, *Captain*," snapped the Major.

"Yes, Sir."

"Well my idea, Miller, is to send young Liz over there. I think she would be a great asset to the Brigadier with her particular gift. What say you?"

"Splendid idea, Major. Do you want me to arrange it?"

"Yes, if you would." He hesitated.

"Problem, Major?"

"Er, she IS young and has no-one. But I know Old Kingsley, and I know he will take her under his wing."

"I hear she is no wimp, Sir," the captain added. "She can hold her own in a scuffle, and is clever and quick judging by her exam results."

"Good." The Major smiled. "Right, I will leave the arrangements to you. I will contact the Brigadier now, thank you, Captain."

"Sir." Miller saluted smartly and left.

Jean was in the outer office as she had this space all to herself. The captain walked over to her. She arose and came around the table. He caught her mid-flow and they kissed. His hand went straight between her legs. She moved forward trapping his hand between them. The moment was broken by, "Jean, get me Brigadier Kingsley, would you?" a voice from the Major's office.

"See you tonight, my lovely," he whispered.

"If you're lucky you might," was her reply. A quick kiss and he was gone.

Liz took the position and was looking forward to being part of this war. She had her father's strong will and her mother's quick mind. She wanted to make her parents proud, she did not want their deaths to be in vain.

Liz looked out of the train's carriage window, and cleared the condensation from the glass with her glove. It was a dark and grey day, the view of fields, rivers, and small villages seemed to fly past. She started to ponder on what was she heading into. What would the Brigadier be like? Where would she be staying?

She glanced down at a small brown leather suitcase. Everything she owned was in that case. It wasn't much to look at. She thought about the shops on the Island and what they were like. What did they sell being a small Island stuck in the middle of the Irish sea?

I hope they have some nice clothe shops, I need new bits. She read that over eight thousand the men folk on the Island had been called up, and the women were doing their bit. Good news for the Island economy, Vickers had moved their balloon manufacturing over there.

Liz settled into her Army issued book on Morse-code. She passed the time testing herself. She tapped the "Dar" and "Dit" on her knee with her fingers and started to make up sentences. If anyone looked it may have seemed she was tapping out a tune or song.

The train slowly pulled into Liverpool's Lime Street Station. She walked to the gates, but stopped and looked around. The noise and the steam of the eight, giant black trains standing there, the people around her all seemed happy.

"I suppose the war is up here," she whispered to herself.

"Ya Orright lover," came the call from one of the porters. "Won elp wif ya case?" He pointed to her suitcase.

"Er, oh I see, no thank you I can manage"

"Only askin luv, tarra well."

Am I in another country? She giggled to herself. *They all seem very friendly.* she thought.

Out in the street she studied her surroundings. She thought she might spot someone in uniform looking for her, but sadly no. She decided to ask for directions to the I.O.M. Ferry.

"Excuse me."

"Why wot ya dun?" The throaty voice came from the smiley face.

"Erm." This confused her, but decided to carry on. "I need to get to the I.O.M. Ferry"

"Well, luv. you look big enough and ugly enough you could walk it in about twenty minutes or grab a taxi. Cost ya about a Tanner."

"Sixpence for a taxi? I'll walk."

"Right. Ya can't go wron' if you keep goin' down hill, luv. Turn down there." He pointed. "And just keep goin, be lucky." He was gone.

70

Big enough and ugly enough. She smiled to herself. The way it was said, she just could not take offence.

He was right, after about ten minutes she could see the sea.

That must be the River Mersey. Liz found herself smiling as everyone she passed seemed to be doing the same and saying, "hello," "Good day," "Looks like rain," etc.

One woman on passing called out. "Nice coat, luv. Wanna sell it?" Liz smiles and mouthed a NO *What a friendly city.* Liz reached the ferry terminal.

"Yes, sweetheart?"

"I want the I.O.M. ferry, please."

"You've got 45 minutes before boardin. Go get ya self a cup of tea and a piece of cake and we'll call ya over the Megaphone."

Liz did as he had suggested, and sat overlooking the river, watching the several small ferry boats crossing back and forth. She was mesmerised at the floating pier and the tunnel walkways leading down from the land to it. As the ferry boats docked against the large black rubber tyres used as fenders the pier would move.

This must go up and down with the tides. Her thoughts were broken by the "Tanoy."

"The I.O.M. ferry is now boardin'. Please make ya way to the boardin' area, she will sail in one hour, thank you."

There was about a hundred people waiting to go on board.

The Mona's Queen, what a strange name for a ship, she thought.

The gang-way was lowered and on they went. People filed on and went their separate ways in order to find the best seating. Liz walked around the ferry and decided to sit outside in the fresh air. And the air was *very* fresh with slight a nip in the south westerly breeze. But having sat on the train for all those hours, this was most welcome.

Liz jumped when the whistle blew. She walked to the quay side guard rail just to see the ropes being brought aboard and stowed. She watched as the gap between the ferry and the pierhead widened. Suddenly she felt alone. Leaving Liverpool felt as if she was leaving everything she had ever known behind. A cold shiver ran through her body, a tear came to her eyes. She shook her head in defiance.

"Don't be silly, you're stronger than this," she whispered to herself.

After taking a deep breath she looked out to see the whole of the waterfront, that building with the two giant birds on the top, that was so much a landmark

71

for the port of Liverpool. Two Navy ships, the dry docks, small launches and tugs going about their business. Except for the naval ships, one would never think the world was at war.

Liz stood holding on to the rails at the stern looking down at the wake, the movement between white against the blue-green water quite hypnotic. Slowly her eyes went from the stern to the wake, then followed the wake until it stopped, faded and became the sea again. It felt as if all she knew disappeared with the vanishing wake. After a while she started to feel a bit cold and the need to eat. She went to find the galley. She settled for a bowl of Irish stew with crusty bread and butter.

When in Rome, she thought.

The crossing was uneventful, the sea flat for the first four hours. However, swells started to build, and the wind began to bite. It all happened quickly. The ferry started to bob up and down. Liz found it hard to walk along the deck without wobbling.

"You okay, Miss?"

She turned to see a crew member standing a few feet away.

"It's going to get rough, you should go inside. Just a few hours more, and we will have you back on dry land."

Liz had to hold on to the rail while the sailor stood there as if his boots were nailed to the deck.

"Is it always this rough?" She asked.

"Ooh it can get much worst that this, Miss. The Irish sea is known for it, one minute calm next force eight" He offered his arm.

"I'll be fine, thank you."

He stepped aside, however the firm set of his jaw told her he was going to make sure she went inside. As she walked past, she wobbled and he grabbed her arm.

"Got ya, Miss."

"Thank you." She steadied herself and made her way to the saloon door.

He followed to insure she made it okay. Liz. took a seat, the sailor smiled and walked on.

People started to make horrible noises; people started to be sea sick, women ran to the toilets while the men staggered to the ships guard rail. She was determined not to be sick and stood by the door on the lee side of the ship out of the wind. This gave her the badly needed fresh air.

The storm was a North Westerly, the wind turned a full 180 degrees as they approached the Island, which offered some shelter. The land had taken away most of the wind.

Only about 45 minutes to go. Seeing the Island made her relax a little.

They docked in the shelter of Douglas. She was glad to be back on dry land, although it was far from dry. It was raining "stair-rods." She stood alone and wet, holding all she had in her left hand while her right held onto her hat. She spotted an army uniform standing by an army car.

Please let it be for me. She walked over to the waiting Sergeant. She was about to speak, "You for Brigadier Kingsley, Miss?"

"Yes, yes I am."

"Best get in then before you catch your death."

She did not need to be told twice.

"Bit of a storm, Miss. You just got in in time, it's going to get worse or worser."

Worser – is that a real word? she smiled to herself. She was grateful that she was expected, and started feeling much happier.

"Be about twenty minutes, Miss, and you will be in front of a log fire with a glass of something strong I wouldn't wonder, knowing the Brigadier."

Liz nodded, the cold had seeped into her bones, right down in the marrow. She knew if she didn't get warm soon, she would be in for a cold.

They arrived at Cove Manor. As soon as the car stopped, she was out and running up the stone steps. The large castle like wooden doors opened and she flew in. Morris had heard the car and was there to greet her. The man was about 55 and looked as he might have been a jockey in his younger days. He was around five foot six inches slight in build and had a gold riding whip lapel badge.

"Let me take your coat, Miss. Good God, you're wet through, follow me." Off he trotted with Liz close behind.

She followed him into a large room with a massive open fire blazing in the hearth. She was there like a shot.

"You stay there and warm ya bones, Miss. I'll tell the Brigadier your here."

"Don't worry, I'm not going anywhere." She got as close to the fire as she dared.

Liz had her back to the fire when in came the Brigadier. He studied her for a moment, spun on his heel, and was gone. Liz stood, unsure. He returned.

"Just told Biddy to run you a nice hot bath. Should be ready in about twenty minutes. I'll get you a whisky, or would you prepare a Sherry or Gin?"

"A whiskey please, sir," she spoke through chattering teeth. She had never had whiskey, it just seemed the right drink on this occasion.

"Champion. I think I'll join you." He offered Liz the glass of neat whiskey, a good double.

"Thank you, sir."

"Bottoms up." They chinked glasses.

Liz took a large gulp, then regretted it. it was strong and felt as if it had burnt her throat. She coughed and spluttered, but kept it down, and it did warm her.

The Brigadier gazed at her and after a few moments spoke softly. "You do look like your mother, but you have your father's eyes. I see you use your mother's name?" This was a question and a statement in one.

"Yes, sir. Monaco avoids the unwanted questions, as you can imagine."

"Of course."

"Bath is ready for the young lady, shall I take her sir?" smiled Biddy, she was one of the staff.

The Brigadier nodded. Liz finished the whiskey with a small cough. She felt a little light headed but steady enough to walk and followed Biddy.

The Brigadier shouted after them, "Come down when you are ready, have some dinner. No rush."

Liz laid back in the soft hot water. Whatever Biddy put in the water felt and smelled heavenly. She started to feel human again as warmth returned to her bones. After about an hour, the water started to cool and she decided to get out. She wrapped herself in a large warm towel and padded across the soft carpet to her bedroom where a fire blazing awaited. As she dried herself, she noticed her wet clothes were gone.

She opened her suitcase and placed the contents on the bed. It all needed ironing. The nightdress was draped over a chair to warm in front of the fire. She put on a pair of trousers and a woollen jumper, before brushing her hair back and holding it in place with a Tortoiseshell comb her mother had given her on her thirteenth birthday. This made her stop and think of her mother. They were close, but as her mother was away for weeks on end, in the latter years never spent real bonding.

Liz shook herself. *Right, this will have to do. I look like a labourer, but I'm warm. Liz made her way downstairs to the dining room.*

"Hello again. Feeling better?" The Brigadier asked.

"Yes, thank you, sir."

74

"We have already eaten. Do you mind dining alone this once?"

"Not at all, I'll be fine. Is it alright if afterwards I just go to bed?" Liz hoped for a yes.

"Yes, of course. See you at breakfast. Goodnight and sleep well." He left right as Cook brought in dinner.

Liz sat, at the large polished Mahogany table there was a bowl of French onion soup followed by Cottage Pie.

"That will stick to your ribs, Miss." Cook smiled and introduced herself. "I'll leave you to it, call if you need me"

"Thank you, Cook." Liz realised she was ravenous and ate the soup too quickly. It was still hot and burnt her throat, forcing her to slowed down.

She donned the nightdress before pulling back the bedclothes to find they being were warmed with two stone hot water bottles. She moved them from the middle to down where her feet would be and got in. The last thing she remembered was watching the dying embers in the grate before sleep overtook her.

Liz woke with a start. it was Biddy with Liz's freshly cleaned and ironed clothes.

"Sorry, Miss, just brought back your clothes and bits. They have been washed, dried and ironed all ready for you."

"Thank you, that's wonderful." Liz was pleased.

"Erm it's gone ten, Miss, the Brigadier sent me to wake you."

Liz sprang out of bed. "Oh damn! My first day and I'm late. I must have slept a full twelve hours." She looked helplessly at Biddy.

"You get yourself together, Miss, and we'll see you downstairs all in good time." smiled Biddy.

Liz got herself together, dressed in the same clothes as she arrived in yesterday but they felt fresh and like new. She made her way downstairs. On hearing voices from a room she made her way towards that door. She popped her head around the doorframe.

"Come in, come in." Smiled the Brigadier. "Well you look a bit better than last time I saw you."

"Thank you, sir. I'm sorry I'm late I—" She was cut short.

"Don't let it happen again." The Brigadier spoke gruffly, but his eyes were kind. "I thought we could have breakfast together this morning, so I waited for you."

Liz started to speak, however, the Brigadier held up his hand as to stop her.

"We have to talk."

They walked to the dining room and took their seats. Cook appeared and served two plates of food, one in front of each of them. The tantalising scent of cooked salmon teased her nostrils and the egg looked delicious.

"Salmon and poached egg, to your liking?" The Brigadier asked.

"Yes, sir,"

"Help yourself ."

For a while the only sound in the dining room was that of clinking silverware and people eating. The Brigadier finished first and took a tentative sip of his coffee before clearing his throat.

"I was saddened with the news of your mother and father. they were both very special people very brave you should be very proud. I met them both when I was stationed in London a few years back. I was pleased with the transfer, and the news I was to have you stationed with me, it made perfect sense" He was hoping she would have the same strength and loyalty.

"Now, the Island is to be made a centre for the people from the mainland with German, Austrian, and Italian back grounds. It would appear they are being targeted, it is getting very Unpleasant. So, it's for their own safety. They may not see it as such, but there we are. This is where your language skills will be of use, and the main reason you are here. You will be staying here and report to me and me only, understood?"

"Yes, sir."

"Good, now living with me is my daughter Doris Woodgarth. She is married to a Captain, I am not at liberty to tell you more, and their daughter, my grand-daughter, Lucie. Lucie is a few years younger than yourself. You will meet them in time. Morris, Biddy, and cook you have met. We have estate staff and Tom in the stables.

"Now, I don't want you getting involved with Army work just yet. I am told you are bright and well able, so I am going to leave you to explore on your own. I imagine you will need to go into Douglas at some point. Tell me when and I will arrange transport. Oh, do you ride?"

"Yes, sir, I do," Liz replied.

"Wonderful. Speak to Tom in the stables. Right well that is all for now… no it's not. You will receive £5 per week, this is just for your own use. All the services here at Cove Manor, food, board, cleaning etc. etc. will be at your disposal.

What do you think?" He could see from the beaming smile on her face she was delighted.

"I am delighted with the arrangements, sir, and thank you."

"Least I could do under the present situation. I will leave you now as I have my duties to perform, I must organise somewhere for the poor sods to stay." He stood up. "I hope you enjoy your time here." This was said with genuine feeling.

Liz was warmed by the gesture.

"I forgot to say, my daughter and granddaughter are due back from their shopping spree in London in three day's time, all being well. We have property there on York Street. It'll give you some female company, er I hope. That's it" with that he left.

Liz couldn't believe it. *Fantastic, this is just fantastic. £5 a week to do as I please. I will be able to save a little, well I'll see after I have cleared all the fashion shops in Douglas.*

She spent the rest of the day walking around the estate. Morris sorted out a pair of much needed Wellingtons. The estate had two working farms giving good revenue as far as she could fathom. The stables housed several horses, and she decided to check them out.

"Morning, Miss." Liz was taken-a-back, she had not seen him but, he had spotted her.

"You must be Tom"

"Yes, Miss. I'm son of one of the tenant farmers." He doffed his cap.

This tickled her. Tom was about thirty about five foot ten inches and shall we say robust, he was heavily built broad shoulders and girth. The thick, heavy leather belt with a large brass buckle holding up his trousers looked as it had come from a Shire-Horses harness… "Could you show me around the stables, please?"

"Be my pleasure, Miss. This one here is Tony, he belongs to the Brigadier's daughter and this one is Breeze. She belongs to the granddaughter." He seemed pleased to be able to show off a bit. "I tend to all the stable duties. Are you looking for a ride?"

"Oh, not today. I need a new riding outfit. Which horse can I have?"

"I would give you Door—as she bolts."

Silence.

"Sorry about that, Miss, my sense of humour."

Liz laughed. "I get it."

"This one's name is Dream; she should be ridden more. She is an ex-track horse, wilful and strong. As I said, she needs to be ridden"

"Well, perhaps she will. Thank you, Tom. Oh, what about the Army horses?"

"They keep them themselves."

"Thanks again ." Liz headed back to the Manor.

She settled in over the next few days. She liked the staff and they liked her.

"No airs and graces, that one," she overheard cook say.

"And she speaks several languages, she's clever," answered Biddy.

This made Liz feel warm and secure.

Chapter 4

"Mother, I'm going out. Some last minute shopping," said Lucie.

"Okay, darling, take your time there's no rush," answered her mother.

Doris Woodgarth was delighted and went straight on the phone. "She's just gone out shopping, she'll be hours. Can you come around now? I want you."

"I'll be with you in ten minutes. B.U.R.M.A…" (be undressed and ready my angel) whispered Major Jack Bowen. He hung up. "Just going out for a few hours, Corporal."

"Yes, sir."

She unlocked the front door, quickly got undressed and freshened herself, and got into bed. Her hand between her legs, making herself ready. She got wet just thinking about him. She never felt so physical in her life, this time she was going to do something she thought she would never do again. She heard the door close; she shut her eyes in anticipation. In he came, looked at her, and started to undress. He stood there naked and hard, his body toned. She threw back the bed sheets.

"My God, you are beautiful!" These words barely left his mouth when she jumped out of bed, fell to her knees, and took his penis to her mouth.

His head fell back, his eyes to the ceiling then down to her. He held her head for a moment before pulling her away. She rose and they kissed. He pushed her back on to the bed, knelt on the floor and with both hands under her arse, lifted her as he went down on her. She arched her back and moaned in total ecstasy. She pulled him up. He was inside her. He stayed close, rubbing against her. They both came at the same time.

"You are one hell of a woman! God knows that was fantastic."

"You bring out the animal in me Jack." She smiled, caressing his back. They kissed.

"I must be going, there's a war on you know." Jack kissed her hard, got up, and dressed.

She covered herself and lay there. "Jack, Lucie and I will be going back tomorrow. I don't know when I will see you again." Her voice was direct.

"Times are so uncertain, darling. What started out as just a fling has now become too important to us and too real. You're a married woman, and John is somewhere out there in France," he said, concerned. Jack had known John, they had worked together. Jack knew John to be a good sort, this made jack feel more than a little guilty.

"Please don't say any more, Jack, it's what he wanted." She rolled over and looked at the floor.

He bent down and kissed her; his hand slid under the sheets.

"Stop it!" She laughed, throwing her arms around him. When she spoke, her voice was tender. "Please be careful, darling."

"I will, my love." With this he was gone.

She lay on the pillows, staring at the ceiling. Closing her eyes, she went through the last hour in her mind's eye. They only met two or three times a year, but each one was like the first.

She heard the front door open. She flew into the bathroom, ran the bath, cleaned and powdered herself, wrapped herself in her robe, and sat on the toilet.

"I'm home! Wait till you see the handbag I have just bought, Mummy, it's sublime," Lucie's voice got closer.

"You weren't out long, darling. I'll be out in a moment and you can show me then."

The Major walk back to his office. "Anything for me Corporal?"

"No, sir."

"Very good." He sat down and as she had done, pondered on the last hour. He knew his feelings for her where real, and knew she felt the same.

This affair started some years ago, they met when Her husband was stationed in the United Kingdom. The attraction was instant. Lucie would have been only seven at the time. Her husband, Captain John Woodgarth, was an Army man through and through. The Army was all he knew and really all he needed.

The physical side of their marriage was never spontaneous. She wanted him to work his way up the ranks, but he was happy just being a captain. and a good one. Whether he knew what was going on or not, as long as she was happy, he was.

"Captain Woodgarth."

"Yes, sir?"

"Good news, the new weapon of destruction you showed so much interest in has borne fruit. You are to return to England and report to H.Q. for briefing."

"Thank you, sir." The captain tried to appear calm.

"Don't thank me. Nothing to do with me, I want men like you here with me."

Captain Woodgarth had shown great interest in the new weapon, the "Tank," being built in Birmingham by Fosters Metropolitan Carriage and Wagon Company. It was now December 1915. He spent the time helping to develop the Mark 1 – Tank. He would advise on the type of fire power and secondary equipment. He worked alongside its co-designer, Sir William Tritton M.D of Fosters and Major Gordon Wilson.

During John's time with them he only went to see his wife and daughter twice. He could have visited much more if he had wanted to. The trip from Birmingham to Liverpool was an easy one.

The Mark 1-Tank, so called as it resembled the water tanks used in the field, nick-named "Little Willie" was complete. It stood at fourteen tonnes, with a top speed of five miles per hour. The powers that be were very pleased with the trials in September and with the forceful backing of Mr Winston Churchill, Little Willie went into production.

As it happened it was not long before "Tanks" showed their worth. It was early November 1916 in France, on the Upper Reaches of the River Somme. A battle to end all battles. Millions of men died on both sides, the conditions were dismal at best. It was here Captain John Woodgarth died. His tank exploded, he and his crew died instantly. No one was sure what happened. Was he hit by an enemy bomb? Or did a shell explode within the tank? There was nothing left to send home, He died doing the one thing he loved: which is all that can be said. And to think that when this happened His wife and the Major were in bed, her husband was the last thing on her mind.

Chapter 5

Cove Manor

"Hello, you must be Liz Monaco," observed Mrs Woodgarth while her daughter hung back a bit.

"Yes, I'm very pleased to meet you." Liz held out her hand, yet it was not taken by either of the women. Instead, their coats and hats were handed to her. Morris was just in time.

"Thank you, ma'am. May I say welcome back. I'll take those. Your father is in the drawing room."

They both walked past Liz and Morris.

"Sorry about that, Miss," offered Morris.

"Please don't be, not you're doing." She was confused as to what they knew, or may have been told. Meanwhile, the disappeared into the drawing room.

"Ah, you are both back safe, good. Have a nice trip?" inquired the Brigadier.

His daughter looked out the window. "Looks like rain, shame I was going to take Tony out."

"Yes, thank you, Grandfather, it was lovely. Spent lots of money, bought lots of things," Lucie offered.

"Perhaps you could show me all these lovely things," he suggested.

"They would be of no interest to you, Daddy," Doris butted in.

With that they flounced out of the room, leaving the Brigadier a bit deflated. Liz was outside the door as both of them walked past without a word. She tapped on the door and poked her head around.

"Do come in, no need for all that knocking carry on." His voice was angry.

"Everything ok, sir?"

"Yes, I only thought, well, does not matter. Would have been nice to have had a son." This was more of a whisper. "What can I do for you?"

"Nothing really. I borrowed a bicycle and went into town, bought my new riding clothes, and a few other bits and pieces. I thought I would go out tomorrow, weather being good."

"You cycled into Douglas? Splendid stuff." The Brigadier was outwardly pleased. "I did say I would arrange transport, but well done, well done. I have calls to make, I'll see you at dinner, and will introduce you to my daughter and my granddaughter."

"Yes, thank you, see you then." Liz went up to her room and sat on the bed, gazing out the window. "Well I don't think much of those two. If they think I am going to be at their beck and call they have another thing coming," she whispered.

The Brigadier and Liz arrived for dinner at the same time. Shortly afterwards the daughter and granddaughter joined them. Morris pulled out a chair for one, then the other. Mrs Woodgarth scrutinised Liz for a few seconds before sitting.

Liz took this act as a 'You should have stood as I was seated.' *This is not nice,* she thought.

Nothing was said till the first course was finished.

"Doris," was as far as the Brigadier got.

"I am told my father knew your parents when he was based in London. Your mother was French I believe. Do you speak any French?" Doris asked, loftily.

Liz saw this a chance to get even. "Oui je parle Francais, Allemend et Italien, comme un natif, c'est pourquoi je suis ici et sera un grand atout pour ton p'ere, vous?"

(Yes, I speak French, German and Italian, this is why I'm here. I will be a great asset to your father. Do you speak any?)

Silence fell. The Brigadier was trying not to smile and used his napkin to cover his mouth.

"I got a little bit, but far too fast for me," Lucie replied.

Her mother glared at Liz.

Liz, after a few moments, offered again "Vous?" She was ignored.

Doris turned to Morris. "I am famished, where is dinner? Morris more port, please."

After dinner Doris spoke, "I feel so tired, I'm going upstairs. Please bring supper to my room, will you, Morris?"

Morris nodded.

"You must be very clever, Liz. I could not retain it all," said Lucie.

"I am sure you have gifts I don't. We all have something we are good at." Liz, smiled, grateful Lucie appeared to not have her mother's aloof manner.

"I can't think of anything I'm good at. Except spending Grandfather's money." She giggled.

"You have a natural gift for that, my dear." The Brigadier chuckled.

Lucie stood and said, " Au revoir."

Liz replied with, "Bonne nuit, Lucie."

Off she went.

"I'm sorry about my daughter, Liz. She's not as bad as she may seem. Her husband is in France."

"I hope so, sir, I do hope so." Liz sighed. *I can match anything Doris throws at me, but it doesn't make for a pleasant atmosphere.*

The following morning Liz went down to breakfast. Doris and Lucie had starting eating, yet the Brigadier was nowhere to be seen. Liz helped herself to some smoked Kippers and poached egg from the breakfast board and sat down.

"Bonjour comment allez-vous Lucie?" Liz greeted the younger woman.

"Oh erm, erm—bien merci," said Lucie, looking very pleased with herself.

"Have you always sat here for breakfast?" Doris interrupted.

"Yes, Mrs Woodgarth, your father and I talk business." This was met with silence. "I see you are both dressed for riding," she tried again.

"Yes. Do you ride, Liz? Do say yes!" begged Lucie.

"Well yes I do. I bought a new outfit a few days ago, have yet to try it out."

"Come with us now, it will be fun!"

"Thank you, Lucie, but I have a meeting with your grandfather this morning."

"Do you have a mount here ?" questioned Doris.

"No, Mrs Woodgarth, I spoke to Tom and he offered me Dream."

"Dream is an ex-race horse, Liz, and quite strong." Lucie's brow furrowed with concern. She was about to say more when her mother spoke over her.

"Good choice, Dream needs to be ridden."

"But, Mother, you said—" Lucie was cut short.

"We must be off. Come along, darling." They rose and left.

Liz was pondering the events of the past few minutes the Brigadier came in.

"Sorry about this, Liz, but I have to leave you to your own devices again today. In three days' time I will need you with me. We have set-up two camps for the poor sods. One in Douglas, an old holiday camp and the other the other side of the Island at Knockaloe, near Peel. It's going to get busy, and I believe it's men only. Don't like the sound of that. Speak to you this evening." He disappeared as quickly as he appeared.

Good, Liz thought, *that gives me time to get to know Dream.*

She changed into her riding attire, took two apples from the bowl in the dining room, and made her way to the stables.

"Good morning, Tom."

"Morning, Miss, you joining Mrs Woodgarth and her daughter?" He greeted her.

"No, Tom, I am going to get to know Dream. If that's ok with you."

"That's fine by me, Miss."

Liz waited by the stable door and admired the fine animal, Dream stood still and returned the look. Slowly, she unlatched and walked in, closing the lower half of the stable door behind her, Tom observed from a few feet away.

Liz took out one of the apples, cut it in half with her father's penknife, and offered it to Dream on an open hand. After a few moments Dream sniffed and ate. They stared at each other, eye to eye. Liz then offered the other half which Dream ate.

"That's all for now, Dream. Tom?"

"Yes, Miss?"

"Could you pass over a chair, please."

This was done. Liz sat, still talking to the horse and waited. It took fifteen minutes before Dream came closer, bit by bit until she was within a foot of Liz's face. Liz took a deep breath and blew up Dream's nostrils. The horse did the same. Liz took out the second apple, cut it in half and Dream ate it right away, then touched Liz's hand the one holding the last half.

"Okay, okay, steady now."

As Dream took the last piece of apple Liz stroked the purebred's head before working her way around to the neck and under her chin. This done, she sat down on a overturned wooden bucket, took out the Morse-code book, placed it on the bucket and started to read. Dream snorted, and ate from the hay basket. They had bonded.

It was dinner time before Liz stood and stretched her aching body. She had sat in the stable with Dream for over four hours.

"Well, we are friends now, Dream, and tomorrow we ride like the wind."

Tom, who had come to check on them while doing his chores, could see Dream was totally relaxed. "It seems you know what you are doing."

"I hope so, Tom, see you tomorrow then."

"Bye, Miss."

Tomorrow came.

"I see you are dressed, are you taking Dream out?" Doris's tone was almost judgemental.

"Yes, Mrs Woodgarth." Doris was about speak, but Liz kept talking. "Perhaps you and Lucie would like to join me?"

Lucie became excited. "Oh yes, that would be fantastic. It will only take Mother and I a few moments to get ready."

"Good, I'll see you both at the stables then." Liz took a sip of her coffee.

Mrs Woodgarth said nothing, but knew how Dream could be. Her thoughts were not kind at all, and she was looking forward to Liz breaking her neck.

They got to the stables as Liz was saddling up Dream. She had told Tom the others were coming, so he had Tony and Breeze ready. Liz gave Dream half an apple before Doris and Lucie arrived and as they were busy getting themselves sorted, slipped Dream the other half.

All three walked on for about a hundred yards until they were in the field. This was their usual route: Across the field, over the three foot hedge, and to the water. Dream kept pulling at the reigns, eager to go, but Liz held her back.

Once in the field, Lucie went first and was soon at a gallop, followed by her mother, then Liz on Dream. Soon Liz and Doris were neck and neck. Liz held Dream back so they continued side by side. About fifty yards from the hedge, Liz let Dream go, it was as if Doris was standing still. Over the hedge and on to catch Lucie. Both Liz and Lucie reached the sea together. Lucie looked back to see her mother heading back to the Manor.

"Strange," Lucie muttered, "still that just leaves us, Liz."

The girls got on well. They talked about fashion, horses, and boys, However, soon it was time to return.

"Beat you to the road!" Lucie shouted and was off like a shot.

Liz followed and kept Dream back, she wanted Lucie to win. The pair reached the stables and left Tom to wipe down their horses while they went in search of Doris. They found her in the drawing room.

"What happened to you, Mother?" inquired Lucie.

"Oh nothing, darling. I think Tony may have got something in his hoof." Mrs Woodgarth glared daggers at Liz. *So, the bitch can ride as well. She will have to go.*

"Captain, may I introduce you to Miss Liz Monaco. She speaks several languages and will act as your interpreter."

"Pleased to meet you, Miss Monaco. You are just what I need." Captain Glover removed his cap and shook her hand.

He held on to her hand just a bit longer than perhaps he should have. The attraction was mutual. Liz started to blush. The captain was about 25 years old, tall, slim with dark brown eyes, and black wavy hair. She cast a quick glance at his left hand, but there was no ring.

She swallowed. "Pleased to meet you, too, Captain."

"I will leave you in the captain's capable hands. I'm sure he will get you back home when he's finished with you."

Liz found herself giving new meanings to the words just spoken, and was feeling a bit flushed.

"Right then, Miss Monaco."

"Please call me Liz."

"In public I will call you Miss Monaco, it's only proper. In private I will call you Liz. My name is David, in private, Captain Glover in public, agreed?"

"Yes, agreed, Captain Glover."

"Let's get started, Miss Monaco."

The days went by and soon became weeks and weeks months. The steady stream of men of all ages filed by with their papers and endless questions. The older ones asking the younger ones, some were related, fathers-sons, some brothers etc. This is where Liz came into her own. She could talk to the older men in their native language whose hold on the spoken English was not as good as their sons, and of course they liked her.

In the end there were over 22,000 internees in lnockaloe when the powers that be thought around 5,000. It was 5,000 in the camp in Douglas alone.

It was almost five months before Captain Glover for all his front and apparent confidence got to ask Liz out on a date. And he did it while taking her home one afternoon.

She thought this moment would never happen, despite dropping enough hints to show she was interested and began to accept that perhaps he just did not fancy her.

"Do you like motorbikes?" David asked.

"I don't know. I have never been on one, but sounds exciting."

"I will pick you up at 1500 hours here. I suggest you wrap up very warm," he offered.

She got out of the car and watched as he waved, turned around, and sped up the drive to the main gate. He turned right and was gone. It was 1 p.m. Liz went up to her room to get ready.

At last, she thought.

She was eighteen and he was 25. Over the last few months they had got to know bit about each other's back ground. She only let him know the bits she wanted him to know. He appeared very open and spoke about the girl he had back home in Portsmouth. But this had run its course and was over before he was stationed on the Island.

She suspected he must have done it several times, while she never. This caused her to panic a little. What was he expecting? Would he want to do it with her? What would she be expected to do to him? She knew she did want to do it, she felt ready and she really liked him. Yet should she do it on the first date? Would he think her a bit … loose?.

"What shall I wear? Oh My God, get a grip!" She whispered to herself. "Right it's cold, there's a clear blue sky so it won't be dark till about six o'clock. And I'll be on a motorbike."

She stood naked and studied at herself in the full-length mirror, she knew she was pretty, tall, and slim. Although, she felt that her breasts were too big.

It's what men like. That and long hair.

She settled for her riding breaches they were lined and warm, her long woollen socks, riding boots, vest, shirt, and the thick Arran Sweater she just bought. She finished with her hooded waxed jacket and gloves.

It was 2.45 p.m. when she went down stairs and met the Brigadier.

He looked a bit concerned. "Not going ridding at this time, surely?"

"No, Brigadier. I erm, Captain Glover is picking me up on his motorbike at 1500 hours."

The Brigadier smiled. "I see. Hang on a minute." He went to the kitchen while she waited in the hallway. Ten minutes went by before he reappeared. "Take this, it's to keep you both warm if you stop to look at the stars. It's new it a Thermos flask, in it is something warm and it will stay that way. Clever don't you think?"

"Yes, sir, thank you."

"Go and enjoy yourself, you deserve it. Glover is a good sort, and will look after you. He knows it, or he will have me to face." He stood looking at her, and her him.

Over the time she had been at Cove Manor with the Brigadier they had become quite close. Liz and his daughter tolerated each other and Lucie was okay when she was not under the wing of her mother. He was the grandfather she would have wanted, and she the granddaughter he would have wanted.

They both heard the sound of the motorbike. He waved her out the door. She smiled and went outside.

"Hello" David said.

"Hello." She beamed.

"On you get, put your arms around me so you won't fall off," he instructed.

She got on, hesitated, then wrapped her arms around his waist, and leaned into him.

"Waaaaa!" She screamed as they sped up the drive and onto the road.

He turned left, this road took them to the south east side of the Island and out of the biting North Westerly wind. Liz could not stopped smiling and hung on to her hero, loving it all.

They rode for about thirty minutes, before stopping. The view was fantastic; the sea was smooth not one boat in sight.

"This is where I come to get away from it all, hope you don't mind?" offered David.

"I don't mind at all, it's a lovely spot."

He looked at her. "Not too cold I hope?"

"No, I enjoyed the ride and can see the attraction. I might get one."

"I have packed some Army blankets. They are so warm, I thought we could walk to the cliff edge and sit a while, I have made us some Butties."

"Butties?" Liz frowned in confusion.

"Sandwiches, it's what the Scouses call them, that's Liverpudlians."

"It would appear I need to teach myself another language." Grinned Liz.

They both laughed. She walked behind him, it took around fifteen minutes to find a shaded and sheltered spot overlooking the sea. The thick woollen Army issue blankets, one on the ground the other was put to aside. He caught Liz looking at it.

"One for if you get cold you can cover yourself in it."

There was a quiet moment as both tried to fathom out what the other was thinking.

They spoke about day-to-day stuff, and a little background. Time flew by. It started to get dark, "Fancy a Butty?" He asked.

She, for a fleeting second thought he was asking something else, and blushed.

"Yes, please and I have something the Brigadier gave me. He said it keeps the drink warn for hours." She produced the Thermos from her large inside coat pocket. She opened it and took a sniff. "Smells like coffee." She offered it to him.

"It's coffee alright, but with a bit of rum, in fact a lot of rum, very warming." He poured and handed it to Liz, the smaller cup that was inside the large cup he had. "Best if I'm to ride us back safely."

Liz sniffed and took a sip.it was a warm feeling that went straight to her toes. "Oh yes, I like this ."

He sipped leisurely. "I agree I could get use to this, Liz."

The Butties, cheese and ham, went down well with the coffee. The next few hours flew past, it was now pitch black. It must have been gone seven. The only light to be seen was the hundreds of lights at the Internees camp about three miles further north along the coast.

The date had gone well, Liz felt completely at ease. They listened to each other's tales. She invited him to share the blanket as she could see he was getting cold. He shivered. She fell back and gazed at the night sky, full of stars, he stretched out beside her, then rolled onto his side.

She glanced at him, he brought his hand up to her face and touched her cheek, Her heart thumped in her chest, her mouth became dry. He slowly came close and kissed her. She closed her eyes.

This is so much better than I could have ever imagined.

His hand caressed down her neck and cupped her breast, she felt herself getting ready, the tingling damp feeling between her legs.

Suddenly he froze. She went to speak, but he covered her mouth and placed his finger to his mouth to signal no talking. He slowly sat up, as did she. There standing no more than thirty feet away were three men, their silhouettes out lined by the moon. To their horror, all three came within twenty feet from where they lay.

They started to speak in German. David looked at Liz, she waved her finger in front of his face as to say don't speak or move, then pointed to her ear. David understood and turned to study the trio.

They must be from the camp. How did they get out and why? she wondered.

Then, roughly a hundred yards from shore came a low rumbling. The couples' eyes widened when they saw a German U-Boat break the surface of the water. They didn't move a muscle. A few flashed suddenly emitted from the U-Boat.

David arched his eyebrow at Liz as if to say, "Well?"

She whispered in his ear, "U-Boat—U-87."

One of the men started to signal back with his torch. Liz got "Alles ist gut, fahren sie fort." David also was able to see the face of the one with the torch, one of the others called him Fredrick. David thought he recognised him from the camp, he was a bit of a trouble maker.

With that the men started to walk along the cliff back to the camp. The U-87 slid beneath the waves. For a moment they sat in silence staring at each other.

Liz spoke first. "They signalled, *'All is in order, proceed'*."

David repeated it to himself. "I think it's safe now, I must get you back and me to the camp."

They moved as quietly as they could, grabbing the blanket and any rubbish just in case the men returned in the day and found something that would indicate they had been seen and overheard. Liz was dropped off at Cove Manor.

"I will have to arrange a meeting in the morning with my C.O., you, and the Brigadier for a talk and debriefing. You okay?" He asked.

"Yes, David, I'm fine."

He could see she was calm and in control. "You are a very special lady, Miss Liz."

They stood under the porch light.

"You have a fantastic pair of—"

Liz sharply looked at him with a face like stone.

"Of intelligent eyes" her face softened.

He smiled. "You thought—well they are okay, too." They kissed. "Must go, see you in the morning." He kick started the bike and was gone.

"I thought it would be you, Miss," came the voice of Morris.

He was standing in the doorway, a small smile playing with the corners of his lips. *How long was he there watching?* she wondered. "Where is the Brigadier, Morris?"

"In the lounge, Miss."

"Thank you." Liz marched straight in.

The Brigadier and his daughter stood by the fire.

"This is a private conversation," spouted Doris.

"I need to speak to the Brigadier urgently."

"Can't it wait till morning?" She insisted.

"NO, it cannot, Mrs Woodgarth."

She stormed past Liz, muttering under her breath. Liz walked to the Brigadier.

"Whisky, Liz?"

"After, I have important news."

The Brigadier's spine stiffened. "Fire away."

"Captain Glover and I witnessed a German U-Boat surface and communicate with three men on land."

"WHAT?" the Brigadier cried.

"The signal was in German it said, *'All is in order, proceed.'* Afterwards, the three men returned to the camp. Captain Glover recognised one of them, he's gone back there now. He said he will arrange a debriefing at daylight."

The Brigadier let it the news sink in for a moment. "Well done, Liz, well done. That whisky now?"

"Yes please sir, thank you, sir."

"My God, a Bosch U-Boat in our waters, you have proved your worth to night, Liz. Splendid, now I must make a call."

No sooner had he said it than the phone rang. He went to answer it while Liz sank into the high backed horse hair chair by the fire with a large whisky in her hand. She was excited as her thoughts went back to what happened between her and David. She felt so alive.

I may never sleep again. Her thoughts were broken by the Brigadier's return.

"I just received a report from the C.O at the camp. They have all three in custody, you and I will go there first thing in the morning. Best get some sleep, Liz. I'll call you in plenty of time and well done again."

"Thank you, sir." Liz finished her whisky and went to her room.

As she left the Lounge Mrs Woodgarth was in like a shot. Liz heard her say, "well, what was so important?" Liz stopped in her tracks.

"That young lady has decoded a message from a German U-Boat located off the coast of this little Island, and uncovered German spies in the camp at Knockaloe." The Brigadier knew he had said to much, but he knew his daughter understood the seriousness and would remain silent. The room fell silent, Liz, smiling, continued to her rooms.

The relationship between Mrs Woodgarth and her since the news of her husband's death had been manageable, the only respite was when she went to London about once a month and stayed for up to a week. As far as Liz was concerned, she could stay there for good. Lucie, on the other hand, was happy at Cove Manor, had become a good friend and companion.

Liz fell back on her bed, looking up at the ceiling. She felt warm from the whisky, her thoughts where of David. She would have given herself to him, she knew that now. She undid the belt on her jodhpurs, undid the buttons and opened the fly buttons. Her hand went inside her knickers and found the spot, she was wet.

Slowly, she moved her middle finger up and down, up and down then slid it into her. She arched her back, her breathing became heavy and rapid, her hung mouth open. She kept her finger inside her and used the other hand to stimulate. She started to sense the feeling rise inside her very being, closer and closer. Then she gave a muted sigh, followed by another, her pelvis jolted several times. She kept her hand on the spot for a few seconds more, sheer pleasure and wishing it was him inside her.

Chapter 6

The Brigadier's driver took them both to the camp at Knockaloe. There they were met by Captain Glover.

"Good morning, sir, good morning... Miss." He almost called her Liz.

"Good morning, Captain," replied the Brigadier.

"Good morning, Captain." Liz dipped her head in greeting.

"Morning, Miss," the captain spoke softly. Then again, loud and clear, he was back to being an Army Captain, "Please follow me."

They followed into the make-shift cell block. The camp C.O. stood one side of the table with the German spy sitting handcuffed on the other side with two M.P. (military-police) flanking him.

The C.O, a Major William Sutter, spoke. "Captain, is this the man you witnessed signalling to an enemy ship known as U-87?"

"Yes, sir it is," answered the captain.

"And you, Miss, I will not mention your name, will you confirm that you were with Captain Glover and also witnessed this man signalling to U-87? In fact, it was you who informed the captain of the content of the message."

Liz swallowed. "Yes, that is correct, sir."

The prisoner lifted his head, looked at Liz, and smiled arrogantly. "Du bist zu spat." With this he returned to looking at the wall.

"He said, you are too late," Liz translated.

"Thank you, Miss, you may leave us. Please stay on camp in case we need you."

"The good captain will look after you, I'm sure," the Brigadier added. "And thank you."

Liz and Captain David Glover walked over to the N.A.A.F.I and had breakfast.

"We think there are more involved in this, perhaps up to six internees, to be able to get out and back in they must have help. We are watching their hut, all three are in the same one along with several others, some Italian."

Liz. listened, and said nothing. He stopped and studied at her for a moment.

"I erm, I really enjoyed our time together yesterday, Liz."

This is what she wanted to hear. "So did I David."

"Can we carry on where we left off? Are you free tonight?"

Liz smiled. "I'd like that."

"I have informed the Navy, Major, they are sending someone over," informed the Brigadier.

"Thank you, sir." The Major signalled to the M.P.'s. "Put him back with the other two, and nil by mouth until further notice."

"You can't do that you, English bastards!" shouted Fredrick Hindz.

"Oh yes I can," replied the Major.

The German was led away, still shouting and struggling against the M.P.'s.

"Major?"

"Sir?"

"Send in Sergeant Major Woodiwus. He frightens me, they should be terrified."

"Yes, sir." Major Sutter did as instructed.

Sergeant Major Woodiwus was one of the older personal, he was in his late forties, maybe early fifties. He was the Army's retired, undefeated Heavy weight boxing champion, and still at his age no-one in their right mind would challenge him. He stood 6ft 6inch with shoulders as wide as a door, his belly, although not always, was almost as big. He had no neck, his large head seemed to just sit on his massive shoulders, and when he shouted, everybody heard the bull like bellowing of a voice.

"Sir, you sent for me?"

The C.O. looked up at this mountain of a man. the room had become dim as the doorway was blocked by this vision of shear power, just his presence felt menacing. "Yes, I did. I would like you to just talk to our guests, and let them know what to expect if they do not cooperate. I have placed them on nil by mouth."

"Yes, SIR." The bellow shook the rafters.

"Thank you, Sergeant Major." the C.O. quickly put his hand up to stop another glass shattering, "Yes, sir."

The M.P opened the cell door, the three men inside were sitting, but quickly arose and gazed in horror at this vision of hell that stood before them.

He stooped, entered, and ever so quietly spoke. "Close the door, lock it, and lose yourself, boyo."

"But, sir," insisted the M.P.

"Don't you BUT SIR MEEEEEE!" This sound went right through everyone. The M.P. did what he was told.

Sergeant Major Woodiwus just stood there in silence; the prisoners looked at each other with eyes like dinner plates. After about ten minutes, Fredrick Hindz opened his mouth to speak.

"SILENCEEEEEEEE!" Enoch Celwyn Woodiwus started to dribble and shake. He towered over him. "I will tear you apart with my bear like hands, starting with your balls, then your manhood, and while you bleed and scream, I will pull out your eyes, then you tongue by the roots.

"THEN I WILL SHOVE MY TWELVE INCH DONG RIGHT UP YOUR ARSE TILL THE BLOOD STARTS TO FLOW. It will take about thirty minutes for you to die. I have done it before and served my time, but for you three I will risk going back inside."

He grabbed the man to his left by the balls and lifted him till he was on tip-toe. The poor sod screamed so loud the M.P. ran in and opened the cell door. The man fell to the floor and was sick. Woodiwus stood, arms straight, his hands making fists. He turned, slowly stooped, and walked out but whirled about as if he might go back in.

The prisoners backed themselves against the cell wall with a look of sheer terror. Woodiwus saw the smaller of the pair had pissed himself. The M.P. closed and locked the cell door. Woodiwus left. The higher ups were waiting outside the door.

"Well, Sergeant Major?" The C.O. asked.

"I think they will talk, sir, give them a few hours. Then get the small Italian alone. He is the weak one, he will talk."

"Thank you, Sergeant Major."

"Sir." Woodiwus saluted.

"More tea, Miss?" Captain Glover held out the tea pot.

"No thank you. I'll prepare the coffee we had last night." Liz smiled.

"I'll go and check if they still want you to hang around. If not, I'll drive you back. You stay here in the warm room, I won't be long." He left Liz sitting at the table holding her last cup of tea.

She felt the call and went to the ladies. She caught sight of herself in the mirror and played with her hair. This did nothing at all. As she returned to the table, she spotted him standing by the door. He spotted her.

What a lovely looking man, such a warm smile. She sailed over to him.

He swallowed hard, his heart skipping a beat. *Wow, you are something special.*

"Do they still need me?" She broke his trance.

"No, they said you can go, but be ready to return if needed."

They arrived at Cove Manor at lunch time.

"Can you stay for lunch?" She asked, "I'm sure Cook can rustle up something…"

"Okay, if it's quick."

They made their way to the kitchen.

"Cook, any chance of lunch for the captain?"

"Anything for you, you know that. Go sit in the sun-room no-one in there, I'll bring it through."

"Where is Mrs Woodgarth and Lucie?"

"Out riding, should be back about now."

Upon entering the sun-room, they chose the window seat with its viewpoint of the lawn and the sea.

"Beautiful view, Liz, you are very lucky to be living here."

"Yes, I do appreciate it, and often walk along the beach"

"Here we are!" Cook bustled in with a tray of food and drink. "You two get on the outside of that and some fresh coffee."

"Thank you, Cook."

"My pleasure, my lovely."

A disgusted voice spoiled the moment. "I see we are feeding the troops now."

97

Liz sighed inwardly, yet kept her outward demeanour pleasant. "Mrs Wood-garth, this is Captain Glover. Captain Glover, this is the Brigadier's daughter Mrs Woodgarth."

He dipped his head in greeting. "Pleased to meet you, I am sorry about your husband."

"It seems ages ago, but thank you, Captain." She scrutinised both of them before flouncing off.

"Don't want to get on the wrong side of her," he commented. "Best be going."

"But you haven't eaten anything," Liz protested.

"It's okay. Shall I pick you up about six? In the car this time, there's a nice little tavern a few miles up the road."

"Sounds nice, see you then."

There was a moment of awkward tension as they didn't know whether to kiss or not. It was decided not. However, she touched his hand. She stayed at the window watched as he drove off.

In her room Liz went through her limited wardrobe, and chose a tartan pleated skirt. Not quite has heavy as a Kilt, but lined and very warm. It came just below the knee, a nice white blouse and the e Arran Sweater. She had never worn nylons, always long skirts socks and boots or trousers. This was the time to wear the knee length leather boots she bought.

She stayed in her room reading a book she had found in the library, *How To Become An Accountant* by A.J. Bore. It was dull, but she saw the importance of managing her money, so persevered.

5.45 p.m. Liz looked in the mirror and was pleased with what she saw. she knew she was attractive and the clothes fitted well. She was excited and appre-hensive. She saw the lights of a car coming down the drive and hurried to meet it. She didn't even wait for him to knock, rather went out to the porch. He easily braked to a stop, alighted, opened the passenger door for her then went around to the driver's side and got in.

"You look nice," he offered.

"Thank you. Your uniform is different from this afternoon."

"I do have several uniforms, it's not always the same one. This is my best one and fresh on. Enough about clothing, off we go!"

They got to the Duck and Grouse. The building showed it's age, the window frames and front door were all out of shape, there had been some subsidence over the years, the sliding sash windows had moved in shape to match the window frames. How the class had not broken was a miracle. The paintwork was cracked and dry. The lighting inside was dim due to the blackout rules, there were only a few locals in up the far end of the bar.

"Well, Liz, what would you like?"

"Can I have a whisky please? I don't suppose they have that sort of coffee?"

David went to the bar. "This is a long shot. Do you have any coffee?"

"Coffee? I could make you a cup."

"Two, please, and no milk. Oh and two large rums, please." He took the rums to their table.

Liz looked confused.

"He is making us two black coffees. I thought when they come we could put the rum in the coffee like last night."

Liz beamed.

A portly man bustled over to their table, coffee in hand. "Here you are, sir, as you requested."

"Thank you." They poured the rum into the coffee.

The barman's face was a picture. a look A of surprise and disbelieve "Well, I've seen it all now." With that off he went to the other end of the bar. They could hear him talking to the locals, They finished their Rum and Coffee.

David paid for the drinks. "Shall we go for a drive?"

"Yes," answered Liz.

Without saying anything, they both knew what going to happen. After a mile or so, he pulled in.

A few moments later David spoke, "I have the blankets in the car, do you fancy finishing what we started last night?"

"Okay," was all she said.

They found a spot overlooking the bay. He placed the first blanket on the ground. They stretched out and he covered them both with the other. They lay on their sides facing each other, not a word was spoken. As before he placed his hand on her cheek and kissed her mouth.

He felt her move closer, his hand crept under her sweater and started to un-button her blouse. That done, he cupped her breast, his thumb caressing her nipple. She sighed and arched her back. He felt her nipple harden under his touch. Her breathing was rapid and shallow.

He was hard and it hurt being in the confines of his trousers. He lifted her skirt, his hand trailed up her thigh until he felt her pants. She rolled to her back and held his face. His hand was now in her pants. She lifted her hips to make it easier for him, her pants were off. His hand was again between her legs, he knew what he was looking for and found it.

She sighed and moved her hips up and down. She had never felt so delirious. Her sighs became more and more frequent. He undid his trousers and rolled on top, he was in. Liz gave a long, low moan. He lay straight armed and moved in time with her. Her eyes were closed, as that feeling started to rise within her. It became far more intense than she had ever felt until they both climaxed at the same time. She held him to her, he kissed her neck and lovely face. They lay like this until he felt himself become soft. He got off and held her close.

"I wish we could stay like this forever. David, you do like me, don't you?"

"Liz, I adore you. You are very special to me. I have never been one for one-night stands, I just can't do it."

"Then why did it take you so long to ask me out?"

"Liz, I—I thought of you as being out of my league. I'm only a captain and the Army is all I have. You live at Cove Manor and are educated. You speak several languages, you're class and could marry a millionaire."

"Have you ever read a book called *Pride and Prejudice*?" Liz asked.

"No, there you go you're educated."

"It's about two people from different backgrounds who are kept apart by their own pride and prejudices. They wasted so much time when they could have been together. It really doesn't matter as long as they love each other."

" It would be so easy for me to fall for you, but these are so uncertain times."

Liz. put a finger to his lips. "One day at a time, David."

They lay in each other's arms admiring the stars.

A little while later. "David?"

"Yes ?"

"I'm getting very cold."

He kissed her. "Let me get you back. If you got a cold I would be blamed and the old man, er, Brigadier will have me on Jankers for life."

It was gone midnight by the time they reached Cove Manor.

"Drop me here at the gate, I'll walk," Liz said.

"No way, Miss! I'll turn out the lights and drive slowly."

All one could hear was the crunching of the gravel under the tyres. They stopped fifty yards from the main door. They both got out and met in front of the car.

"Thank you for a wonderful evening, David."

"I should be thanking you, Liz."

"It's an evening I will never forget." She kissed him and went inside.

He stood still until she was gone. Only then did he leave. The house was quiet, her eyes soon adjusted to the dark interior. She tried to creep up to her room. As she passed the lounge, a light suddenly spilled out.

"And what time do you call this, young lady?" It was the Brigadier.

"I—erm—you see," she tripped over her tongue.

"He's a good chap, should go far. Make sure he treats you well, or I'll have his guts for garters." He smiled, and she smiled back.

"Good night, sir."

Once in her room, she lay on her bed, thoughts going around her head. "I've done it. I'm a woman," she whispered. "And he is wonderful."

However, at breakfast she was back to being all business.

"Any news on the U-Boat business, sir?"

"Yes, Liz, the Navy is arranging to collect them in a few days' time and take them back for questioning. We are going to have a go at the Italian later today. You might be needed, is that alright with you?"

"Yes, of course, sir, that's what I'm here for."

"It's a lot for young shoulders."

"I'll be fine."

He nodded acceptance.

The Italian gave three more names without too much trouble. He was more scared of Woodiwus as made it part of the deal that he never see that unmo dell' inferno (man from the devil) ever again.

All six internees were classed as spies. There were two U-Boats in the area, U-87 and U-91, and they were to operate between Liverpool and The I.O.M. This was passed on to the Navy.

The Navy was due to collect all at 18.00H later on that day. It was 10.00H when there was a racket coming from the cells, Two M.P.'s went to investigate. One man was on the floor screaming.

Fredrick shouted, "He's not well. Get him out! Get him out!"

The M.P.'s acted quickly. Just as the cell was opened, Fredrick pulled a gun and put it to the M.P.'s head while others took their guns. Fredrick signalled for the M.P.'s to go first. On entering the main guard room, they were met by Captain Glover and four armed M.P.'s pointing their guns.

"Drop your guns now," ordered Captain Glover. "I said NOW."

Fredrick, seeing it was hopeless, screamed, fired and ran forward. The M.P.'s opened fire. All six men within seconds were dead. It was only then did they spot Captain Glover slowly falling to the floor. They grabbed and laid him down. He was dead before he touched the ground.

In ran the Major, out of breath. "Oh for Christ sake, not Glover!" He looked around at the stoic faces. Captain Glover was well liked by the men and would be sadly missed.

"Clear up this mess, take Captain Glover to the chapel. Then someone best tell me what the bloody hell happened, I want a full report. I go for a piss and this."

The mess was cleaned, the Navy told not to bother. The Major sat at his table and muttered, "What a waste of a life." He took a deep breath, gave a long sigh and reluctantly picked up the phone.

"Brigadier, it's Major Sutter. I have some bad news. Captain Glover has been killed in the line of duty. The six internees are also dead. I have informed the Navy, and I will give you a full written report as soon as." Silence. "Sir?"

"Yes, Major, I'm here. What happened?"

"Attempted break-out. They had an army issue Webley and Scott revolver. I have yet to find out how."

"Thank you, I'll be along shortly" The Brigadier put down the phone and sat on the arm of the study chair. *She must be told, and the sooner the better.* He went out to the hallway. "Morris, have you seen Miss Liz?"

"I think she is in her room, sir. Shall I fetch her?"

"No, thank you."

"Are you alright, sir?" Morris sensed a sadness in the Brigadier's voice.

"Keep it to yourself for now, Morris, young Captain Glover has been killed."

"Oh no!." Morris's shoulders fell.

The Brigadier climbed the stairs as if he has divers lead boots, pausing outside for a moment then knocked.

"Come in, it's unlocked." She sounded so happy, he was about to break her heart.

He opened the door.

"Oh, it's you sir. Please come in."

He came in and closed the door behind him. His face was pale and she thought he looked old.

She stood. "Are you well, sir?"

"Please sit, Liz."

She sat, then stood then sat.

He took a deep breath "It's bad news, I'm afraid. There was been trouble in the camp, and Captain Glover was shot. He's dead."

Liz started to shake. She tried so hard to stay in control, but the tears started to roll down her cheek and her lip trembled. He started to walk to her when she flew at him, threw her arms around him, held on as if her life depended on it, and sobbed. He, too, felt a tear. He cradled the back of her head against his chest and held her close.

The service took place, with full honours, Captain David Glover was awarded the C.S.O (Distinguished Service Order) and his body was taken back to his home town of Birkenhead for burial. Liz met his parents, they knew who she was as he had written to them about this lovely, bright and clever girl he knew and how he might ask her out one day. His mother was glad to meet this girl and learn how close they had become.

"It makes me feel much better knowing he had you." Both his mother and Liz shed a few tears that day. But somehow meeting each other gave both women much comfort.

Liz was not the same after David's death, only to be expected. She lost weight and couldn't sleep. The Brigadier kept a close eye on her. Lucie was good, she tried her best to keep Liz's spirits up. They went riding often, but her mother kept Lucie close.

Two weeks before Christmas Mrs Woodgarth took herself and Lucie to London shopping, they would be back Christmas Eve. The Brigadier did ask his daughter if she would take Liz, but alas it would be too inconvenient.

"Liz?"

"Yes sir?"

"Good news, the Navy, God bless them, found the U-87 and have been tracking it for a few days now. No sign yet of U-91. They found it after it sunk a cargo ship entering Liverpool bay. Let's hope the sink the Bugger."

"Yes, sir." The news, although good, did nothing to lift her spirits.

"I wish there was something I could do to help." The Brigadier sighed.

"I'll be fine, it's all part of growing up and life" She left without another word.

He could see she was getting upset and let it go. However, he didn't want her moping about the house and made a decision.

"Liz, I need you to come with me to the camp, we have a lead on who may have given them the gun. Grab your coat the car is waiting."

"Yes, sir." Liz grabbed her coat, got her boots on, looked in the hall mirror messed with her hair, it did nothing as per usual (her hair was long and thick, lovely condition, just a lot of it) and ran to the car. The Brigadier was already waiting.

When they arrived at the camp, they were waved through the checkpoint.

"Good day, sir, Miss Monaco," the Major greeted them both.

"Good day to you, Major," answered the Brigadier. Liz managed to smile weakly and nod.

Seated at the desk was two internees, one young about twenty while the other must have been in his late sixties.

"These two have information on the gun used, sir," the Major said.

The young one started to speak to the older one in broken Italian, then turned to all assembled. "I don't speak good Italian, my grandfather he speaks no English. His grandfather muttered something in Italian."

Liz picked up on it and smiled. "I giouani di eggi non hanno rispetto per la loro storia."

The old man brightened up. "Si Signora si, Antonio." He pointed to himself.

"What is happening?" The Major sounded a bit put out.

"I told him, Antonio," Liz nodded to the old man, "that the youth of today have no respect for their history. He said, *'Yes, Miss, yes'.*"

Antonio started to talk to Liz. "*Signora, Ho sontito uno di lorodire chi il prete lo portera stasera al recinto, questo e tutto quello chi ho sentito.*"

The room was silent all eyes were on Liz.

"Well, Miss Monaco?" The Major asked.

"He heard one of them say the priest is bringing it to the fence tonight, that's all he heard."

"The Priest? Are you sure?"

Liz turned to Antonio. "Antonio, Prete?"

"Si Signora si."

"Thank you, Antonio. Please see he is looked after. Sergeant, take them both to the N.A.A.F.I."

"Yes, sir. como thisa awayo."

The Major looked at his sergeant in disgust. Antonio grabbed Liz's arm, "Vuoi sposare mio nipote, ho soldi?"

"Non, Antonio."

"Peccato." With that he squeezed her arm and went with the Sergeant.

"What was all that about, Miss Monaco?" the Major inquired.

"He asked if I would marry his grandson, he said he has money, I declined. He said, *'Pity.'*"

The Major shook his head and sighed. "Shall we get on?"

"So, a priest? That can only mean our Chaplin on the Islands," the Brigadier said.

The Major picked up the phone. "Bring me the file on The Chaplin please, and on the Q.T. understood? Good."

"I will see to the civilian side of this," stated the Brigadier.

"Yes, sir."

The Brigadier and Liz were driven back to Cove Manor.

"Must be lunch time, my belly thinks my throat has been cut," joked the Brigadier.

As they ate, Liz observed the man, having never seen him so excited. The Brigadier had the bit between his teeth, action at last. After lunch and a large Rum and Coffee, this had become their drink, he got serious.

"Right, Miss Liz, I am going to put something to you. You can say yes or no, but I think it is just what you want and dare say it, need."

Liz pasted on a pleased smile, yet deep down was a little apprehensive.

"It's going to be an undercover operation. I want you to join the church, can you sing? No don't answer that. You will need to get to know the Vicar, and Christmas is the perfect time. You will have to give yourself a complete makeover and a new name. As you are known I think it best if you start to live in town, just come over from London to start a new life here. You will report to no one but me. What do you think?"

"I can do it!" Liz answered right away.

"Yes, I know or I would never of asked. I will make the arrangements in Douglas. You go and think of how you plan to do it. We will talk again this evening as it's only nine days to Christmas."

Liz spent the afternoon going through some old fashion magazines borrowed from Lucie: The *Chiffons La Mode* and the *Delineator.*

At Dinner that evening the Brigadier was eager to see what she had come up with.

"Well, Liz, what have you for me?"

"I need to go to Liverpool, sir, I need an allowance of £20 for clothes, make-up, shoes, etc."

"I see."

"And I need to go tomorrow."

"Fine, I trust you, Miss Monaco. Bring back the receipts, won't you? I look forward to seeing what you have in mind. I have made arrangements for you to stay with a Mrs O'Rorke at Harbour House down by the Pier, you have a suit of rooms, with your own bath etc. I will arrange the rent and out of pocket expenses to be paid into your bank account. Please keep all receipts, and your new name is Miss Biddy Bell."

She laughed. "That fits exactly with the idea I have in mind."

"Really? I was joking" His bushy eyebrows went up in surprise. "I look forward to seeing the new you. Wait here." He was gone only a matter of moments. "Here is £25, I assume you will be staying overnight?"

"Yes, sir, I will."

"Right, I have work to do and I imagine so have you. Good luck, Liz, I will see you the day after tomorrow, I will tell Private Ryan to have the car warmed and ready for at 0500 Hours." He took his leave and Liz retired to her room.

She sat facing the fire. in her mind's eye she had Miss Biddy Bell. *Yes, this is what I needed.* head become a little hardened since David's death, but this would prove an asset.

Chapter 7

Liz was back at Cove Manor. Morris helped her carry several boxes of various sizes up to her room.

"You're back I see. Successful trip I take it?" The Brigadier greeted her with a peck on each cheek.

"Yes, sir, I have put all the receipts with a detailed list of items bought. No change, in fact you owe me £1-10-04d."

"My God, all you women are the same it's never enough. Sorry, Liz, I didn't mean to include you. Not you, there is something different about—I—can't think what it is. I'll let you get on and see you at dinner this evening."

In her room she took off her big hat, but no hair fell down to her waist. It was now in a modern bob, all the rage in Paris. She unpacked everything she bought and spread it around.

"Just wait till they see me in this," she whispered.

One outfit was a bright red number, skirt with wide black waist band and s hem that stopped just below the knee, blouse with frills, red fitted jacket with black buttons to match the skirt, stockings, suspender-belt, red shoes with a court heel, and hat to finish.

Liz set about with the make-up and hair. She thumbed through the magazines, checking out the lipstick, powders and whatnot. This was a completely new experience for her. She had watched her mother do it and wished she had paid closer attention. Or perhaps the woman could have spent more time showing her daughter. To be fair, Liz was not that interested she was more fascinated with in horses and tractors and how they worked.

She spent hours getting ready. When she was done, she looked in the full-length mirror for the first time. She could not believe the women that stared back, she did not recognise herself at all. This tall, elegant, sophisticated, and stylish woman about town. She tried a few poses and dissolved into laughter.

The opening and closing of a door followed by familiar male voices told her the Brigadier had returned. She peered around her door and waited until he almost got to the study door when she called out, "Sir, could you please spare me a minute?"

He looked her way, muttered something to Morris, and started up the stairs. With an excited giggle, she closed the door before he reached the top step. He knocked. A voice he did not recognise said, "Do come in, Brigadier." He opened the door, his jaw dropped.

"Close the door quickly, sir." This voice he did recognise.

He was dumb-struck for several moments before he managed to find his tongue. "Miss Liz Monaco is that really you? My God, Liz!" He gave a short laugh, "Miss Biddy Bell I am so pleased to make your acquittance. I'm not sure Douglas or the Island is ready for you."

"Will it do, sir?"

"Yes, indeed it will. We have to create a plan. How do we get you out and down to Mrs O'Rorke? How do I explain your sudden going? How are we to meet or communicate?

"You are a remarkable young woman. You have your mother's gift for the theatricals, your parents would be so proud if they saw you now and knew what you are about to do for England and its people. I will leave you now, I have urgent work, I unfortunately must attend to, we will talk first thing in the morning. Good night, Miss Biddy Bell, sleep well."

"Good night, sir."

Breakfast came soon enough and Liz was bursting with curiosity to find out what was going to happen. Thankfully the Brigadier didn't keep her waiting.

"I have talked it over with the Major, Liz, and we have decided to hold off till the New Year. The Major and I think it is too soon after the event. Whoever is involved will be on their guard and on the lookout for anything out of the ordinary. We do have a tail on the Vicar, and have cleared the camp Chaplin. He was away at the time, but we will keep an eye on him. It does point to the Vicar."

"Or the Verger, there could have been some confusion," volunteered Liz.

"Yes, indeed good point. I'll set a watch on him, too. Now tomorrow is Christmas Eve and the ladies will be back, no doubt spent out. Liz, I want you to phone Mrs O'Rorke and explain why you will not be taking up the room till after New Year. Some personal problems or whatever you can concoct. But the rent will still be paid, can I leave that to you?"

"I'll do it now." Liz hurried to make the call.

"The number is in the book under Harbour House," the Brigadier called after her.

"Hello is this Mrs O'Rorke? Miss Bell here. I won't be over and taking the rooms till after the New Year. I will give you 24 hours' notice of my arrival, the rent will be paid as agreed. Yes. Good, and the same to you, Mrs O'Rorke, good-bye." Liz was smiling.

"You enjoyed that Miss Monaco."

"I did. If that's all I thought I would take Dream out for a few hours."

"Yes, yes, you go ahead."

Christmas Eve, 10a.m.

Liz was back to her old self, except for the hair. So far only cook has made any comment.

" Oh, my lovely what have you done to all that wonderful hair?" Later she apologised and said, "I believe it's all the rage in the big cities."

That made Liz feel better. She was beginning to realise just how easy it was to manage and dry.

"I don't believe it!" Snarled the Brigadier as Liz walked in, "Problem, sir?"

"That was my daughter on the phone, they are staying until the 27th, I mean travelling back on the 27th. They have been invited to the Christmas bash at H.Q."

"So it's just you and I then?"

"Not if I can help it. Why should they have all the fun?" He picked up the phone and dialled. "Good morning, Major. Yes thank you. You will have two more guests for tomorrow's Christmas dinner, Myself and Miss Monaco. Good. While we speak any developments? Good, yes very good. See you at 19.00Hours."

"That sounds fantastic." Her eyes twinkled mischievously. "Do I come as Miss Monaco or Miss Biddy Bell?"

"I think Miss Monaco. I do not want to see the officers dribbling down the best uniforms into their soup. Er, er, not that you would not,"

"I know what you meant." She let him off the hook." Shall I tell Cook we will have our Christmas dinner on the 27th or 28th?"

"Good idea, let's say the 28th."

Cook was not pleased at all. But with a lot of tut tut tuttering, it was settled.

Christmas Day 10.30 a.m.

Liz returned from her ride. Her and Dream were now the best of friends and enjoyed each other. She ran to her room, got changed, grabbed the present for the Brigadier his daughter and Lucie, and joined him for a Christmas breakfast. She placed the presents under the tree with the others. others being his to them.

Morris with vthe help of Biddy had decked the table beautifully. Breakfast was Manx Kippers with poached eggs and green beans. There was Port, sherry, and champagne with fresh orange juice. Liz was like a child, excited and impatient.

"Would you like your present, sir." With a look of don't say no, and the Brigadier did pick up on it.

"Yes, and you can open yours at the same time."

Liz brought them both to the table. "You open yours first."

"I am the commanding officer here, young Miss Liz." He smiled. "And I give you a direct order, you first."

"Yes, SIR." Liz unwrapped the beautiful paper, it was a box. She opened the box and found a very beautiful pair of black riding boots with tan leather tops and finger pulls to match, "Thank you so much! This is just what I needed." For a moment she forgot herself and was about to go and give the Brigadier a hug.

He, realising what was happening, half shouted, "Right it's my turn now. Er, I wonder what it is."

He unwrapped the small box, and removed a lead crystal Whisky glass. It was quite plain with a small repeated patten around the square base. But the bit that got a tear in the Brigadier's eye was the beautiful inscription:

To Brigadier Kingsley,

A small thank you for all you have done for me.

Miss Liz Monaco,

Christmas 1916,

He whispered, "Thank you" stood and strode over to the large bay window overlooking the sweeping lawn down to the sea.

Liz sensed how he felt. "I'll go and try on my new boot ." She vanished up to her room, put on the wonderful boots, taking her time to give him a while to compose himself and returned to the breakfast room.

"They are perfect, sir! Just perfect."

The Brigadier stood with his arm outstretched, in his hand was "The Glass" and almost full of whisky. "Yours is on the table."

She picked up her glass; they chinked and toasted good health and an end to this stupid war.

"My God, Major, what a splendid turn out. First class, well done," the Brigadier exclaimed.

"Thank you, sir." The Major held his head high, proud as a peacock.

They were shown to their seats, prime position. The mess hall looked fantastic, one would never know a war was on. One long table with an officer then a lady, officer, lady, and so on. The Brigadier and Liz where in the middle.

The food was to die for, drink everywhere, and lots of lively conversation. Afterwards, everyone filed in to the side rooms while the table and chairs were removed to make way for the band and dancing.

Liz was asked several times, but declined for two reasons. First, she cannot dance at all, and second, too many young men in uniform made her think of David.

She tried her best and hid it well, only the Brigadier sensed the truth.

It was about 20.00 Hours when in ran the Signals officer waving a piece of paper. He wove through the people on the dance floor and handed it to the Brigadier. The latter read it and walked to the stage and the microphone.

"Gentlemen and ladies, good news. The Royal Navy, with our help I might add, found U-87 and has sent her and her crew to the bottom of the deep blue sea." A mighty cheer went up, almost lifting the roof, "We sunk the bastards!" Came this bull horn of a voice it was Sergeant Major Woodiwus.

The Brigadier, Major, and Liz went into one of the side rooms.

"Major it reads, *'At 17.00Hours H.M.S. Buttercup spotted U-87 when she surfaced in the dark, fifteen miles west of Liverpool bay. Action was taken to head for her at full speed. This was successfully carried out, she was hit midships and sank with the loss of her full complement of 45 officers and crew, no survivors'."*

"I'll drink to that," the Major declared.

All three went back to the party which was in full swing. Dancing, singing, and plenty of drinking. If the Bosch landed now, they would take them all without a fight.

Liz could not stop thinking of those poor men drowning and their families back home. Some were fathers, brothers, husbands, uncles… Her thoughts were broken by a captain heading her way.

He was a bit worse for drink. "That was all down to you and your Captain Glover. So his dying was not in vain, Miss."

Her throat constricted and tears burned her eyes, but kept it together. "Thank you, please excuse me." She walked outside for some welcome fresh air.

London, Christmas Eve.

"Enjoying yourself, darling?" Major Jack Bowen asked as he waltzed Mrs Woodgarth around the floor, trying to not bump into anyone. Most of all the Colonel and his large wife, both seemed oblivious of all other personal on the dance floor.

"Very much so. This must all cost a small fortune."

"Poor old tax payer, darling. Good old tax payer I mean." Captain Jack grinned.

Lucie was not short of dance partners and revelled in the attention.

"Jack, have you had a word with your men with regards to Lucie?" Doris cast a nervous glance at her daughter, her mind painting all sorts of picture where the constant male attention might lead.

"Yes. darling, they will be on their best behaviour." Jack looked into her eyes. "Do you know what I am thinking?" He spoke low and pulled her tight against him.

"I think I might." She winked.

He grabbed her hand and led her through the throngs of dancing couples, off the dance floor, into a side room leading to the back stairwell, and up to his quarters.

"Where are you taking me?" She giggled, her mind full of anticipation. He made her feel twenty years younger, and more of a woman than she had ever been. God knows he made feel so alive.

He opened the door and took a quick look to see if he could spot anyone, no-one. He pulled her roughly into his arms, she gasped as he kissed her hard. It had been a long time since she'd been treated like this, and she was loving every second. He kissed her neck then down to her half-concealed breasts, his hands grabbed at her skirt and lifted it high. Finding her knickers, down they came faster than a ship's sail in a hurricane.

She whispered, "No," which shouted a, "Yes! Please!" Sex with him was like nothing she ever experienced.

He gently threw her face down onto his bed. Her skirt bunched up around her thighs, he pulled her into the kneeling position and was in her. His hands squeezed either side of her pelvis as he pulled her onto him pushed, pulled, pushed, pulled.

She whispered, "My God yes! Yes! YES!" She never felt so basic. This was the roughest he had ever been and she was loving it. She felt him come, and with this he playfully slapped her arse. "Harder please, harder"

She could not believe these words were coming from her mouth. He was taken a-back for a moment, but he did as instructed. She moaned and moved her arse from side to side and tilted her hips towards him. He smacked her hard with both hands. Her cheeks were getting red. She started playing with herself, her body arched, she gave out a long moan as she slowly slid forward and lay flat on the bed. He stretched out on top and moved her hair away from her sweaty face and kissed the back of her neck.

"Darling are you okay?" He had been pleasantly surprised, and was not expecting that from her.

"You bring out the whore in me, Jack. I want you so much, and now we can plan our life together. Now I'm free."

"Where will we live? And I can't give you the sort of lifestyle—."

She cut him short. "We will live here in London on York Street, and part of the estate at Cove Manor is mine. I will have money."

This was just what he wanted to hear; it was all starting to come together for him.

"You go back the way we came; it will take you past the ladies powder room. I will go around the front, it's best we are not seen entering the party together, darling. You go first, I will follow in a few minutes." Doris tentatively made her way down stairs and back to the ballroom. On entering the room she was grabbed.

"Mother I've been looking for you everywhere," remarked Lucie.

"I needed some fresh air darling, felt a bit faint."

"let's find somewhere to sit I want to tell you something."

"I er, prefer to stand Lucie er, if you don't mind" she was feeling a little tender.

"I could live in London for ever. It's so boring at Grandfather's. Do we have we got to go back?" Lucie sighed.

"For now, darling, yes." Her mother realised what she had said. However, Lucie did not pick-up on it.

The Brigadier replaced the phone, walked out into the hall, and down to the kitchen. His driver, Private Sean Ryan, often sat there when not required.

"Go and fetch my daughter and granddaughter, will you? They have just arrived and are waiting for you at the ferry."

"Yes, sir." Off he went.

The Brigadier returned to the lounge and poured himself a whisky in what was now his favourite glass. He looked at the words etched on the glass.

What a lovely thing to have had done, he thought. *If only I had a son, I would make the blighter marry her.*

There was a fuss at the door, the Brigadier went to investigate. There, he beheld his daughter and granddaughter along with a mountain of boxes of various shapes and sized.

"Morris, do be careful. Is that all of them?" She asked the driver.

"Yes, Mrs Woodgarth." Ryan looked at Morris and threw his gaze skyward.

"Good to have you both back," the Brigadier said. "Seems as though you have bought up the whole of the West End."

"Hardly, Father. Morris, please take them to my room, and Lucie's to hers."

"Yes, ma'am." Morris looked at the dozen or so boxes, and glanced at Lucie as her mother had gone into the lounge. "Which ones are yours, Miss?"

"That's mine, and that, and that one, and that one."

"Yes, Miss."

Lucie then followed her mother into the lounge and left Morris to his duty. The Brigadier wasn't far behind them.

"Christmas dinner will be at 20.00Hours," he announced.

"Good, I'm starving," piped up Lucie.

"That gives you both a few hours to sort yourselves out. Cook has been beside herself and on tender hooks all day."

They both left, the Brigadier went back to his whisky. Lucie raced up the stairs, but not to her bedroom.

Knock, knock. "Liz are you in there?"

Liz answered the door. "Lucie, you and your mother back? Was it a good trip?"

"Fantastic. I had men fighting for me, for a dance that is, no duels or pistols at dawn. I could have stayed in London or Paris or Rome. I got you a present, it's under the tree."

"Yours is there, too," Liz offered.

"Well, I have to get ready for dinner, I'm starving. See you at eight." Lucie ran across the hall to her room.

Only two years between us, but Lucie is still a child. Liz stared at the partially left open door. She reflected on how she had grown up over the last few months. The way her life had gone the pressures the decisions she had made.

The time passed quickly and after dinner everyone gathered around the tree.

"Open your present, Grandfather!" Lucie urged.

He picked up a square shaped box with a fancy bow on top. Removing the lid, he pulled out a Deer Stalker Shooting hat. "Oh, Lucie, it's just what I needed."

"Well, put it on," Lucie ordered. "It's from Mother and me."

He humoured her. "Do I look the part?"

"Yes you do, Grandfather," said Lucie, looking very pleased with herself as it was her idea.

Doris opened her present from her father; it was a beautiful diamond broach that had belonged to her grandmother.

"I thought you should have it now, darling, than wait until I'm dead."

"Thank you," was all she said.

The silence was broken by the Brigadier. "Look what Liz got me." He showed off the whisky glass to them both, clearly unable to conceal how pleased he was.

"Yes, that's nice," remarked Doris.

Lucie took the glass from her grandfather and started to read out the wording. She got as far as "a Small thank you" when her mother interrupted, "That's very personal" in a tone of, *'Who do you think you are? You are not family, you are in my father's employment.'*

Liz met her demeaning gaze head on. "Your father bought me the most wonderful pair of riding boots; you will see them when we go riding next."

"The travelling was very tiresome," said Doris. "If you would excuse me." She rose and left.

"It's only 10:30," the Brigadier objected.

"I think I will go, too. See you in the morning." With that Lucie left.

"Just you and me, Liz. Whisky?"

"Yes please, sir."

"I don't know why she act's the way she does towards you. I feel I must apologise on her behalf."

"There is no need, sir. Your daughter thinks I am getting above my station, after all I am only in your employment."

"You are more than that as well you know, here drink this."

Liz took the whisky and stood by the fire. She wanted to return the complement, but it didn't feel right somehow.

It was New Year's Eve, and tomorrow would be the start of a new year 1917. Snow started to fall and settle as the weather had been quite dry over the last few days. Liz gazed out of her window at the wonderful view, the sight was fantastic. It was early only 6 a.m. She got dressed and went outside.

She walked in the virgin snow and looked back at her foot-prints. She was the first, she stood still, there was not a sound. The snow was heavy and thick, she had never seen such large snow-flakes before. They settled on her gloves in perfect shapes. She took a deep breath and thought how alone she felt at that moment. If it was not for the Brigadier and Lucie, and perhaps the staff they were fine, but kept their distance really. Cook was good.

Her thoughts went to David and what might have been. She felt a tear forming in the corner of her eyes, shook her head, and walked on. She strode to the stables, Tom had just arrived, and got busy with the day's duties.

He had a lot of work to do today, as it was the custom that the Brigadier took the four wheeled carriage out and his daughter and granddaughter would follow on horseback. They would go up the hill a mile to a spot overlooking the sea, share a bottle of "Bubbly" and some cold meats and cheeses. They would meet the Fothergills and their two daughters from the neighbouring estate.

After breakfast while all were assembled, there was a bit of tension in the air. Doris kept glaring at Liz, clearly unhappy she was joining them.

It's not my fault I'm coming. Liz recalled the conversation with the Brigadier she'd had earlier in the week.

"Liz, I want you to come with us on our annual post-Christmas drive," the *Brigadier announced.*

"Oh, I couldn't, sir, it's a family affair," she declined, while thinking, *'Mrs Goodgarth would have a fit.'*

"Do I have to give you a direct order, Miss Monaco?" He smiled.

She accepted.

The snow stopped, the temperature dropped, and the snow crunched beneath the foot. They gathered around the front entrance. The carriage looked polished, the Brigadier in his cloak new hat and whip, the three ladies looking very smart. Mrs Woodgarth scrutinised Liz's new riding boots, and said nothing.

Lucie tried to ease the situation. "You look lovely, Mother, and I like your new boots, Liz."

"Thank you, Lucie I think we all look the part." quipped Liz.

The Brigadier got in the driver's seat, cracked the whip, and off they went. The horses' hooves made marks in the snow.

They reached the rendezvous. The Brigadier spotted the Fothergills and shouted, "Happy New Year!" and cracked the whip playfully. It smacked the horse square across the head.

The horse reared and bolted, but could not get a hold of the ground as ice had formed beneath the snow. The poor animal, now distressed, fell to its knees. The carriage and horse started to slide backwards. Breeze tried to get out of the way, and began to panic as she too was clawing at the frozen ground and lost her footing. She fell, throwing Lucie in the way of the sliding carriage. It was as if it was all in slow motion, Lucie was stunned, and lay motionless.

"LUCIE MOVE YOUR LEGS!" Liz screamed.

It was too late. The sound of Lucie screaming as the rear wheels of the carriage ran over her lower legs and the noise of braking crushing bones was something Liz would never ever forget. Liz jumped off Dream and drug Lucie away from the carriage as it slid into the snow-covered bank and there it stopped.

Crimson blood stained the white snow. Lucie had passed out and her mother was beside herself, frozen to the spot with her hands to her mouth. Liz did not wait to be told what to do, she mounted and rode back to Cove Manor as fast as she dared. Morris was clearing the snow from around the main entrance and saw Liz coming down the drive by herself and much too fast. He sensed something was wrong and ran to meet her.

She jumped from Dream and shouted, "Morris, where is the driver? We need to get Lucie the hospital."

"He's in the kitchen," Morris answered.

She flew inside and into the kitchen. She spotted Ryan reading the newspaper. "Get up to the top, we need to get Lucie to the hospital."

He jumped up and ran out. Liz darted to the lounge, and grabbed the phone. "Hello, operator? We need an ambulance at Cove Manor now, it's a matter of life and death." She then phoned the Major at the camp. "Major, listen the Brigadier's carriage has run over Lucie's legs, she is in a terrible state. I have called the ambulance, is there anything you can do? Yes sir, will do." She slammed the phone down and ran out just in time to see the car leave the drive.

She jumped back on Dream and rode up to the main gate. She whispered to herself, "The ambulance has to come here, I will direct it to where they are. If they have Lucie in the car, they can swap when they meet." She anxiously scanned the road. "Come on, come ON!" She heard the bell.

It seemed to her the ambulance was going ever so slow, but it was doing the best it could in the elements.

She waved it down. "Keep going, it's about a mile further on."

The ambulance was almost out of sight when she saw it stop.

Must have met the car, she thought. She sat atop Dream, watching the Ambulance turn and head back. It went past her and on to Douglas. The car turned into the drive and stopped, in the back was the Brigadier. She looked at him, he stared back ashen-faced and shook his head.

"Take him home," she said to the driver, "Yes ma'am." He nodded and drove down to the Manor.

Liz had never seen him so shaken, he seemed so old and pale.

He probably blames himself. She climbed on Dream and followed the car to the Manor.

The driver helped the Brigadier out of the car. and into the house.

"Take him into the lounge please."

"Yes ma'am, anything else?"

"I take it Mrs Woodgarth went with Lucie?"

"Yes ma'am she did. Shall I go and wait for Mrs Woodgarth?"

"Yes good idea."

"Very good, ma'am." However, he hesitated, obviously reluctant to leave the Brigadier. This man whom he had worked for and respected looked totally finished.

He left as Morris came in with a blanket and put it around the Brigadier's bent and shrivelled shoulders. Morris's eyes darted between Liz and the Brigadier. She went over to the drink cabinet, poured a large brandy, and gave it to him. He stared at brandy.

"It was not your fault, sir, just one of those things." Liz knelt and held his hand.

He dissolved into tears and wept.

Lucie was saved, but she lost both legs just below the knee. She returned and kept herself to her room. She became very bitter.

"I thank you again, Liz, for your quick thinking on that terrible, terrible day. I am in your debt."

"It's time Miss Biddy Bell made a comeback," said Liz.

The two of them stood by the large Inglenook fireplace. It was a large stone construction big enough to have a bench seat either side of the "Dog-Grate," that space now being used for storing and drying the logs.

"The major and I have been talking and it would appear it has gone quiet," the Brigadier said. "But the Admiralty have had intelligence that another U-Boat is in the Irish sea. Its aim, they say, is to sink ships approaching or leaving Liverpool with supplies and whatnot.

"The Major keeps tabs on the church, and has come up with nothing. We think it would lean more to the Catholic church being involved, with their Italian connection than the Church of England. But we cannot rule them out. We must come up with a plan as we spoke about just before Christmas. We have to get Miss Liz Monaco out of Cove Manor and Miss Biddy Bell into Mrs O'Rorke's. I take it that you are still up for it, Liz?"

"Yes, sir, very much so."

The Brigadier nodded acceptance. "I bid you a good night." He downed his whisky and looked at the glass it was in. "You know, I am convinced the whisky tastes much better from this glass, good night, Liz." He smiled at her and left.

Liz stood looking at the flames, in the dying embers, her thoughts were of her David. She knew that a small part of her died that day. She knew also that if his killer was to walk into the room at that moment, she would kill him.

"Oh, you still up?" It was the Brigadier's daughter.

"Yes, I'll go up when I have finished my drink." Liz wouldn't look at her.

"You and my father do seem to have a lot to talk about, does the whisky help?"

"We are at war with Germany and this little Island has become important. My languages have proved very useful and may do so again, that's all I can say." Liz still stared at the fire.

"All very cloak and dagger, I must say." Not getting an answer, she sniffed in disdain and flounced out of the room.

Stupid woman. She went to the drink cabinet and poured herself another whisky, with equal amount of water. She returned to the fire and sat in one of the high backed chairs. She held the glass in her hands to warm it a little and gazed into the fire.

It was gone midnight when Liz woke, she felt cold, and shivered. The fire was out and her glass empty. She went to her room.

"Good morning, sir."

"Good morning, Liz, sleep well?"

"Yes, thank you."

"Try the Kippers, Liz. Wonderful, only trouble is they stink the place out."

"Father." Doris entered the room, her face pinched in an unattractive pout.

"Morning, darling, joining us for breakfast?"

"No, Father, I'm too upset. I have been searching for that lovely broach you gave me. You know Grandmother's diamond broach, I can't find it anywhere."

"When did you last see it?".

"Yesterday morning."

"It will turn up I'm sure."

She stormed out and down to the kitchen. "Would you all kindly assemble in the hallway at once." She stomped off before anyone could respond.

Cook looked at Morris and Biddy and Tom as he had come in for his breakfast and at each other in turn. Morris shrugged his shoulders. They went upstairs and all stood in line.

120

"Where are Joan and Sally?" She snapped.

"Up stairs doing rooms, ma'am, I should think," volunteered Morris.

"They should have finished by now," snarled Doris.

"Should we call Lucie?" Liz offered.

"No there's no need to disturb her," Doris fired back.

Just then Joan and Sally appeared at the top of the stairs. They looked a bit shocked and red faced.

"Well, what is it?" Doris snapped.

"Er, ma'am, we found this." Sally opened her hand to show the diamond broach.

"Where did you find it?" Doris asked.

Both girls looked silently at Liz. and stood silent.

"Well?"

"In Miss Liz's room, ma'am. I'm so sorry," spluttered Joan as she burst into tears.

Liz looked straight at the Brigadier and he at her in return. She shook her head as in a "No."

"Well, darling, you have found it," said the Brigadier. "Right, all back to your stations."

They returned to the kitchen, mumbling amongst themselves. Doris scrutinised Liz who had not said a word.

"I'm calling the police." She all but ran into the lounge, followed swiftly by her father.

"No, darling, don't do that; we will sort this out ourselves." The Brigadier put his hand on the phone.

"She should be locked up, she's a thief."

"Darling, leave this to me, please."

"She has to go as far away from you and this house as possible." She marched to the hallway.

Liz had not moved; Doris slithered up to her and whispered with a faint smile, "Good bye, Miss Monaco."

Liz gazed straight through her, never blinking. Doris was a bit taken-a-back. The younger girl's stir went right through her. She slowly retreated up the stairs. As she reached the turn, she glanced down where Liz was standing. She had not moved, her expression and gaze unchanged. Doris was unnerved and carried on to her room. Liz's gaze followed and did not leave her. Doris knew and felt it.

The Brigadier put his hand on Liz's shoulder, beckoned her into the lounge, and closed the door behind her. He could see the muscles in her jaw flexing. He went over to the corner cupboard, and opened the bottom draw. He stood still for a second then closed it. He walked over to were Liz stood; she still had not said a word.

"The pass key is missing, she has taken it to get into your room. I imagine by this evening it will be back in the draw."

Liz's jaw went taut. "Sir—"

He cut her short. "My own daughter, Liz, my own daughter." She could see he was angry his face stern his fists clenched, and this somehow calmed her.

After a few moments of silence, she could see his face change. he started to relax, he looked as if a light in his brain had just switched on.

"Liz, she has given us the way out. She wants you to go. I know how you must feel leaving under a cloud, but it's the opening we need. I will phone the Major and tell him just what he needs to know." He went over to the desk and started to call the camp.

Still frustrated by the morning's events, Liz wandered down to the kitchen. She could hear the staff talking as she drew closer. She stood at the door; it went silent.

"Oh, come here, my lovely," Cook grabbed her hand and pulled her in. "We know what has happened, Miss Lizzy. I spotted her acting a bit strange yesterday evening. She was looking all around as if to see if anyone was watching. She must have done it then; I think you were asleep by the fire in the lounge at the time."

Liz's face brightened. She looked around at the faces she had come to love, and they her in return.

"She's wanted you out from day one she has, pure jealousy that's all it is. You're young, clever, and beautiful" Morris stated. They all looked at him, he blushed. "Well she is."

"Thank you, it means so much to me, but I will have to leave. If I don't, she will get the police involved."

"Where will you go, Miss?" Biddy asked.

Liz tried to hide a smile when she thought about the name Biddy. "Back to London, I have distant family there," she lied. "I will miss you all, and thank you for making me feel so welcome."

122

"We will miss you, Miss Liz, and so will Dream. Who will ride him now?" Tom spoke with a slight tremor, he looked down at the floor.

"When will you be going?" Sally spoke up.

"Very soon." Liz decided to head back to the lounge. She could hear the staff talking, the voices grew fainter as she reached the lounge door. The Brigadier was still on the phone.

"I agree, Major. Oh, here she is now. Goodbye." He replaced the phone and waved her in. "I know it's short notice, but we have to strike while the iron is hot. First, I have checked on the ferry and one is due in tonight at 19.00 Hours. A car from the camp will pick you up at 17.00 Hours, and take you to the ferry. There you will be transferred to a wagon. This will give you time to become Miss Biddy Bell." He stopped mid flow. "Er, will two hours be enough time?"

"Yes, sir."

"Good, you will call on Mrs O'Rorke and take up residence. All communication at present will be through the local Library in Douglas, which will also be our meeting place once you're settled. The Major is sorting that out as we speak. What do you think so far ?"

"I'm looking forward to it."

"Splendid." He wanted to say how much like her mother she was, but felt this may open up wounds that have healed. He visibly softened he gave a faint smile and relaxed. "I will miss having you around the place, Miss Lizzy." He half smiled. "No doubt I'll get over it and sooner than I should."

"I'll go and start packing. But first I must phone Mrs O'Rorke and let her know I will be there around 20.00 Hours."

"Yes, yes of course." He turned his attention out the large bay window overlooking the grounds and the sea.

"Hello, Mrs O'Rorke? It's Miss Bell, I will be arriving at eight this evening. Could you please freshen my rooms? Thank you. Yes, that will be fine. Goodbye."

He was still staring out across the land. She studied him, her heart went out to him.

What must he be thinking? His own daughter to play such a low, underhanded trick. It could have ended a lot worse, if she had gotten the police involved. She took this opportunity and slipped out of the room.

She packed. *I am leaving with a lot more than I came with.*

She went out to the stables, spent some time with her horse, gave him an apple, and said her goodbye's.

"Until we meet again, Dream." She took a deep breath, sighed, and exited the stall. It was then she spotted Tom. "Goodbye, Tom, and thank you for all you have done." He smiled. "Until we meet again, Miss."

Chapter 8

The plan worked well. She was able to become Miss Biddy Bell in the back of the truck, and in the dark managed to blend in with the passengers leaving the ferry.

"Carry your bags, Miss?" A porter asked.

"Yes, please take them to Mrs O'Rorke at Harbour House."

"Will do, Miss. You staying long?"

She ignored him and walked on in front. She knocked and the door opened. "Mrs O'Rorke?"

"That I am, and you must be Miss Bell?"

"Indeed, Mrs O'Rorke."

"Fred, don't just stand there. Take the lady's bags to her room. Up the stairs, the door straight in front of you, you can't miss it."

Both ladies stepped aside to let a "tutting" Fred pass. Liz followed him into her new world.

"Thank you." She gave him a sixpence.

"Thank you, Miss." He came down the stairs with a grin holding the coin between his thumb and fore finger. "Look what she gave me, a tanner," he said as he walked past Mrs O'Rorke.

"Be gone with ya," was her reply. She ascended the stairs to check on her newest tenant. "Now, Miss, have you eaten? I only ask as dinner has been and gone, but—."

Liz interrupted her. "I am fine, thank you, Mrs O'Rorke. I would like to unpack and settle in."

"As you wish. breakfast is six to eight in the morning. Well, it wouldn't be any other time of the day, now would it?" Chuckling at her own joke, she left Liz in peace.

Liz looked at herself in the mirror. Suddenly it hit her, this is for real. She, as far as the outside world is concerned, was Miss Biddy Bell.

She sank into a high backed chair by the fire. The familiar feeling of loneliness crept over her. She was alone and already started to miss the Brigadier, Cook, Morris, and all the staff and Cove Manor.

"My God!" She said out-loud as she thought, *How long will I have to keep up this charade? How and what am I supposed to be doing?*

She arose and walked around the room, one hand on her brow the other holding her stomach. Panic started to rise within her.

"I can do this, I can do this, I can," she whispered. Her thoughts went to her mother and father. *If only you were here for me to talk to.* Her thoughts went to David and her spine stiffened. She now knew why she was doing this, for them.

Unpacking helped her calm down. *God knows I could do with a whisky.*

As she put away the lovely dresses, coats, shoes, tops, and blouses it was then she noticed a small bag she didn't recognise. She picked it up it, noted it felt heavy, and opened it. Her eyes opened wide with delight; it was a bottle of whisky a single malt along with a note: *AS AND WHEN.*

She knew it was from the Brigadier it was his favourite, the Peaty-Laphroaig. It was an acquired taste, but one she had got used to during her stay at Cove Manor. Now she did not feel so alone. She found a glass, poured herself more than she should have, and toasted the Brigadier. Soon she started to felt MUCH better.

With a bit of a head, Liz made her way down for breakfast.

"Ah, good morning," Mrs O'Rorke greeted her cheerily. "Your table is over there by the window. Every room has its own table, folks then know where to sit. Now will you be wantin' the full Irish or something else?"

"I would like the poached egg on toast and black coffee, no sugar."

"One or two, Miss?"

Liz frowned, perplexed.

"Eggs, one or two?"

"Two, please." Liz sat looking out the window at the people passing by, and felt a little excited at the prospect of the day. In no time at all Mrs O'Rorke bustled up with a plate of delicious smelling food.

"There ya go, Miss, fresh from me own hens. Yal get no better."

Liz enjoyed the eggs, more so the black coffee. It was then she noticed the rest of the room, all men. Some looked like travelling salesmen, others not sure. She witnessed something she had never had before, men gaping at her. They would look away if she court them. It was a bit unsettling at first.

Out in the street she strolled down the way, looking in all the shops as a new arrival would. She soon found out if she put on some airs and graces, people treat her completely different, as if she were someone important. Gentlemen would touch their hats, others in doing so would say, "Good morning, ma'am." Women would either move to one side or nod their heads, some would totally ignore her.

Liz made her way up Hill Street to the Catholic church, St. Mary's. She stopped at the large black ornate iron gates and slowly walked up to the polished oak doors.

"Can I help you?" Came a voice from behind.

Liz jumped and whirled about. It was a small man of around five foot seven inches and around 40-ish with a dark complexion, his face was smiley. his hands were clasped together, and his posture slightly bent forward and to one side.

"Did I make you jump? So sorry. I am Anthony Land, the Curate here at St. Mary's."

"Hello, pleased to meet you Curate. I have just arrived on the Island and plan to stay for a while. I'm afraid I have let my religion lapse, and would like to help the church in any way I can. I would like to get involved; my name is Miss Bell."

"We are always looking for volunteers, Miss Bell. Would you like to come inside?"

"Thank you yes." She followed him into the church and up to the altar.

He knelt and genuflected before moving to one side. Liz followed. A man wearing a long black robe emerged from a door to her immediate left.

"Ah, Father Clancy this is Miss Bell. She has just arrived on the Island and would wish to get involved and volunteer."

Father Clancy was in his sixties and quite plump. He thin white hair retained a yellow, gold tint to the sides, and a broken veined red faced as if he had been and the Sacramental wine.

"Very pleased to meet you, Miss Bell." He held out his hand, which Liz shook.

"I will leave you in the good hands of Father Clancy. I have things to do. Lovely to have met you, Miss Bell, and I look forward to seeing a lot more of you." He disappeared into the darkness of the Church's walls.

"The Curate must be a great help to you Father," Liz remarked.

"Yes, indeed," he agreed.

"I sense, Father, that he has been here for years." Liz had a feeling about Mr Land. Hard to explain, a sixth sense, something not right not true.

"Oh no, he came here around the time the people started to arrive. You know the Internees, poor souls. My heart goes out to them. Just because of their backgrounds… Sorry, Miss Bell, I do ramble on at times, but I do feel for them. He was my replacement after the last one died suddenly from a heart attack. He had always been a fit man, but the Lord works in mysterious ways." He rubbed his jaw thoughtfully and seemed to just drift off.

He has a kind heart and caring eyes, Liz thought. *But he also seems disillusioned with life, or is starting to lose his mind. Or both.*

As Liz walked back to town she remembered what Father Clancy has said about the Curate, he arrived with the Internees.

He must have been sent there by the Church. Liz opened the front door of the boarding house.

"Oh, Miss Bell, there's a letter for you."

She was handed a letter.

"Thank you, Mrs O'Rorke." Liz took it and went up to her room. It was post marked "Chester," she slit the envelope and out fell a letter. It read:

'In the Library at the end of aisle three, at the end of the History section there is a small wooden box marked 'Suggestions.'' It has a removable lid, although it may not look it. This will be our two-way line of communication. The box will be checked twice a day. B.K.

Destroy this letter.'

B.K.? she thought. *Brigadier Kingsley, got it! Okay, right let's try it.*

She wrote:

'The Curate Mr Anthony Land, how did he get the job? Where was he before? Any personal history? Was there anything suspicious about the previous Curate's death?'

Liz made her way to the library, filled in a form to join, and went in search of the "Box." She found it with little trouble; it was just as described. She was hesitant at first, looked around saw no-one, and placed the note in the slot. Her heartbeat quickened. So as to not arouse suspicion should anyone be watching, she chose a book on the history of the I.O.M. signed it out, and left.

Four days later Liz went as normal to check for a reply from her note. The librarian was a woman of about sixty with grey hair tied back in a French bun, she wore half round spectacles perched on the end of her nose, had a knowing smile, and clear intelligent eyes.

I wonder if she is also a contact, Liz thought.

Sure enough, a response awaited her in the box. Excitement ran through her at the prospect of what the note might say. However, she waited until she was back in her room.

'Curate based in Liverpool, joined the church in 1913. Previous history un-known at present. Volunteered for present position on death of previous Curate. Destroy this note.'

Fascinating! She let the note fall to her lap. *My gut is telling me the Curate is the informer. I must try and get closer to him. I've been playing it cool and going to Mass for three weeks. But now I must up my game.*

She must now find the evidence to prove it. She went to the vicarage, stopped, and looked at the house for any signs of life. There was none. She was about to knock on the door when Father Clancy appeared around the corner.

"Hello, Father Clancy, I have come to see you."

"That's lovely. You're a sight for sore and old eyes, Miss Bell. Please do come in." He opened the front door walked in, Liz followed.

"To what do I owe the pleasure, of your visit, child?" He gestured to a seat. "Please do sit down."

Just then in came the Curate.

"Oh, Anthony, would you be kind enough to make Miss Bell and I some tea?"

"Yes Father" he nodded and left.

"How can I help?" Father Clancy eased his large frame into a chair opposite Liz.

"Well, Father, I was wondering if there was anything more I could do to help around the church or the Vicarage. I find myself with plenty of time on my hands."

"I've been meaning to ask. If you don't mind, what was it you do or did?"

"I was in fashion in London, and er, did rather well. I told them I was taking a year out."

"How wonderful!" replied Father Clancy.

In came Anthony with the tea.

"Miss Bell here was, is in fashion and taking a year out. How wonderful" Father Clancy beamed.

"Yes indeed we thought as much. You always look so…" He started to colour-up. "Er fashionable."

He likes me, I can use this. Oh thank you. Do I call you Curate? Or can I call you Anthony or Mr Land?" She smiled coyly.

"Anthony would be nice, if you wish."

"Anthony it shall be." Her eyes roved around the room for anything she could use or show an interest in. Nothing until she spotted a small crude painting of the Vicarage. "Do you paint Father?"

"Oh no, child, that's Anthony's work."

Liz went to examine the painting. "It's very good, Anthony, such detail." She turned to face him. His gaze was transfixed on her.

"You're being kind," he sputtered.

"No I'm not, do you paint portraits? I would pay if you think you could paint me. I would love a portrait."

"There you are, Anthony, only last week you mentioned you would if you could only get someone to sit for you. Your prayers have been answered." Father Clancy rubbed his hands together in delight.

Best strike while the iron is hot. "When can we start? Where shall we do it?" Liz hoped this sounded a bit suggestive.

"Er, tomorrow. Could you be here for about two?" Despite his red face, a pleased grin played with the corner of his lips.

"Yes, Anthony, I'll see you at two. What shall I wear?" She looked him in the eye.

"Whatever you want to really," he half stuttered.

"How exciting. Thank you for tea, Father, till tomorrow."

"I'll show you out, Miss Bell." He followed her to the door. "Erm."

Liz sensed he was going to say, *"What can I call you?"* So jumped in, "Thank you, bye for now." She walked down the path to the gate, but glanced over her shoulder to see he was still at the front door. He waved.

Till tomorrow. Liz walked on, feeling very pleased with herself.

130

"Hello, Father." Liz smiled.

"Hello, child, you are here for your first sitting I believe. Anthony is very excited; he has not stopped talking about it. Do come in" beckoned Father Clancy.

Liz hadn't gone more than five paces before she was greeted by the Curate.

"You came, and on time! I, er, well shall we? I use the back room, it has a lovely view across the fields." His eyes betrayed the nerves and excitement he felt at the prospect of having this beautiful elegant woman sit for him to paint.

Liz was well aware of how Anthony felt, and hoped to use this to gain the information she needed to prove her gut feeling. She was also aware he thought she was a lot older than her nineteen years. In fact, she could pass for mid-twenties.

"Where would you want me to sit, Anthony?"

"Just on the chair if that's alright.?" He nervously tugged on his collar.

Liz positioned herself on the allotted chair and focused her gaze on the book shelves. She tried to read the titles as he got himself organised. After a few puffs and sighs, he started to draw.

Liz noticed a newspaper folded with a post-mark wrapping.

"Could I read your newspaper, please?" She moved to pick it up.

"NO! I—I mean er, not until I have, I er, have this thing about reading it before anyone else. Being the first, it's fresh and unopened." He was a bit alarmed and took the paper out of the room. He reappeared a few moments later.

"Put it in my room." He nervously offered.

"What paper was it?" She asked.

"The Liverpool Echo. I get it delivered every day. Good to keep up with what's going on."

He composed himself and carried on. After two hours he stood and stretched. "I think that all for today, Miss Bell. Same time tomorrow?"

"Very well." She walked past, pretending to be put out. "Till tomorrow then." She glanced at the paint box he was using. A cold shiver went right through her body and she felt her knees weaken. The label on the lid which was not quite out of sight read, *Hergeslellt in Deutschland—Produced in Germany.*

He nodded as she walked out. At the bottom of the landing she turned to catch him staring at her. He quickly turned towards his room. She noted which one it was. She could not get out of there fast enough. Suddenly it had become very real, and this frightened her.

"Goodbye, Miss—" was as far as Father Clancy got.

"Goodbye, Father, I'll be back tomorrow." It took everything in her to not go flying down the hill. She stopped, she leaned against the wall, her mind going crazy.

Oh My God! Her thoughts were trying franticly to make sense of it all. *He is the one!* She took a deep breath to collect herself. *Right, to the library.*

She entered, greeted everyone, and went to the Suggestion Box. She wrote down the important bits and placed the note in the box. The task complete, she decided to spend the rest of the day at the boarding house. Once there, she poured herself a large whisky and sat on the edge of the bed. It was only then that it really hit her just how serious this was and just how dangerous it could become. The whisky went down and another was poured, but taken a bit slower this time. She had told the Brigadier she was up to the challenge.

"I must stay strong, I must," she muttered to herself.

Liz slept well and after breakfast she walked to the library. She was the first and only patron there. The Librarian had just opened and hadn't even returned to her desk. It was only then t Liz noticed the Librarian's name plate, Mrs Bookshaw. Liz had this feeling that all was not as it seemed.

"Good morning, Mrs Bookshaw." Liz looked right into her eyes. *That cannot be her real name.*

With a knowing smile she replied, "Good morning, Miss, good to see you."

She says it as if she wasn't expecting to see me. Good God, I'm starting to get paranoia.

She browsed, pretending to look at some books towards the end of the shelf. She ran her finger across several then picked one and removed it. She glanced through it.

Oh my, tropical diseases. Some of the illustrations where so shocking she put it back. She scanned her surroundings to see if anyone was about. She lifted the lid and removed the note, relieved there was something to retrieve.

"I return this book and wish to take this one."

Mrs Bookshaw took the book, stamped it, and handed it back to Liz. The younger woman went to take the book from the Librarian's hand but, she held on to it. Their eyes met for a few seconds. Mrs Bookshaw gave a small nod and let go the book. Liz knew then that Mrs Bookshaw was on her side.

It's more than likely it's her who takes and replaces the notes.

This made Liz feel a bit more secure and not so alone. It also made her feel stronger and more determined to expose Anthony Land as the collaborator.

Despite her impatience, she didn't dare read it until she reached the privacy of her room.

The note simply said: '*Good, we are looking into his background. Will report any findings.*'

Liz looked out of her window. She had seen the Postman on his rounds early in the mornings and had a thought.

The Curate has his Liverpool Echo delivered every day by the Postman. Now why would he not allow me to read it before he had? Was there something inside that he did not want me to see? I have got to get to it before he does.

With this in mind she threw on her coat and went out into the street and followed the Postman. He started to walk up Hill Street towards the Vicarage. She quickened her step and got to him about twenty feet from the Vicarage gate.

"Good morning, Posty."

"Oh good morning, Miss."

She could see he liked being called Posty by a very attractive young woman. He was in his fifties, grey hair, and sprightly.

"I'm just about to visit the Curate Anthony and Father Clancy. Can I take any post you have for the Vicarage? It would be no trouble."

"Well, I shouldn't really. But just this once, Miss. Only the Curate's newspaper, every day without fail."

She took the folded paper.

"You're a sight for sore eyes, Miss, if you don't mind me saying so."

"Thank you, Posty, that's very kind of you." She pretended to curtsy.

He chucked, nodded, and carried on up the hill Liz watched him walk on, he then turned and waved. She pretended to open the gate and waved back. He was soon round the grassy bank and gone.

She walked a small way back down the hill so not to be noticed. She slid the franked cover from the Echo and opened the paper to see numbers written on the inside of the cover. A series of numbers to be exact. She tried to remember them, then remembered the small note book and pencil she kept in her hand bag but never used. She started to copy the numbers, 34-12-8. 102-31-9. 223-5-4. and so on there where seventeen groups of numbers in total.

She replaced the cover and looked at it to make sure it appeared as if it had not been tampered with. Satisfied she walked to the front door and knocked. It was 9 a.m. the Curate answered. His eyes went right to the newspaper.

"Good morning, Anthony. The Postman gave me this for you." She handed him the paper. "I have called early because sadly I can't make it this afternoon. Can we make it tomorrow please? I'm so sorry."

"Er, yes of course, Miss Bell, are you alright?"

"Yes, thank you, merely feeling a bit under the weather. I'll may stay inside to day. Bye." She left before he could frame a response. She thought she could feel his stir on the back of her neck, On reaching the gate she turned to look back, he was gone and the door was shut.

Liz waited in the tea shop next to the library for Mrs Bookshaw or whoever she was to arrive and open up. It was 10 a.m. when Liz spotted her. She finished her tea and cake and gave the Librarian time to open and get settled before she paid and left.

"Good morning, Miss." Smiled Mrs Bookshaw. "You're bright and early anything. I can help you with?"

"No thank you. I want another book please."

Mrs Bookshaw only gave a slight smile and played with papers on her desk.

Liz was not one hundred percent sure about this Mrs Bookshaw. She went and placed the note with the numbers on with some explanatory lines into the box.

I'm going to test this Librarian, Liz thought. She walked around the room so she would have to pass the desk where the woman sat. She did this quite slowly, carrying no books.

Liz watched her out of the corner of her eye. The woman lifted her head, gave that slight smile, and went back to her papers. No mention of, *'You have no books, I thought that was what you came in for'* nothing! Liz went back to her room and poured over the numbers. She tried, but could make no sense at all. Angry, she gave up for the time being.

It was around 11. 30 a.m. when there was a knock on her room door.

"It's only me, Miss Bell. It was Mrs O'Rorke. I noticed you were not at breakfast this morning."

"Correct Mrs O'Rorke," Liz said, stony faced. being Miss Bell is so opposite to her real persona but she must keep up the aura of being cold and distant.

"Mrs Bookshaw from the library gave me this to give to you. You left it on your visit this morning."

"Thank you."

Silence.

"Er, well I be going then."

"Thank you again, Mrs O'Rorke."

"I'm a bloody post man now," Mrs O'Rorke muttered as she shuffled out of the room and down the stairs.

Liz opened the brown paper bag. It was a book titled, *We Are As One*. She opened it and in the folds was an envelope.

She is on my side this proves it. I knew it. Liz felt very pleased with herself.

The envelope contained a railway ticket and a note that said: *'Take the Mountain Railway 2 p.m. this afternoon.'*

This was the Snaefell Mountain Railway. It ran in a loop around the south of the Island, stopping at Peel on the west coast, and back to Douglas. There was a hotel and tearooms at Tholt-y-Will. Taking a train ride was something she had wanted to do anyway as the views were said to be breath taking. She went down to lunch. she had nothing and was ready for it.

Liz walked to the station. She was fifteen minutes early and stood on the platform looking around at all the faces also waiting for the train. There was one man she thought looked possible. He was tall, stood straight with his hands clasped behind his back as a soldier standing at ease looked Military.

The train arrived. Liz boarded, found a seat by the window, and waited. What she was waiting for? She had no idea, But God knows this is exciting she found herself smiling as the train pulled away.

The train reached Port Erin, still nothing. As they pulled away from the station the man she had spotted on the platform strode up the carriage towards her. Her heart quickened as her eyes widened. He sat down beside her. Liz stared out the window in silence.

"Miss Bell, the Brigadier sends his regards."

"Who are you?" Liz asked, nervously.

"You don't need to know that, and there is no need to feel nervous. You are being watched by us 24 hours. It was the Brigadier's instructions, he must value you. Miss Bell, the numbers you gave us, we think we know the meanings. It's a simple code, the first number is the page number, the second is the line number and the third is the word in that line.

"We need you to find the book he is using to de-code the numbers. We could arrest him now, but we want to get all who is involved. His contact on the main land, in Liverpool, and anywhere else. Do you understand, Miss Bell?"

"Yes," was all she could say.

"Good, enjoy the rest of your trip. They do a very good hot chocolate in the tearooms. Good day, Miss." He walked away the same way he had come.

Liz sat in silence, hardly believing what had just transpired. *I am being watched 24 hours a day, the Brigadiers orders.* This made her feel a lot more confident and secure. *Yet now I must think of a way to get the book. But what am I looking for? What kind of book? How large? How small? What colour?*

He must keep it in his room. Yes, that's where I should look first. It makes sense. She almost found herself speaking out loud. She quickly looked around, no one was within hearing distance.

The rest of the journey was really quite pleasant, Liz found the clickity clack of the wheels on the rails soothing and relaxing. Her thoughts took her right back to when she was about eight years old, when her father explained what the noise was.

"Well, my Lovely, it's when the wheels hit the gap in the rails. You see there is an expansion gap at the end and the beginning of each rail. This is to allow for the rails in summer to expand and not buckle."

She could see his face smiling at her as he spoke. She would sit on his knee, his arms around her. She remembered the feeling of being completely safe, and secure. What she would not give to be in his strong arms now. A tear fell from the corner of her eye; she bit her bottom lip to stop it quivering and folded her arms around herself.

She got back to Harbour House just in time for evening dinner. Walking from the station, she tried to recognise anyone who may be looking out for her. As her contact on the train had told her 24 hour surveillance .

She imagined all sorts; him with the newspaper leaning on the wall, or that woman standing pretending to look in the shop window. She shook her head and walked on.

Lying in bed that night she imagined how tomorrow's sitting would go.

Now, how do I get into his room without him knowing? Or perhaps he has some of his paintings in there, as I have only seen the one. Yes, that's it I will ask to see more of his paintings and once in there I could have a look around to see if anything seems likely. Her mind finally relaxed, she was soon fast asleep.

After lunch, Liz headed to the Vicarage. She took a deep breath, her legs felt a bit like jelly. *He expects nothing, so pull yourself together.* She spotted Father Clancy in the front garden admiring his handy work. "Good morning, Father,"

"And a good morning to you, Miss Bell. Feeling better I hope."

"Oh yes, Father, thank you." She paused to admire the flowers. "They are lovely. You're very clever. I know nothing about gardening."

"Thank you, I could show you if you are interested."

"One thing at a time, Father."

Anthony appeared at the front door. "Hello, feeling better?" He smiled.

Liz tried her best to appear normal, and smiled back hoping her eyes wouldn't betray her emotions. "Yes, thank you, shall we go on up?"

The Curate moved aside and beckoned her to follow him. Once in the room her mind moved quickly.

"I don't see any more of your paintings, Anthony. Surely you have more."

"I do have more, but they're not very good." He prepared his paint and brushes.

"I'm sure they are fine. Please let me see them, I do have contacts in the art world in London."

"Really?" His face lit up. "I keep them in my room, are you sure you want to see them?"

"Yes I am, Anthony." This was said with a bit of an edge.

He put down his pallet and brushes. He said nothing as he led the way to his room with Liz right behind him. He unlocked the door to his room, opened it, and walked in as Liz followed. The room was immaculate, she stood at the door studying her surroundings.

"Please come in."

His eager tone made her uneasy and reluctant come in any further, but did so as to not arouse suspicion. He was obviously pleased to have her in his room.

"I keep them over here." He walked to a dark corner of the room and pointed to the window. "This one is the view from the window."

" I can see that, very detailed."

While his back was turned her eyes searched the room.

"This one is my best I think. It's of, well you can see." He offered the painting to Liz.

"Father Clancy!" She exclaimed pretending to be very impress. "My word, this is good, Anthony."

He started to relax a bit and was eager to show Liz all his paintings. He responded to the attention and the flattery as he moved paintings around in order find a particular one. It was then that Liz spotted it, *Die Bibel. It had been hidden on the floor behind the painting.*

She swallowed hard and started to shake a little, but got control of herself in time, and hoped he did not notice.

"Miss Bell," he started to say.

Did he notice? Her eyes were wide.

Suddenly from down stairs, "ANTHONY! Quickly, please! I'm bleeding!" Came the trembling voice of Father Clancy. "ANTHONY, where are you?"

Anthony looked at Liz, she could see a thousand thoughts going through his head. She put her hands up to her face and sank back into a chair as in a faint. He hesitated then ran out and down the stairs. As soon as he left the room, she went for the book. Her hands shook as she opened the Bible and noted it was by Dr. Martin Luthers dated 1905. She replaced it and ran out and downstairs were Anthony and the Curate stood. He was busy attending to the wound, "Silly old me." Father Clancy trembled.

"It's not bad, Father," offered the Curate. "Walk through to the kitchen we can clean the cut and bandage it."

"I think I will go, Anthony." Liz tried to look shocked at the sight of blood. "I—I will see you tomorrow." She flew out the door before he could object.

She went straight to the library, excited, and concerned. She slowed her walk to normal and regained most of her composure, although her thoughts going a hundred miles an hour.

A "German Bible". What is he doing with a German Bible? This is the proof I needed, this has to be the book.

Once at the library, she paused to talk to Mrs Bookshaw, as she now knew the woman was one of the Brigadier's people. Mrs Bookshaw, on seeing Liz's face and guessing her intention, shook her head no. Liz changed direction and went to the Box.

She wrote, *'German Bible found. "Die Bibel, Dr. Martin Luthers, 1905."*

She retrieved the note already in the box, put it in her pocket, and put her note in its stead. The job done, she grabbed the first book she could find.

"May I have this book, please?"

Mrs Bookshaw took the book, stamped it, and handed it back to Liz with a nod.

Back at her room she read the newest note. *'Newspaper intercepted, and Curate under surveillance.'*

Liz sank into her chair, feeling very pleased with herself. "GOD, this is exciting!" She poured a small whisky and water and tried without success to relax.

Her mind was everywhere. She went over every detail, every word spoken during that visit.

"I can do no more," she said to herself. She heard the dinner gong, and went down to eat.

Nothing happened for the rest of the day. The next morning at breakfast Liz sat at her table, surveying her surroundings. There were some new faces among the regulars. As she ate, she became aware of voices in the hall. She looked up; it was the man from the train.

"Is there any chance of some breakfast? I was passing by, and the aroma wafting from your door was too much. I would really appreciate it. What's your name?"

"Mrs O'Rorke, and you have kissed the Blany-Stone right enough to be sure. I suppose I could squeeze one more breakfast. Sit yourself down, and I suppose you'll be wantin' tea?"

"That would be fantastic, Mrs O'Rorke. You are an angel."

"Get away with ya." She smiled as she made her way back to the kitchen.

He came and sat as close to Liz as he could, but made no contact. Liz drank her coffee, wondering what on earth is going on. In came his breakfast.

"Now get yaself on the outside of that, stick to ya ribs so it will." Off she went back to her kitchen.

Liz watched him out of the corner of her eye as he sat there and ate. He finished and stood; it was then he made his move. He pretended to trip, and in doing so grabbed Liz's table.

"Oh, I'm so sorry, Miss!"

She spotted the envelope under her plate as he pretended to straighten his crooked lapel. She used her napkin to cover it as she slipped it into her bag.

"What's all the ruckus?" Mrs O'Rorke bustled in through the door.

"Nothing, everything is fine. That was lovely, Mrs O'Rorke, and thank you again." Tipping his hat to the portly woman, he left.

"What a lovely young man, such manner's. Make someone a nice husband," she commented, clearing Liz's table.

Liz ignored the remark and went up to her room, eager to find out the contents of the letter.

She opened the envelope: *'Correct book, have now got codes, suggest you take back seat, from now on, well done. B.K.'*

Liz was a bit disappointed, to say the least, and felt robbed of something. "No way!" She spat these words aloud. She paced the floor, anger building up inside her. *Is that it? What do I do now? Sit and wait?*

After a short while she calmed down and sat, still holding the letter, she read it again. After a big sigh she went to the table and lit the letter and the envelope, she watched as the white turned to dark grey then ashes. She made up her mind.

I am going to keep the two o'clock meeting.

Liz left at 1.45 p.m. and walked to the Vicarage, she stopped a few yards from the gate, doubting her decision. Something was telling her to go back. She started to turn yet stopped, clenched her jaw, and dismissed this as just nerves. She looked across the road, there was a man sweeping the gutters along the road. She waited for him to turn and look at her, but he kept on brushing.

Taking a deep breath, she opened the gate and walked to the front door. As she walked each step felt heavy, all her being was telling her to run. On reaching the door she raised her hand to knock, but noticed it was open just off the latch. The house felt strangely quiet. Her pulse quickened; her breathing followed.

She pushed the door open and half shouted, "Hello?" She heard a door open at the top of the stairs leading to the room where the painting took place. Out walked the Curate.

"Miss Bell, lovely to see you and on time. Please come up." There was something different in his manner, something more forceful, more authoritative.

She hesitated.

"I am ready for you." he added. She climbed the stairs, forcing a smile. He stood at the top with both arms behind his back. With his head he gestured for Liz to go into the room.

Her heart dropped as she felt something in her back.

"Keep moving, Miss Bell or whoever you are." The Curate's voice took on a sinister tone. He pushed the barrel of the German Luger harder into her back, forcing her to stumble forward. She stopped with a gasp; there was Father Clancy tied to a chair and gagged.

"Sit," was all he said.

Liz did not need telling twice, her legs were trembling. She crossed them, afraid she might wet herself.

"I know you found Die Bibel, don't bother denying it. I placed a match in it, and the match was moved, So who are you?"

"I—I am in fashion and taking a year out to—"

"Don't lie to me! I will ask you again; tell me the truth, or I shoot the priest."

Liz glanced at Father Clancy, he looked as if his heart was about to give out. His eyes were wide and terrified, his breathing fast and laboured.

Anger started to build in Liz. *If I'm going to die, I am not going to do it sitting down, the bastard.*

She stood, this shocked the Curate. He stepped back, obviously surprised by her actions.

"Sit, I said." He waved the gun again.

Liz stared him down and in her best High German said, "Erschiebe das irische Schwein mien name ist Helga Von Stasonburg. Ich wurde geschickt um dich zu beolrachton wie du es vermasselt hast und Deutschland ein U-Boot, gekostet hast."

(I was sent here as you messed up and cost Germany a U-Boat)

This completely threw him; she saw he was visibly shaken.

"My, my German is not good." He was not sure of what exactly was happening.

Liz took the initiative so continued, "Du Dummer Mann!" (You stupid man) then switched to Italian. "Sono stato mandato perche hai perso la Germania un U-Boat."

"Sona stato tradito!" He replied, defensively. (I was betrayed).

He lowered the gun and shifted from one foot to the other while his poor brain tried to make sense of what happened. Suddenly he straightened up, and pointed the gun at Liz.

"Qual e il mio nome?" (What is my name?)

"Antonio Olandio." This was a wild guess. She had known an Italian girl whose sir name was Olandio.

He lowered the gun. Liz went to the window and looked out, strangely at ease, as if reconciled to her fate.

"Drop the gun," a deep voice commanded.

She spun on her heel to see the road sweeper, and two other men had their guns trained on the Curate.

"Take him away, and try not to be seen." The road sweeper was the man she had seen on the train. He picked up the Lugger and handed it to Liz. "Souvenir, Miss Bell?"

"No thank you." She untied Father Clancy, knelt beside him, held his shaking hands. "It's all over, Father, what an afternoon."

He dissolved in to tears.

"Father Clancy, I am Captain O'Connor. I know how you must be feeling, but I have to talk to you and ask you to pretend that the Curate has been taken ill with let's say—appendicitis.

"This would mean hospital and as the Army one is the closer, it's where he has been taken. No one should question you, because that is where he will be seen to be taken."

Father Clancy stood, a little shaken. Liz had hold of him. He straightened himself as best he could.

"My heart must be stronger than I thought if it can withstand that, it can withstand anything. I will be alright, bless you both. I never suspected, and would never have guessed."

"The church will have to find you a new Curate, Father," the captain remarked.

"At one point, Captain, a new Priest, too." Father Clancy forced a smile. "It may sound strange, but this experience has made me stronger I feel better than I have for years,"

"Shall I make you tea, Father?" Liz offered.

"No, child, thank you. I think you and the captain have things to talk about." Father Clancy hobbled out of the room.

"Miss Bell, thank you for all your help. We could not have done this without your input, and if you are willing, we need your skills further."

"I will help in any way I can."

"What you did just then was remarkable, very calm and clever. He was completely taken in; you took control and got him to confess when he said, *'I was betrayed.'* I speak a little Italian."

Liz's eyes widened. "How do you know all this? You must have been outside the room all the time." Her voice rising as she spoke.

"Almost all the time," the captain admitted. "Now, the Brigadier would like the company of yourself and I at Cove Manor for a de-brief. I have a car waiting."

This was just what Liz wanted. During the ride there, she sat in the back, excited to see the Brigadier again.

I will meet them all again, but I will have to be Miss Biddy Bell. God, I hope they don't recognise me. I'm looking forward to meeting Mrs Woodgarth, the bitch. With this thought in mind, they arrived.

It felt like years had passed, when in reality it had only been a few months. Everything was exactly the same.

What am I thinking? What was I expecting?

Morris opened the car door. She almost said, "Thank you, Morris," but caught herself in time. She stepped out and waited for the captain to come around to her side. This was deliberate, as it meant standing next to Morris for about ten seconds. No reaction.

If only he knew it was me, Liz smiled to herself.

"Miss Bell, please follow me," instructed the captain. He led her into the lounge, a room she knew very well.

"Miss Bell, good to see you, I am Brigadier Kingsley." He held out his hand, she took it and held on to it a shade longer than perhaps she should have.

"Pleased to meet you, Brigadier."

"Captain, perhaps you could organise some tea."

Liz knew he could have just rang for Biddy. The captain, being sharp, took his time with the tea.

"So glad to see you, Liz, and what a fine job of work you have done. Absolutely splendid."

"It's good to see you, sir."

There was an awkward silence, a time when family may have hugged. It was broken by the captain and Biddy with the tea and freshly made biscuits.

This will be a test, Liz thought. "Hello, did you make the biscuits yourself?"

"No, Miss, all the cook's doing. If they were mine, they would be burnt, that right sir?" answered Biddy.

"I'm afraid so, Miss Bell" the Brigadier agreed, knowing what Liz was trying. Biddy left the room. "No one would know, the transformation is remarkable. Now we must get down to this business of the Curate." With this the Brigadier sat at the end of the large dining table full of maps, nautical charts, papers, and Die Bibel.

Liz and the captain sat each side of the Brigadier.

"The good news is the Curate, and as you so rightly named him Anthony Olandio, has been very forthcoming. We offered him a deal in exchange for all the information on his part and of others on the mainland. It would appear we just got him in time, tomorrow night at 02.00 Hours U-91 will surface a few hundred yards off shore at Laxey Bay north east of here in order to collect provisions that Mr Olandio has collected over the last few weeks.

"These are in a small twelve foot long rowboat hidden at Laxey Bay. We have found the rowboat. U-91 will surface and give one three second light, this will prompt a reply from the shore, the same one as you did for U-87."

Liz nodded.

"The Admiralty will have a ship downwind at the ready, they will attack as soon as they see our signal from shore. Did you know they can only stay underwater for a max. of two hours?"

Both Liz and the Captain answered at the same time Liz "No," the captain "Yes."

"It's best you stay here tonight, Miss Bell," the Brigadier suggested. "We can finalize details tomorrow, thank you, Captain."

Captain O'Connor saluted and took his leave.

"You can have your old bedroom, I have had it prepared for you. Now, young lady, how about a whiskey?"

"That would be nice and thank you for—"

The Brigadier waved aside her thanks. "Yes, yes, yes, here we are." they chinked glasses and enjoyed their drinks by the open fire.

"How are you, Lizzy?"

"At one point, sir, I thought my number was up. But up till then I have really enjoyed it."

Silence settled over the pair, broken only by the Brigadier's next comment.

"I couldn't lose you." He spoke quietly into his glass, cleared his throat and spoke in his normal voice. "Anyway, all good stuff, and well done again. Well done. It would seem that after tomorrow night, Liz, you may be free to resume your true self."

"That would be nice. Although I have really enjoyed it, it has been a strain, it would be good to be me again."

The moment was spoilt by the arrival of an unwanted visitor.

"Father I—oh sorry I was not made aware you had company." It was his daughter, Mrs Woodgarth.

He stood. "Ah, Miss Bell, this is my daughter Mrs Woodgarth. Doris, this is Miss Bell."

Liz faced the bitch. "Hello pleased to meet you, Mrs Woodgarth."

"Pleased to meet you, Miss Bell, and may I say you must tell me where you buy your clothes. That outfit is to die for."

144

"I buy all my clothes in Paris, at Paul Poiret on the Champs-Selysees. Perhaps you know him, he is often in Vogue Magazine," Liz replied.

"I—I may have," Doris stuttered.

In your eye, you cow. It took every ounce of willpower for her not to roll her eyes.

"I thought I'd find you in here, Mummy. Oh hello."

"Ah, this is my granddaughter Lucie, Lucie this is Miss bell," the Brigadier announced with a sideways glance at Liz.

"Pleased to meet you, Lucie," said Liz.

"Do you ride Miss, Bell," Lucie asked.

"I'm afraid not and especially in these shoes," Liz cajoled.

Lucie laughed.

"Do you get to London, Miss Bell?" inquired Doris.

"Not as often as I would like."

"We have property in York street, you would be made most welcome. Lucie and I would love to spend time shopping with you and perhaps the theatre."

"Thank you I will try. If I remember correctly, there is a splendid Fishmonger at the end of York Street."

This took the bitch completely by surprise.

"Erm, yes there is," was all she could say. *If she knows that, she must know the type of property, and they are far from grand.* "What a shame we are leaving early tomorrow. Lucie and I are spending a few weeks in London. I would have loved to have got to know you better, Miss Bell. As I said we would love to entertain you in London. I'll say goodbye now as we won't see you in the morning. I will phone you, Father."

Lucie kissed her grandfather on the cheek and they both left.

They waited a few moments then both Liz and the Brigadier burst out laughing.

"Ha! Ha! Well, I never if only she knew. Liz, you were fantastic you are a natural, Ha! Ha!"

"Perhaps I should not have enjoyed that as much as I did." She sniggered.

All was ready, it was 01.35Hours. Captain and his men were armed and lying in wait. Liz was in dark overalls and boots, and held the flash-light in readiness.

Her hands kept sweating, and she constantly wiped them down the leg of her overalls.

"You okay, Miss?" Asked the sergeant standing next to her.

"Yes, thank you, Sergeant."

Time seemed to drag on. It was a quiet night, no wind and the moon shone through the clouds when it felt like it. Not a word was spoken, all present just waited for a sign. Ten minutes to the time of 02.00 Hours. everyone heard a low rumbling sound coming from the water.

"This is it, Miss, are you ready?" whispered Sergeant.

"Yes," was all she could say, her throat was as dry as a bone. She quickly wiped the sweat from her hands for the last time.

No more than a hundred yards from the shore U-91 started to surface. First the conning tower, then the rest of the hull followed. Just then the moon broke through, Liz could see and hear the hatch being opened. Men appeared, two ran aft and two ran forward. All went quiet, a few seconds passed, then the moment arrived Liz had been waiting for and dreading at the same time. She stood firm and straight. One three second flash. She swallowed hard and replied, "Alles ist in ordnung, weiler."

The world exploded; something was very wrong. Machine gun fire came from the sub and returning fire from the shore. The sergeant grabbed Liz and pulled her to the ground.

"Stay here, Miss, don't move and keep your head down."

She did not need telling twice. Bullets whizzed past her head. She looked up as the sergeant hit the earth few feet from where she lay. He wasn't moving, blood pooled around his head and his lifeless eyes stared at her. She put her hands to her mouth to stop herself from being sick.

Suddenly the night lit-up and within seconds the shooting stopped. Liz dared to take a peek; the U-91 was lit in full silhouette. A dozen or so strong search lights shone from H.M.S. Dragoon, she had been fitted with the latest underwater detection the "Hydrophone."

It was all over. It was too late for the sub to dive, there was no way out. Men ran along the hull of U-91, some had their hands in the air. and there was shouting. Liz stood shaking uncontrollably and feeling physically sick as Captain O'Connor appeared at her side and moved her a few yards away from the sergeant's body.

"Are you alright, Miss?"

"Yes, Captain, what went wrong?" her voice wobbled, she tried to remain calm, "I signalled then all hell let loose, I don't understand."

"It will all come out in the de-briefing, but we got ourselves a U-Boat and crew. Well, the Navy has."

The de-briefing was held at the camp in Douglas that afternoon. In the middle sat the Brigadier, to his left the Major, to his right the captain. Standing was a sergeant and sitting a corporal taking down the minutes.

Liz was the last to go in. She felt bit nervous as she took her place in front of said bench. She looked searchingly at the three faces, there was a faint smile on all of them. She relaxed a little. She still felt somehow responsible for what happened earlier.

Not twelve hours ago she had seen a man shot and killed right in front of her eyes. She had tried, but could not seem to get that image out of her head. Only a few moments before, he was protecting her then—gone.

"Miss Bell," The Brigadier spoke first, "let me tell you how pleased we are at your behaviour in a strange and difficult situation while under fire. You have had no formal training, though your actions were professional. The Navy has taken U-91 and the remainder of its crew. Four crewmen were killed in the exchange, and we, as you are aware lost one, Sergeant Higgins. It was a great success, and mostly down to you, Miss Bell. Is there anything you wish to add?"

"Yes, sir. I got to bed around 05.00 Hours, yet could not sleep. The message kept going around and around my head. You told me that the Curate had said the same signal as before, *'Alles ist in ordnung, Weiter'* meaning, *'All is in order, proceed.'*"

"But I am sure it was different before. It was something like, *'Alles ist gut, fahren sie fort'*—*'Everything is fine, continue.'* The signal changed, and that is when the shooting started."

The Major turned to the corporal. "Could we have the statements from them please, Corporal?"

"Yes, sir." she (the corporal) stood and left the room.

"If you are right, Miss Bell," said the captain, "this would indeed explain what happened."

"You are correct, the shooting from U-91 did start halfway through your signal."

There were a few moments silence, before the Corporal returned with the paperwork. The Major took them and handed it to the Brigadier. Everyone held their breath as he scanned the documents.

"Here we are, excuse my German. It is, *'Alles, ist'.*" He looked at Liz.

Liz nodded. "*'Gut Fahrien sie fort.'* You are right, The Curate must have known that and gave us the wrong signal."

"The bastard!" the captain snorted. "Sergeant Higgins was one of the best, he leaves a wife and two children"

"Captain! NOT here," the Major reprimanded him.

"Sorry, sir, may I be excused if we are finished here?"

"You may, Captain, and nothing you may regret later, understood?"

"Understood, sir."

The Brigadier set the papers down. "If you would excuse us, Major, I wish to talk to Miss Bell. May I use your office?"

"Of course, sir."

Liz and the Brigadier went into the Major's office.

"Liz, I am so proud of you! I don't think you realise just how important a part you played in all this. We could never, well, it would have taken much, much longer and we may have missed the boat, in this case the U-Boat." He sat back in the Major's chair. "I think it's time Miss Bell had a long holiday, perhaps as Miss Liz Monaco. On all accounts it would appear this damn war could be over in a month or so. October or November."

"A Christmas without war, sir?" Liz thought for a moment. "I think you are right, Miss Bell is in need of a holiday."

"Splendid! Now, to get you back to Harbour House without suspicion."

"I could walk it's only just over a mile and I would welcome the fresh air. If I'm asked, I shall think of something."

"Of that I have no doubt." The Brigadier chuckled.

There was silence, Liz stood and slowly replaced the chair under the table, not sure what she was doing.

"Liz, I would take it as a great honour if you would come back to Cove Manor as Miss Liz Monaco. If only for a while as the other two will be in London. I have a feeling they may be there some time. I think I know what is keeping my daughter there, not sure about Lucie, probably enjoying all the attention and Dream—"

Liz interrupted him. "I would like that very much, sir, very much indeed."

Both were getting emotional. Liz started to walk out, "See you in a day or two."

Chapter 9

The war ended on the 18th of November, 1918. Mrs Woodgarth was now Ms Kingsley, having reverted back to her maiden name. She and Lucie spent the whole summer and autumn in York Street, Liz the whole summer and autumn at Cove Manor. But all good things must come to an end.

"Liz, I have just had a call from Doris. She and Lucie are coming back on Friday, two weeks from now, Christmas eve." The Brigadier could see the look on Liz's face. a mixture of Disgust and maybe a little anxiety. "As it happens, we need the services of Miss Bell. It's a small job, and I'm afraid there's no real danger."

"I will take up my rooms at Mrs O'Rorke forthwith, sir." Liz stood upright and saluted.

"Thank you, Liz, no need for all that. It should only be for a month or so. We will use the same contact as before. You know Mrs Bookshaw is on our team?"

"Yes, I did guess that." Smiled Liz. "I will go and say my goodbyes."

"Let me know when you are ready and I'll get Sean to drive you to town under the cloak of darkness as before."

"I'll start packing."

They both nodded. Liz phoned Mrs O'Rorke to confirm her rooms had been paid for and kept.

That task over, she went to her room and sat on her bed. She felt sad, but also excited at becoming the very stylish, sophisticated Miss Biddy Bell once again. However, the staff didn't take too kindly to the announcement of her departure.

"It's wrong you going just because she is coming back, ran out of money most like." Scowled Cook.

"Needs a good smacking that one, if you ask me," offered Morris.

"I will probably see you all next year sometime," Liz assured them.

"I hope, so my lovely, look after yourself," Biddy piped up.

"Find yourself a good man," added Morris.

"You offering, Morris?" Cook teased.

"She could do worse," he retorted.

"But not by much." Giggled Cook.

"I will miss you all." Liz sighed. "Have a great Christmas and happy new year."

"And you, too, my lovely." Cook's bottom lip started to quiver. Liz gave her a big hug before heading to the waiting car.

Just as before, she arrived just as the ferry passengers were leaving. In the truck she became Miss Biddy Bell and joined in the walk from the Ferry.

"Bags Miss—Oh it's you, Miss Bell, long time no see. Still at Mary's, er, Mrs O'Rorke's?"

"Yes, it's Fred if I'm not mistaken."

"Yes, Miss, fancy you remembering my name. He was over the moon and couldn't wait to brag to Mrs O'Rorke."Miss Bell remembered my name!"

"Lovely to see you again, Miss Bell, your rooms are ready."

It took Fred two trips to take all the bags to the room.

"Thank you." She handed him a shilling.

"No, Miss, thank You." As he passed Mrs O'Rorke he had the shilling between his thumb and forefinger, "A shilling this time."

"Be gone with yis," she scolded.

Next morning after breakfast Liz went to the library. It was a cold and crisp morning, the North east wind felt as if would cut right through her. Liz looked fantastic in her fur coat with a Russian style hat to match, worn for the first time. People she passed acknowledged her in several ways; she began to feel that perhaps this was a little too much for the folks of Douglas. The feeling soon passed.

"Good morning, Mrs Bookshaw."

"Good morning, Miss Bell, you look very cosy and warm." She gave a nod of approval.

Liz walked to the Box, it was exactly the same. She opened, it took the letter, replaced the lid. She felt a little excited at the new assignment. Back at Mrs O'Rorke's Liz opened the letter. *'Take up your position at The I.O.M. "News and Times" as their fashion editor, this is a new venture for the paper. You will report to Mr Fredrick Cockburn, Owner, at the office here in Douglas. Your outside contact will be Captain O'Connor. The Chief Editor Mr Mike Shaw is suspected of gun running and may have contacts in the camp at Douglas. IMPORTANT— OBSERVE ONLY and report. Destroy this letter.'*

"Fashion editor," Liz whispered to herself. "Right, better get some fashion books and magazines."

Before heading to the library, she burned the letter, watching as it became ash.

"Back already, Miss?" Mrs Bookshaw said.

"I'm in need of a few things."

"I have some books and magazines that may be of interest you." She handed Liz several fashion magazines. It was as if she knew the contents of the letter and had anticipated Liz's needs.

"Oh thank you." Liz looked around, except for an elderly gent at the far end the place was empty. Liz took the magazines and went back to her rooms to study.

The following day was bright, clear and still. It was 8.30 a.m. when Liz made her way across to the offices of The News and Times. As she approached the entrance, she surveyed the building. It was old and built of dark red brick with Herringbone brick features panels, the main doors were arched and heavy surrounded in wedge shaped brick to form the arch. The year 1847 was carved above the arch.

She looked up to the first floor window. A man in his forties with glasses and moustache, smoking a cigar and with Garters holding up and back his shirt sleeves stared straight at her. He was motionless, just staring. Liz strode up to the reception desk. The girl behind the desk looked about the same age as her, around nineteen or so.

She seems friendly. "Hello, I'm Biddy Bell. I'm here to see Mr Cockburn."

"Hello, is he expecting you?"

"Yes, I'm going to be the papers fashion editor. Please call me Biddy."

"That's fantastic, just what us girls wanted. How exciting. I'm Brenda, I'll take you up." Brenda wore make-up and was dressed modern.

Liz followed Brenda up to the second floor and to the back offices. One door had "Chief Editor," no name and the other "Mr Fredrick Cockburn." Brenda knocked.

"Come in," came a very thick, deep Scottish tone.

Brenda opened the door and walked in with Liz close behind. "Miss Bell to see you, Mr Cockburn,"

"Thank you, Brenda, now back to your desk." This was said in a half joking way.

Brenda smiled at Liz and closed the door behind her.

"So, you are my new fashion editor, Miss Bell." He winked of an eye and tapped his nose.

"Yes Mr Cockburn."

Silence settled on the pair. Finally he rose from the large chesterfield leather chair.

"Follow me."

Liz did just that, out of his office, and next door to the "Chief Editor." She fully expected to see the man she saw at the window, but there sitting behind his desk was a small man no more than 5 foot 6inches with dark hair to the sides and bald on top. He had the most blue piercing eyes she had ever seen. On his desk was his name plate Mr Michael Shaw. Standing quietly in the corner was the man she had seen in the window. This office went from the front of the building to the rear.

"Miss Bell, this is Mike Shaw our chief editor and this is" walking towards this man, "our main man in the print shop. Without him we would never get the paper printed, Mr Harry Howard."

"Pleased to meet you both." Liz studied each in turn. Harry Howard showed no expression or emotion.

"I'll get back then" was all he said, walking past all three of them and out the door.

Liz surveyed her surroundings. There were several desks, all covered with bits of paper and personal stuff.

"Your desk is that one." Mike pointed to a desk by the window. "Make yourself at home, no pressure at this time, Miss Bell."

"Call me Biddy, please," Liz piped up.

"Miss Biddy it is. As I said no pressure this week, but I want a full page from you for midday Wednesday next. That's when we put the paper to bed. I would expect as your first page, for it to contain at least 20% advertising revenue. How you get it is up to you okay, Miss Biddy Bell?"

"His bark is worse than his bite, Biddy," chipped in Mr Cockburn. "I'll leave you two to get acquainted."

Liz took her briefcase to her desk and started to unpack, up until now it had been quiet. Suddenly she heard the starting of clanking of machinery, in a rhythm similar to that of a train on the tracks. Then the phone rang on Mike's desk, several people arrived and took their positions at their desks, there was exchanges of greetings and hellos for Liz. It was as if she had always been here, there were no questions. For the next few hours it seemed like madness. Everybody talking on their phones, to each other, and shouting across the room with bits of news and stories.

Liz tried to think in this madness. It was about 10 a.m. when a woman in her fifties named Jill came to her.

"Cup of tea or coffee?"

"Er, coffee please, Jill."

"Got your cup, sweetheart? No? I'll lend you one of mine, bring yours in tomorrow. Sugar and milk?"

"Just milk please."

Jill left the room, a few minutes later a mug of coffee was placed on her desk.

"Talk more after lunch," Jill whispered.

The atmosphere in the office was as if there was no tomorrow, then the penny dropped. As Mike had said midday on Wednesday they put "the paper to bed." It was Wednesday.

Liz found out Jill was one of the reporters on the paper. The two sat at Liz's desk.

"So, you are our new fashion editor? I think it's a fantastic idea, and I can see from your fashion sense you know what you are talking about. It may take a few weeks for the Island women to take note, but I think it's a winner Biddy. Biddy…? What is it short for?"

"Oh it's a family nick name that stuck."

Jill just nodded. "Right so what has the old Fart given you for next week?"

Liz giggled a little at Jill's 'Old Fart.' "He wants a full page with at least 20% advertising revenue."

"Any ideas?"

Liz shook her head.

"Get out there and talk all the outlets on the Island that have anything to do with fashion. No matter how distant into spending money on buying "space" on your opening feature. The more space you sell the less editorial you have to write, and the more the Old Fart will love you."

"How long have you been at the paper, Jill?"

"I started delivering as a 'paper girl' in Douglas the year Henry the VIII took the crown."

Both laughed. Liz got home that night exhausted from doing it appeared very little. Her mind was full of the day's goings on.

I have a week to do this full page it would be the last one before Christmas, she thought. *It's a good time to get the shops and outlet to advertise their Christmas goods for sale. First thing tomorrow I'm out around Douglas.*

After dinner Liz went to her rooms and poured herself a large whisky. She stood looking out onto the street below at people going about their business and thinking, *If only they knew.* She held her glass up to the window and whispered, "Thank you, Brigadier. What have you got me into?"

Over the next week Liz walked the streets of Douglas and most parts of the Island, with a great amount of success. She had managed to get 50% of her "Feature Page" in advertising revenue. She really enjoyed it and found it quite easy. The women owners of local business took to her, were truly excited about a regular fashion page, and were keen to support every week with a smaller advert.

As far as the men folk, well, they would have given Liz anything she'd care to ask for. She loved it. It's something she would like to have done full time; she had to remember what it was she was sent to do. On that score, the pressure and pace of life on a newspaper gave her little time to pay any attention to "the Quest" at hand.

Back in the office Liz gave all her adverts in a very rough form to Annette, 'Netty.' As the paper's artist it was her job to make up the individual advert for each business. She sat in the corner of the same office surrounded with bits of paper, it looked like complete chaos to Liz. But Netty assured her she knew where everything was.

Liz, made a mock-up of her page, showing how the various size adverts made up a half page, then typed very slowly her copy for the editorial. She found this so easy to do, she had completed her first full page fashion feature for a newspaper.

She sat looking at her work, quite pleased with it. *And to think the people of this little Island would be reading it on Friday morning.* The shops and outlets all looking at their own adverts, and reading what she had to say about fashion. She couldn't wait to see what her page looked like. All those hundreds of copies with her feature page in it.

The bubble was about to burst. On Tuesday morning Liz took her page to Mike at his desk.

"I have done as you asked, and here it is." She handed him her mock-up. "I managed to get 50% advertising revenue." She stood looking very pleased with herself.

He looked up and with those bright blue eyes looking right into hers he said, "What do you want, a medal? Give all you have to John the reader." He pointed to a desk in the opposite corner. "He will check it out for you and take it down ready for printing. What's your ideas for next week? I want a full page from you every week, think you can do it, Miss Biddy?"

Liz was stunned. "Erm, it will be the New Year edition."

"Correct."

"I will start on it right away," was all she could think to say.

Mike's phone rang, he answered it and carried on as before. Liz sat at her desk, feeling a bit deflated. It dawned on her.

I have to do this every week; this is what they all do week after week after week. The pressure to fill a Newspaper. She smiled to herself. *At least the days do go fast.*

I now have a bit of time, before starting all over again tomorrow afternoon.

She decided to take a look at the shop floor, as so far she had not seen Mike leave his desk. Someone else would be watching him after work. She decided to go in the way the workers entered rather than through the offices. She left the building, walked around the corner, through the gates, and up to a door where two men stood talking and smoking. One of the men was Mr Harry Howard, he was giving the other man something wrapped in a cloth.

He saw Liz walking towards him. His eyes widened in panic and he whispered to the other man who walked away without looking, back the package held in front of him.

"What you doing here?" he barked. "You're not allowed around here, get back to your office. No one is allowed around here without my permission."

Liz stopped in her tracks, her immediate reaction was to challenge him, then thought this might make him suspect. So she decided to fake it and became a wimp. She pretended to get upset and ran out the way she had come. She stopped as she reached the corner and peeked back. He was shrugging his shoulders in a manner of, *'Well that frightened her, won't see her here again.'* He disappeared back inside.

After work Liz walked to the library, gave Mrs Bookshaw a knowing nod, and went to a desk at the far end of the room. She took out her little note book and wrote the following: *'I think your man is the print-shop foreman Harry Howard. He handed another man a small package wrapped in some material about the size and weight of a handgun. The man was around thirty, 5 foot 10 inches, ginger hair and beard, with glasses.'*

She placed the note in the box, then seeing several people around walked to where Mrs Bookshaw sat. "Have you anything by Winston Churchill?"

"No sorry, Miss, I will put your request on my list."

"Thank you."

Liz thought she would treat herself to a coffee and piece of cake. The tea shop "Lily's" was at the far end of the town, but well worth the walk. She past various shops that she had visited while filling her fashion page. She smiled and waved as she walked by. One shop owner Nora Kemp owner of "Old Sew and Sew" came out.

"Hello, again, I'm looking forward to this Friday's paper. It's a grand thing you are doing, I think it will be very popular."

"Thank you, Mrs Kemp, I hope you like the feature."

"I'm sure I will. It's all very exciting."

Liz was just about to enter the tea rooms when Captain O'Connor appeared and stood pretending to gaze at all the cakes on display in the window. He stood a few feet away, bent looking in the window.

"Got your note, very interesting. Meet me at 9 p.m. tonight at the ferry." He slipped away.

Undeterred, Liz walked in and sat down. Ordered a tea and a slice of Victoria sponge. Her mind doing overtime, *tonight at 9*, all very Cloak and Dagger, Liz sat looking out of the tea Shop window thinking about Captain O'Connor and what tonight will bring, she started to have romantic thoughts then shook her head as in—*stay focused* .

Back at Mrs O'Rorke's Liz had her dinner and waited in her room until 8.50 p.m., then made her way down stairs.

"Going out Miss Bell? Going anywhere nice?" Mrs O'Rorke was ignored as usual.

Liz walked down to the ferry terminal, it was cold and the North west wind cut right through her. They say it was going to be a white Christmas, it had just started to rain.

If this freezes over night, she thought, *tomorrow is going to be like a skating rink.*

"Over here," came a voice from the dark, it was the captain.

Liz walked towards the voice. They stood together.

"Are you okay? Are you warm enough?" He asked.

Liz was not expecting this personal attention. but was pleased. "Yes, I'm fine, thank you."

"Good I do erm, worry about you. Anyway, down to business, we think you are right. We found the other man you described, and now have him under surveillance. He has a previous, as does your Mr Harry Howard.

"We think they are manufacturing guns here on the Island, and selling on the mainland. Not quite Army business, we have the local police involved, but at present only on a need to know basis. We don't want them to involved, local bobby could jeopardize with his size ten feet."

He hesitated. "I was wondering if you would let me… if we could meet up socially?"

This took Liz completely by surprise. And tried to not smile. She thought him handsome and attractive, but never thought he was attracted to her. And David still very much in her heart.

"Erm that would be nice, what do you suggest?"

"Would you be my partner at the Christmas Ball?"

"Yes, I would love to, thank you."

"Fantastic! I'll give you the details, times, and transport. We will have to play it clever, we can be seen together at the camp, but not before. Right, I'll let you get back into the warmth of Mrs O'Rorke's, good night."

"Good night." Liz hurried off. *Well, what about that? What a turn up for the books.* She was very pleased. *WHAT I'm I going to wear?*

Friday morning,

The paper was out on the streets, and copies on each desk. Liz opened her copy and found her page. She was excited as she scanned the adverts with her finger, noticing the faint ink on her hands. She felt responsible; people entrusted her with how their business would be seen. She could find no mistakes, all looked good.

She sat and looked around, Others were doing just the same, she had never heard the office so quiet. She spotted Jill, who turned her copy around so Liz could see it was the fashion feature page that she had been looking at. Jill smiled and gave Liz the thumbs-up.

"Thank you," Liz mouthed She then looked at Mike, she felt she needed to know she had done good, perhaps a little recognition.

158

Mike must have sensed this, lifted and turned his head slowly. He studied Liz with no expression for a few seconds, then shrugged his shoulders and mouthed "Not Bad."

he did have a hint of a smile, or did Liz just hope that is what it was?

Liz spent the day going around to the people and business's that had supported her. The response was fantastic, early days, but most of them wanted to repeat for the next issue. She was over the moon.

What a fantastic experience this has been! It had gone great and was well received. She already had enough support for the next issue, and she found the copy so easy to write. She called in at the library.

"Good morning, Miss Bell, very impressive." Mrs Bookshaw pointed to the copy of the Paper on her desk, "Oh thank you." Liz wore a Cheshire cat grin.

She retrieved the envelope from the box and left. Back at Mrs O'Rorke's she read the letter. *'Brigadier Kingsley's driver Sean will pick you up at 20.00 Hours from the ferry terminal. He will also return you as and when, C.O.'*

Christmas Eve,

The first Christmas without war for over four years. People all over the Island were really pushing the boat out, the feeling of relief was almost tangible. Shop owners filled their shop windows with whatever looked Christmassy, the Town Hall had strings of lights festooned across the building, and there was a genuine feeling of joy to all mankind. To top it all, it was snowing.

Chapter 10

Liz looked out her window into the most Christmassy Christmas card picture she had ever seen. The snow had fallen for several hours and had settled. Pure white. People were taking it easy for sake of falling, one poor mother with her three young children struggled with her shopping and trying her best to keep her young family under control. All they wanted to do is play in the fresh snow. Two other women arm in arm giggling with the odd scream as one slipped and the other trying to hold her up while trying not to slip herself.

She had a little giggle herself, she spotted an elderly woman with her little dog, the dog it would appear did not like the snow. Probably never seen it before and was trying to climb her skirt. She kept pushing it down and telling it to behave. Poor thing all its bits must be in the snow and freezing. She ended picking it up and carrying it, much to her displeasure. She was probably thinking, *I'm have enough trouble keeping myself safe.*

The sight made her think of her last Christmas at Cove Manor when she ran through the virgin snow. How she looked back at her foot prints she had left behind. So much has happened since then, there had been great excitement, and heartache. She realised how she had grown not only as a woman, but as a person in her own right.

Her thoughts where suddenly brought back by a soft bang on her window. Two boys of around ten had thrown a snowball up at her, and were now laughing at how clever they had been. Liz smiled and drew the curtains, only to hear another soft bang on the window. She ignored it and started to concentrate on what she is going to wear for tonight. She smiled as she thought of Captain O'Connor, this made her feel like a school girl on her first date. She opened her wardrobe and stopped. her mind went to her David. Her heart sank.

It's too soon, I don't want to give the captain the wrong idea, I'm not ready. Then she spoke out loud, "For God's sake, girl, get a grip, it's the first date." *It is a date, or did he just want a partner for the evening?*

She took a deep breath and started to pick out something appropriate. She had all her outfits thrown across the bed.

This will go with that, yes, but if I tried this I could wear that.

She finally decided on the red dress with a white blouse and black accessories, very seasonal. She looked fantastic and knew it. She poured herself a whiskey with the same amount of water. It was 7:45 p.m. it was only five minutes to the ferry terminal. She sipped her drink and made sure everything was correct before making her way down stairs.

"Going out are we? Going anywhere nice?" Mrs.O'Rorke questioned.

Liz smiled and walked by and out the door. She heard Mrs O'Rorke mumble something under her breath as she closed the door. Liz did not want to encourage any closeness, she wanted to maintain the impression of being stuck-up. And aloof.

Liz smiled. *If only she knew.*

In the darkest area she spotted the car just as Sean spotted her. He was out and held the car door open.

"Evening Miss."

"Good evening, Sean, and thank you."

"My pleasure. Oh, Miss, the Brigadier asked me to give you this." Sean handed it over the seat.

Liz took it and smiled to herself; it was a bottle of what she presumed to be whisky. "Thank the Brigadier for me please, Sean."

"Do that yourself, Miss, he, his daughter, and granddaughter are at the ball."

"Oh, this is going to be a challenge," she half whispered, "Sorry, did you say something?"

"No, Sean, thank you."

As the car pulled up outside the Officer's mess, out came Captain O'Connor in full dress, looking very handsome. He opened the car door and helped Liz out.

"Wow, Miss Bell, you look fabulous. The other women are going to hate you." He held out his arm, she took it and in they went.

They did look the business, everybody gawked at this handsome couple. Liz spotted the Brigadier he was gazing at her with a look of pride and admiration. They were offered a glass of champagne and joined the throng of people.

Liz made her way across the room to the Brigadier. She was introduced by the captain to all and sundry, he was very pleased with his partner for the evening. He knew he had the most beautiful woman there.

Eventually, they reached the Brigadier's group. Before Liz had time to speak, Mrs Woodgarth started gabbing, "Ah, Miss Bell, how wonderful to see you. You look fabulous. We, Lucie and I have read and enjoyed your feature, and look forward to comparing ideas."

Before she had chance to carry on, she was cut short by Liz.

"Good evening, Mrs Woodgarth, Brigadier so good to see you."

"And you too, Miss Bell."

"It's Ms Kingsley, I have reverted to my maiden name, Lucie also."

"Ms And Miss Kingsley it is." Liz confirmed.

An elderly officer came and asked Ms Kingsley to dance. she was dragged off, protesting, but he was not taking No for an answer.

Liz turned to Lucie. "You look well. Are you admiring the view?"

Lucie looked at Liz with a quizzical expression. For a split moment she thought Lucie might have spotted something, however it passed.

"Aren't they all very handsome in their full dress uniforms? Not so much a question as an observation," offered Liz.

"Yes, they do," answered Lucie. "I wish we could spend some time together, I feel as if I have known you for ever. It's a pity you don't ride." A young officer came and asked Lucie to join him on the dance floor, she was off like a shot.

"Thank you for the whisky, sir."

"My pleasure, Miss Bell. Your sixth sense is spot on, we are close to making an arrest. They have been supplying the Irish with arms, your part may soon be over." The Captain arrived with drinks, "Ah Captain, I have been looking after and standing guard protecting her from any enemy infiltration."

"Thank you, sir."

"Look after her, Captain, she is very precious."

Liz took the captain's arm and joined the couples on the dance floor.

He whispered, "I think the Brigadier wants to bed you himself."

"What!" Exclaimed Liz. She stopped and glared at him with a face like thunder.

"I-I didn't mean that, I was just joking. I'm sorry, I should never have said it," he hastily apologised.

Reluctantly she joined him in dancing. It was Army talk, that's all. She did like him, but she had seen a side of him she didn't care for.

Liz and Lucie where never short of dance partners, the night went well. Food was to die for, the band was fantastic and the party games towards the end. Well, this was the Army after all, but some of the games left little to the imagination. Passing the long balloon held between your knees over to another pair of knees of the opposite sex. Liz never thought of herself as a prude, but this was not for her. Lucie, however, found it very entertaining.

Captain O'Connor stood by the drapes watching Miss Bell dance, his thoughts where in the bedroom. Behind the curtains he heard some muffled drunken laughter.

"Miss Bell, well she is the Bell of the ball."

"Ha, ha!" laughed one, not knowing the captain heard every word.

"I'd give her a right ding dong."

"Ha, ha, ha! She can play with my clanger anytime."

"Ha—"

The captain heard enough. "Sergeant Riley and Sergeant Taylor."

Both bolted upright and saluted, their faces like death.

"Do you both enjoy being sergeants? Cos if you don't, I can arrange for you both to become corporals."

"Sorry, sir, that was not for your ears, sorry sir."

"It's the drink, sir, meant no offence."

"Get out of my sight, both of you."

They saluted, stomped their feet, and marched off. The captain smiled to himself; they had only said the words he had been thinking.

"Father, I think Lucie and I will be getting back. Could you call for Sean?" Ms Kingsley was trying her best to appear no worse for drink, but she was plainly pie-eyed.

"Sean, take Ms and Miss Kingsley home and return for Miss Bell, thank you," ordered the Brigadier.

"Yes, sir. This way, ladies." Sean led them both to the car. Liz and the Brigadier watched quite amused at the spectacle unravelling before them. Both Ladies had obviously enjoyed the liquid hospitality, holding on to each other and trying their best to appear normal, without success.

"Captain, thank you for inviting me this evening. I have enjoyed myself," Liz said.

"It was my pleasure." He noted the Brigadier at her side. "I-I was wondering if you would do the same on New Year's Eve."

"I would love to, thank you." Smiled Liz.

"I have arranged for my driver to take Miss Bell home, Captain."

He looked most put-out. "Thank you, sir. I'll say good night. Miss Bell," then to the Brigadier, "Sir."

"Goodnight, Captain," answered the Brigadier.

The captain saluted and departed.

"Glad to have you alone, Liz, I would very much like for you to spend some time in the coming week up at Cove Manor. If you feel able to cope with those two, I do feel they are no match for you. It would mean you arriving in the dark and going back in the dark, perhaps stay over one or two nights. I could have some intelligent conversation at last, and we do need to talk business…"

"I would like that."

"Let me know through the normal channels when to send Sean for you. Speak of the devil, here is your carriage, Miss Bell."

"Thank you, sir."

He merely nodded. It was 1:30 in the morning when Liz crept up the creaky stairs to her rooms. She spent Christmas day and Boxing day at Mrs O'Rorke's. The woman did put on a lovely Christmas dinner with all the trimmings, also homemade Christmas Pudding with a choice of Brandy sauce or custard. It was quite a feast. Some of her guests complimented her on the wonderful table settings and the food.

Looking at Liz she said, "I'm not all stew and cottage pie. I used to cook for Gentry when I was younger, and there will be a special Bubble and Squeak tomorrow, Boxing day."

"It is very good Mrs O'Rorke."

"Well thank you, Miss Bell, coming from you that is a compliment." She left for the kitchen.

Liz sat and thought, *What does she think of me? This persona I portray is not the real me, I am really quite nice.* She enjoyed the theatricals and excitement, but Liz was beginning to tire of Miss Bell. Her mind went to Captain O'Connor. *He likes Miss Bell, will he like Liz Monaco as much?*

Liz spent the 27th and 28th at Cove Manor. It was stressful and how she wanted to take Dream out for a gallop. She confided in the Brigadier, she told him how she felt. He was very sympathetic and understood. He said it would only be for a few more weeks, a month at best. They still needed her to watch and report. Liz accepted this and felt better.

It was New Year's Eve, and again it was the same arrangement as Christmas Eve. Liz was met by the very handsome Captain O'Connor, and escorted in to the proceedings. She was beginning to like the captain more and more.

The evening was, as to be expected, a fantastic success. They even had a piper to bring in the new year. Liz developed more feelings for this dapper and popular captain. She started to think there could be a future for them both. It was helped along by nearly everyone commenting on how they looked good together, what a handsome couple they made. Liz now saw him through a different pair of eyes, and felt a little pang of jealousy when he danced with another women.

Ms and Miss Kingsley were entertained by several officers, and played several silly games. It was plain to see they both revelled in the attention. It was 2:30 a.m. and time to go. Most had gone, just the die-hards remained. Ladies Kingsley departed a good half hour ago. Liz was with the captain.

"I have my own quarters here on camp. Would you like a night cap before you go? I can take you back, I have a staff car on hand. Say you will, please?"

Liz thought for a few moments. "Okay, just for a night cap."

"Fantastic!" He smiled and escorted her to the officers' quarters. "Just here." He got the key and let Liz go in first. He turned on the light, drew the curtains, and poured them both a large whisky.

"Can I have a little water with mine, please?"

"Water? This is a single malt, you can't ruin it with water." His voice was not as soothing as she would have liked.

"The Irish add a small amount of water, they say it brings out the full flavour, I agree." She smiled.

He downed his in one gulp. Liz added water herself, and watched him pour himself another and offered to top up her glass.

"Please sit, what do you think of the place?"

Liz walked over to the window and looked back at the room. "Mmmm, very masculine."

"Well, I suppose it would be. I'm a masculine sort of chap." He walked towards her, placed his glass on the table and came close. He wrapped his arm around her waist, pulled her to him, and kissed her hard. Liz pushed him away.

"I—I don't feel ready. I didn't mean to give you the wrong idea I—."

He grabbed her behind her neck and kissed her again, this time he had his other hand on her breast.

"No, please no! I do like you, but—"

"Bit of a cock-teaser are you, eh? Say no and you mean yes, you can look but don't touch. I'm not the first captain, am I?" He grabbed her around the waist, his other hand straight up her skirt and between her legs. "Like it a bit rough?" He smirked.

She tried to push him away, but he was too strong. He tried to pull her down to the floor, she was frightened and beginning to panic. He had his hand over her mouth, her eyes were wide and wild. She remembered what her father had shown her; first and second finger straight out and in the eyes. This she did.

"Ahhhhh, you bitch! You've blinded me, you stupid cow." He covered his face with his hands.

She ran out, along the corridor, down the stairs, and into the night. She flew towards the lights of the main hall, and could see people cleaning up.

"Are you alright Miss?" A concerned corporal asked.

"Is the Brigadier still here?" Liz asked. Her voice was shaky, her heart beating like a drum beads of sweat ran from her forehead.

"Yes, Miss, he's over there in the corner office with the Major finishing the whisky. I'll—"

"No, it's ok I'll go, thank you."

"If you are quite sure."

Liz got her breath back and nodded. She went straight in, tried to keep her composure, but burst out sobbing.

"What on earth is the matter, Liz?" The Brigadier and Major jumped up and rushed to her side.

She got herself together as best she could and was about to speak when the tears again started to fall.

The Brigadier, with a firm voice, spoke, "Liz, tell me what has happened now."

Liz looked at him and stood straight, her voice trembling, "Captain O'Connor just tried to rape me."

"HE WHAT?"

The Major ran outside. "Corporal, call out the guard NOW." It was no more than twenty seconds later in ran a two M.P.s "Captain O'Connor, get him here now. He should be in his quarters, and send someone to the ferry just in case,"

"Yes, sir."

The M.P.s and Major disappeared into the night.

"Liz, are you sure?" the Brigadier asked. The look she gave him said it all the Brigadier acknowledged the look. "Sorry, of course you are sure, I trust you one hundred percent."

The Major ran in. "He left the camp in the staff car. He must've left just after you came in, this proves his guilt, the stupid bugger."

The Major and the Brigadier looked at each other.

"He has just thrown away a very promising career," said the Major.

"What was he thinking, for God's sake?" The Brigadier poured a large brandy and gave it to Liz. "Drink this. Corporal, ask my driver to come in. You are coming back with me, young lady. Major, he must have panicked, he knows he can't get far on a small Island."

"Indeed, sir," agreed the Major.

Sean arrived. "Car is ready, sir."

Both Liz and the Brigadier sat in the back as Sean drove them back to Cove Manor.

"If you feel up to it, Liz, can you tell me what happened?"

Liz had composed herself and now began to feel angry with herself and a little guilty. Angry because she let it get to her, and guilty, did she lead him on? Was it a little bit her fault?

She relayed the whole terrible experience, not missing out a single item. This made her feel a bit better, and she felt safe with the Brigadier. "And to top it all, he said, *'You don't put water in whisky'*."

The Brigadier, just for a moment, had a face full of 'What'? He saw Liz tried to smile.

"My God, Liz, you are one hell of a woman. Retain your sense of humour at all cost, eh. Well done, that's my girl."

Liz desperately needed a hug, and the Brigadier desperately wanted to give one. But alas none was forthcoming.

Once at Cove Manor the Brigadier poured another large brandy, this time in a warmed glass. He handed it to Liz. "How did you escape?"

"My father showed me the two fingers in the eyes. He sounded really hurt, I hope I haven't blinded him."

"What? I'll have the bastard hung, drawn, and quartered," mumbled the Brigadier.

"I have been thinking, sir, I-I don't want to press charges."

He stared at her, in shock. "You must, Liz, if this is the kind of man he is, He needs to be dealt with. He might try it on another woman, think about it, please."

"I'll sleep on it."

"That sounds like, *'I have made up my mind, so please say no more'*."

"Something like that. I'll say goodnight." Liz finished the Brandy and went to her room.

She sat on the bed in and thought, *The year can only get better.*

And so it did.

"Sir, we found Captain O'Connor in a ditch, the car went off the road in the snow. The captain is in sick-bay, the car is in the workshop."

"Thank you, Sergeant." The Major phoned the Brigadier and relayed the message.

"She does not want to press charges, Major. She has this silly idea that somehow she may be a little guilty about going to his room late at night. I told her he needs to be dealt with as he may try it again. Yes, I agree, Major, I'll be with you within the hour."

Sean drove the Brigadier into the camp and up to the Majors office.

"Morning, sir," the Major greeted him.

"Morning, Major," he replied. "Right, bring him in."

The two men seated themselves as Captain O'Connor was helped in by two M.P.s one on each arm. His arm was in a cast, a bandage over one eye, and looked very shaken.

"I am struggling, Captain, to find words. What was you thinking? Your career could be over. I have your doctor's report here, it says that all your injuries will heal but your eye is another matter. If you lose sight, your Army days as you know it are over. I must inform you that Miss Bell will not be pressing charges."

"It's her word against mine," he protested. "I'm a serving officer she's just—"

The Major cut in. "I would choose your words very carefully, Captain."

"I don't think you fully understand the seriousness of your situation." The Brigadier was doing his best to remain calm. "Miss Bell is a British intelligence Officer." He paused. "And holds the temporary rank of Major."

This hit the captain right between the eyes, he visibly shook.

"This changes everything," the Brigadier continued. "Not only do you stand accused of attempted rape, but the attempted rape of a Superior Officer."

The room fell silent. Captain O'Connor knew he was done for: Court marshalled and thrown out of the armed forces, and a dishonourable discharge.

"It is only because of your record to-date that we will allow you to keep your rank. You will be sent to help clean up the mess left in Europe. Do not seek promotion, you will be under surveillance and report daily to Sergeant Major Woodiwus. He has volunteered to look after you."

Captain O'Connor and all assembled knew that from now on, his life was going to be a living HELL!

Chapter 11

It was now February 1919. Liz carried on at the paper, and was enjoying its surprising success. In fact, Liz now had an assistant, the young lady from reception Brenda. Brenda was beside herself with excitement. She hinted to Liz whenever she could how wonderful the fashion feature was, and how ordinary women and girls could now get patterns and make their own dresses and tops in the latest styles.

Brenda's enthusiasm had no boundaries, it was good to watch. She went to it like a duck to water. Her first assignment was to help Liz fill two pages, this was to correspond with the first fashion show in London since the war. In the back of Liz's mind was the fact that Miss Biddy Bell will soon, and it couldn't come soon enough, cease to exist and when it does Brenda could step into her shoes.

Liz felt good about this. She had developed a good rapport with all the staff, but kept her distance. She knew they all thought of her as very much "Up-Herself," but this was the price she had to pay for doing her job. And knowing it was only a temporary arrangement helped her on days when she felt extra lonely.

She had been given instructions by her new contact, a Captain Harper. Liz had met him at the "New-Year do." She still had a cold shiver run down her spine whenever "that do" was mentioned.

They were getting very close to finding the source of the arms. they knew arms where being taken by fishing boat from the Island East and West. Boats were being watched. They did not want to intercept until they had the full gang. It was the Making, the factory they wanted. It had to be large for the amount of arms being produced.

But where it is still remained a mystery. It began to dawn on them that the operation was bigger than they originally thought. Small arms and rifles had been appearing in Ireland and mainland U.K. but where they are being manufactured still alluded them.

Liz took it on herself to investigate. She knew her mission was to "observe and report," but she had a gut feeling about the shop floor headman. Over the weeks she had seen how people feared him, at first it just seemed his manner, but she felt it was more sinister than that.

She decided to stay behind after hours, and planned to hide in the store room. She knew the cleaners came at 18.00 Hours and left around 19.30 Hours. Sometimes Mike would stay an hour or so, but the place would be empty by 20.00 Hours.

She left it as late as possible, telling Brenda she was tying up some loose ends before going home. Brenda wanted to stay and help.

"No thank you, Brenda, I'll be fine."

"But, Biddy, I want to learn, I have nothing else to do, Please let me help, Please."

"Brenda, go home. I will see you in the morning." This was said with some authority.

Brenda reluctantly gave up and left. Liz sat at her desk.

Mike was still at his, and without lifting his head said, "There is more to you than meets the eye, Miss Biddy."

Liz froze.

"I see you achieving great things, you will go far. I have seen it before, you are a bit special." This was the most her had ever said to her in one go. He stood, looked at her, smiled. "I will see you in the morning, Biddy Bell."

She had never seen this playful side of him before. There was a warmth in his manner. Yet he always appeared unapproachable.

What I'm I doing? What am I looking for? What am I hopping to find? God knows and He won't tell. She got serious. *I better leave some form of note, if something goes wrong.*

She wrote a letter to Captain Harper.

I am staying behind tonight (4th Feb.)
I think all this is something to do with the shop-floor. If you are reading this note, I am in trouble I have not returned to my desk to destroy this note.
B.B.

Liz placed it in an envelope and wrote; *Please give this to Mrs Bookshaw at the Library.*

She left the envelope in plain view on her desk, went to the toilet as a precaution, and met the cleaners on her way to the store room. The key was always in the lock. She looked around, no-one, went in and locked the door from the inside. She sat on a box of A4 paper in the dark. After a while her eyes became accustomed to the dark, she found the light switch and turned on the light. She could hear the cleaners working away with the odd chatter and laughter.

"Right you lot," came a woman's voice that sounded as if she must be smoking forty fags a day. "Got no homes to go to, I'm going over to the "Legs of Man" for a drink."

"Filthy cow, it's all sex, sex, sex with you, Mavis."

Laughter all around. The lights started to go out one by one, the last one being the hallway leading to the stairwell and also to the store room. Liz quickly switched off the light. Her heart jumped as the door was tried, the handle going up and down.

"Bloody hell." It was the same rough voice. "They've locked the bloody door."

Another voice spoke, "They have sussed you out, Mavis, no more free envelopes a stuff for you."

"Bollocks!" Shouted Mavis as she kicked the door. Then mutterings as they went down the stairs and out.

Liz heard the doors being locked; she waited a few moments before letting herself out into the darkness. She could hear the clickety clack of the printing press in the distance, and made her way towards the noise. She got to the office door that led onto the shop floor. She tried the door, it was unlocked, she opened it slightly and closed it quickly.

The sudden clatter and noise from the machinery was overwhelming. She looked through the Georgian Wired frosted glass, but could not pick out anything moving like a person. So she opened the door, only this time was not shocked by the noise. She slipped inside and crouched down behind an old filing cabinet and looked around. Her mouth was dry, her heart pounding.

There was several men in several positions watching the machinery as it printed. There were three men at tables making up the pages, they all looked to engrossed in what they were doing to notice her, so she hoped.

She spotted him, Harry Howard, he was talking to a man in a nice overcoat, hat, and gloves. He was not one of the workers, that was for sure.

She watched the two men talk, then Howard turned and looked around the shop floor. All the workmen appeared to be looking the other way on purpose, away from the cold gaze of Howard. Then both men looked down at the floor and seemed to disappear into it. She knew she must have a closer look, so slowly worked her way around the room, stopping to check all was okay.

She spotted a large clock on the opposite wall, she had lost the track of time it was 3:45 a.m. She got to within ten feet of the spot, when a trap-door opened. She froze, hardly able to swallow and her heart about to burst through her chest. Up came Howard followed by the well-dressed guy. She could not make out what they were saying for the noise and clatter of the presses. She crouched, motionless. Something inside of her made her take out a handkerchief and tie it to a rail behind her. And only just in time, she was spotted.

Liz stood and held on to the rail. She had been crouched for so long, her legs decided to cramp. Howard grabbed her by the arm.

"Who ARE you? What are you doing here?" His face was twisted with rage.

He slapped her across the face with the back of his hand. She felt she was going to pass out. He threw her at the trap door, she fell to her knees and managed to grab hold of the side to stop herself from falling down into God knows what lay beneath.

"Get down!" He snarled.

Liz saw blood spots on her blouse and skirt as she stumbled down the wooden stairs and into a large room. He followed, grabbed her arm, and pushed her onto a chair. He slapped her again to make sure she stayed put. He tied her to the chair and dragged the chair into the corner. He stood there his chest heaving in and out and a face showed real hatred.

I'm going to die, she really thought. *He is going to kill me, if not now then soon.*

"I'll deal with you later." He went up top and slammed down the trap-door.

She had tears in her eyes and was shaking like a leaf, but stayed strong. She took stock of her surroundings.

This is it, this is where they made the guns and rifles. She was right after all, which made her feel a bit better.

She spotted a woman walking towards her. She looked hard-nosed, stopped, and walked away. A few moments later she reappeared. Liz, not sure of what was about to happen, stiffened up. The woman had a cloth in her hand.

I'm going to be suffocated. "NO! Please, no!" Liz screamed.

The woman spoke in a very thick Irish accent. "Just goin' ta clean ya face, darlin.' Don't want spoilin' those lovely clothes." She cleaned Liz's face. "Shame, a cryin' shame, so it is." The woman left. Liz knew she was going to die.

Liz looked at all the wooden boxes, most closed some still open and being filled with rifles, then nailed closed.

What a set-up, she thought. *No one would hear the sound of this machinery over the sound of the printing press. Surely, the men upstairs aren't part of this, but they must know what is going on.*

She wracked her brain until she remembered a story that appeared in the paper some six months ago. A fishing trip that went wrong, some men from the shop floor drowned in a freak accident a few miles of Douglas. The upturned boat was found all died except the owner who somehow got to shore. Her mind ran wild, that was not an accident, they were killed to stop them from talking. No wonder they all looked frightened to death and looked the other way.

The clock on the wall said 7:30 a.m. Liz was so glad she went to the toilet before all this started. She looked around counted five men and two women including the one who had offered to clean her face… They kept working and ignored her. Her nose and jaw was starting to hurt, she felt the swelling in her lip and her left eye started to close. She had a headache to beat all headaches.

It was 7:50 a.m. she knew that people would be starting work. She prayed Brenda would see the envelope and take it to the library.

Oh my God, it doesn't open till ten o'clock! It may be too late.

"Good morning, people." Brenda smiled as she walked through the room to Liz's desk.

This was okay if you are, as Brenda was, a morning person. But unfortunately most of the room was not. She was answered with moans and grunts. This did not deter her from feeling good as she was doing the job she loved with someone she liked. Brenda picked up the letter and put it in her handbag. She got her bits together, told Mike she was going out selling space. All she got and expected was a nod.

I'll do the letter first, she thought.

So popped it through the letterbox at the library. It was 9 a.m. and went on her merry way. Mrs Bookshaw was inside re arranging and tidying up and heard

174

the letterbox go. She left it for about ten minutes while she finished what she was doing. She made herself tea, then sat at her desk with her tea and a few small cakes. Halfway through she remembered the letterbox. She picked up the letter and walked back to finish her breakfast. She opened the letter. The world stopped.

She ran out, grabbed her bicycle, and peddled as fast as she could up to the camp some two miles away. The corporal on station watched her approach with interest. He was amazed at the speed for an old woman.

"My code name is Library, this is a life and death. Code Red situation, give this letter to the Major now."

The Corporal hesitated.

"NOW!"

Having heard the woman shouting, a sergeant came to see what the ruckus was about. She grabbed the letter from the corporal and gave it to him.

"My code name is Library. Give this letter to the Major, this is a Code Red situation."

The Sergeant understood and handed the letter back to the corporal. "The Major NOW and run, damn you."

"What do you know?" He asked.

"Only that it means Miss Bell is in danger. I'll get back to the library before I am missed." Off she peddled.

The Major contacted Captain Harper, and briefed him. The captain had twelve men fully armed and briefed. They were all part of this undercover operation and knew their positions. They used the back of the Rolls Royce Ambulance, this would give then the cover they needed.

They set off down to Douglas and the paper. They drove normal as not to raise suspicion. On arrival they backed the ambulance up to the rear entrance gates. They surrounded the workshop. no resistance, not a sound. Captain Harper led four men to the back door, nothing. He nudged it open. Two men flew in and stood left and right, guns at the ready. Still nothing, just looks from the men on the two printing press.

The other two men came in. All four and the captain stood in silence, surrounded by the noise of the room. The captain glanced at the workmen, a bit confused. Here was the army armed and ready, and they carried on as they were not there.

This can only mean this is not a surprise, the captain mused.

175

He spotted the handkerchief tied to the rail. As he walked over to retrieve it, he stepped over the trap door. He heard the squeak of loose boards, stopped, and examined where the door edges were and could make out the hinges. He looked up, the face of one of the press workers peered straight at him and without expression nodded.

The captain stepped back, and indicated for the men to stand around the trap door, guns at the ready, He was banking on the noise of the room not giving him away. He slowly lifted the trap door and on his knees peered in. On the other side of the room people stood working on their machines, completely unaware of what was about to happen.

He started down the stairs, followed by his men, till all five gaped at this vast underground workshop. The captain signalled for two to go left and two go right. When they were in position, he crept forward twenty feet and fired his pistol. The noise echoed around the room and had the desired effect. The men and women jumped and whirled about. One went for a pistol close by, but thought better of it when he had one pointed at him.

It was only when Captain Harper turned to climb back upstairs leaving his men to round up and bring up-top did he see Liz. He flew to her, untied her, and helped her back up to fresh air and freedom. She was trembling and in shock. He put his arm around her and took her to the waiting ambulance. Here the medics took her in.

"You're save now, Miss, all over. You are a very brave woman." He turned to the medic. "Take Miss Bell to camp, give her your very best, and return for my men and I."

"Yes, sir."

He watched the ambulance leave. A crash followed by shouting erupted from the open doorway. He raced inside to see what the commotion was. His men had got the well-dressed man and Harry Howard.

"Got them coming through a secret hole in the fence, sir."

"Well done, Sergeant, well done men. Why is this man bleeding, Sergeant?" He was referring to Harry Howard.

"He tripped and hurt himself, sir."

"I see." Smiled the captain. "Make sure he does not self-harm any more, Sergeant, we need him awake for questioning."

"Sir."

"You'll get nothing from me, you filth!" spluttered Howard, just as the sergeant's elbow met his nose. "Bastards!"

"Take him away."

"Yes, sir, with pleasure."

When they got back to the camp, the Brigadier was already there. He was at Liz's bedside.

"I told you *'Observe and report,'* young lady, not take them on single handed. You could have been." He stopped.

She touched his hand and tried to smile; she could see his bottom lip start to go.

"I feel tired, sir, I think I'll now sleep. The pills they gave me are starting to work." She pretended to fall asleep. She heard him stand and walk away, but soon she was really asleep.

A local bobby was sent round to inform Mrs O'Rorke.

"Thank God for that, officer!" She cried. "I was going to report her missing. What happened? You can tell me now, Robert."

"Mrs O'Rorke, you know I can't," he began.

"Don't you *'Mrs O'Rorke'* me, Robert Jones! I've bounced you on my knee many a time, and don't you forget it."

"Good day to you, Mrs O'Rorke." He walked away.

"Wait till I see your mother!" She shouted after him. She was not happy.

The Brigadier arranged for Liz to spend her recovery with him at Cove Manor. It was two weeks before she looked a bit like herself again. Lucie was good. Liz had to be so on her guard, and kept her face covered as much as she could. Ms Kingsley came and spoke a few times, asking opinion on styles and make-up, but never stayed. This suited them both. Brenda sent flowers from them all at the paper, and now the Paper had the best story ever. And would probably never be topped.

The Brigadier told Liz all what transpired. "Another day and we would have lost Mr Big. He would have been back in Ireland or the UK. and he would have disappeared."

"I take it he was the well-dressed man I saw with Harry Howard," Liz guessed.

"Yes, my dear, it was. It was a hell of a thing you did, against orders I may add. It's time Miss Bell went, don't you think?"

"Yes." Liz nodded. "I must do a few more weeks at the paper, and get back to Mrs O'Rorke's tidy up loose ends."

"As you wish, Liz, I promise not to give you any more missions."

"Good to have you back Miss Biddy," offered Mike. The others mumbled the same sort of thing.

"I have kept the fashion page going, Biddy. I hope you like what I've done." Brenda smiled.

Jill gave Liz a knowing look. *You are not what you seem.* She suspected something, but she did not know what. She was good at her job, but experience told her not to pursue this one.

Things settled after a few weeks. Mrs O'Rorke gave up trying to find out what really happened. Liz settled in at the paper and Harbour House, and kept her distance from the camp and Cove Manor. It felt best to keep a low profile for the time being. Liz would decide when to kill off Miss Biddy Bell.

Chapter 12

The war is over and we won, but the cost is almost unbearable. So may young lives taken, so many families shattered. I just hope like millions that the powers that be have learnt a lesson and there will never be another war.

It's February 1919, things are about the same. I am still at the boatyard. Business is good. Everyone I care about is well. Auntie and Jack are not getting married, they thought it better just to carry on as they have been. Jack has never stayed overnight, but they enjoy each other's company and they look after each other.

Nelly and me are great, I stay over in Tom's room whenever I can and help around the farm. Nelly and me have set a date, the 4th July 1920.

I was working on the drawing of the latest boat, writing down a cutting list for the timbers required. In came Mr O'Hara.

"Kev lad, will you see me in my office when you're ready?"

"Yes, Mr O'Hara, I'll only be a few minutes. I'm almost complete."

He said nothing, turned, and went. I looked at Jimmy and Pat. They pulled a face shrugged and carried on.

I knocked.

"Come in, Kev lad. Come in. Sit ya self-down."

"Here is the cutting list for the O'Brians new boat." I handed him my paperwork.

He took it and put it to one side. "I have a problem, not a bad one, but a problem all the same. You know I have a brother in the same business on the Isle-Of-Man, in Douglas?"

I nodded.

"Well, he passed away a few days ago. His lungs had gone and he was a drinker, never married."

"I'm sorry to hear that," I offered.

"Yes, thank you for that, Kev lad. All he had is now mine, and I need to go over there and sort things out. I want you to join me, I may have a proposal for you. That's all I can say at present. It will mean going by steamer from Belfast. I have arranged transport to get us there for eight in the morning. We should be at the docks by one or two. We sail at 3 p.m…"

I was taken aback. *This sounds exciting, how I need an adventure, having not gone roaming a few years back as planned.* "Thank you, Mr O'Hara, I look forward to it."

"Feel at liberty to tell Jimmy and Pat. I don't want any misunderstandings. Pack for three days."

"Right, er, do you want to go over the cutting list, Mr O'Hara?"

"No, no, I'm sure it is as it should be. I'll get the timbers ordered." With this he started through the cutting list.

I went down back to the workshop.

"Well, what was all that about?" spouted Pat.

"I'll make us some tea and—" I was cut short by Jimmy.

"No, Mr O'Keefe, you sit yourself down, and Pat will make the tea." He was smiling, Pat was within ear-shot.

I started. "Did you know his brother had died?"

"Yes, we know," said Pat.

"How do you know that?" I asked.

"Not important, go on," Jimmy urged.

"He asked me to go with him to the Isle-Of-Man to help him sort things out. That's all," I said.

"That's all?" Pat echoed.

Jimmy jumped in. "He is going to offer you the chance to run the business."

"What? that can't be right!" I exclaimed.

"I bet you a week's wages on it," said Jimmy.

My mind was full of questions and very few answers. As I mentioned before, a moment's thought is an hour in words. We settled into work .

It was Wednesday and Nelly would be meeting me at dinner time as normal. *What do I tell her?*

Lunch time came, I was working on the planking around the port-side away from the workshop doors when.

"Kevin, it must be time for you to go to go and meet your maker," Jimmy teases.

"What are you talking about?" I answered.

"I must be right, Kev, as an angel has come for you."

I turned. "Very funny. Hello, sweetheart."

"Hello, darling."

"Hello sweeeeeetheart, hello darrrrrrling," Jimmy and Pat mimicked us.

"I think I'm going to be sick," Jimmy pretended to gag.

Nelly and I walked outside. We sat on the same bench we sat on for the last two years.

"So, woman, what have you brought me for to eat?"

"Kind, sir, it is but simple fare. Tis prepared by my own fair hand."

"Then all the sweeter it will be." I unwrapped the small very neatly wrapped packet… "Not cheese and pickle again." I sighed.

"Careful," she warned, "or you won't get the hardboiled egg I was going to give you."

"I take it all back! I would do anything for a hardboiled egg."

Her eyebrows raised. "Anything?"

"Er, I'll reserve judgement until I have tasted it."

There have been moments lately, when we are finding it more and more difficult to keep our hands off each other. A few days ago I was at her farm, we were just laying among the hay bales and the feeling was so strong.

Nelly looked away and said, "Kevin." Pause.

"Yes?" I prodded.

"I know how you men do it to yourself."

Oh my God, I couldn't believe she just said that. I was too stunned to reply. "I saw Tommy doing it. I was in the big barn day dreaming when in he came. I lay still, he was only about ten feet away and I saw him do it. He never saw me."

I held her close and stared up at the sky. She looked up at me and started to undo my belt.

There are going to be times, I thought. "You make it very hard for me… you know Nel, to—." I stopped.

She had her hand on my penis. "I want to see," she whispered, eyes like dinner plates. It took a few seconds for the penny to drop.

"Nelly Kelly!" I tried to appear shocked.

"Don't you Nelly Kelly me, Mr O'Keefe." She settled with her head on my chest, her hand moving slowly up and down.

I thanked the gods above. It was not long before I felt the feeling rise. I tried to stay calm, no chance. My breathing became shallow and rapid. The feeling built and built until I exploded. Nelly gave a small scream and stopped.

"Don't stop, Nel, just a few seconds more."

This she did, then sat up. "It's in my eye." She used her sleeve to wipe it away. "I didn't know it went that far. Did you like me doing that?"

"You can do that anytime you want, sweetheart." I hesitated, not wanting to ruin the moment.

Back to the present It's now or never. "Nel, Mr O'Hara asked me to go with him to Douglas for a few days to his brother's boatyard to help him sort a few things out."

"Why you? What's wrong with Jimmy or Patrick?"

"He wants me, he can spare me. Jimmy and Pat are needed in the workshop, they can carry on," I offered in my defence.

"You do more in that place than anyone, you told me he is giving you more responsibility."

"Well, yes."

"When are you going?"

"Tomorrow for three days. I'm looking forward to it a little adventure, a ferry out of Belfast and all that. I have never been to the Isle-o-Man. I'll bring you back a present."

"You better." She was not happy and sat silent for a few moments. "Right then, Kevin, I'm going back to my gran's. I'll see you on Sunday, be careful." She kissed me, more of a peck, on the cheek. I watched her walk away. She did not turn.

"Everything alright?" Jimmy asked.

"Yes." I did not sound convincing enough.

"You told her then?" Pat guessed.

"And I take it she is not happy," Jimmy piped up.

"Don't fret, they do get very possessive. You'll have to watch that, they like to feel in control," said Pat. "She'll come around, she's a good lass that one. Just think, you have never done anything like this before, bring her back something nice. and all will be forgiven."

The next morning I was at the workshop 7:30 a.m. as normal, I was called upstairs by Mrs O'Hara. I was surprised to see Jack standing there.

"There has been a slight change of plan," said Mr O'Hara. "Jack here is going to take us to Belfast. I was let down by the transport I had arranged for today. So, with no further ado, let's be off."

I liked this arrangement better, I knew Jack's boat and it was a fine day for it. I could see that Mr O'Hara was also excited at the trip ahead.

"It's been years since I last tripped on your boat, Jack," said Mr O'Hara.

"You are always welcome," Jack replied. "After all, you built her over forty years ago for me father."

"And it's still afloat, Jack, a miracle."

"Don't put your mouth on it just yet, Sean O'Hara."

We all laughed. I'd never seen Mr O'Hara so jolly.

"I must do this again before I get too old," said Mr O'Hara.

"I don't think Mary would take too kindly to you wandering around the seas at your age," Jack commented.

"I suppose you're right, Jack." Mr O'Hara sighed.

We settled down to the trip. I threw a line of hooks over to try and catch some mackerel. We approached Belfast harbour. There she was, the S.S. PATRIOTIC. looking very grand.

Jack shouted out, "There she is! They used her as a troop ship, just finished the re-fit. Kev lad, get ready to jump."

We pulled alongside behind the stern of the ship. We were met with, "You can't tie-up there!"

We turned a deaf ear. I jumped and made fast. Mr O'Hara got off and Jack passed us the bags. I untied, pushed the bow out, and off she went with Jack waving. We walked along the quay, to a gap in the barrier.

Again the same voice, "You're not supposed to do that, you know?" It was a Job's – Worth Minor Official. Mr O'Hara stood close to this fellow.

"We promise never to do it again," he whispered in his ear.

"Make sure you don't," came the reply.

Off we went to join the queue.

What an adventure, this is fantastic. My Nelly would love this. We found seats, Mr O'Hara soon fell asleep. *Great, I can have a wander.*

I went to every part of the ship I was allowed, and some places I wasn't. I got to the entrance to the engine room and looked down. *My God what a job, being stuck down there all day. They must earn every penny.* Got myself as close to the bridge as I could.

An officer came up to me. "Are you lost, sir?"

"No, no it's my first trip on a boat this size. I build wooden fishing boats in the village Carrickfergus" I nervously replied.

Another officer joined the first. "You don't work for O'Hara?"

"Yes, I do, he's on board."

"Come on up," came the reply.

I was on the bridge, a dream come true.

"You say Sean O'Hara is onboard." This was the captain.

"Yes, I left him asleep,"

"It must be thirty years since I left O'Hara's Boatyard, and you are?"

"Kevin O'Keefe."

"Well, Mr O'Keefe, Captain Connors at your service. Would you like to take the helm, Kevin?"

I stood at the big polished wooden wheel. I was King or Captain. *Steady at as she goes, Mr O'Keefe.* No words can explain the feeling, I could not stop grinning. *What would Nelly say if she could see me now?*

"Kevin," said Captain Connors, it's a long-shot, but are you in anyway related to William O'Keefe? I worked with him at O'Hara's, he was married to a lovely lady, Winny, short for Winifred."

"I am their son!" I exclaimed.

"What? They left it a bit late," smiled the captain.

"I was a surprise."

"I bet you were. Well, I never did. I have some wonderful memories of that man; he would help anyone and she worked at the Castle. They must be near retirement, not still working are they?"

"I lost them when I was fourteen in1913. Both died within minutes of each other."

His face went stern. then softened. "So sorry, Kevin, how sad. So, you have taken over from your father then. Yes. Married?"

"Not yet, the date is set for next year."

"Can I ask her name?"

"Nelly Kelly."

"That's a name you won't forget in a hurry. I knew a Kelly, John Kelly had a big farm about 7/8 miles outside of Carrickfergus. Can't recall the name of the farm."

"Fergus farm," I offered.

"Yes, that was it. So, John Kelly must be Nelly's Grandfather. Well, well, well, would you believe it? It's been grand talking to you, Kevin. If your father could see you now, you would make him very proud, Now, hand back the wheel to Mr Green here. Any longer and you'll want paying."

I shook hands and left them to it. I found Mr O'Hara in the bar.

"Something to eat, Kev, lad?"

"No thank you I have sandwiches. Mr O'Hara, do you remember a Mr Connors? He worked for you some thirty years ago."

"Yes, Barry Connors, why?"

"He is the captain of this ship and asked to be remembered to you. He remembers my father."

"Good God, you don't say? damn-it, if I'd known that I might have got free tickets."

We docked in Douglas and were met by a tall skinny fellow of about fifty. He spoke very slowly as if every breath would wear him out.

"Hello, Mr O'Hara, nice to see you after all these years. Sad about your brother."

"Yes, thank you, Enoch."

We put our bags on the barrow he had brought. Off he went, we walked a few yards behind. I looked at Mr O'Hara.

"Don't ask, Kev lad, don't ask."

We walked for about a mile, then I could see a sign above the entrance to J.P. O'Hara—Boat builder—Est. 1869. It started to rain. I followed Mr O'Hara through the workshop and into the office at the far end. We passed three benches, two were occupied. By the first one stood a man of about forty, he took of his cap as we passed. At the second bench sat a man of about fifty stocky, and unshaven. He totally ignored us.

He was sharpening a chisel and spat on the sharpening stone as we passed. In the shed was a half-finished fishing boat of about eighteen feet. It looked small in such a big shed. The shed was untidy and upswept.

"Shall I take the bags to the house Mr O'Hara?" Enoch asked.

"Yes, please, is it all ready?" said Mr O'Hara.

"Oh, yes. Mrs O'Frarity has lit the fire and all. I'll take the bags to the house then." He disappeared around the bend.

His mother must have dropped him on his head as a baby, I thought.

The first carpenter came, cap in hand.

"Oh, Kevin, this is Mathew Evans."

"Hello," I said.

He looked at Mr O'Hara. "Shall I lock-up? It's gone six."

"Yes, that's fine. Tell Bill to come in, will you?"

"Bill's gone, Mr O'Hara."

"Right, see you in the morning."

Evans started to lock-up. I watched him, all the tools were left out. He put them all away, locked the screw/nail cabinet and the store/stock room.

I asked, "Have you a broom?"

He did not answer, just brought it to me.

"Do you want me to stay?"

"No, Mathew, thank you."

Mathew touched his forehead, nodded, placed the keys on the bench, made sure I saw him do it, and left.

I started to sweep up. I found nails/screws/fixings and a riveting tool. It took about an hour. I could not find any sacks to put the pile of sawdust/shavings in, so left it and went into the office.

Mr O'Hara leaned back in the chair with a sigh. "Not good, Kev lad, not good at all. Fresh start in the morning."

We got to the house. It was big and in its own grounds, proper set of iron entrance gates. It was sound, but unloved, it needed a bit of tender loving care. We were met by Mrs O'Flarity.

"It's wonderful to see you, Mr O'Hara, it's been years. Your brother often mentioned you—"

Mr O'Hara cut her short. "I find that very hard to believe, Mrs O'Flarity. Are there clean sheets on the beds?"

"Oh yes, and fresh water in the bowl and fresh towels and all," she replied.

"Thank you, have you food?"

"No I thought you would be eating at the Legs-o-Man."

"Probably for the best." Was his answer.

"I'll be off then. Sleep well." With this, this scarecrow of a woman vanished into the dark and was gone.

I was shown my room, large with a massive fireplace, a little fire in the grate, and a four-poster bed with all round curtains. It must have been four feet high, there was a single wooden step built into the bed frame. If my Nelly could only see all this, she would be mine.

We ate well, and I had a pint of porta with a whiskey chaser. It was insisted upon by Mr O'Hara.

"It will help you sleep, Kev lad."

And it did. Just before we left, I asked at the bar was there any one in from the stables. The barman had a look around, went in the public bar. I followed and spotted Bill. He saw me and glared. I stared at him until he blinked first. I could tell he did not like this or me, he looked like trouble. I was wrong.

"Ah, Barry, this man wants a word or two with you,"

I said, "Thank you" and shook hands with Barry, he was around 25 and smiley.

"What can I do for you?"

"Kevin, Kevin O'Keefe." I offered.

"Barry Murry at your service."

"I have a very large pile of sawdust and shavings at O'Hara's, going begging."

"I'll be around first thing in the morning with me cart. You the new owner then?" He looked at Bill then me.

"No, I'm here to help Mr O'Hara sort things out." I looked at Bill as I said this. Bill muttered something under his breath and turn away to face the bar.

"Thank you, Barry, I'll see you in the morning."

"Ah, that you will," replied Barry.

We had breakfast at the Legs-O-Man, then down to the yard. It was around 8:30 a.m. Barry was already to leave fully loaded.

"That's grand, Kevin, call me anytime. I always need clean floor/bedding for the horses. I'll be off then."

"When did you arrange that, Kev lad?" Mr O'Hara spoke with a note of surprise.

"Last night at the tavern."

"Good job, lad, good job."

We walked through the workshop to the office. Mr O'Hara sat at the table which was table was full of papers, drawings and the like.

"Kev lad, I am going to spend most of the day going through this lot. My brother was not the best of bookkeepers. I have an appointment with the bank at eleven, and the undertakers at two, so, I want you to stay in the shop and get a feel for what's going on and such. You know what I mean, lad, you know what I mean."

I went into the workshop. Mathew was working on the boat, Bill was standing by his bench with his back to me. I went over and stood the other side of his bench. I held out my hand, "I'm Kevin."

"I don't shake hands." He wouldn't look up.

"It would appear there are lots of things you don't do." I waited for a reaction. He sharply looked up and stood straight.

"You are the foreman, Bill, as I am back in Carrickfergus. You don't seem happy."

"Happy?" He snapped. "Why should I be happy? He's going to close us down, ain't he?"

"Who?" I asked.

"Him in there."

"The new owner, Mr O'Hara you mean?"

"And why are you here?". Bill asked with a suspicious snarl.

"Mathew, would you come and join us please?"

Mathew came over a bit sheepish.

"When was this boat due to be finished?" I put the question to both.

Mathew spoke first. "Two weeks ago."

"Well, it looks as if another week would do it. I can understand how you may be feeling with your Mr O'Hara dying, not knowing the future and all. But if I know this his brother here, he will do his best to keep this yard afloat. So, what I propose is we all work together, finish this boat, and show him what you two can do.

"You are both alive and fit, not like the 30,000 that did not return. You both have jobs and wages every week. You're the foreman here, Bill, so I will follow your lead."

Bill walked off and stood outside, Mathew turned to me.

"It might be best to go easy with Bill, he lost his only son and his brother among that 30,000."

"Oh, shit!" I said to myself. I walked to him. "Bill, I had no idea about your loss, it must really hurt."

"What do you know about loss and hurt eh?" Bill voice was bitter.

"I lost my mother and father at the same time when I was fourteen."

Bill's head dropped. "Sorry to hear that."

"It does hurt and make you think, *'What is the point.'* I keep them alive in here." I pointed to my heart and head. "I talk to them."

Bill studied me for a second. "That's madness."

"I have a good friend back home that said once, *'It's being mad that keeps me sane'*."

"There's a bit of Irish logic in that I suppose." Answered Bill reluctantly.

"We are all a bit mad." I smiled.

Bill returned to the workshop. "Come on, Taffy, we have work to do."

Mathew blew a sigh of relief and got to it with renewed vigour. Bill joined him.

"Bill!" I shouted.

He stopped and faced me.

"The lads back home told me about a Bill that worked here, he was known for his fine work and carvings on boats up to fifty feet long. People gave this yard contracts because of him, do you know him?"

Bill seemed to debate whether or not to tell me. "He's still around here somewhere, I'll try and find him." He touched his forehead and nodded.

We worked well together. They both could see I knew what I was doing, and Bill was now out to prove to me he was better. And this I welcomed.

Mr O'Hara came and went, we worked till 5:45 p.m. I had made the tea during the day.

"If it's ok with you, Bill, I'll start brushing up."

He only nodded. The shop was tidy all tools cleaned and put away. He said to Mathew, "You go, I'll lock-up."

Mathew smiled and looked brighter.

I said to Bill, "I'll go sit in the office and wait for Mr O'Hara. See you 7:30 a.m. in the morning ." I headed to the office.

I heard Bill lock-up, the place fell in silence. The day had gone well, at this rate we would have the boat done a day sooner. I studied the drawings, clipped to one was a letter saying, *'We accept your costings and would wish for you to have the contract. Could you please provide us with a completion date'?*

The letter was dated four weeks since. I finally found the cutting list and costings that Mr' O'Hara's brother had done some eight weeks since before falling ill. I put all the relative paperwork together and examined the drawings. The vessel was a 42 foot Schooner with a square topsail on the foremast, very sleek, and nice scroll-work at the bows.

Bill will like that work, I thought. *And that's what all that timber is for.*

The yacht was to be named *LUCIE KINGSLEY*, the customer was Brigadier Kingsley, of Cove Manor, Douglas. I found myself touching the name with my finger, The *LUCIE KINGSLEY*.

Mr O'Hara said, for me to go ahead and he would follow after he had attended to business that day. It was a cold rainy day with a light sea-mist, no wind to blow it away. I opened the boatyard at 7 a.m. and had the kettle on ready. Mathew arrived at 7:20 p.m. followed by Bill who was clean shaven and looked better in himself. I made no comment. They put their dinner boxes on their respective benches.

"Would you gentleman like to join me in the office?"

They looked at each other, a moment's thought is an hour in words.

"Nothing to worry about," I added.

"Sit down, I'll be Mother." I smiled to myself. *These two have no idea how to take me.* I poured the tea and sat in the big chair; they sat in front of me, searching my face.

"I stayed behind last night, and went through these papers and drawings." I paused. "We have a 42 foot Schooner to build, have you seen the drawings?" I passed one to Bill and one to Mathew. They looked at each other.

Bill spoke, "I thought Mr O'Hara lost this one."

"What makes you say that, Bill?" I felt concerned. *Have I jumped the gun? God, I hope not.*

"I heard old Kingsley gave it to Riley's over the other side."

Mathew butted in. "They don't have the workforce or the expertise. They have never built anything over 25 feet, and all open craft. Nothing like this type of vessel."

"Tell me where er," I glanced at the paperwork, "Cove Manor is, and what is this Brigadier Kingsley like."

"A crusty old bastard. His daughter is a posh cow, wipe your feet, tradesman entrance, doff thy cap, kiss my arse."

"Thank you, Bill, for that. Give me some history."

"His missus is dead, lost his son-in-law in Flanders, Captain Woodgarth. So there's him, his daughter, and his granddaughter."

"And all the staff," added Mathew.

"How do I get there?" I inquired.

"Out of the yard, turn left, and keep walking a good two hours," replied Bill.

"A good seven or eight miles must be like," chipped in Mathew.

"I am going to leave you to carry on, I'll get back as soon as I can. When Mr O'Hara arrives tell him where I've gone."

They nodded and started work. I gathered up the paperwork. As I passed Mathew shouted, "We should have all the planking done today, boy'o."

I stopped. "Boy'o?"

Mathew went red.

"It's Welsh for laddy'o," said Bill.

"Well, laddy'o is a friendly phrase," said I.

The rain had stopped, but looked as if it could start again at any time. The path around the coast was well worn. The views did remind me of home, I started to feel guilty.

I thought for the first time, *I like it here I feel as if I have come home, as if this was meant to be. Mr O'Hara mentioned a proposition, what did he mean? Take over the running of the boatyard? I felt I have already started to treat it as if I had.*

What am I doing, going to see this Brigadier Kingsley without asking first? What if O'Hara has to sell, or at worse close down?

I had given Bill and Mathew hope and they responded positively. I have to bring back the contract, it's a good price, and the timber is in stock, hope to God it's paid for. Perhaps not as no deposit had been paid as far as I could see. Five months would complete the *LUCIE KINGSLEY*, and at that there would be a healthy profit.

I reached the gates to the drive, and could see the Manor House some quarter of a mile away, I should make it before it started to rain, Spoke too soon, I reached the main entrance before the heavens opened. I yanked the bell-pull, and waited. I heard footsteps; the door opened.

"Can I help you, sir ?" I assumed this must be the butler.

"Yes, thank you I'm here to see Brigadier Kingsley."

"Does he expect you?"

"No, But I need to speak with him urgently."

"May I ask the purpose of your visit?"

"Yes, I need to speak to him with reference to the *LUCIE KINGSLEY*."

"Who is it Morris?" A woman's voice asked.

"A gentleman wishes to speak to The Brigadier, Ms Kingsley."

The same voice replied. "I didn't hear a car."

191

I stepped past Morris and stood in the doorway. I removed my hat and faced an attractive lady in riding clothes.

"It's really started to downpour, Ms Kingsley, I don't think the horse would enjoy it," I informed this lady who I presumed to be Ms Kingsley, the daughter.

"Do I know you?" She asked.

"No, I am Kevin O'Keefe from O'Hara's Boatyard. I was hoping to speak to your father about the Schooner"

"You walked here?"

"Yes."

She smiled. "I am quite impressed Mr.O'Keefe, and you are right, Tony, would not enjoy the wet. Please follow me."

"Can I take your coat?" Morris held out his hand.

"Yes, thank you Morris. Tony?"

"The horse," winked Morris.

I followed in to a large room facing the sea. It felt strangely familiar. She left, I stood there looking at this fantastic view and noticed they had their own moorings. There was no boat to be seen. I looked around the room and spotted photos of a small Ketch of about 24 feet long.

"O'Keefe."

I turned to see Brigadier Kingsley, just as I imagined; tall, moustached, and straight.

"You walked here I am told?"

"Yes, just a stretch of the legs Mr Kingsley."

He looked me up and down. "Well, O'Keefe—" I cut him short.

"Mr Kingsley, my name is Kevin O'Keefe. Please call me Kevin or Mr O'Keefe." I thought I was going to be shown the door. his hands formed fists, I could see the muscles in his jaw twitch.

"You're not one of those Irish trouble makers are you?"

"No, in fact the opposite. I believe that man should live as close to the Ten Commandments as humanly possible, and that is it."

"Religion, eh Mr O'Keefe?" was all the Brigadier offered with emphasis on the Mr.

"Everyone goes to war with God on their side."

"Politics, Mr O'Keefe?"

"The only time a politician tells the truth is when he calls another a liar."

We looked at each other for a few seconds.

"Morris, MORRIS."

The man came running. "Yes, sir?"

"Set another sitting for lunch, Mr O'Keefe will be dining with us today. Tell Cook."

"Yes, sir."

Mr Kingsley chuckled. "You have a very old head on those young shoulders. I have a very good Irish whiskey, will you join me, Mr O'Keefe?"

"Thank you, Mr Kingsley."

"Please sit. So, this is about the yacht?"

"Yes, I wanted to confirm that O'Hara's still have the contract," I spoke firmly.

"Sorry to hear about old O'Hara, he hasn't looked that good for a while. I believe his brother is here to sort things out."

"Yes, I work for him in Carrickfergus."

"And you hope to take over here?"

"I would like that very much but, nothing has been mentioned."

"The fact that you and you alone came to see me shows me that it must be O'Hara's intention." He smiled, "Mr O'Hara does not know I am here, Mr Kingsley."

"We could have done with you."

I assumed he meant in the war.

"Anyway, I have given the contract to Riley's, however I don't think they would cope. Yes, Mr O'Keefe, the contract is yours, and I do mean yours. I am not sure what it is, but I have warmed to you, and I do not say that lightly."

"Thank you, Mr Kingsley."

"Daddy." In came his daughter. "I am told Mr O'Keefe here is staying for lunch. I'm so pleased. Mr O'Keefe do you ride?"

"Sorry, no," I admitted.

"Pity, Lunch in twenty minutes." She sashayed out of the room.

"You should learn," the Brigadier commented. "Mr O'Keefe, do you shoot?"

"Alas, no."

"Again, you should learn, I would be happy to show you."

"I might take you up on that, Mr Kingsley."

We both acknowledged with a nod of the head. I was relieved to say the least, the contract was mine and to find him not as stuffy as described by Bill and Mathew. In fact, I found him to be very lonely. He must miss his son-in-law terribly, and no grandsons, He was the type who would enjoy male company. He would enjoy teaching a grandson fishing, sailing, shooting, and riding. I enjoyed the Jameson's whiskey.

I was shown to my place at the dining room table. It would seat around twelve, we three sat at one end. The food was a cold meat selection, cooked veg with red wine, and pudding was home grown apple pie with cloves and cinnamon.

I heard Morris say to Ms Kingsley, "Shall I take lunch up to Miss Kingsley?"

She filled a plate with bits and pieces and Morris left. I said nothing. We talked about boats and sailing. His daughter was a keen sailor and knew her way around the rigging. I asked about the name, there was an exchange of glances.

"My granddaughter's name," came the reply and no further information.

"Does she enjoy sailing, Mr Kingsley?" I inquired.

"Biddy!" Mr Kingsley half shouted.

A woman of about sixty came in and started to clear the table.

"Well, Mr O'Keefe, it has been an unexpected pleasure to meet you and I look forward to being invited to view the build."

"Yes, for sure, Mr Kingsley. There will be items that will need to be sorted during the build, fittings, interior, and the like. Please tell your cook the apple pie was to die for."

"Oh, she will be so pleased. I will tell her," said Ms Kingsley. "Morris, show Mr O'Keefe out, will you please?"

"Yes, Ms Kingsley."

We walked to the door, when I heard a loud, "Take this away and bring me a fresh one. NOW!" It came from upstairs; the voice sounded young, very bitter and cruel. I looked at Morris.

"It's Miss Kingsley, Mr O'Keefe."

"What's the matter?"

"Not my place to say."

I so wanted to go and find out for myself. I felt indescribably drawn to the voice, as if I was being pulled up the stairs. Morris had the door open, I reluctantly walked through. and out into the day. It took me a few seconds to get my walking pace up to speed, my feet felt like divers' lead boots.

I got halfway to the gate, turned to look at the house, and was drawn to one window on the first floor. I stared, my trance was broken by, "Mr O'Keefe are you alright?" It was Ms Kingsley on horseback.

"Yes. thank you, this must be Tony," I remarked.

"Yes." She smiled. "Enjoy your walk back to Douglas, Mr O'Keefe." She kicked Tony's sides and galloped off.

I arrived back in the workshop around five o'clock. The boat was looking good and fully planked. Both Bill and Mathew stopped and looked expectantly at me.

"We have 42 foot schooner to build, so get this tiddlier finished," I said.

I think Mathew would have hugged me given the chance. Mr O'Hara was in the office. As I approached, he looked at me and smiled.

"Come in, Kev lad, come in. Close the door. Sit yourself down." His brow puckered as if to say, 'Where do I start'? "Right, first things first, the yard can be saved here, and I have just heard you have a Schooner to build." He hesitated, studying my face.

"YOU have a Schooner to build. Kev lad, you have done exactly as I hoped you would. Without any encouragement from me, you took over and started to run this boatyard as your own workshop. Securing a well-priced contract in the bargain. How do you feel?"

I could not stop grinning.

"I take it then, that this is what you want?"

"Yes, I suppose it must be, sorry Mr O'Hara. I have only now realised what will be involved. I must give you a letter for Nelly Auntie Kathryn to take back with you."

"So, I take it you won't be travelling back with me?" He looked concerned.

"I have too much to do here that can't wait. I have to get the one in the yard complete and out to its new owner. Sort out the office, paperwork, get the Schooner started—"

He stopped me. "I want you to go find somewhere quiet and really think this through. Think of what life you will be leaving behind, not to mention the people who care about you."

I knew exactly who he meant. "This is what I want, Mr O'Hara, this is my fate. I just know it, I feel it inside."

"Sleep on it, Kev lad, sleep on it. I'll lock up. I have things to do, see you at the house later."

As I walked out, I heard Mr O'Hara say, "Well, lads, there goes your new boss. What say you?"

I heard paused to hear their response.

"He'll do," Bill said.

I smiled and carried on walking. It was cold and damp, I felt numb as I sat down at the foreshore and looked out at the water. I thought of my Nelly. Tears rolled down my cheek. I knew I would never see her again.

This will break her heart, I thought. *You can't do it, you must go back and tell her to her face. If I do that, I know I will never come back here. What am I thinking? Why can't she join me here? Why have I just cut her off?*

My mind went back to the window at Cove Manor. What is it that is pulling me to the place? How can I just cut off the one person I have loved for all these years? Planned to marry, have children with, her parents, Auntie Kathryn, Jack, Jimmy, Pat, and Terry.

I shook my head. *I will write a letter, to Auntie, and enclose one for Nelly. I will ask them to give me a month to come back and collect my stuff and bring Nelly back with me. Perhaps Jack could bring us back, save money, as he fishes close to the Island.* I felt better, but was surprised at my first reaction. Not at all like me.

I wrote the letters, gave them to Mr O'Hara, then we both went to the Legs-O-Man to eat.

"Well, Mr O'Keefe," said the barman. "I believe congratulations are in order. Am I looking at the new Gaffa of O'Hara's Boatyard?"

He kept talking before I had time to answer.

"Bill's in the other bar, he told us all about it. A new yacht built for the Brigadier, Tonight's on the house."

I looked at Mr O'Hara. He simply raised his eyebrows and smiled.

"Thank you, barman, we will have a large whiskey."

"Call me Joe."

"Thank you, Joe."

"My pleasure, gents, it's good to hear business as usual. I know of two persons who are very relieved." He was referring Bill and Mathew.

We sat and ate.

"Kevin lad."

I got my full name.

"There are things I have to do. And things we both have to agree on." He paused. "I have to sell the house; this will pay for all the expenses and give the business a good bank balance. I have drawn up a contract for both of us to sign. You must read it, agree, and sign.

196

"I leave here at 2 p.m. tomorrow, I want it all to be done and dusted by then. I have had an offer for the house, so, I think you will have to find yourself accommodation soon. You probably have a few weeks to find somewhere. I think you will find I have been fair and probably a bit too generous. But, Kev lad, I trust you one hundred percent as I did your father. It pleases me to be able to do this for you, and I know Mrs O'Hara will stop bending my ear. We have no children as you know, and we have, well, never mind all that now." He slid a document across the table to me. "Read and sign, I'll say goodnight to you. See you in the morning."

That night I lay in bed, reading the contract. Basically, the yard was mine to run as I saw fit for as long as I wished. Ten percent of nett profit went to him, all the property, material, stock, etc would belong to him. It must be properly maintained. he had the right to visit once a month to see how things are going. No set wage as ninety percent of nett profit was mine.

I cannot believe my luck! I could have never dreamed this would happen. What a chance to be given, what an adventure. My God I feel so alive, I want to get started. I will make this a success. I may never sleep again.

I signed, put it on the nightstand, and tried to get some sleep. The next day I shook hands and watched him go onboard. I waved him goodbye.

My God, this is it! I went to the yard.

I sat behind the desk. That morning we had sat here and went through all the paperwork, it was now all filed. The bank statements showed a very healthy balance. We could finish the *LUCIE KINGSLEY* with our own money. But good business practice is a form of interim payments with the balance on completion or delivery. I set about writing a letter to the Brigadier.

As I finished the letter, I leaned back in the chair, my thoughts went to Nelly.

What will she think on reading my letter? I hope she writes back, that would be nice a letter from her to me.

I went to post the letter to the Brigadier but stopped to talk to Bill and Mathew.

"We need a lad in here to help, clean up, make tea, help on the tools, errands and the like. Do you know of anyone ?"

Mathew spoke. "Bill, how about Andy, your brother's boy?"

"I'll ask him," said Bill.

I could tell this pleased a large grin beamed across his face. him. I got to the Post Office and went to the counter.

"Mr O'Keefe, good day to you. How can I help you?" This was a very prim and proper lady of around 50-ish. She stood straight with hands clasped across her middle.

News travels fast, like back home. "I would like to post this letter please."

"My pleasure, Mr O'Keefe. I am Mrs Cottrell."

"Pleased to meet you, Mrs Cottrell."

"Will your wife be joining you?"

Here we go. "I have no wife, Mrs Cottrell, not here anyway. I am looking for accommodation. Perhaps you know of somewhere?"

Her face was a picture. I could see she was pleased to be helping me. "Well, there is Harbour Guest House, respectable and overlooking the harbour. Mrs O'Rorke, know her very well, she'll be in now if you wish to visit."

"Thank you, Mrs Cottrell. I'll find it. Good day." I left before she had time to say a word.

I would imagine, Mrs Cottrell and Mrs O'Rorke will have plenty to say to each other after my visit. I found Harbour Guest House. It stood alone and looked as it may have been part of the harbour at one time a custom house kind of thing. It was well kept and appeared clean. I knocked; the door opened. A woman filled the doorway.

"Oh, hello come on in."

"I am—"

"Mr O'Keefe, yes, I know. You'll be looking for accommodation now that Mr O'Hara's old house is sold."

My God! I thought, "Yes you are right, Mrs O'Rorke."

"Well, you are in luck, I have the best rooms in the house waiting just for yourself. I'll show you." She shuffled towards the steps and I followed.

Up the stairs and to the left, she held open the door.

"What do you think, Mr O'Keefe? You'll not find better in all of Douglas. Lovely view of the harbour and the sea. You have your own water closet and bath, there are two rooms as you can see plenty of space for entertaining, bedroom and parlour. I do breakfast from 7 a.m. to 9 a.m. and evening dinner 6 p.m. to 8 p.m. There'll be no smoking or drink in the house. Will you be staying tonight?"

It was very nice. "Yes, Mrs O'Rorke. I'll take it."

"Of course you will. Now, come down and I'll make us a nice cup of tea and you can tell me all about yourself."

"Thank you, Mrs O'Rorke, but I'll be getting back to the yard. See you tonight."

She looked most put-out. She would have my life story over a cup of tea, then tell it all to Mrs Cottrell.

Over breakfast I met Mrs O'Rorke's other guests. There was only one other permanent, a Miss Biddy Bell. An attractive woman of about 24, far too much make-up, but stylish. The rest were salesmen and crew. Miss Bell sat by herself in the window, no rings on her fingers, none at all.

I was the first to leave. Got to the yard by eight. By the office door stood a Matthew, Bill, and lad of about fifteen. He saw me and removed his cap.

"Good morning, men, and you must be Andy."

"Yes, sir." He bowed.

"Come on in, sit down. Has your uncle Bill told you what we need of you?"

"Er, yes, sir."

"And what would that be?"

"Sweep up, keep the shop tidy, help wherever I can, run errands and the like."

I looked at him with a stern face "You have missed the most important job, Andy."

His eyes widened in shock.

"Make the tea." I smiled and so did he. "When can you start?"

"Now, sir."

"And what is your first job?"

"Make the tea, sir."

"You are right."

"Yes, sir."

"Don't call me sir, in public or in front of customers. It's Mr O'Keefe, between ourselves it's Kevin. Mine strong with one sugar."

He ran up to Bill. The older man's weathered face broke into a broad grin and he slapped his nephew's shoulder. They stood for a while talking.

"Any time this morning will do," I shouted, "Bill, show him were everything is."

"Yes, Boss." Said Bill, I must admit I liked the Boss bit.

The little fishing boat was done and looking good, the paintwork and varnish excellent. As it happened, the new owner a Mr Fisher called in.

"Pleased to meet you, Mr Fisher." *Very apt,* I thought.

"And you, Mr O'Keefe. I heard the news and thought I must go see for my-self."

"Let me show you your boat. There she is."

"Very nice. Mr O'Keefe, I was worried with what's happened. I thought I might have never have gotten My Lady."

"I will ask Bill to paint her name on the bows and transom. When would you want us to deliver her?"

"That's ok, I'll send the wagon around as we live the other side of the island."

"When will that be, Mr Fisher?"

"Tomorrow."

"I'll have her ready. Now about the last payment. I have the paperwork in my office. Andy, a cup of tea please for Mr Fisher and myself. How do you take your tea, Mr Fisher?"

"Milk, two sugars, please."

We sat down in the office. "Er, Mr O'Keefe about the last payment. I would pay you at the end of the month."

This was four weeks away.

"Mr Fisher, I have just taken over this business, and I am running on a tight budget. I could do with the payment now before you take ownership, or we will keep *MY LADY* till the end of the month. You do understand, business is business." I handed him the invoice and shouted out to Bill. "Bill, please can you stop what you are doing and sign write MY LADY both bows and stern, in gold shadowed in black? Thank you."

"Yes, Boss," smiled Bill.

"I suppose you would like cash?" Mr Fisher said.

I nodded.

"I will be back shortly."

As he walked past his new boat I shouted to Mathew, "Put a second set of oars in *MY LADY*."

Mr Fisher and I exchanged nods of acceptance.

What a week, as all this happened in only one week. My Nelly should get her letter on Sunday, Auntie will give it to her then I should think.

I introduced myself to Mr Butler the Bank Manager, and he opened a private account in my name. I took out the men's wages and mine, ten shillings for the petty cash, and the rest of the cash into the boatyards account. I paid myself the same as I was getting back home. I put my rent as a business expense, yard running cost paid on invoice.

So far so good. I stayed at the yard most of the weekend, and spent time on the yard launch.

I gave the engine a full service, replaced the ropes, and took it for a chug up the coast. I found myself approaching the quay at Cove Manor. The house and grounds did look wonderful from seaward. I turned and went back.

Monday I called the three of them into the office first thing. Andy made the tea and played mother.

"Today, men, we start the *LUCIE KINGSLEY*, we have got to do the best job possible. The build is a high specification, teak is expensive so no mistakes. The Brigadier has many rich contacts, he could give this yard a lot of good paying work. I have told him four months." *Though in reality I told him six months.*

They looked uncertainly at each other.

"The four of us should do this with no problem," I added. "We must work closely together, and make sure we are not running low on any material, fixings, or fittings. We cannot afford to lose any time due to waiting for deliveries. I need to know as soon as a problem is spotted so I can deal with it there and then. And to finish, there will be a good bonus for you on completion."

"Bonus?" Mathew said. "I've never had a bonus before."

"Nor me," Bill commented.

"Well, what are we waiting for?" I spoke with eyes wide.

It was good to see Bill take charge. He and Mathew worked with renewed vigour. Andy was proving a good hand. I took it upon myself to get a telephone installed. This seemed to be the way forward.

Second week I was late in it was on purpose, I peered around the door; they were at work, the keel was laid.

I walked in. "Good morning."

"Good morning, Boss."

I went into the office, there was a package on the desk. I picked it up, it was quite heavy and softish. I opened it, it looked and smelt like fruit cake. Mathew came up to me looking a bit sheepish, but smiling, "It's Bara-Breath, Welsh it is. The wife, Gladys that is, thought you might like it, it's made with tea."

Tea? I thought. "Let's try it with tea. Andy, tea if you please, we can drink and work." There was enough for all. "Mathew tell your Gladys she can do this again anytime she pleases. That was good."

"It will keep you anchored to the floor in a wind." Smiled Bill. "A diver won't need his lead boots—"

"Thank you, Bill." It was all in good humour. "Right, back to work."

"Don't think I can move taffy."

"That's enough, Bill." We all laughed. Mathew looked pleased. The atmosphere felt good.

Bill, Mathew and I worked really well together, they were good, as was I. I showed Andy how to use the steamer. He was bright and picked it up quickly. One hour for every square inch. of hardwood. This became his job.

The phone was installed. I ordered new letter heading and sent a complement slip to all my contacts and suppliers. I sat staring at the phone for a while. I jumped when it rang. I hesitated.

"Hello, O'Hara's Boatyard. Mr O'Keefe speaking."

"It's Brigadier Kingsley here. Are you in all day?"

"Yes, Mr Kingsley."

"Good, I will be with you within the hour. Trust I will have something to look at."

"Indeed, Mr Kingsley."

He rang off. I was working when I heard a car outside and a honk of the horn. *I'm not going out, he can come in,* I thought.

In he came. "Mr O'Keefe, my daughter would like to have a word."

"Right." I went to the car. She was in the driving seat of the Lanchester.

"Hello again, Mr O'Keefe."

"Ms Kingsley." I nodded.

"I am worried about the state of our Quay, the last boat was only 24 feet. I'm concerned it may need up-grading somewhat. Would you kindly come and give advice as to what you think will be required?"

"Yes. I would be pleased to, and thank you for thinking of me for the job."

She smiled. The Brigadier came out of the office.

"Looking good Mr O'Keefe? Are we on target?"

"Indeed we are."

"Good, has my daughter spoken to you?"

"Yes, Father, Mr O'Keefe has agreed to help."

"Good, hop in, Mr O'Keefe, no time like the present."

"I must tell the men what I am doing. Just a second. Bill, I am going up to Cove Manor. If you need me that's where I am. The number is in the directory."

We arrived at Cove Manor.

"You drive well, Ms Kingsley."

"Too damn fast if you ask me," the Brigadier grumbled. "Have us all killed."

Chapter 13

We walked around and down to the Quay. I stood on the walkway; the seabed was only five to six feet.

"It's low water in about an hour, Mr O'Keefe," said Ms Kingsley.

"So, it must be down to three feet. The *LUCIE KINGSLEY* will need six feet and should be floating all the time. So, another two or eight feet in total and this woodwork will need a lot of up-grading. In fact Ms Kingsley, I would recommend a complete new build."

"I thought as much. Mr' O'Keefe, would you be willing to take on the work? I mean oversee the construction."

"Yes, I will draw the new Quay and give you costing."

"Lovely. Will you please join us at the house for some tea before I drive you back?"

"Ms Kingsley, I will walk."

"I insist, Mr O'Keefe."

"Well, thank you, I accept."

"All sorted, Mr O'Keefe?"

"Yes, Mr Kingsley."

"Good."

By now we'd reached the house and found our way to the lounge. Biddy came in with the tea and scones.

"What? No apple pie?" I exclaimed.

Ms Kingsley's face stiffened, I sensed she thought me to familiar. "Biddy, tell Cook to get a slice of apple pie for Mr O'Keefe."

"No, please I was only joking."

"Apple pie please, Biddy." Ms Kingsley played mother.

A few seconds later Biddy returned. "Ma'am, Cook wants to know hot or cold."

I spoke first. "Cold will be fine, thank you."

After a few minutes Cook brought the apple pie herself. "Sorry ma'am, Biddy was busy." She was beaming, "It's Mr O'Keefe who thinks your apple pie is to die for," Ms Kingsley spoke with a note of intolerance.

"I have warmed it and put custard and cream on the tray," smiled Cook.

"My God, I don't get this kind of service in my own house," the Brigadier grumbled playfully.

I sat and pretended to dither between custard or cream. Cook waited to see which one I went for. Custard. I poured the hot golden liquid over the flaky crust.

"Thank you, Cook." The Brigadier rolled his eyes to the ceiling and gave a few tuts. "Charm the knickers off a nun," he said to himself.

"Daddy, what did you just say?"

"Nothing, darling, nothing."

My mind went right back the day the Titanic sailed by. I am on Da's shoulders asked him what do you know, He answered, *"Nothing, son nothing."*

I had been accepted by this very wealthy people, and felt at ease. Then, that same voice I had heard before from up the stairs.

"I want to come down, can anyone hear me? HELLO."

They looked at each other in shock.

"That's a first." The Brigadier seemed embarrassed. "She, my granddaughter, normally won't come down if there are visitors in the house. Morris," he shouted, "give me a hand, will you?"

"Can I help?" I asked.

The Brigadier was visibly shaken. I didn't wait for an answer, walked out into the hall, stood at the bottom of the stairwell. I looked up. It was all in slow motion; on the landing was a vision of loveliness in a wheelchair. I felt the pain in my lower legs, her beautiful face was hard and stern. I was being pulled up the stairs towards her.

Our eyes never left each other. After what seemed like an age I reached the landing, our eyes still locked. She was in my head and I in hers. I took hold one side and Morris the other. I don't remember doing it, we were at the bottom of the stairway. Everyone was silent. I glanced at Ms Kingsley, tears were rolling down her cheek. The Brigadier's eyes were wet. He spoke with a mild tremor, "Mr O'Keefe, this is my granddaughter Lucie."

"I meet you at last, Lucie," I spoke, quietly.

Lucie said nothing and cast her eyes down to the floor.

"My granddaughter had—"

I interrupted. "A riding accident involving a carriage, New Year's Day a few years ago."

"You knew?" Ms Kingsley gasped.

"Yes, Ms Kingsley, I have always known."

"I don't understand, Mr O'Keefe," the Brigadier stammered.

"Sorry, I'm not making any sense, please forgive me. It must be the apple pie." I smiled, yet no one else did.

I took hold and pushed Lucie into the front room and up to the bay window overlooking the Quay. No one followed. I stood looking out the window as did Lucie. No words were spoken, it didn't seem necessary.

After a few moments in came her mother. "Are you alright, darling?" She looked puzzled. No answer.

"I must be getting back to town. Ms Kingsley, is that offer of a lift still on?" I asked.

"Yes, of course." Her voice held a note of inconvenience. She knelt next to Lucie. "I won't be long, darling, I'll just take Mr O'Keefe into town, anything you need from there?"

Lucie continued to look out to sea. Again, no answer.

I bent down and whispered in her ear, "You know don't you?"

She raised her hand and briefly touched my hand. Ms Kingsley, stood up sharply, her face was full of emotion, and confusion, her eyes searching mine. "I don't understand. What is going on, Mr O'Keefe?"

"Please, Ms Kingsley, just give it time. Don't ask me now, but I can assure you things will only get better. Can we leave?"

Ms Kingsley turned to leave the room. Morris was coming our way, but paused on the threshold.

"Till we meet again 'Lucie No Legs'," I said.

There was a gasp from Morris. Her mother exploded.

"How dare you!" She screamed, "How could you say such a horrible thing?" She rushed to Lucie. "Oh, darling."

"Ms Kingsley, Lucie is not offended," I stated.

Lucie touched her mother's hand with hers. The Brigadier rushed in.

"What on God's earth is going on?" He roared.

Ms Kingsley, still kneeling holding her daughter's hand could only say, "I really don't know, Father. I really don't know."

"Mr O'Keefe, you seem to have made things happen in this house we never thought," his voice trembled. "We have wished and prayed, but never thought would ever happen, I thank you. Now, get yourself together, girl, and take Mr O'Keefe back to town. I think we have had enough excitement for one day."

We drove back, in silence, Ms Kingsley was close to tears most of the way. She from time to time glanced across to me with a confusion expression. We stopped just before the yard gates.

"Mr O'Keefe, my mind is about to explode, I have so many questions. My daughter since the accident has never come down from her room when there are visitors in the house, and has never held my hand since the accident. I still don't understand how you knew." Her lip started to go and the tears flowed.

"And most of all no one but Morris has ever been allowed to push her. Who are you? I'm frightened, but so pleased. I don't know what to think, and when you called her that horrible name... What were you thinking?"

"You mean 'Lucie No Legs'?"

If looks could kill, I would be dead.

"Ms Kingsley this will become a pet-name that all the family, including Lucie, will enjoy. You must believe me."

She studied me for a moment. "I will hold you to that, Mr O'Keefe. Good day to you."

I got out and she drove off.

Lucie No Legs, were in God's name did that come from? I shook my head. But, I knew that this was all meant to be, why I was here.

Nan's words came back, *"She won't be what you would expect, she is not from these parts. And when you win her heart, you will have everything."*

My heart sank. *Nelly, what am I going to do? I now know who it is I am to spend the rest of my life with.* I would always love Nelly, but no longer in the same way.

I locked up, did the paperwork for the day, made a note about the new Quay at Cove Manor, and walked back to Mrs O'Rorke's. I arrived the same time as Miss Biddy Bell.

"Good evening, Miss Bell."

She scrutinised me.

"Kevin O'Keefe, I moved in the other day."

"Oh, yes, hello." She strode up to her room.

Mrs O'Rorke was standing at the bottom of the stairs, waiting to hear her door shut. "No better than she should be that one. So far up herself it's a wonder she can walk. We are make do, she's a buy new."

"Mrs O'Rorke!" I exclaimed.

"Oh, I do beg your pardon, Mr O'Keefe, but she wouldn't give you a sniff of an oily rag that one. You go on in, it's Irish stew with my own dumpling and lovely if I say so myself and nice crusty bread."

I went in and sat down, nodded to the others. In she came.

"Here we are, Mr O'Keefe, what won't fatten will fill, stick to your ribs that will. Just shout if you want more."

It was delicious. Afterwards I went up to my room, had a good wash, and laid on the bed with the days goings on running through my mind.

What a day.

Morning came and I went to see Barry at the stables. "Good morning, Barry."

"And the same to you, Mr O'Keefe. To what do I owe the pleasure?"

"I am going to need a pony and trap now and then, have you got such a thing? Or know where I could hire one?"

"Just a two-seater you're after then?"

"Yes, I suppose so."

"Well, Mr O'Keefe, your guardian angel must have sobered up as I have only yesterday bought old Ma Clancy's. It's around the back."

I followed him through the rear door.

"It will need a day or two, I could have it ready for Friday. Have you handled a horse and trap before?" Barry inquired.

"Er, no."

"Right, I have a nice quiet horse for you. She's an old Welsh-Cob and has pulled before. But don't push her too much, she'll walk all day or trot most of the day. But her galloping days are over."

"Sounds about right for me, Barry, how much?" I asked.

"I've never hired before, let me have a think. See you Friday."

I went back to the yard, and joined the others. The *LUCIE KINGSLEY* was taking shape.

"Bill, were is that off-cut of oak from the stem-post?" I asked.

He pointed. I took it in to the office and propped it next to the door. It was about four feet. long and four inches by four inches. square. I went back to work.

I do enjoy working with wood. The smell, the feel and to see a boat start to take shape by the hands of man. A skill handed down, a sense of pride in creating something that others will use and enjoy. And the day of the launch, no other feeling like it.

Friday arrived. I opened up, shortly after 7:20 a.m. in came the lads. A routine had been established; Andy made the tea, and drank it as we worked. I had post from yesterday not yet opened, I told the lads so, and that I will join them as soon as I have sorted things.

There were letters from suppliers, invoices, people who would wish to become suppliers, and an enquiry for a new build a 28 foot motor fishing boat, an inquiry as to whether I would be interested in repair work on a eighteen foot Gaff. And then I spotted it and hesitated. I knew it was a letter from Nelly. I held it for a second or two, then opened it.

'My Darling Kevin,

I hope you are keeping well and looking after yourself. I think of you every day, I miss you so much. I'm worried you may never come back. Mr O'Hara has told me all about it, and I understand it is a wonderful opportunity for you, and I'm sure you will make a success of the yard. But I love you so much. I would come to you, alas I am needed at home, and Mammy's cough is getting worse.

Please write me soon, darling. I need to hear you call me sweetheart, again. You must have saved up dozens for me.

Your loving Nelly. X'

I sat back in the chair, and recalled how little I had thought of her over the last few weeks. *I can't let her go, yet I must. I will have to tell her about Lucie. I* jumped as the phone rang. *Will I ever get used to it?*

"Hello, O'Hara's Boatyard." That's as far as I got.

"Kev lad, Sean O'Hara here. I see your spending our money."

"Hello, Mr' O'Hara, I don't understand."

"The telephone, Kev lad, the telephone."

"Oh, I see. It's the way forward Mr O'Hara, I will be with you around 10 a.m. on Monday. I have people to see papers to sign and whatnot. I take it all is well in your world."

"Yes, Mr O'Hara, we are three weeks into the Schooner. It's starting to take shape."

"Good, look forward to seeing it. The house is sold, so, could you book me into the Leg-O-Man for two nights."

"Yes, of course." I was going to ask about Nelly but…

"Bye for now, see you Monday." He was gone.

I could ring him back, but decided against it. I went out into the workshop.

"Mr O'Hara is paying us a visit on Monday for a few days. I'll go and book him in at the Legs-O-Man. Consider it a chance for you, Andy, to meet the owner. He might not like you, he's very fussy about how he takes his tea. Back home he sacked a man for not leaving the tea to brew long enough."

Andy nervously twisted his cap in his hands.

"He's pulling your leg, lad," laughed Bill.

"By the way, Mathew, is there a chance of that wonderful Bara-Brith? I'm sure Mr O'Hara would love to try some."

Mathew beamed. "I'm sure of it like. I'll get my Gladys to make some Sunday night ready for the morning."

"Can she make a big bit?" queried Bill. "We need ballast for the schooner."

"Very funny, Bill Makem, your bit will have rat poison in it, you can count on it," Mathew declared.

I made the reservation and walked down to the stables.

"Hello, Kevin, it's all ready," Barry met him in front of a stall. "Come with me."

I followed him.

"What do you think?"

"It looks great."

"Aye. I have greased the wheels, repaired the tear in the seat and new reigns, spit and polish and all. Now when do you want it? Sunday?"

I nodded. *This will be a new experience.*

"That's just grand, I'll have Nelly in the shafts ready for say ten o'clock."

I laughed.

"What's so funny?" Barry demanded.

"Nothing, it' all good, see you Sunday."

"Don't you worry none, I will give you a few tips before I send you off."

"I will welcome that Barry" *A horse called Nelly*. I shook my head in disbelief.

The day ended and I stayed behind to cost the new Quay at Cove Manor. The material and design was easy to do and price, but I needed help with the labour. *I'll ask Bill in the morning if he knows any labourers that could do such work.*

I looked again at the piece of oak leaning against the wall. I started to sketch the idea I had in my mind: Wooden legs for Lucie. I can shape and I have an idea for hinging the foot and toes, but how do I attach to her leg?

I left around 8 p.m. and called in the Leg-O-Man for a drink. I just felt like one. I ordered a whiskey and a little tap water and left it for a few minutes before sipping. The barman walked through to the public bar. I heard laughter yet thought nothing of it. In came a man I had seen around the harbour, thick set and about thirty. He came up to me as if he was going to whisper in my ear.

"Well, Mr O'Keefe, I hear you have been up to Cove Manor. Trying to get your LEGS under the table."

The room fell silent.

"Now, Patrick," said the barman.

"I hear the granddaughter has a nick-name, Lucie No Legs. Ha, ha! My uncle is Morris, he told me."

My blood ran cold, my hands made fists, I squared up to him. "If you want your uncle to lose his job, say that again."

"If he does get sacked, I'll know who told the Brigadier, won't I?"

"I will ask you once, Patrick, that was a private conversation and I want you to promise me you will never mention it again."

"Bugger off. Who do you think you are?" He laughed.

"Promise me, Patrick."

"Patrick," warned the barman, "you are out of order. Back off, or you are barred."

"Taken his side now are you?" Patrick moved away and drew his hand back.

It happened, the rest mist shrouded me like a cloud and before I knew it, I had him by the throat. He was big, but went down on his knees, gasping for breath. I came to, and let go. The red mist cleared. He was sat on the floor, gasping and trying to speak. It was the closest he had ever come to death and he knew it. The room was still, everyone stared at me in complete shock.

"Let me apologise to you all. I am sorry you had to see that. But I was only protecting the good name of the lady."

I finished my drink and left. I was shaking, Jack's words came flooding back, *"You will kill someone one day if you don't learn to control it."*

I did. I let go, didn't I? I thought. That's a start, yet I don't remember starting it.

I got back to Harbour House around 8:30 p.m. I walked in. Mrs O'Rorke stood as if she had been waiting for me.

"Good evening, Mr O'Keefe."

"Good evening, Mrs O'Rorke."

"Have you eaten?"

"Er, no as it happens."

"Go in, sit yourself down. I have one dinner left I've bin saving for you." She appeared with a plate full. "Now get yourself on the outside of that, and don't for one minute think you will get this sort of service again. Eight o'clock I finish, I won't say it again now, I don't boil me cabbages twice, you know."

"Thank you, Mrs O'Rorke."

I had just finished when in came Miss Biddy Bell, dressed in red and black.

"Oh, er, I'm looking for Mrs.ORorke."

"I think see is in the kitchen."

"Thank you." She hesitated then went to find the woman.

I noticed that her skirt of red had a broad black band at the waist. I heard her coming back.

"Miss Bell," I called.

"Yes?" She stopped at the bottom of the stairs.

"I—" I pondered how to say this. "I noticed from your skirt."

She looked slightly alarmed.

"The black band at the waist, is it elastic?"

"Why do you want to know?"

"I have an idea I am working on, and I am looking for that sort of thing."

"Yes it is." She put her long elegant fingers in it and pulled it out a bit to prove it. "It's the latest thing in fashion." She gave a smile that said, *'You have no chance',* and off she went.

"Miss Bell."

She stopped and from my chair I heard her give an annoyed sigh. "YES?"

"Where would I buy some?"

"Try the dress makers around the corner," she called over her shoulder.

Mrs O'Rorke stood there with her hands on her hips. "Thinks she's the whole cheese when she's only the smell."

"Mrs O'Rorke. where do you get these from?" I chuckled.

"And you're not as green as your cabbage looking. I have plenty more where that came from."

"I bet you have, Mrs O'Rorke."

We both laughed. The day started as it usually does, I mentioned to Bill about the new Quay at Cove Manor. He knew lads who do that sort of work for cash in hand.

"Ask them to come and see me please, Bill, as soon as possible."

"Yes, Boss."

Sunday morning came. I was quite excited at the thought of a day out with pony and trap. Mrs O'Rorke had packed me some lunch and a bottle of beer. I walked round to the stables. Outside was Nelly and the trap, I stood and looked, out came Barry.

"All ready for the gentleman, but I hear not so much of the gentle."

"You heard?"

"Hard not to," said Barry. "You frightened Patrick, he thought he was going to die."

"Is he okay?" I nervously inquired.

"He'll be fine, Patrick is, shall we say, a bit slow. If you get my drift."

"I understand," I said. "Now, Mr Murry, what do I do?"

"First, give Nelly this apple, break it in half and give her half at a time. Hold your hand flat, or you may lose a finger or two. I think she likes you, right get on. Now hold the reins like this with this bit between your fingers like so. Good. Relax, relax. This has a hand brake over the wheel see?"

"Yes, got it." I nodded.

"I have put some feed in the sack there, and Nelly will need water. Ready?"

"I think so." I sighed.

"You'll be fine. Brake off, walk-on, Nelly."

The trap jerked forward.

"Nelly stop," shouted Barry. "Pull the reins to stop and left to go left and right to go right."

"Okay," said I. "Nelly walk-on." The horse did as instructed.

I soon got the idea, and rested in the knowledge that no way was Nelly going to gallop away. Nelly, why Nelly? It's my Guardian Angel having a bit of fun, for sure it is.

For some reason I chose south, this road would take me past Cove Manor. The trip was great, time to see and view the coast and sea. A few boats out there, no pleasure craft, all fishing boats and a few white horses must be blowing four to five. Then I saw it. I had never seen a full square-rigged ship before.

It must be one of those tea-clippers, the last of a fantastic breed of man. If I had been born thirty years hence, that would be me. What a life, what an adventure.

It's all steam now. She must have doing twelve to fifteen knots with a following wind. I watched for a while as she passed, probably on her way to Liverpool with wool and such. I was about a mile from Cove Manor gates when I saw a horse and rider.

"Hello, good morning, Ms Kingsley."

"Good morning, Mr O'Keefe, are you calling on us?"

"Erm."

"Please do, I will follow you back." She rode on.

I arrived at the gates and turned in, just as she galloping passed. I was ready for Nelly to do something, but no. Ms Kingsley stopped and dismounted as I arrived. A new stable boy hurried out to collect the animals.

"William, take care of the horses, make sure they are fed and watered. Please, Mr O'Keefe, do come in."

"What happened to Tom?" I asked.

"William is his helper"

I entered the hallway and heard a bit of a commotion from upstairs.

"I am still a bit confused about the other day, Mr O'Keefe." Her face stern.

"There is nothing to fear, Ms Kingsley."

"I certainly hope so, Mr O'Keefe."

Lucie appeared at the top of the stair. Morris held the wheel chair. He looked at me then down. He knew his whole way of life was in my hands. I slowly climbed the stairs, until I reached the top. I looked him square in the eyes, he lowered his head in reconision.

"Will you take the left? I will take the right," I instructed.

"Yes, sir, of course, sir." He looked relieved.

"Just before we start, Morris, I think payment is due."

He frowned, puzzled.

"I wonder if Miss Kingsley here could perhaps give us a smile as payment." I stepped down so I was face to face with Lucie. She stared straight ahead, her mother stood at the bottom of the stairs with a face like stone.

"Morris, perhaps a smile might crack her," I softened my voice so only she would hear, "lovely face."

She glanced at me, I saw a tear in her eye.

"Well?" I said.

She gave a smile, but it was ever so quick.

"Sorry, Miss, I blinked, I must have missed it."

"You won't get another."

I got close. "Oh yes I will. Right, Morris, after three."

"What after three?" Questioned Morris.

"1-2-3 and we throw Miss Kingsley down the stairs."

Lucie grabbed the arms of the chair. "You are insufferable and arrogant!" She managed to say through gritted teeth.

"1-2-3."

Lucie screamed, but in laughter. Morris and I carried her down to the hallway. Ms Kingsley had tears in her eyes with a look of total bewilderment.

"I'll take over now, Morris, thank you." I wheeled Lucie into the drawing room with those wonderful views over the water. The Brigadier was red faced eyes blotchy.

"It's." He cleared his throat. "Good to see you, Mr O'Keefe. And you, too, Lucie. I'll see if I can get us some tea." He left.

I knelt down and looked Lucie in the face. "Lucie, these good people love you so much. It was not their fault, they deserve better from you. Imagine how they must feel seeing you so unhappy, it's making their lives very hard, your mother more so. You are her little girl, and she feels so useless. It's slowly killing her seeing you like this."

Lucie glared at me. "Who do you think you are? You are not the one sitting in this bloody chair. This is it for the rest of my life! Who the bloody hell do you think you are?"

"Lucie, you know who I am. I held her hands. I am the one for you and you are the one for me. We knew that from the very first time our eyes met. I felt your pain on that New Years. I had no idea what had happened until we met."

"I don't believe you; how could any man want this for the rest of his life?"

"Lucie, listen to me, you must trust me with all your heart. You must believe me when I tell you, you will walk again."

"How dare you say such a thing! You, you must be evil!"

"I am the father of your unborn children, I will be with you forever."

Her gaze turned cold as ice said. "You are mad, get out of my sight."

"Show me your thumbs," I commanded.

"What?"

"Show me your thumbs."

"You are mad." Lucie straightened her thumbs.

"I knew it!" I exclaimed. "Stubborn, my God, so stubborn, so single minded."

"What? So you're a fortune teller now are you? Unbelievable."

The room fell silent. In came the Brigadier followed by Ms Kingsley, then Biddy with the tea, lastly Cook with the apple pie. They must have been waiting outside.

"Mummy, this—man is, is, as mad as a box of frogs! And WHAT is so special about this apple pie? I want to try some… please."

The Brigadier was shaking, he was holding back the tears. Stiff upper lip and all that. Ms Kingsley was laughing and crying at the same time. Biddy ran out, Cook dished out the apple pie. Ms Kingsley went to Lucie."

"I'm so sorry, Mummy, but I feel so unhappy and alone, I keep thinking I will never ride again or sail. I'm only sixteen I can't bear the thought of my whole life like this. I wish sometimes I was dead."

"Oh, darling!" They hugged and cried.

"Well, Mr O'Keefe you have done it again. I don't know how or why, but again I thank you. Today is the most we have ever got from Lucie since that terrible day. I think we should leave them alone."

"Yes, Mr Kingsley, I will be going."

We walked outside and I got on the trap.

"Nelly, walk-on." As we reached the gates, I looked back. The Brigadier was still standing there, looking my way.

"Everything okay for you, Mr O'Keefe?" Barry asked.

"Yes, thanks. I enjoyed it. What's it like to ride a horse?" I hopped out.

"My advice, stick to the trap."

"You're probably right. Thanks again."

Monday morning, I'm down at the pier.

"Good day to you, Kev lad."

"Hello Mr O'Hara, good trip?"

"Yes, looks like a great day."

We walked to the Inn. I got Mr O'Hara booked in and settled.

"What do you want to do first?" I inquired.

"I have to sign a few papers at 3 p.m. this afternoon. Other than that, I'm all yours."

"I think the yard first, then lunch?"

"Lead on, Kev lad, lead on."

"Just a thought, Mr O'Hara, would you like a ride out of town this evening? I hear there is a nice pub about six miles out, we could eat."

"Sounds good to me."

"I'll just go and arrange it. If you want to make your way over to the yard, I'll catch you up." I hurried to get Nelly and the trap. "Barry?"

"Yes, sir."

"Can I have the trap this evening?"

"What time?"

"Say—five?"

Barry nodded, "See you then."

I found Mr O'Hara in the office, going through the banking. I grabbed Andy.

"Tea for myself and Mr' O'Hara, he has milk and three sugars."

"Yes, Boss."

I walked into the office and sat in silence. Andy came in with the tea and the Bara-Brith on a plate and on a tray.

"Thank you, Andy." *Plate and tray?* "Mr O'Hara this is Andy, a valuable member of the team."

Mr O'Hara looked up. "Hello, Andy, thank you for the tea."

Andy smiled at me and left. After a few minutes Mathew hovered around the office door.

"Mr O'Hara," I spoke aloud, "please try the Bara-Brith."

He looked up. "Try the what?"

I handed him a slice.

"What's this?"

"It's Bara-Brith a speciality of Mrs Evans."

Mathew popped his head around the door. "It's Welsh for speckled bread, Mr O'Hara."

He took a bite. "Rather spicy. That's really nice, goes well with a cup of tea."

"It's made with tea," said Mathew.

"Thank you, Mathew," I said.

"My wife Gladys with be tickled pink." He went back to work, I heard him say to Bill, "He likes it."

Bill muttered something and they laughed.

"Well, Kev lad, shut the door."

I did.

"I see you are on top of the finances, that's very important. I see what you have done with the cash from Mr Fisher, that's good and fine. And you have half payment from Brigadier Kingsley, with a monthly interim payment, final payment on delivery after sea trials. How you got the him to agree to that… Well, Kev lad, I am pleased in the way you handled yourself and the yard." He studied me, I could see a glimmer of pride in his eyes. I think he would have said as much, but perhaps he had no need to.

We walked around the place. The yard did look good, clean tidy and the *LUCIE KINGSLEY* was taking shape. I was pleased with the way things had progressed.

"Now, Kev lad, if you don't mind, I have a dinner appointment with the bank manager, and as I mentioned have to sign papers at 3 p.m. So, I will catch you at five." He walked off.

I joined the others on the *LUCIE KINGSLEY*. We had started the planking, four inches by one inch finished size in best Larch. Andy had several lengths in the steamer, they were clamped in position and left to set. She was going to be a real eye catcher. I will have to think about some form of publicity on the launch. The yard could take up to fifty feet and the launch trolley, winch and tracks, max thirty tonnes.

I left the yard at 4:15 p.m., back to Mrs O'Rorkes, get cleaned up then pick up the trap at five. I was walking back when I spotted Mr' O'Hara striding towards the yard, I caught him up.

"I'll just get the trap and see you back at the yard."

He nodded.

"Hello," Barry greeted me, "All ready for you."

"Thank you, Barry, should be back around 10-ish."

"That's fine, just knock on the door."

I got myself sorted, "Nelly walk-on." I couldn't help but think of my Nelly.

Chapter 14

We set off for the village of Braddan some six miles outside town and the Horse and Plough. The evening was warm and sunny. We spoke about the views, the houses and farms we passed, and waved at folks along the way. After a while we fell into an awkward silence. I sensed he wanted to talk about Nelly, or was it me feeling guilty?

The silence was broken when I spoke, "Nelly, trot-on." I thought I would get in first. "Have you seen Nelly Kelly?"

"Yes Kev lad, she is very concerned," My heart sank, "about her mother the feeling is it's Pneumonia, not good at all."

"I am sorry to hear that, I did notice she had a bad cough a while back." I remembered the time I was with Nelly and I got that picture and feeling of her mother in pain.

"If she goes, it will leave only Mr Kelly and Nelly to run that farm, and that size farm needs around four to run correctly. I don't know if they can afford it, they may have to sell land or the farm as a whole." He looked at me, I knew what he was thinking, "Mr O'Hara, my life is now here I know that. And, my feelings for Nelly—"

He cut me short. "Nelly and you are none of my business. However, I know you will do the right thing." We both knew what that meant.

We arrived at the Horse and Plough in good time, about just gone seven. The lad took Nelly around the back.

"My treat Mr O'Hara, what would you like?"

"Well, that's very kind of you Kev lad."

"It's the least I can do as a thank you for giving me this opportunity to prove myself. I hope I have done you proud."

He cleared his throat, I sensed he had become quite emotional.

"A bottle of your finest red wine, landlord, and I will have the bass," I said.

"And make that two bass, landlord."

We took our seats and toasted to the future of O'Hara's Boatyard and good health to each other. The bass was delicious as was the wine. We had been there for around an hour, just finishing the bass and looking for a pudding when I heard a car and looked out the window. It was the Lanchester driven by the Brigadier. The lady getting out was a complete surprise, none other than Miss Biddy Bell. This was again another instance of a moment's thought is an hour in words.

Why should I think there was anything underhand? His wife was dead, but he must be forty years older. Was she a gold digger?

They strolled in and sat in a dark corner.

So, they don't want to be seen? Well, that's not good.

The barman brought them drinks. They must be known to the staff to bring drinks without being told. I went up to the bar.

"Can we have the Spotted Dick please? And may I settle the bill now?"

That done, I re-joined Mr O'Hara. We finished our food and wine.

There is no way we can leave without them seeing us. Sod it, it's not my problem. I have settled the bill. "I think we should be heading back," I suggested.

"A brandy, Kev lad, my treat. Landlord!" He shouted. "Two large brandies, if you please."

This prompted the Brigadier to look in our direction. We stared at each other, his face stern. Miss Bell offered a small smile. I sat back, the brandies arrived in a warmed glass. Oh, it did taste good.

What's done is done, what will be will be.

We left and headed back to Douglas. Mr O'Hara was totally oblivious of what had just transpired, I dropped Mr O'Hara at the inn and made my way back to the stables. Barry must have heard me and came out to greet me.

"All good?" He asked.

"Yes, thank you. Er, could I have a better horse next time?"

Barry covered Nelly's ears. "SHHHH, our Nelly has feelings, too."

We both laughed.

"I do have an ex-race horse."

I was a bit taken-a-back.

"Only joking, I do have another trap pony if you feel you're up to the challenge. But she does tend to shy a bit and is a wee nervous. And here I thought you and our Nelly were getting on so well."

"Okay, okay, Nelly will be just fine."

"Good man, good man."

"Good night, Barry."

"And the same to yourself, Mr O'Keefe."

I walked back to Mrs O'Rorkes. It was lovely night, so I decided to go to the harbour only a few yards from the house. I gazed out at the sea, the harbour lights twinkled like stars, the buoyage lights flashing their position. The ferry was lit up, the cleaners at work.

I thought back to my childhood days back in Carrickfergus when I would do the same as I am now. I became very emotional, I felt eyes filling with tears, but what for? Homesick? No, Nelly? Yes, I did miss her. What the hell am I to do? I miss Nelly and the fun and closeness, the things we had done.

My thoughts went back to the time on the boat and the time in the hay. After all I have known her practically all my life, I do believe I really loved her, and she me. All the memories we shared, yet we were so young.

If I had stayed in Carrickfergus, we would have surely got married and had lots of children and that was that. Am I fooling myself thinking that Lucie was the one? Okay, I do get on with her and her family, and there is a mental bond between us like me Ma and Da. And Nan did say she would not be what I would expect, she lost her lower legs and is in a wheelchair.

But this doesn't matter as I will get her walking again, I know I will. I am a tradesman, I don't own any property or business. What have I got to offer the Brigadier and her mother? I'm sure they would thank me for getting Lucie walking, however would a big thank you be all I got? And if so, would Lucie come with me and forsake all she has? I really don't know. I must accept my responsibility and be a man and tell Nelly how I feel.

I turned to walk back, yet stopped in my tracks, The Brigadier's Lanchester pulled up a little way from the front door, Miss Bell alighted and headed inside the boarding house. The Brigadier drove off. I reached the front door just as she did.

She said, "Good evening, Mr O'Keefe, did you and your friend enjoy your meal?"

"Yes, it was delicious, and you, Miss Bell?"

"It is not at all what you may be thinking, Mr O'Keefe. I am not at liberty to tell you, but I can say that the Brigadier holds you in high regard. Good night." She went to her room. I went to mine. I lay in bed.

What was all that about? Not what I may think it is? What else can it be? I will have to find out what it is that Miss Biddy Bell does.

I opened up as normal at 7 a.m., we sat having tea by 7:20 a.m. and all four of us at work by 7:30 a.m. I asked Bill about the men he thought would do the new Quay at Cove Manor.

"They are to drop in at dinner time to see you," Matthew replied.

Mr' O'Hara came in around 11 a.m. with his bags. "Walk with me to the ferry will you, Kev lad?"

I helped with the bags.

"I'm quite pleased with the way you have done things. Do you feel settled?" He asked.

"Yes, I do, I really think this will be the making of me."

"I would agree. Well goodbye, Kev lad, see you in about a month."

I waved him off and returned to the yard. There were two men talking to Bill.

"Ah, Mr O'Keefe." The first one held out his hand, I shook it. "I am Ian Daley and this is my brother Gordon." I also shook his hand.

"Will you both come into the office, please." I led they followed. We all remained standing. "Here are the drawings of the proposed new Quay at Cove Manor. My idea is that it would be much easier to build further out and wider, another thirty feet, and we are into six feet of water at low spring tides. We need this for the Schooner.

"The specification is heavy, we must think of the worse storms here in the Irish sea. The boat will be beam on to any Northerly weather during the winter months. As you can see, I have designed a U-shape Pontoon, to enable the Schooner to enter between and be secured both sides. This will help with cleaning and maintenance. What do you think?"

"Well, Mr O'Keefe it all looks grand. One question, what is the bed made of? Sand, mud, or clay?" Ian asked.

"Soft clay," I answered. "I have driven in a pointed three inch diameter spike with some effort."

"Sounds ideal to us," was the enthusiastic reply.

"What equipment do you have?" I inquired.

"We have a barge with a pile drive hammer, this will be well within our abilities." Ian nodded to his brother who nodded back in agreement. "Did Bill tell you we done the pier for the tug?" He added.

"No, but if Bill has recommended you, that's fine with me. Now, it will be labour only and cash on completion. How does that sound?"

"That's fine by us," Gordon confirmed.

"Have you transport?" I asked.

"Only by water, the barge will have to be towed around to the site," said Ian.

"That's not a problem, we can use the launch. Are you able to come with me now? We can go by launch, I want to show you the site before you give me a price."

"No problem, Mr O'Keefe."agread Ian.

"Bill, you go and get the launch ready. I'll telephone the Brigadier and let him know we are on our way." I placed the call. "Hello, operator, can please you get me Brigadier Kingsley? Thank you."

"Hello Mr O'Keefe," said the operator, "I'll connect you, putting you through now."

It rang four or five times then, then a voice answered that I recognised. "Kevin."

"Lucie."

"Yes, I knew it was you, I just knew. Where have you been? It's been over a week since I saw you."

I was a bit taken aback with the use of first names. She has never called me by my first name and I have never been invited to call her by her first name. It felt good.

"Well, Lucie, I am bringing round two men to look at the moorings. So, I will be with you in a few hours, we are coming by sea. Will you please tell the Brigadier?"

"Yes, It will be lovely see you."

We arrived and tied up.

"I'll go up to the house, leave you to do your bit." I started to walk, and got onto the lawn when I saw Lucie coming towards me being pushed by Morris.

"Kevin!" She shouted with a big smile.

"Good afternoon, Miss Lucie." I caught the look of surprise on Morris's face at the use of first names.

I stood in front of her. She grabbed both my hands in hers and we gazed deep into each other's eyes.

"You feel it, too," I said.

She nodded. "Thank you, Morris, Mr O'Keefe will take over the reins."

"Yes, Miss Kingsley." He bowed turned and left.

"What if I don't want to take over the reins, Miss Kingsley?"

"Then I will never speak to you ever again, Mr O'Keefe."

"Every cloud has a silver lining."

"You are so sure of yourself, so-so…"

"Good looking?"

"No, well, yes."

"Overbearing? Arrogant?"

"Yes." She smiled.

I knelt beside her, my face inches. from hers, and looked in to those sky blue eyes.

"Don't you dare kiss me?" She said with a hint of surprise and expectancy.

"You flatter yourself, young lady, I might catch something."

"Why I let you get away with the things you say, I have no idea."

"Oh yes you do." I smiled.

I pushed her to the top of the steps and explained what was happening. The men were testing the seabed and measuring.

I shouted, "Everything okay?"

"Yes, give us another half hour, Mr O'Keefe," Ian called back.

I waved and pushed Lucie back to the house. Her mother was standing by the open French doors.

I smiled. "Good day, Ms Kingsley."

"Good day, Mr O'Keefe."

I sensed something was off. Did Morris mention the use of first names? Did she overhear Lucie on the telephone?

"Is the Brigadier at home, Ms Kingsley?" I finally asked.

"Yes, he is here." Ms Kingsley frowned. "I'll go and fetch him." Off she went.

"Lucie," was as far as I got.

"I have been thinking about all you said and told me when you were here last," she spoke over me. "I do feel it, too, but, Kevin, I am frightened. Look at me, no one will want me. I could never be a proper wife or mother." Tears welled up in her eyes.

The Brigadier joined us. "Good day to you, Mr O'Keefe."

"And to you, sir."

"Doris, would you look after Lucie while I go with Mr O'Keefe down to the moorings?"

"Yes, Father. Lucie and I have things to talk about." As Ms Kingsley said this, she glared right at me. I felt as if I had just been turned to stone.

The Brigadier and I walked in silence, then he stopped halfway.

"Mr O'Keefe, I feel I need to explain about the other night."

"No explanation required, Mr Kingsley."

"Thank you for that, but." He looked at me for a few moments. "I feel I do, I trust you, Mr O'Keefe, and I know if you give me your word that what I am about to tell you will never be repeated to anyone." He paused.

"I give you my word, Brigadier."

He continued. "Miss Biddy Bell, and that is not her real name, is an intelligence officer working for the British government. She was stationed here during the war. I was her contact. She will be going back to London in a few months' time. That, Mr O'Keefe, is all you need to know. Do we have an understanding?"

"Yes, we do." I nodded. We shook hands and continued on.

I showed the Brigadier the drawings and explained my ideas. The lads told him how deep and far apart the piling would go. He was pleased and gave me the go-ahead. Just let him know how much in due course. I was asked to stay for dinner.

I said, "I would be honoured. But before I go." I turned to the lads. "It's a contract."

Gordan started to whoop in delight, but thought better of it with the Brigadier right there.

"Take the launch back to the yard and make preparations to start as soon as possible. I'll need a written quote for the labour content."

The brothers wasted no time in casting off. The Brigadier and I walked back to the house. I felt closer to him, probably as he had confided in me, it felt good. Upon our arrival I noticed Lucie appeared a bit glum while Ms Kingsley looking pleased with herself.

I went to Lucie. "Your grandfather has given me the contract for the new Quay, Lucie." she looked down, "Miss Kingsley please, Mr O'Keefe" her mother instructed.

I looked at her mother. I couldn't help myself and stood next to her.

"Romeo and Juliet comes to mind," I whispered.

"In Shakespeare's Romeo and Juliet, Mr O'Keefe, both families were rich."

I had just been put in my place.

Chapter 15

Dinner over, the Brigadier and I had warm brandies and spoke about the LUCIE KINGSLEY, the new Quay, and a bit of shooting. I was offered to join a Shoot, but declined. Ms Kingsley went out riding, this gave me time to say a long good-bye to Lucie. I got her alone.

"Lucie."

She looked a bit concerned.

"I know what your mother has said, and I fully understand how she would feel. This is your life and only you can live it."

"Mummy said you will change your mind and how can someone like you want someone like me."

"Lucie, I will not give in, you know who I am."

She nodded.

"I want to look at your legs."

Sheer panic crossed her face. "What? No! Please no! Go now, please." Tears filled her eyes.

I bent down and slowly lifted the blanket from the bottom. I glanced at her, she was doing her best to hold back the tears.

"Do you trust me?"

Lucie nodded.

"Do you want to walk again?"

She whispered through the tears, "Yes."

I put the blanked above her knees, she had stumps from the knee down. "Lucie, can you bend at the knee?"

She did.

"That's really good. I must measure, okay?"

She nodded. The left stump was six inches, the right one eight inches. I took the circumference just below the knee, left twelve inches as with the right. Both tapered the same. I put the blanket down. Lucie was searching my face, I smiled, she grabbed my hand.

"It's fine. Lucie, what would your mother say if she knew I had seen her daughter's knees? Shock and horror."

Lucie gave a small laugh.

" I want you to try and start walking on the stumps."

Her response gave me surprise and delight.

"Kevin, in my room alone I do. It was very painful at first, but now I can stand and walk holding on to chairs and things."

"That shows me just how strong a person you are, that could not have been easy. Straight thumbs, stubborn."

She smiled. I said my goodbyes, and left her by the French doors looking out over the green sea. I found Morris.

"Morris, can I trust you?" I asked.

"That you can, Mr O'Keefe. And thank you for saying nothing about, well, you know what."

"I am sure you meant no harm. I need Miss Kingsley's riding boot, do you know where she keeps them?"

"I'll fetch them." He returned with them in a canvas bag.

"Not a word to anyone, Morris, please."

"My lips are sealed, Mr O'Keefe."

I started the seven mile walk back, going along the coast path, I didn't want to meet Ms Kingsley and have to explain the canvas bag. I got back around 8 p.m. The launch was moored and the yard locked up. I put the boots in my office and left.

That night I lay in bed sorting out in my head how I was going to make those wooden legs work.

I can carve the legs and make the toes and the ankles move. I can use elastic to bring the toes and ankles back, the movement is about 45 degrees. But how do I attach the wooden bit to the real leg? This will depend on the width and strength of the elastic sheet as I saw on Miss Bell's waistband. I will have to visit the dress makers in the morning.

Speaking of the woman, what was all that about Miss Bell working for the British government? The war was over and she will be going back to London in a few months.

Wow, she's a British spy. This really caught my imagination. Yes, I can see it now. so confident, so in control.

I wondered what her job was and what she had seen and done. I saw our Miss Bell in a completely new light.

Next morning, I left the yard and walked to the dressmakers. The little bell rang as I entered the door.

A matronly woman stood behind the counter. "Good morning, sir, can I help you?"

"Good morning, I hope so. I require some black elastic band; do you have any you could show me?"

She pulled a draw out from under the counter and placed it on the counter top.

"Have you any wider, say six or eight inches?"

"No, sir, six inches is the widest they do. I can order some in for you if you wish."

I held the four inch that was in the drawer. "Can you get thicker, stronger?"

"The six inch can be ordered in double."

"That sounds just right, please can you order say, two yards?"

"Yes, I will need payment now if that is acceptable?"

"Thank you, how much?"

"One shilling a yard plus carriage, that's three shillings."

I paid. "How long will it take?"

"Should be ready for collection week from today, Mr O'Keefe." this was spoke with a look of—I know your name.

"Oh sorry, can I have a yard of the four inch you have in the drawer?"

"Six pence, please."

I paid and left. *The four inch can go at the back of the boots, make them stretch, easier to get on.*

I went back to the yard to fetch the boots and took them to the Heel and Toe cobblers around from the bank.

"Mornin'," was the greeting I got.

"Good morning, I want some professional advice."

"Then why come in 'ere?" He spoke with a straight face.

"That is not a local accent," I said.

"You're quick I can see that. I only jest, I be from a place called Cornwall, ever heard of it?"

"Yes, I have, somewhere on the south coast of mainland England."

"To the west, sir. Now how can I help thee?"

I took the boots from the sack and placed them on the counter.

"Fine boots sir, nout wrong with 'em."

I then produced the elastic strip. "I want you to undo the back stitching and place this elastic inside on both sides so the boots look the same. But open up at the back, much easier to pull them on. Can you do it?"

He pondered, looked at me, the boots, me, then the boots several times. I believe he was thinking: *Is he in his right mind?* And by his manner would have said so.

"What do you think?" I prompted.

"Ye sure about this, sir? They're lovely boots."

"Yes."

He picked up the elastic and held it to the boot.

"Down inside like this, stitched down both sides twice, maybe thrice. Open up the back, so when it be done the boot will look the same."

"Aye, I can do that. Give me three days."

I paused.

"Why are you still here?" He carried on with the job in hand.

I left and joined the lads in the yard. The Schooner was taking shape, one could now see the size of her hull. 42 feet overall, not including the bow sprit, 36 feet at the water-line, 12 foot beam and six foot draft. Rounded counter at the stern, so a following sea will lift her stern. Fitted with a 25 hp.

Kelvin Marine—Petrol/paraffin engine with the new feathered propeller, the blades fold back when sailing so as not to give drag, and centrifugal force when the engine is in use throws the blades out and gives thrust. She will be painted gloss black with gold-leaf coach work. She will be a beauty, just like her name-sake.

That evening I walked past the town hall just as Miss Biddy Bell, or whoever she was, came out.

"Good evening, Miss Bell."

"Good evening, Mr O'Keefe."

"Are going back to Harbour House?"

"Yes."

"May I walk with you?"

"If you would like to, I don't mind." Her tone said, *'Don't expect anything from this.'*

I said, "I wouldn't flatter myself, Miss Bell."

"Pardon?" She exclaimed.

"I don't expect anything from this."

She was taken a-back. We walked on in silence. She was a handsome woman and she obviously knew it. I had watched her as she walked down the Town Hall steps, her legs were fantastic.

I had a thought, *I could model Lucie's legs on hers.*

She was about 5 foot 8inches. Lucie's mother was about that height, maybe an inch taller. The riding boots were size five. We reached the front door, I stood in front of Miss Bell and stopped. She stopped abruptly, surprised by my actions.

"Miss Bell, I need to ask you a question of some importance, what size shoe are you?"

"What? Er five, size five. Why do you ask?"

"The Brigadier told me about you." I offered waiting for a reaction.

"He WHAT? God, he must trust you."

"I am making wooden legs for Lucie, er, Miss Kingsley."

"I know who Lucie is." She indignantly.

I continued. "I plan to make them as close to the real thing as possible, and as lovely as yours."

She laughed. "I think I know where this is going."

"Do I take that as a yes?"

"It depends on how you plan to copy them."

I could see she was enjoying the thought. "I will draw them then add the measurements, simple."

"And when do you want to do this, Mr O'Keefe?"

"Tonight, after the house has gone to sleep. I will call on you say twelve?"

"Will it take long?"

"About half an hour."

"I will see you then." This was all very matter of fact. She could have said no, but she said yes.

In we went into the dining room, sat at separate tables, and never said a word or exchanged a glance.

I waited until the house was quiet, removed my shoes and with measure, pencil, and paper crept to her room. I noticed the door was not closed. I opened it and walked inside in the dark.

"Shut the door," came a command.

I did, the light came on. Miss Bell sat in the chair, wearing a night dress that showed her knees. Her legs were crossed, but she soon uncrossed them. Not a word was spoken. I knelt and started to draw her legs, pleased with the result. I placed another sheet of paper to the inside of her left leg and drew the profile right down to her big toe, then at the back and drew that profile including the heel.

I drew around her foot, going between each toe. I started to measure from the ankle at inch intervals, all the way up to just below the knee, transferring the measurements to the outline. I glanced up for the first time since I started some thirty minutes ago. She was looking straight at me, her bosom rising up and down faster than normal. I was getting hard.

We rose simultaneously. I held her face and kissed her, her hand went between my legs, and started to undo my belt and buttons. I pulled off my shirt, kicked off my pants and socks. She stood there naked, as did I. She pivoted me and pushed me onto the bed. I lay on my back, she on top kissing me. She sat up, and put me inside her. I was in heaven; the feeling was like nothing I could have ever imagined or describe.

There was the warmth of her body heat. I held her as she moved, her breast cupped. I grabbed her and rolled her over. I was strangely at ease, I felt guilty and thought of Nelly then Lucie. It soon passed. I was with this beautiful woman. I grabbed a pillow, lifted her, and slid the pillow under her bottom.

I was then able to sit on my legs, one knee each side of her. I held my self and slowly pushed inside her. She lifted her hips and arched her back to meet me. I placed my open hand on her toned belly and let my thumb move down to touch her vein. She opened her mouth and gasped, her eyes were wide and conveyed a message: *You know and what's more you know where it is.*

I moved my thumb slowly up and down, up and down, up and down. She lowered her head with a whimper then shook. I stopped for a few seconds and moved slowly inside her, then started again. I felt her nails in my chest as I exploded inside her with a feeling that went from my head right down to my toes. She shook again and quickly put her hand to her mouth. She straightened her lovely legs and pushed me over, she now on top of me, I kissed her face, and rolled us both over I was back on top. I kissed her neck and shoulders, still hard and inside her. Our breathing slowly came back to normal, we both turned sidewards facing each other.

"You must go, Kevin," was all she said.

I said nothing, it finished as quickly as it started. I got my pants and shirt, gathered up the drawings and the rest of my clothes, and went back to my room. This was not the heart beating as with Nelly, this was pure lust. And it was fantastic.

I lay on my bed going through every movement again in my head. I felt it all happened far too fast to really be into the moment and understand what was really happening. I wanted to go back and do it again. I now felt ready to take it slower. But, but-I smiled to myself.

In the morning we sat at our individual tables. We said good morning, and that was that. I finished my breakfast and left for the yard. I was on my back under the boat when the telephone rang.

I said to the others, "Leave it."

It stopped, yet a few minutes later rang again. I pulled myself from under the boat and went to answer it. It stopped again. I waited, it rang, and I answered.

"O'Hara's boatyard," was as far as I got.

"Kevin? it's me Nelly, I'm in Mr O'Hara's office, he said I could use the telephone. How are you?"

"I'm fine how are you?" It was on the tip of my tongue to say "sweetheart," but all I felt was guilt.

"I-I'm well, thank you." She started to cry.

"Kev lad, it's me O'Hara. Sad news, Mrs Kelly died last night. Nelly wanted to tell you herself. Here I'll put her back on."

"Sorry, Kevin, I want you back here. Please come home!" She started to cry.

I heard Mrs O'Hara talking in the background, "It's me again, Kev lad, I will let you know the date of the funeral. Try and make it, son." He rang off.

I slumped in the chair, staring down at the floor.

"Cup of tea, Boss?" offered Andy.

"Er, yes."

After a few seconds, Andy spoke again, "Are you ok, Mr O'Keefe?"

"Someone I knew back home has died."

"Oh, so sorry to hear that. I'll fetch the tea and some of Mathew's funny cake, er Bara Brith."

I said nothing, Andy hesitated then left without another word. My mind was everywhere, last night, Nelly, Lucie, I was so confused. I felt for Nelly, and wanted to be there for her, I must go for the funeral, I owe that to Nelly and her father. But no way can I tell her about Lucie, not then.

I started to doubt myself and what I thought my destiny was. Where I wanted to be and who I wanted to be with. Ms Kingsley made it very clear about my lowly position. so, perhaps I will never be able to marry Lucie. Is my fate to help her, then go back to Nelly? Nelly can't leave her father to come here to be with me.

I finished my tea and Bara-Brith, I don't remember doing either. I walked outside, got in the launch, and headed out the harbour. I needed to be alone for a while.

I got clear of the headland out of harm's way and stopped the engine. I drifted on the tide. My mind was nowhere, almost blank, I sat and stared at the sea. A few hours must have passed, I slowly came to, started the engine, and headed back, my mind a bit clearer.

Right, one thing at a time. Miss Bell, over and done never to be repeated, the moment had passed. I knew that. Nelly, wait until I hear about her mother's funeral date. Lucie's legs I will make a start after work tomorrow. The boat, that's the only thing I can say is sorted and on schedule.

I got back and spent the last few hours with the men on the Schooner. The workshop day was over, I locked up and sat at my desk looking at the drawings I had made and the oak by the office door. My mind went back to the bliss of the night before. I could still see her face and feel the smoothness of her skin, the little noises she made. I smiled to myself.

Well, this will not do, I must make a start. I stood up and felt exhausted, as if I had been drained of energy. I shook myself, grabbed the oak and took it into the workshop. I cut the four by four oak in two equal parts, then cut one into two bits one eight inch this was the foot and toes. This left sixteen inches for the leg. I traced the shape of Miss Bell's leg onto the wood, again I smiled at the memory. I worked for around three hours. I had two legs, two feet and ten toes all very roughly shaped I called it a night.

Work as normal, it got to ten o'clock, tea time. I told them I was going out for twenty minutes. I went to see the cobbler. I was looking forward to seeing what he had managed to do with the elastic and the riding boots.

"Mornin', you've come for them boots I would imagine." He was smiling.

He must be pleased with the result, I thought.

Indeed he was. He placed them on the counter with certain amount of pride and proceeded to explain and show me what he had to do to make it work. Double stitch here and there.

"This elastic is a beggar to stitch, but well, what do you think?" He asked.

I was pleased with the work. They looked normal until you pulled the back apart, and there was the elastic and it sprung back into shape. Perfect. I paid and thanked him. I was just about to leave.

"Sir, can I ask were you get the elastic from?"

I stopped and walked back to the counter. "This was my idea, and I would like it to remain that way," I retorted.

"But, sir, I thinks you 'av somethin.' It makes puttin' on ya boots much easier."

I studied him. "A gentleman's agreement, you do nothing until I have secured the idea with the patent office. I will inform you when it is done, and you will be able to do the alteration from that date. I will require ten percent of profit from all alterations and new make." I held out my hand, he shook it and agreed.

He held onto my hand. "I will be the only one on the island?"

"Yes. You will have sole trading rights."

He shook my hand with both of his.

"Well, good day to you, sir."

I set out for the yard, my head full of what had just happened. I remembered the six inch elastic. I changed direction and went to the dressmaker's. Ding went the bell over the door.

"Mr O'Keefe, I was just thinking about you. Er, I mean your purchase has arrived." She coloured up and placed the parcel on the counter.

"Any more to pay?" I asked.

"No, it's paid in full."

I could tell she was busting to, as me, what I wanted the elastic for. I thanked her and left. Back at the yard, I placed the boots in the corner of then office and put the parcel inside the left one.

Mathew came in. "Cup of tea, Boss?" He looked at the boots.

"Yes, please, Mathew."

He hesitated.

"That would be nice, Mathew."

"Er, yes Boss." off he went.

"Mathew," I called him back. "I'll have it in the workshop."

I wanted to get the engine in position today and to see how far back we could get it. This will give more room in the main cabin. The design put the fuel tank above the engine, I thought this was a fire risk if the tank leaked petrol onto the engine. I was going to place it forward, away from the batteries. A full tank was the same weight as the engine, this would balance the boat better.

I locked up and started on Lucie's legs. I managed to carve the ten toes, complete with toe-nails. I was pleased with the result as they looked real. I made notes. I took off my boots and socks. Toes move from flat to fully up at about 45 degrees. And a foot at the ankle fully pointed to fully up travels through about 45 degrees down and 45 degrees up from the flat.

There is movement left and right about the same, but I was not going to try to do that, just up and down. The toes will be held in position with a quarter inch brass rod passing through holes in them and through the corresponding hole in the foot. The toe end of the foot will have slots to take the toe, and I will place elastic to the underneath of the toes to the under part of the foot.

This will bring the toes back to level after being bent as in walking. Same with the ankle joint, a one inch oak dowel will pass through where the ankle bone is to hinge the foot with elastic attached to the back of the ankle to under the heel. Again this will bring the foot back to ninety degrees to the leg as in standing. This should work, it does in my head anyway.

The Daley brothers had started on the new Quay at Cove Manor. I could only hope the weather held. They were taking the material to site by their barge towed by the launch, all seemed good. They gave a contract duration of three weeks, I think probably four. One week gone and all the piling is done, they could do it in three, we'll see.

The telephone rang, Andy was the nearest.

"Answer that please, Andy." I was under the boat.

He hovered from one foot to the other.

I looked at him. "Go on, it won't bite."

He did as instructed. "It's Mr' O'Hara, Boss."

"Tell him I'll call him back." I knew what that would be about, the funeral date.

I called him back, I was right, it was eleven o'clock the following Monday, three days away. I decided to go over on the Sunday and stay with Auntie Kathryn. I asked Mr O'Hara to tell Auntie I'd be with her late afternoon Sunday.

"If you see Nelly, tell her the same," I requested.

After dinner the telephone rang, it was Lucie.

"Kevin, when will I see you again? It's been over a week."

"Does your mother know you called me?" I asked.

"No, I was told not to call you."

"The last thing I wanted is to come between you and your mother."

"But, she will have to accept how we feel about each other at some point."

"Lucie, we have the rest of our lives, so, we will just have to be patient. I planned to come tomorrow, I need to check on the new Quay. So, I'll be at Cove Manor about eleven o'clock."

"Kevin…"

"Yes?"

"I think I love you. And—" The telephone went dead. I suspected her mother had arrived. gave a big sigh. The words—We have the rest of our lives. Nelly said that to me. I felt a bit disillusioned. Just then I got a mental picture of an Army officer of around forty, good looking, and in jodhpurs. I think I have had this vision before. What it is all about God only knows, and He won't tell.

Chapter 16

That evening, I worked on Lucie's legs. All the bits are finished, just had to put them together. They do, if I say so myself, look life like and have a lovely shape thanks to Miss Bell. The hardest bit was hollowing out to take Lucie's stumps. I will allow an extra quarter inch all round to permit a soft wool lining.

This had to be right in order for her weight to be on all of the stump and not just the ends. I had to attach the six inch elastic around the tops, then paint as close to Lucie's skin tone as possible.

Barry brought the trap round. It was a bright still day, not a breath of wind. But there was a bit of a chill in the air with a ground mist. The sun would burn it off in a few hours. I reached Cove Manor and turned into the drive. The stable lad William met me and took Nelly around to the stables. Morris answered the door within seconds, Ms Kingsley was behind him.

"Mr O'Keefe, would you go around to the side? I will ask my father to meet you there." She spun on her heel and marched off.

Morris looked at me with embarrassment on his face.

"It's okay, Morris, not your fault. I will play her game for the time being."

"Very good, Mr O'Keefe."

I walked around the side to the tradesman's entrance. Again, I had been put in my place. After a few moments, Morris arrived with Lucie.

"Good morning, Miss Kingsley." I pretended to doff my cap.

"Good day to you, Mr O'Keefe."

"I'll take Miss Kingsley from here, Morris," I offered.

"Certainly, sir."

I pushed Lucie to the top of the steps leading down to where the new Quay was taking shape. The Daley brothers had done well. They caught sight of us and waved, we waved back. The Brigadier bustled towards us.

"Good morning, Mr O'Keefe."

"Oh, good morning, Brigadier. The Daley brothers are doing well," I commented.

"Yes, indeed I'm pleased with the progress, you're a good man to know, Mr O'Keefe."

I was taken a back. "Thank you, Brigadier."

He nodded. I saw this as an opportunity to mention the legs. "Mr Kingsley, I have something to tell you."

He straightened, not knowing what to expect. "Yes?"

"I have been making legs for Lucie."

His eyebrows went up in shock, but he said nothing and frowned thoughtfully at Lucie.

"Lucie, you know about this?"

"Yes, Grandfather, I do." Lucie held my hand.

"I see, and how long has this been going on may I ask?"

"From the start, Brigadier," I answered.

"I have been blind." He smiled. "I have never seen my granddaughter so happy as I have these last months. Please don't think I have not tried. I know a Mr Marcel Desoutter, an aviator he lost a leg. He and his brother Charles designed a replacement, they were willing to help Lucie. Yet she would have none of it. Being very stubborn, she kept to her room for over six months, and would never allow a word on the subject until now. Until you, Mr O'Keefe, this combined with the loss of Lucie's father…" The Brigadier's eyes started to form tears. "Well." He got himself together. "Lucie, does your mother know."

"No, Grandfather." She looked at me.

The Brigadier sensed it. "Spit it out, you two, what's the problem?"

I looked him in the eye. "Ms Kingsley does not approve of me, or I should say does not approve of Lucie and I."

"Ah, I see," he mused. After a few silent moments, "One thing at a time, Mr O'Keefe, when do we see these new legs?"

"I need a few more days, Brigadier."

"You are a strange one, Mr O'Keefe, however, and I don't say this lightly, I do like you. And I do trust you to do the right thing, er, whatever that may be."

Just then, Morris came sprinting down the path. "Excuse me, sir, you have a visitor, a Major Bowen."

"Major!" the Brigadier shouted.

The Major had followed Morris and was halfway across the lawn. The Brigadier went to meet him, Lucie and I watched.

"Wonderful to see you, Major, just wonderful."

They shook hands. and walked towards us.

"Come and see my new project, a new harbour for my new yacht."

I looked at the Major. *This was the man I saw in my mind's eye. This was scary!*

"May I introduce you to Mr O'Keefe, and of course my granddaughter Lucie."

"Please to meet you, Mr O'Keefe, and the last time I met you. Miss Kingsley you were only this high."

"Yes, I was about eleven or twelve, Major," volunteered Lucie.

"Your Grandfather told me about the accident, so very sorry."

"I will be walking soon," sputtered Lucie.

"Oh, really?" said the Major, a little surprised.

"Yes, Mr O'Keefe is making me new legs, aren't you Mr O'Keefe."

The Major eyed me. "This is your line of expertise?"

"No, Major I'm a boat builder. My yard is building the Brigadier's new yacht, and I'm overseeing the new Quay."

He appeared confused and only managed to say, "I see."

I felt sure this was not the case; another case of a moment's thought is an hour in words. He had no idea of what to make of me, I smiled to myself and imagined in his mind he saw something that Long John Silver would have worn.

"Well, we will leave you two. No further business, Mr O'Keefe?"

"No, Brigadier."

"Good, if you need me, I'll be in the house." They left us alone.

"Lucie" I started, "I saw the Major in my mind a few days ago. He is going to play a major part in your family."

"Very funny, Kevin, a MAJOR part."

We both laughed.

"So, you are now going to tell me you are a Wizard or Warlock."

"Well now you mention it, I will cast a spell on you."

"You have already done that, as well you know."

I knelt down and gazed into her lovely face. The hardness of months ago had faded, her eyes were large and sky blue, her hair as blue, black as a raven's wing and down to her waist, her skin showed signs of being an outdoor girl, still had a faint sun kissed brown. I tried my best to remember this shade to colour match the legs. After a few silent moments I spoke.

"I like tall women, so I have made your legs so you will be 6 foot 2 inch."

"What? Please don't joke, Kevin, I am really quite frightened at the thought. They will work, won't they?"

"It will not be easy, they will probably hurt until you get hardened, but the pain will be so worth it. I'm excited and apprehensive. It will be up to you, yet I believe you have the inner strength to persevere."

"Are they well, woman shaped?" Lucie inquired with her serious expression.

"No, I modelled them on an old donkey."

"Not funny, Mr O'Keefe" she said, half smiling.

"I have never looked so close at ladies' legs. I have gone out of my way to walk behind dozens of women, staring at their legs."

"YOU Can Stop Right There, Mr O'Keefe."

We both had a good laugh.

"Can you please take me back to the house?" She asked, urgently.

"Are you okay?"

"Yes, thank you."

I pushed as fast as I could. *She needs the toilet.* I took her to just outside the toilet door.

"Thank you I can take it from here," Lucie said, kindly.

I was right. I went to find Morris.

Ms Kingsley appeared looking very smart in full make-up. "Yes, Mr O'Keefe can I help you?"

"No thank you, Ms Kingsley. I have just taken Lucie to the privy."

If looks could kill! I knew this would get to her.

"I will get Biddy to attend Miss Kingsley, please don't trouble yourself."

"It's no trouble."

Her face was thunder. As if to break the awkward silence, out came the Major and the Brigadier.

"Major, how wonderful to see you, what a lovely surprise," said Ms Kingsley.

"Ms Kingsley you look beautiful! You must have a painting in the attic, you get younger."

Doris giggled like a school girl "Major, please."

The Major nodded. I smiled to myself, I could see where this is going, well, well, well. The Major and the lady.

I had a thought, *The major has fallen on hard times, he's hoping to marry into this rich family, I know I'm right.*

The Major and the lady went into the drawing room followed by the Brigadier, I don't think he knew he was playing Gooseberry. The lady had forgotten about her daughter. I went over as Lucie came out.

"I must be going, I will be away for a few days back home." I felt uncomfortable about saying home. I sensed Lucie felt the same, perhaps for the same reason. "I have a funeral to go to. I will be back on Tuesday late I should think. Lucie, I think the Major is after your mother."

"I think my mother is after the Major." She smiled.

I bent down and kissed her. She held her hand to her mouth.

"So, it's ok to kiss you now?"

"I never said you could not."

"Oh, yes you did."

"That, Mr O'Keefe, was then."

"I'll see you Saturday next." I walked out to where Nelly waited. Morris was holding the reigns. "No lunch time invite today, Morris?"

"No, sir, safe journey ."

"Thank you. Nelly walk-on."

I felt a chill as I rode and looked out to sea. It was like a mill-pond. I left Nelly with Barry at the stables and walked down to Mrs O'Rorkes. I went to my room; only a few minutes later there was a knock on the door.

"Come in."

Mrs O'Rorke poked her head into the room. "Mr O'Keefe, have you eaten? I bet you have not. A nice young man like yourself has to keep up his strength, Now, I said this before, don't expect this kind of service all the time."

I butted in. "You don't boil your cabbages twice."

"Indeed, I don't. Do you want a dinner or not?"

"Yes please."

"I'll bring it up. You can have it in your room as I have cleared the dining room and I don't want a mess." Off she went, and returned with a tray of cottage pie, crusty bread and butter and a mug of tea. "Don't be letting it get cold now, eat it while its hot. good day to you." And she was gone.

I cleared the plate, dipped the bread into the gravy, and wiped the plate clean with the remaining bread, lovely. I opened the top draw of the bedside cabinet to get paper and pen. It was only then I spotted the Tarot cards that Nan had given me. I took them out and placed them on the table.

Memories started flooding back, I was six or seven at the time, sitting on the floor. Nan and a neighbour sat at the table. She spoke of the major and the minor cards, she would ask the sitter to shuffle the cards and think of the question or problem that was troubling them. Then take the cards one at a time from the top of the pack and place one at a time, telling the sitter the meaning of each card as she went until a cross had been formed. Then four cards to the right-hand side, that's ten cards in all. She called it the Gallic or was it the Celtic Cross? I can't remember the meanings of the cards. But she did say I would know instinctively.

Well, let's find out. I wonder what my future is. I shuffled the cards, my mind a Kaleidoscope of questions.

I placed them to the left of me, and took the top card and placed it in the middle of the old and well-worn silk handkerchief they had been wrapped in. Just as I had seen Nan do. The first card was The Magician, *Is this me?*

It showed a man standing by a table with all four symbols and sun flowers around his feet. He looked as if he was about to grant a wish. I got the feeling he could make dreams come true.

The second card I placed across The Magician was The Emperor. A very important looking man sitting on a throne holding a key of some-sort in his right hand. I felt he was in a position of power, perhaps legal, but had a kind face. Someone in this position could help or be on my side.

The third card was The Two of Cups, a young couple both holding a cup each offering each other their cup, as if they are taking vows. I got the feeling that this couple were on a much higher level than just emotional, more spiritual.

Is this me and Lucie? I placed this card below. *So, below, past? This would make sense.*

The fourth card was Five of Wands, this showed five young men fighting each other with wooden staffs. I felt this could be opposition from one quarter, yet, no one was getting hurt. So, not that serious.

Ah, could this be Ms Kingsley? I placed this card to the left of cards one and two. so, ongoing?

The next card was The Chariot, this showed a man in a two wheeled chariot pulled by two sphinx, one black and one white. I got from this car, being pulled in two directions at once. Is the black negative and the white positive? But the man appeared in control, holding on while being pulled in opposite directions or decisions, I could make sense of this. This card went above, so, the future? The next card the sixth is The Sun, this card showed a young boy naked riding bareback on a white horse holding a flag with the sun large and smiling above.

This says to me total freedom, in control, as if all wishes have been granted. This card was placed to the right of cards one and two. so, distant future? The next card the seventh is The Six of Cups, this card showed a village scene with a couple sharing flowers, an older couple. They appeared settled, easy with each other. I got a feeling of quieter times, things now past, I felt as if I needed to go back in order to find peace. This card I placed to my right separate from the first six cards. I felt this position was the inside of me, perhaps fear of making a mistake?

The next card the eighth is The Seven of Cups, this card showed a man standing with his arms open, looking at seven cups. This card said to me a time of outside confusion, to many decisions, which way do I go? Which cup do I choose? 1people and things around me, outside my control. I placed this card directly above the last.

The ninth card is The Three of Coins. This card showed a tradesman to the left and a rich man to the right, there were three Coins built into the buildings entrance.

Is the tradesman being paid for his work? Or being appreciated for work done, and promise of future work? Perhaps the Brigadier? I thought.

Now, the last and tenth card is The Wheel of Fortune, this card showed a sort of compass and four animals, one in each corner, I got a feeling of good fortune, as if the power of the four corners of the world were behind me giving me great strength.

I sat back and studied the cards lying in front of me. *Have I been right in my interpretation?*

I started to tidy up the cards when one card fell from the pack, it landed face down on the floor. I bent to pick it up and turned the card, it was the Grim Reaper dressed head to toe in a flowing black gown and a scythe in his thin bony fingers. A cold shiver ran down my spine.

I looked closer; the card showed lying on the ground around his feet were severed hands, feet, and two heads one male and one female. But both heads were smiling and the sun was shining, flowers blooming.

I think I know; this is a complete cutting off of the past, life, beliefs, emotional ties and beginning of a completely new start. This made sense. *Only time will tell.*

If so, it all does make sense of my life at the moment. Anyway, right or wrong, it has made me feel good and hopeful that I will sort out any problems that may arrive. I slept well.

I awoke and drew back the curtains, I could not believe what my eyes were telling me. I could not see anything past the window, a thick fog or sea mist had totally obscured the view from my window. I washed and got dressed, went down and out the front door. The visibility was a few yards at most. And as still as the grave, not a sound, it made me shiver. I went back inside. Mrs O'Rorke was getting the breakfast room ready.

"Mr O'Keefe, have you seen outside at all? I have never in all my years seen a fog that thick, and no sign of lifting. Not much will be doing today, I've got a man going to Liverpool. I don't think he'll be going anywhere."

"I was hoping to go to Belfast later, Mrs O'Rorke. I have a funeral to attend tomorrow back in Carrickfergus."

"Well, if you ask me, Mr O'Keefe, if you go out to sea in this it could be your own funeral you be attending."

After breakfast I decided to go to the yard. *I will telephone Mr O'Hara, tell him the situation, and I can do some work on Lucie's legs.*

I inched my way to the yard, almost walked into a lamp-post. The walk would normally take twelve to fifteen minutes. This time thirty minutes, and my coat was wet through. I made a cup of tea and sat down in the office, I called Mr O'Hara, and explained the situation. He understood as it was the same over there, no fishing boats had gone out. I asked him to explain to Nelly, he said he would.

Then added, "She does miss you, Kev lad."

I waited for him to repeat himself as always, but no.

"I will write to her." I exclaimed. He rang off.

I felt terrible, pulled in two directions. *That Tarot card of man in chariot, does appear to be true.*

I started on Lucie's legs, I had a whole day. I looked outside now and then, no change, a real pea-souper. It was about 7 p.m. I had eaten nothing since breakfast, it was only now that I had finished the legs that I suddenly felt hungry. I was pleased with the result. I mixed the paint to as near as I could remember Lucie's skin to be, and painted them.

The toes, the shape of the foot, how it hinged, I just hope I have got the correct size. This is where Lucie's stumps will fit.

I had fitted lamb's wool to the inside I hoped it would compress into the small details of her stump's. All I had to do now was attach the six inch elastic all the way around the top, and to the back of the ankle. I had another cup of tea, and relaxed, looking at the legs hanging on a wire, the right way around. My mind went back to Miss Bell. and that night. I smiled to myself, and imagined they were her legs again.

I recalled her naked standing there. What a body, and she knew what she was doing. No way was I anywhere near being the first. I felt a closeness, I dismissed the thought as me just feeling this way about my second conquest. If you can call it my conquest, she was not slow in coming forward. I leaned back in my chair, and started to question my actions.

I do seem to just take things over and assume I and only I can fix things and make a situation better, I thought. *It does seem to have done me ok so far, I have done good in such a short time.*

I felt better, I had talked myself around. I took one more look at the legs and said out loud, "Not bad, if I do say so myself." I locked up.

I walked back to Mrs O'Rorke's just in time for evening meal. The sea-mist had not lifted, and this was the topic of conversation around the dinner tables. Miss Biddy Bell sat alone as normal, and spoke to no one. All though several people tried, one fellow looked as if he fancied his chances, and was met with a blank stir. He gave up. I don't think she blinked the whole time. She stood and as she walked past looked down at me and winked. I took this as a *'That put him in his place'* and not a *'Come to my room.'* I hope I was right, but must admit, I was a bit disappointed.

Monday morning the mist had lifted enough for folks to go about their business. I heard the ferry fog-horn blow. I took this to mean service as normal, but too late for me. I made my way to the yard.

I had forgot I had left Lucies legs hanging in my office. I arrived same time as the men. It was too late, they had been spotted. I went into the office and took them down; they did look good.

In came Andy. "Tea, boss?"

"Yes, thanks, Andy."

Bill came into the office. He had no need, he knew what he had to do.

"Any change to the work for today?" He asked, looking at the legs.

"No, Bill, I will be with you in a few moments."

He hesitated then went to work. It was lunch time we stopped.

I said, "Just going over the road, I'll have my tea when I come back."

I went to see a solicitor, the same one Mr O'Hara had used for the house sale. I gave him the drawings and details for the patent for the elasticated footwear. He said he would let me know in due course the costing and whatnot. He seemed taken by the idea.

You never know, I thought. *Nothing ventured, nothing gained.*

I returned the yard to find all three of them in the office. Mathew spoke first.

"Sorry, Boss, but we couldn't help ourselves see."

Bill butted in. "Do the work yourself? Very nice, if you don't mind me saying."

"Thank you, Bill, coming from you that is a complement."

"We think we know who they are for, Boss," Andy piped up.

A big "SHUHHH!" came from Mathew and Bill.

"This Schooner is not going to build itself, now is it?"

They went back to work with mumblings.

The day passed uneventful, I knew there was one thing I must do. I locked up, and sat in the office. After a few minutes of guilt, I telephoned Mr O'Hara. There was no answer. I wondered how it went, how was Nelly? I should have been there for her. I'd try again tomorrow.

I got a telephone call from Mr O'Hara. Mrs Kelly's funeral went as well as could be expected, some people from miles away could not make it due to the fog. He also said I should have been there as Nelly really needed me, but understood and so did Nelly. He also added she was going to write to me this week, so look out for the letter.

I should be writing to her first. I feared that if I had made it to the funeral and saw Nelly and the people I grew up with, I might never have come back. But that's a daft thought, my future is here. I have position, I have money, I have been accepted, and I have ideas that could really do well here. I have been given a chance and I must take as far as it will go. I could never live with myself if I gave it up for a possibility I might take over the boatyard in Carrickfergus.

I may never be allowed to be with Lucie. She is only seventeen and I am 21. I remembered something Jack Catten once said, *"A man should be at least six years older than the woman to be able to stand a chance of competing mentally."* I do believe there is more than a grain of truth in that remark.

The week went well. The LUCIE KINGSLEY was taking shape. The hull was finished and most of the internal fittings were in. The Heads (toilet) were in, and the separate cabin partitions were in. The lads were making a fantastic job, the workmanship top quality. This boat should bring me some good contracts. I must use this to advertise, the yard. It did look like we would complete in the four months, with a good bonus for the lads.

Nelly's letter arrived on Friday, I left it till the end of the day. After the yard was locked up, I sat in my office holding the letter, almost in dread. I opened it and started to read.

'Dear Kevin.

You were missed on Monday. Terry asked after you, as did several people, your Auntie Kathryn and JackTerry has been very attentive, but most of all me. However I do understand the reason why, many people could not attend because of the weather. I did think you would have made the trip once the weather improved, just to pay your respects. My father is very fond of you and would have loved to see you. I am sure you have your reasons, Kevin. But I must tell you I feel we are drifting apart, please be honest with me. If you have found someone new, it will break my heart I know, but please tell me.

If you have, I wish you all the happiness in the world. You will always be in my heart. I have wonderful memories and will always have those.

Please write soon, your loving Nelly, X'

I could not hold back the tears, they flowed like rain. I could feel her pain, it was unbearable. I wanted to reach out and hold her tight, make the hurt go away. But, I could not. I slammed the desk with my fist so hard it made my tea cup bounce off and smash into a million pieces. I slumped back in to my chair, I went to slam the table again, yet thought better of it.

I must let her go. This was the first time I had thought these words in earnest.

I felt as if I had just lost a big part of me, almost half empty. She was such a large part of my life for so long. The tears fell, I could not stop.

Are these tears for Nelly? Or for the life I knew and left behind? The friends I had? The parents I lost. Is this the true grieving, after all this time? Tears fell like they would never stop. I have never felt so alone. I remembered the words, "Terry has been very attentive." *I bet the bastard has.*

I walked around for a while, got myself together, and headed over to the Legs-O-Man.

"Good evening, Mr O'Keefe," the barman greeted me.

I just nodded. "A large whiskey, please."

He sensed there was no conversation, he must have seen it a thousand times. Without a word he placed the whiskey on the bar and turned away. I sat down in a quiet corner. I had no one to talk to, and didn't want anyone to talk to anyway. I stared at the wall, feeling very sorry for myself. I downed the whiskey in one, and went to the bar.

"Same again, please."

Still without a word the drink was placed in front of me. I downed in one and walked out. I considered really getting drunk.

This solves nothing, I thought. *You forget and wake up in the morning feeling like crap and the problem is still there.*

I headed back to my rooms. I had not yet eaten, and the whiskey had gone right to my head. I opened the door.

"Oh, Mr O'Keefe, are you alright?" Mrs O'Rorke fussed at me. "You've been drinking."

I just smiled at her.

"Go right up to your room, and I'll bring you some dinner. You need something to soak up that rubbish. Go on now before my other guests see you."

I climbed the stairs and opened the door to my room. I was okay, nowhere near drunk, just a little heady. The dinner arrived.

"Get on the outside of that, Mr O'Keefe, your feel better in no time."

I said, "Thank you" and she left.

I finished the meal and lay on the bed; my mind a blank. After a while, the door opened and in walked Miss Bell. I sat up. She sat on the chair opposite the bed.

"Do you mind if I smoke?"

I shook my head. She lit, inhaled, exhaled, and crossed her lovely legs. One arm across her middle, the other holding the cigarette level with her face. She studied me, I had not spoken. Finally, she spoke.

"She will get over it, you know what you have to do. It will be the right decision, you are a good man."

Her face and voice softened, and I sensed she wanted to say something personal. However, it passed.

"Your future is here. It will not be easy, you have opposition in the form of her mother. The Brigadier is on your side." After a few moments she added, "As am I."

I was speechless. She looked straight into my eyes, and I sensed a quiet strength. She sat, and smoked. I relaxed and opened my mouth to speak.

"Please don't ask, I cannot tell you." She finished the cigarette, and with a face that gave away nothing, walked out.

I lay on the bed, my mind doing somersaults. *What was that? How did she know?*

I got undressed and went to bed, it must have been around two or three in the morning before I finally dropped off to sleep.

Morning came, clear and bright, not so my head, lack of sleep and drink, a lovely day. I felt better about my situation, I think. I looked at myself in the mirror and thought how my life had changed in so little a time. I seem to have aged, the boy is now a man, and I'm doing okay.

"I am," I said out loud.

Today was the day I take Lucie's new legs to her. My pulse quickened at the thought, I only hoped and wished they work as well as I planned. I started to have second thoughts. I am playing with peoples' feelings and lives. Was this me being arrogant and overbearing? This had been mentioned before as I recall. I must believe they will work. I took a deep breath and went down to breakfast.

Mrs O'Rorke had a full house. There by the window sat Miss Bell looking fabulous. I noticed some of the men making the odd glance and knew what they were thinking. She sat looking totally untouchable and unobtainable. She stood and with head held high, wafted through the room and out the door.

I smiled to myself. *She is not what she seems. And I know it.*

I went to my room and changed into my best clothes, I had bought new boots that week.

In time elastic would do away with laces, this could be big. I studied myself in the full-length mirror.

I was 6 foot, slim but strong, and my actions were quick. I felt good and ready for any opposition from any quarter. I smiled, even Ms Kingsley.

I went down stairs. Mrs O'Rorke's jaw fell when she saw me.

"My goodness, Mr O'Keefe! I must say, touch me not me names temptation," she smiled. "Going somewhere or seeing someone special? or both?"

"Thank you, Mrs O'Rorke, I think. I'll be back for dinner."

I arrived at the yard and went in to get the legs. I put them in the canvas sack with the riding boots.

"Well, Kev lad," I said to myself, "this is it, today is the day, the moment of truth. Failure is not an option." I walked in to the workshop. "Good morning, men."

It was Bill who spoke first. "Today must be the day."

The other two looked and smiled.

"Could be, Bill, could be."

"Cup of tea, Boss?" Andy asked.

"Yes please, and a new cup. I seem to have broken mine." I continued on to my office.

"Hello? Anybody there?" It was the Brigadier's unmistakeable voice.

"Hello!" I shouted back and walked out into the workshop.

He was standing there with Miss Bell. I was taken-a-back.

"Mr O'Keefe, Miss Bell is leaving us today, and going back to London for good."

"I wanted to say goodbye, Ke—Mr O'Keefe, and to wish you success for the future," she spoke softly.

She kissed me on the cheek. I noticed the Brigadier did not think this at all out of place. I looked into her lovely face, and noticed a softness in her eyes. Her face was not hard, rather full of compassion. She looked at me eye to eye, I felt a closeness, a connection. Just for a fleeting moment.

She turned to the Brigadier. "Goodbye, Brigadier."

"Goodbye, Miss Bell."

She walked to the door. I noticed for the first time her suitcase by the threshold. She picked it up and went. I thought she would turn to wave, but no, not her style.

I was brought back to earth with, "Well, Mr O'Keefe, the *LUCIE KINGSLEY* is looking mighty fine. You and your men have done well. I had no idea just how big she is. Can't wait to take her out for the first time, wonderful. Here is the next payment."

"Thank you, Brigadier, on time as normal."

"Are you off somewhere, Mr O'Keefe?" The Brigadier said after looking at my attire.

"I was on my way to Cove Manor. I have Lucie's new legs here in this bag."

He looked frightened and concerned. "I hope to God-Above you know what you are doing. I fear there is a lot at stake here, it's going to be well—emotional."

"It's going to be a day we will never forget, and for the right reasons."

"You are very sure of yourself."

"I have to be, I have to believe."

He drew a deep breath. "Right, into battle we go. Let's hope the gods look on us with favour, Mr O'Keefe. The car is outside."

We drove in silence and anticipation.

This is a new adventure, I thought, I was starting to feel excited at the prospect of seeing Lucie-no-legs standing up for the first time in over two years. The freedom, she will get her life back, I know she has the strength of character to persevere no matter how hard or how painful.

We arrived at the main entrance. Morris greeted us and glanced at the canvas bag with a quick nod to me. He stood aside, we walked into the Hallway. Ms Kingsley stood still, I could see the muscles in her cheek move as she clenched her jaw, but in front of her father could say nothing. I knew what she was thinking, *The tradesman's entrance.* I smiled and bid her good morning. Before she had time to respond, if a response was in the offing, the Brigadier spoke.

"Doris darling, Mr O'Keefe is here with Lucie's new legs." He tried to sound positive, yet I could see he had his reservations.

"You have taken a lot on yourself, Mr O'Keefe, in doing this. I for one would have liked to have been involved, or at least consulted. Lucie, after all, is my daughter."

"I must agree, Ms Kingsley, it would have been good to of had your input." I felt I had been turned to stone yet again… "Just before your gaze turns me to stone, Ms Kingsley, let's try and get Lucie-no-Legs her life back and walking."

Her face was a picture. She looked as if she was fighting for the right words but just grinned her teeth. I had to turn away. And pretended to fiddle with the canvas bag.

"Ms Kingsley, could I ask you to tell your daughter I am here with her new legs?"

She brushed past without a word and went up the stairs. We waited in the hall.

"Mr O'Keefe, may I see what you have created?" requested the Brigadier.

I opened the canvas bag and lifted out a left leg.

"My God, they could be real! They are a work of art, and the colour. Morris, look at the toes."

"Er, yes, Mr Kingsley, mighty fine work."

"You are a very talented man, Mr O'Keefe."

"Thank you both."

Just then, Ms Kingsley appeared at the top of the stairs in tears. "She will only allow YOU, Mr O'Keefe, to see her." She stood at the top of the stairs. Again, if looks could kill I would be dead and buried.

"Morris."

"Yes, Mr O'Keefe?"

"Would you please get two walking sticks from the stand and bring them up to Miss Kingsley's room? Two that match, if possible."

I started to walk up the stairs, Ms Kingsley was standing dead centre. I had to move around her, only then did she walk down the stairs. I heard the Brigadier say, "Doris darling, Mr O'Keefe knows what he is doing, I think we should be grateful. He and he alone have given us back our beloved Lucie." She hugged him he responded.

I knocked on Lucie's door. "Could I speak to Miss Lucie-no-Legs, please?" I tried the door, it was locked. "Lucie, I know how you must be feeling. I know you would find it heart breaking if you can't get them to work. The disappoint- ment would be too much to bear.But I know you are a fighter, and I know you will not give in. No matter what it takes, I will be here beside you all the way. Imagine, walking again, riding, sailing, and all the other things you used to enjoy, But, above all that, Lucie, I have taken the time to do this for you and it would be terrible bad manners if you did not give them a try. I will be most put out, and may never play the violin ever again."

After a few moments, "You can't play the violin," came a quivering voice.

"How do you know?"

"I just do. If I do this, do you promise to learn the violin?"

"Can I learn the banjo instead, or the ukulele?"

"The ukulele is a terrible sound, Kevin."

"Ok, the banjo."

"It's a deal." Her voice sounded stronger.

"Lucie, now, you have to open the door so we can spit on our hands and shake on it."

The door unlocked and opened, she sat in her wheel-chair.

"That, Mr O'Keefe, sounds disgusting."

"It's what the gypsies do."

"I am not gypsy."

"Do you want to know what a newly married gypsy couple must do in a bucket in front of all gathered before they can—"

"Stop right there! I don't want to know."

"Remind me to tell you later."

She gave me a look of, *Let's just get on with it.*

I walked in, closed the door, and placed the bag on the floor. Lucie's eyes were big. I knelt down in front of her, cupped her beautiful face in my hands, and kissed that lovely mouth.

"Lucie, this is going to be the first day of the rest of your life. Are you ready?"

She drew a large breath. "Yes, I am."

I opened the bag and first took out her riding boots. "Remember these? Look, I have had them altered a little."

"What do you mean? Let me see."

I showed her the elastic back. She looked at me with tears in her eyes.

"Hold onto those tears for a little while longer, sweetheart."

She smiled and squeezed my hand.

"Now, if you think the boots were fantastic, what do you think of these?" I slowly removed her new legs from the bag, I watched closely for her reaction my eyes searching her face. Her eyes like Organ stops, her arm slowly moved, then retracted then reaching forward. She took one from me and examined it closely.

"Kevin, oh, Kevin, I can't believe it! They look so real. I have toes that move." She stared at me for a few moments. "Well, are you just going to stand there, Mr O'Keefe? Or are we going to put them on?"

I suddenly became very unsure of myself. *Oh my God, this is the moment I have worked and waited for and now it's here.*

Lucie was wearing her night dress. She pulled it up over her knee.

"Left leg first?" I asked.

She laughed. "I really don't mind."

My hands shook and my palms were sweaty. I held open the elastic and offered the leg up to the stump, it fit perfectly. Next I pulled the elastic as high as I could over her thigh.

I looked up. "You're wearing no underwear."

"Mr O'Keefe, if you are going to be the father of my unborn children, as you so boldly put it, you are going to see a lot more than that. Now get on with it."

"Yes, Miss Kingsley. How does that feel?"

"Strange and the elastic is very tight, but I suppose it will give in time."

"Yes, I suppose it will." I was surprised by the sudden boldness and confidence. I placed the right leg.

"Kevin, they are wonderful, and the colour matches my skin. I look normal, I feel I should be able to move the toes. Very strange."

With that the tears flowed. She stared at her new legs and I must admit, they looked fantastic. She could not speak for crying. She held on to my hands, I let her get it out of her system.

After a few minutes she wiped her eyes, had a big sniff and said, "Please lift me up."

I swallowed hard, bent over her, put my arms under hers.

"Hold on to me tight, are you ready?"

She nodded.

"After three. One, two, three!"

Up we came. She was standing in front of me, holding on to the top of my arms. I had mine around her waist. She was about four inches shorter than me, this would make her about 5 foot 8 inches. Absolutely perfect. I could not help myself, tears were in my eyes.

With great difficulty I tried to keep control, my heart beat like a drum. Lucie was as calm as could be. She lowered her arms down mine until she had hold of my hands. I stood back a step.

"Are you okay? How does it feel?" I asked.

I got no reply. She looked down at her new legs, lifted one, then put it down, lifted the other then put it down. Not a word was spoken, she gave me a look of pure determination.

I spoke. "Come on then, Lucie-no-Legs, come on."

She lifted her left leg and moved it forward and down. I could see the pain in her face as all her weight went onto her right leg. She lifted her left leg and stepped forward. She had taken her first step.

"Step back, Kevin, step back."

I did what I was told. Still holding her hands, she took another step.

"They feel very heavy. But I will get use to them in time, I'm sure."

Tears streamed down my face. I could not believe what I was seeing, this was so much better than I could have ever wished for.

"Tears, Mr O'Keefe?"

"This is what you wanted, wasn't it?"

We laughed, me through my tears and Lucie through her pain. We stood together and held each other close.

"I can hold you now like a real woman."

"Yes, you can."

"I had no idea just how beautiful you are."

"I must sit down, I can't stand much longer, darling."

"Hold onto the bed, Lucie, I'll fetch the chair." I lowered her into the chair. "Shall I take them off?"

"NO you will not! I will have another go in a short while. Can you get my jodhpurs out from the wardrobe, please?"

"Here you are." I handed them over.

"Right, I want you to help me put them on."

"Lucie, don't over exert it, please." I was concerned she would overdo it.

"Please, Kevin."

I got them to above her knee. "You've got no knickers on."

"Well don't look then."

"I was not looking" I lied.

"Yes, you were."

"I was not."

"Pull me up the same way."

I did, and she pulled up the jodhpurs.

"They still fit, look they still fit!"

I shook my head. *What a girl, what a girl.*

"Sit me down, please and let's get my boots on."

I wanted to see how the alteration worked. I opened the back of the boot as far as I could and put them on. Perfect. I stood back.

"Lucie, you would never know."

"Bring the mirror across please."

I did.

"Pull me up please."

I did. She stood, holding onto me and looking at herself for a few moments.

"Kevin, I don't know how to thank you. You have made me whole again, given me my life back. You said you would and you have. Now I must sit down."

I lowered her back into her chair. "Do you want me to fetch your mother and grandfather?"

She eyed me for a moment.

"I think you should, if you feel up to it."

"Yes, yes please."

I found them exactly where I had left them nigh an hour ago. They both just looked at me, waiting for a sign.

"Lucie wants to see you both in her room."

They ran up the stairs and crowded at the doorway. Her mother went in first followed by the Brigadier. I was last.

"Kevin, would you please help me to stand."

I saw her mother flinch as Lucie used my first name. I walked over, placed my arms under hers, looked into her eyes, and whispered, "This is it, Lucie-no-Legs. It's show time." I lifted her up and held her hand.

Tears rolled down the Brigadier's face and his bottom lip had gone. Her mother had her hands over her mouth as tears ruined her makeup. No one said a word, Lucie stepped forward, then again. A cry came from her mother, the Brigadier held onto his daughter.

Lucie stood tall and proud, but I saw the pain in her face.

"Ms Kingsley, would you kindly fetch Lucie's chair?"

This she did. Lucie sat, she did look tired. Mother and daughter held each other and wept tears of sheer joy. The Brigadier shook my hand.

"Thank you, thank you, Mr O'Keefe!" He stood next to them both, his hand on his daughter's shoulder.

I went outside and looked at the sky. There was a wooden bench just to the left. I eased onto the hard surface feeling drained. I looked again at the sky and whispered, "Well, Ma and Da, I did it."

Morris came over to where I was sitting. "Are you alright, Mr O'Keefe?"

"Yes, thank you."

"Cook, Biddy, and I would like to thank you for what you have done. Is there anything I can fetch for you?"

"I could murder a cup of tea."

He hurried to fetch me a cup. smiled to myself, feeling pleased with myself. Morris arrived with the tea and a large piece of apple pie on a tray.

"Thank you, Morris, and please say thank you to Cook."

"I will, sir."

I drank the tea and ate the apple pie. Morris came over and took the tray.

"Ms Kingsley would like you to stay for lunch, what should I tell her?"

"Tell Ms Kingsley I would be delighted."

"Very good, sir."

I was just about to walk through the main doors when I spotted Ms Kingsley standing in the hallway looking at me. I stopped and put my left arm out with my first finger pointing to signal, Main Entrance or Tradesman's Entrance?

"Please come in, Mr O'Keefe."

"Thank you, Ms Kingsley."

"It should be me thanking you. My father and I can't thank you enough, what you have done is beyond words."

"I did it only," I emphasized the *'only,'* "for Lucie. You must believe that."

"I am ashamed of the way I treated you. Please accept my apologies." These words were no doubt hard for her to say.

"Your apologies are accepted, madam." I did a small bow and sensed a small smile in return.

A small commotion drew our attention to the top of the stairs. Lucie stood there with the two walking sticks.

"Grandfather, stop fussing."

"But, Lucie darling, you must rest. Rome was not built in a day." the Brigadier was by her side.

Her mother went to go to her, but I gently held her back.

"Leave her be. She knows what she is doing."

"You have your father's strength and determination, young lady." The Brigadier's voice trembled.

"Your father would be so proud of you, darling," echoed Ms Kingsley.

"He is with me, I just know it," spoke Lucie through gritted teeth. "Morris, take this." She handed him her left hand and grabbed the stair handrail.

"Come on Lucie-no-Legs, show me what you can do," I said. *I dare not look at her mother after saying that.*

It was now I noticed Cook, Biddy, and the other staff hovering nearby. I overheard one of them whisper, "We know we should not be here, but we will risk it."

258

Lucie called down to me, "This, Mr O'Keefe, is all your doing, If I fall and break my neck, it's all your fault."

"Thank you for those few kind words, Miss," I returned with a smile on my face.

A gasp came from the staff as Lucie took her first step, then her second. Pain was etched in her face as her whole weight went onto one leg.

If you did not know, you just might have thought that she had just hurt herself riding and was a bit stiff, I thought.

She reached the hallway and stood in front of her mother, visibly shaking from the effort, "Could I have a chair, please?"

Morris brought one, and Lucie sat down.

Ms Kingsley spoke, "Now, all of you back to your duties, please." She softened. "And thank you."

Off they went whispering to each other. I pushed Lucie into the drawing room. She was still shaking and now there were tears in her eyes.

"Lucie, that was exceptional. Where does it hurt most?" I asked.

"I think the elastic is too tight," was her reply. "Shall I take them off?"

"Yes." I took off the riding boots.

"Let me look at my toes." Lucie held my hand, and whispered, "Thank you."

"I'll fetch your mother as the jodhpurs will have to come off." I walked into the hallway. "Ms Kingsley, Lucie needs you to help her."

She hurried into the drawing room. "Biddy, fetch Lucie a blanket. Mr O'Keefe, please come here."

"Yes?"

"Lucie requires you to remove her-legs."

"Of course, Ms Kingsley."

Lucie was sat looking a bit better. I knelt and lifted the blanket just above the knee, peeled back the elastic, and removed the left leg. The stump looked very red, and the marks left by the elastic were deep. I did the same to the right.

"I can see you are right, Lucie, far too tight. I think we should stuff the elastic with something. Perhaps a towel or old pillowcase to stretch it."

"I will see to that, Mr O'Keefe. Lucie darling, I can help you to put them on now that I have seen how they are attached."

"I could put them on myself, Mummy"

"Yes, darling, but I am here to help you."

"I think I might have overdone it, my legs are throbbing. However, it was wonderful. What do you think Kevin, er, Mr O'Keefe?"

I waited for Ms Kingsley to say something like, *"I think Kevin is fine."* Alas, no, I am still Mr O'Keefe, perhaps I am asking too much too soon.

I cleared my throat. "I think two hours a day for the first week or so. Then as you feel fit, Miss Kingsley."

I felt a change in Lucie's attitude.

"I think I will leave you good folks, I must be getting back to the yard. The *LUCIE KINGSLEY* should be ready for her maiden voyage in six weeks."

"We look forward to that, Mr O'Keefe, and thank you again for all you have done."

I said my goodbyes and walked out. There was no mention of lunch. I stood just outside the front doors, and pondered.

"Everything okay, Mr O'Keefe?" Morris asked.

"Oh, yes, thank you."

"It was wonderful to see Miss Kingsley walk again. Cook says you are a wonder."

"Morris can I ask you what was Miss Kingsley like before the accident?"

"She was always quite head strong, very much her own person."

"And?" I sensed something else.

"Well, she could be let's say a bit arrogant, very much the, *'I am the Brigadier's granddaughter, and you will treat me accordingly.'* So sorry, Mr O'Keefe, I have said too much, please forgive me."

"Morris, my beginnings were the same as yours. Please speak to me as such, it will go no further, I promise you."

"We, that's the staff and me, thought the accident might bring her down a peg or two. Not that I would wish it on my worst enemy, you understand. And it did seem as such."

"Thank you, Morris." I started to walk.

"Not staying for lunch?"

"No, apparently not." I carried on walking.

I got about half way back when a toot of a car horn made me turn around. It was the Brigadier. He pulled over and stopped.

"Mr O'Keefe, you left without saying goodbye, and I thought you were staying for lunch."

"I did not want to intrude, Mr Kingsley."

"Nonsense, nonsense. Please forgive my daughter. We will always be in your debt for what you have done, Mr O'Keefe. Men like you are few and far between. Get in, we have to talk Schooners."

I walked around and got in. We returned to Cove Manor in record time. Morris seemed delighted I had come back when he greeted us on the veranda.

"Morris."

"Yes, Brigadier?"

"Tell Cook Mr O'Keefe **will** be joining us for lunch, and make sure there is enough apple pie."

Morris smiled. "Yes, sir."

The Brigadier and I walked down to the new jetty. The Daley brothers had done a splendid job.

"I am very pleased with the finish, Mr O'Keefe. I can picture the yacht sitting there. Wonderful. Six weeks, you say?"

"Yes, sir ."

"Let me have your invoice for the new jetty."

"Yes, sir."

We walked in for lunch and were met in the hallway by a rather surprised Ms Kingsley.

"Oh, I thought you had gone, Mr O'Keefe."

"I had, Ms Kingsley, but your father insisted I return."

Lunch was a bit quiet. The Brigadier and I spoke about cars and boats. The woman folk spoke very little. Then Lucie said out loud, "I take it that Breese is still alive? As nobody has bothered to tell me otherwise."

"Yes, darling, of course," said her mother, "This is wonderful Lucie dear, you have never talked about your horse since that day," said the Brigadier.

"I will give myself a month and I will be riding. We can go riding together as before."

"Darling, one thing at a time."

"Mother, I have said so, so it will be."

My God, I thought, *what a change. it looks like I have been dismissed.*

"Mr O'Keefe, I will teach you to ride, you must learn."

"Thank you, but I think I will stick to boats."

"But I insist" Lucie persisted.

"Thank you again, Miss Kingsley, but no thank you."

"I want to go into the drawing room. You can take me, Mr O'Keefe."

"I will when I have finished my apple pie."

"Well, don't take too long."

"Perhaps Morris could," I replied.

"I'll take you, darling." Ms Kingsley took Lucie.

"It's the power of walking again after thinking she never would," I said.

"Perhaps." He took a deep breath. "Yes perhaps. Though I fear we may have spoilt her a bit too much from a very early age. I will take you back if you are ready."

"Thank you, Brigadier."

Once we arrived at the yard, I thanked the Brigadier and went into the workshop. I went past the lads.

"Good day, Boss?" Andy said, more of a question than a greeting. "Cup of tea?"

I nodded and sat in my office feeling totally deflated. Pride comes before a fall.

What was I expecting? Lucie, well, she needs a good talking to, and brought back down to earth.

"Here you are, Boss, nice cup of tea."

All three of them hovered around the door.

"Can I help you?" I offered.

They looked a bit sheepish.

"They were a great success, Miss Kingsley walked again for the first time since the accident."

"I told you he could do it," Mathew said to the other two.

"Well done, Boss," said Bill.

I nodded a thank you. "Now, I need to do some paperwork."

They walked off talking to each other while I just gazed at the table.

A small parcel arrived the following Friday. I opened it to find the wooden ring, the one I made for Nelly. My heart sank. A small note was attached.

'Dear Kevin,

I return the ring. I will always love you, there is a place in my heart no one else can have that belongs to you. Take care.

Nelly Clare Kelly.'

What in God's name have I done? I lost a woman who really loved me, who I planned to marry, she would have been with me till the day I died. I gave my love to a woman who appears to love only herself and her position above all. That has been made quite clear.

It'd been over a week and I heard nothing from Lucie or the Brigadier. Lucie said she loved me, I now assumed it was the "power of the moment." I couldn't go back to Carrickfergus, my life and future was here, and now. I have loved another, I know my feelings for Nelly were not the same and never could be. I had never felt so alone. I had no one. And it was all my doing.

I threw myself into the work. The *LUCIE KINGSLEY* was complete and what a sight for sore eyes she was. Her hull was gloss black with a one inch gold leaf line. Decks of teak with deep gloss varnish on all woodwork, fittings of brass or bronze shone, her name had been carved out at the bows and across the stern, then picked out in gold leaf. The Brigadier had chosen red sails. I contacted the local newspaper and the yachting magazines.

The day arrived, a warm and sunny day, The *LUCIE KINGSLEY* was on the trolley that sat on railway lines. At high tide we would lower her into the water and see the 42 foot top sail Schooner float for the first time. High tide was 13.00 Hours. The lads put up the bunting. I had asked Mrs O'Rorke to supply all the catering, she had done herself proud. Several tables were covered with white cloth and the spread was fantastic, I think Mrs.O'Rorke had thought she was feeding the Five Thousand. The town's brass band started to play; everything was ready. The Brigadier arrived at 12.00Hours with his daughter and grand-daughter, all three looking very smart. It had been five weeks since I had seen Lucie and no contact between.

Lucie was the last to get out of the car. I watched with baited breath. She wore a dress that just showed the ankle, she had white stockings and red shoes. She stepped out, the Brigadier held her hand. She linked her arm with the Brigadier's and they walked towards me. You could not tell. Lucie had mastered the legs wonderfully. There was a low murmur from the crowd gathered, they all knew about the legs, jaws had been wagging.

Lucie spoke first. "Good day, Mr O'Keefe. I trust you are well."

"Yes, thank you, Miss Kingsley. And may I say how radiant you look."

She nodded. I felt very low, there was nothing between us, it was as if we had only just met.

The time came, the tide was high, I gave Bill the word. Slowly she reached the water, then she floated off the trolly and the securing ropes went tight. There was a cheer from the crowd and cameras flashing. The brass band played *"For Those In Peril On The Sea"* I had to smile at their choice of tune. There she sat looking fantastic. Bill and Mathew used the launch to bring her alongside and made fast. I escorted the party of three around to the boat. The Brigadier went onboard I followed, the two women stood arm in arm on the Quay. By the sounds around, everybody was having a great time.

I showed the Brigadier around and made him familiar with his new boat. After a few moments Ms Kingsley shouted down, "Myself and Lucie are going back to the house, we will see you there. I will tell the men to be at the Quay to meet you as you arrive." She did not wait for a reply.

I watched them until they moved away in the car. I turned to see the Brigadier looking at me, he saw the look on my face.

"Right, let's get underway" I walked past him and down into the main cabin.

I started the engine, checked all was well, the ropes were let go and off we went. A great cheer went up from the people as the LUCIE KINGSLEY left the quayside.

The Brigadier was like a boy with a new toy. He was at the helm while Bill, Mathew, Andy, and myself got the rigging shipshape. She glided through the water like a swan. This was the first time Andy had been out on a yacht, and he was loving it.

We cleared the headland, and Neptune was on our side. We had an Easterly breeze. Up ran the mainsail, she leaned to Starboard, then the for-sail and jib over she went and flew. Her gunwales about nine inches from the water. I turned off the engine and silence. Ten knots we recorded. The Brigadier was a very happy man. I joined him at the helm.

"Mr O'Keefe, you have built a wonderful yacht. I take this opportunity to thank you for all you have done. You know what I mean."

"Indeed I do, Mr Kingsley."

The Brigadier continued. "I'm sorry things have not worked out as you had planned. I value the man, not the position he holds in society. And I value your friendship, Mr O'Keefe."

"And I yours, Brigadier."

"Can we have all sail out?"

"Yes, skipper." I saluted. This he enjoyed and laughed at. "Set square topsail and second jib, Mr Mathew."

"Aye, aye," came the reply.

I could see the pride in their faces. We built this with our own hands and skills. She handled perfectly. Within just over three hours we were in sight of the new quay. We dropped sail and motored the last few yards to the new quay, Morris and a few others took the ropes and made fast.

"I do wish you come up to the house and have a drink with me to celebrate."

"Thank you, Brigadier, and after that would it be possible to take us back to the yard?"

"Yes, of course."

We walked up to the house. Ms Kingsley met us just outside.

"Mr O'Keefe, you and your men please stay here and enjoy the view. Morris will bring the drinks out to you. Mr O'Keefe, may I have a word with you?" She waited until we were out of earshot before talking. "I want you to accept this as a thank you for giving me back my daughter and giving my daughter back her life." She handed me an envelope.

I opened it, inside was a bank draft for £1000.

"I'm sure you will agree that is more than generous. My daughter leaves in a few days for finishing school in Paris. She will be gone some years, then probably live in London, we have property there."

I sighed, an acceptance, I felt as though she had knifed me through the heart. "I wish you and Miss Kingsley all you both deserve. Ms Kingsley, the Major will ask you to marry him and you will say yes."

Her eyes widened and she gasped softly.

"He has position, breeding, and he is a gentleman, but he has no money. He is marrying you for your money. You already know this, however, your father does not."

"You will not tell him." She went white.

I stared at her for a moment. I turned and left. The Brigadier drove us back.

"It's all happening today, Mr O'Keefe I have to meet Major Bowden at the ferry. He's coming to stay at Cove Manor for a while." He dropped us off at the yard.

"Well, men, and that includes you, Andy."

He shifted from foot to foot and smiled.

"I thank you for your efforts, I am giving you an extra week's wages I promised. And now a proper drink, not that lemonade rubbish."

They thanked me several times as we walked over to the Leg-O-Man. I sent them home elated. I went to my rooms, feeling empty and alone. I was not one of the lads and I was not one with the rich. Where did I fit in? Nelly, Lucie, the yard, I tried to convince myself that I could go back and start over with Nelly. But no, I couldn't. I had achieved so much, Mr O'Hara gave me this chance, I wouldn't let him down. And my feelings for Nelly were not the same.

I must forget Lucie Kingsley. I will concentrate on work and develop the business. I will succeed. I will get over this.

Chapter 17

It's been four years. and in those years, I hired a secretory come bookkeeper. Her name was Mary, and she happened to be the baby sister of Barry from the stables. Mary was eighteen, pretty, quick, and clever. A valuable asset to the company. There could have been something between us, Mary made that quite clear. But I could not commit. I knew it was not right and did not what to jeopardise our good working relationship.

I also got a housekeeper. Auntie Katheryn died and I got the estate left to me. I sold up and banked the proceeds. Nelly married Terry. I was invited, yet never went. I did send them a gift. They now have a daughter. I sometimes think she could have been mine and feel sorry for myself and wallow in self-pity. That could have been my life, a life I chose to throw away.

Mr O'Hara also died and left me the boatyard, I was now the owner. The royalties from the shoe manufactures of a N.E town – Northampton was paying good returns. Mc.Tagart and Co, solicitors handled that for me, I gave Mr Scilly, the cobbler. He told me his name was a group of islands twenty miles off the west tip of his home in Cornwall. Sole rights to the Isle-O-Man. I also had a patent on a twin saddle for the bicycle. This gave better support as you had a saddle for each buttock and the saddles could be moved along a tee-bar to accommodate the larger backside. Brook Saddles took it on.

I also bought the house that belonged to Mr O'Hara. And with a small bank loan purchased the other boatyard on the opposite side of the island. I moved all the business to Douglas and sold the land for development. The yard is now over twice the size, I build two boats at a time and employ ten people full time. The yard has work for over a year. The *LUCIE KINGSLEY* brought in a lot of good quality work from the mainland. I own a Rover 10 hp. I no longer work alongside the men.

I now own property, have money in the bank and own and run a very successful business. I have known several women over the last four years, but couldn't commit. I had broken a heart, and had my heart broken in return. It wasn't worth the pain. As they say, *"Lucky in love, unlucky in money"* or the other way around. But there were moments I felt I would give all I worked for, all I achieved to have someone to love and love me in return.

I heard the Brigadier was not at all well. He lives alone with the staff at Cove Manor. His daughter married the Major and now lives in London with Lucie. The rumour is Ms Kingsley has taken her money out of the estate, and the Brigadier is feeling the pinch. I kept in touch with the Brigadier through the *LUCIE KINGSLEY* maintenance and up-keep. Over the years I took the Schooner out with the Brigadier three or four times. She is a wonderful sail boat. Sadly the Brigadier went downhill ever since his daughter and Lucie left for London. They have never been back to visit, and the Brigadier has never mentioned the Major. I'm sure I know why.

It was just Ir day, I sat in the office costing up a fifty foot cabin cruiser for a newspaper owner. This will be the biggest craft yet. Except for the empty hole deep within me that wouldn't let me go, all was good.

I missed having someone to talk to, to laugh with, and to share life with. I was successful, but an empty shell of a man. Only I knew it, the outside world thought differently. I ran the risk of becoming very bitter.

The phone rang, Mary answered, "Good morning, O'Keefe's Boatyard."

"Can I speak to Mr O'Keefe, please?"

"Mr O'Keefe, it's the Brigadier."

I took the phone from Mary. "How are you?"

"Can you please come and see me today? Er, as soon as you can."

"Yes, Brigadier, I could be with you within the hour."

"Perfect, I'll see you soon then." The phone went dead.

Well, I wonder what all that was about. "He wants me to go over and see him, Mary" I got into the Rover and drove down to the main entrance as I had many times before. I parked and was met by Morris.

"Good day to you, Mr O'Keefe."

"Thank you, Morris, how is the old boy?"

"Not good. We, that is me and the staff, are very worried. He is in the drawing room."

I hurried inside. He was standing looking out to sea, slightly stooped.

"Good day to you, Mr Kingsley."

He turned to face me. "And to you, Mr O'Keefe. I want you to meet someone." He looked past me to the drawing room door.

A female voice I recognised instantly spoke behind me. "Hello Kevin."

I pivoted to see this beautiful woman standing there holding the hand of a little boy of about three or four years old. I froze. I knew instantly, who this little boy was, there was no mistaking the look and colouring. I was looking at Miss Biddy Bell. It was as if an invisible hand went out from me over to touch her lovely face. No red lips, no make-up, or brightly coloured clothes or heels. Her face was much softer. I was speechless and glued to the spot.

She stood before me. "Kevin, I would like you to meet—Kevin."

I looked at this little boy who looked up at me. I swallowed. "Hello, Kevin." I just about managed to say, "You have the same name as me. Do you know that Kevin is Irish for *'handsome'*? And in our case, it happens to be true." I shook his hand.

"I am pleased to meet you, sir." This little person spoke well.

I had trouble speaking. "I am pleased to meet you, too." My God, I had to really fight back the tears, I studied her, her face was searching mine. No words were spoken between us. There was no need, we understood. It was one of those, a moment's thought is an hour in words.

"Shall we walk in the garden?" I suggested.

"Yes, that would be good." She seemed more relaxed.

"Do you like boats, Kevin?" I asked.

"Yes, I do, sir."

I looked at his lovely mother. "That's just as well."

She smiled. We walked down to the Schooner. I wanted to hold her, touch her, the feeling was mutual.

"There are so many questions that need answers." I said looking directly into her eyes.

"I know, Kevin, and I will answer them all in time. All I will say is that the Brigadier has kept me in touch with you and your life. I know everything that's been happening to you. How you have worked your way in the world."

"Did the brigadier know about Kevin?" I asked.

There was a silence.

"Yes, he knew before I left." She sensed my anger. "Please don't be angry, I will explain in time. I fell for you—and our lovely son at Mrs O'Rorkes, but doing my job I was too involved at the time. I could not show it. I am now completely free from all my responsibilities. I can now be myself. I have dreamed of this day so many times, every time I looked at our son, I saw you. Imagine how I felt, I knew his father, loved his father, and yet could say or do nothing." She had tears in her eyes. "I want you to think about your life. I will not push if you cannot accept me and Kevin."

I could stand it no longer. I held her and kissed her hard and long. We both started to cry. The little boy looked concerned.

"Don't worry, Kevin, we cry because we are so happy," I explained. "Your mommy and father are so happy to be together at last after so long apart."

"You are my father?" He looked at me.

I could not speak.

"You are my father?" He asked again.

"Yes, darling, this is your father," she said. "He has been away and now we are all together for ever."

He seemed to accept this and held our hands. I have never felt so happy so complete. How could this be, this morning only hours ago I felt that I had nothing that really mattered? Now, it would appear I had everything: A beautiful, intelligent, stylish and confident woman and a beautiful son. I have accepted this situation as if it had always been there. And of course, it always had.

My son ran on ahead, we walked hand in hand. She turned to me.

"Kevin, we have so much catching up to do. Please say you will stay here tonight. I'm sure Morris can find anything you may need."

Oh my God! I thought. *I must have died and gone to heaven.*

"If I do, will you promise to be gentle with me?"

She laughed out loud and hugged my arm. "Perhaps Kevin would like a brother or a sister."

This was IT. This was the real thing, what I had been waiting for. This is what my Nan meant, *'Not what you would expect, not from these parts, but when you win her heart, you will have everything.'*

Suddenly my life made sense; what's past has passed, all gone. This was the first day of the rest of my life.

The Brigadier walked out to meet us. He looked better than I have seen him for a while. "It warms my old heart to see you two together. You both mean an awful lot to me." He became emotional. but got himself together. "You are two very special people, I feel proud to have known you both. And it would appear all is well?"

"Yes, Brigadier, very much so."

"You are a lucky man, Mr O'Keefe, I have known Miss Bell." He looked at her as he mentioned her name. "Since her parents died, you were just sixteen at the time. I have always thought of you as one of my own."

She butted in as she could see he was getting upset.

"I have always thought of you as a father figure." She hugged him.

"Yes, well, I will leave you to… to… whatever." He walked off as straight as he could make himself. Seeing us together has been a tonic. To him, we both could see it.

"I know this is all very sudden, Kevin, but I feel there is something I must talk to you about."

"At the moment, sweetheart, I could take on the world, what is it?"

"The Brigadier is in financial trouble. His daughter has left the estate short of cash, he let her have far too much when she and Lucie decided to live with the Major in London. And now she is asking for more. I can't bear to see him like this, the worry is killing him."

"Kevin darling, I know what the estate is worth. It would mean you selling the house. The proceeds, with my money, would be more than enough to buy and run Cove Manor and the estate. This will be our home. And I thought the Brigadier could live his life out here in the house he loves so much. And I also thought you might enjoy paying off Ms Kingsley, and letting her know that you now own Cove Manor Estate."

I looked at her in silence, a moment passed, "I have to admit, that is a wonderful idea. I do enjoy the thought of seeing Ms Kingsley face to face and telling her just that. Her face would be a picture, and not a pretty one at that. My word, woman, you have it all worked out. I must say something to you that I consider important."

Her face became serious.

"I always believed that a man should be at least six years older than the woman in order to have any chance of competing mentally."

She laughed. "I am two years older than you, and you have a very old head on those young shoulders, So, I don't for see a problem, darling."

"Have you mentioned this to the Brigadier?" I asked.

"I would not dream of doing that without talking it over with you first. There is an old saying, Kevin, *'Don't walk ahead as I may not follow, don't walk behind as I may not lead, walk beside me and be my equal, be my friend'*."

"I will be your best friend, you are my soul-mate," I said. "And I think it is a fantastic and wonderful idea. Let's do it."

That evening, we sat and watched our son play and read.

Biddy came in with drinks. "Would Kevin like to come with me to see the nursery?"

"No," I said. "I want to stay here with Miss Bell."

We all laughed, "I think Biddy means me, Father." He stood and wandered off with Biddy.

I gazed at her lovely face. I thought my heart was going to explode. We put our idea to the Brigadier. He was over the moon, you could see his whole being lifted.

"I will start the ball rolling with the house tomorrow. I will instruct Mc.Tagard and Co. to handle the sale."

We toasted with warm brandy. We both put Kevin to bed.

"Good night, Father. Good night, Mummy," he said, sleepily.

I kissed my son on the forehead. This was sheer bliss. I felt "Father" was too formal somehow, He called her "Mummy." Normally he would call her "Mother," but this was more personal bed time, more intermit. I glanced at her, she knew.

"Give it time, darling." She smiled that smile and kissed me.

We went into the bedroom. I undressed as did she, we washed, in front of each other. It was the most natural thing in the world. She climbed into bed naked and I followed. We lay looking at each other, smiling like a pair of demented Cheshire cats.

Then the mood changed. I moved my hand from her shoulder down her back, and to the cheek of her bottom. Her body was toned, her skin so smooth. She moved her hips towards me and held my face, we kissed. My hand brushed around to her belly, then down between her legs.

With this she moved on top and knelt down to sit on my thighs. Her hands holding me, slowly moving up and down, up and down, up and down. I cupped her breast then grabbed her as the feeling started and pulled her up onto my chest as I moved down. She lifted and was now kneeling. I raised my head and let my tongue find and explore that vein. With this she moved rocked her hips back and forth against my tongue. I then brought my hand up and entered her with my thumb, my open hand on her bottom. Arms outstretched, she fell forward against the bed head with an open-mouthed sigh. I could sense had I turned her and was now on top and inside her. It was only a few seconds when we both came together.

I lay with my hands under her shoulders and under her head. This was so natural, so right, we were as one in heart and whole being.

I smiled and said, "If it's a boy I would like the name William after my father."

She cut in with a smile, "And if it's a girl?"

"I'm really sorry, but I'll not have her called Biddy."

She laughed heartily.

"When is your birthday?"

"The 4th of May. Why?"

"That makes you a Taurus, head-strong, bull in a China shop, at times go at things like a tornado."

"Well," she replied, "I do like to get things done and dusted."

"In that case, Miss Bell, will you marry me? And as soon as it is possible."

"The answer is yes, and I have set a date for the 1st of September."

"WHAT?" I gasped.

"Only kidding, darling. Can we agree here and now that we never keep secrets from each other, and never tell a lie? Always the truth."

"Yes, I agree."

"And by the way, my name is Elizabeth. Elizabeth Churchill."

THE END

Or is it? It could just be the beginning…